ST. MARTIN'S

Other titles from St. Martin's **Minotaur** Mysteries

St. Martin's Paperbacks is also proud to present
these mystery classics by **AGATHA CHRISTIE**

BE SURE TO READ THE FIRST EMMA HOWE/
BILLIE AUGUST MYSTERY BY GILLIAN ROBERTS

TIME AND TROUBLE

FROM ST. MARTIN'S/MINOTAUR PAPERBACKS

WHATEVER DOESN'T KILL YOU

GILLIAN ROBERTS

St. Martin's Paperbacks

Library of Congress Catalog Card Number: 2001019154

ISBN: 0-312-98359-X

Printed in the United States of America

St. Martin's Press hardcover edition / May 2001
St. Martin's Paperbacks edition / March 2002

St. Martin's Paperbacks are published by St. Martin's Press, 175 Fifth Avenue, New York, NY 10010.

10 9 8 7 6 5 4 3 2 1

One

The sign above the door said "MOVING ON." Emma Howe wished that were true, that she were free to move on to lunch, instead of embarking upon another sure-to-be futile interview.

This was the sixth such interview and so far Emma had learned nothing useful except that nobody actually had known—or cared about not knowing—the accused. This was, she thought, a record of some sort. Never in her experience had so much energy and breath been expended for such pitiable results.

And she had tried because this case felt different from most. Emma's reputation was based on going the distance, doing solid work. She believed that everyone was entitled to the best possible defense, but that didn't mean she believed in the innocence of 99 percent of the accused she helped.

She didn't believe in Gavin Riddock's innocence, either. She thought he'd killed his best friend, Tracy Lester, in a fit of anger or confusion. She didn't know his motives, and she feared he didn't, either. From everything she'd read about him and the case, and from the interviews she'd already completed, it was clear that nobody really knew the twenty-two-year-old young man.

Gavin was different; robbed of oxygen during delivery, he was mentally slow. Because of that or because of his sense of being different, he was a shy, somewhat withdrawn loner who'd never found a comfortable place for himself.

He couldn't explain himself clearly, couldn't defend himself, and was even more withdrawn, in deep mourning for his lost friend, whether or not he'd killed her. And that terrible image was what stayed with Emma. Not that she had suddenly become a sentimental fool, but still, it bothered her to imagine him shackled, although she knew he wasn't physically bound except by his own neurological and emotional ropes. And she knew his shackles were a life sentence, no matter what the courts ultimately said.

Which left it up to Emma to find the words that would explain Gavin Riddock, and so far, she'd found not a one. She pushed open the door of MOVING ON and took a deep breath.

Fourteen minutes later, when she checked her watch, she was hungrier than ever but no closer to the elusive truth of Gavin Riddock's identity or guilt.

"This is ridiculous," the young woman she'd been interviewing—or attempting to—said. "I don't know anything about that murder, or about Gavin Riddock. Not anything real. And I don't want any PI investigating me."

Emma resisted the impulse to check her watch again. All she'd know if she did was how much more time she'd wasted. "I'm not investigating you. I'm trying to get a better sense of Gavin and Tracy, and you may know more than you think you do."

Marlena Pugh tossed her platinum hair. Emma didn't pay much attention to styles, but Marlena's seemed to belong on an old movie reel. Her parents may have dreamed of a young Dietrich, but the girl was modelling herself after Monroe, with her lemon cotton-candy hair, polka dotted dress, red lips, and high-heeled shoes. Why would anyone want to replay the uncomfortable fifties, Emma wondered.

Monroe herself—even in her current state—would have provided the same amount of information as Marlena Pugh had. But she'd have been more entertaining—even dead. This girl confused looking catatonic with looking sultry.

Emma reminded herself that she was being paid for this boredom. That in fact, the less obliging the Marlenas of the world were, the slower their minds moved, the more hours Emma could bill the lawyer.

This knowledge did not improve her mood. She thought she was on the verge of coming down with something, felt it stalking her, trying to lay a claim. She'd decided she was too young at fifty-five for a flu shot—a possible mistake.

Now she'd be sick, her work undone and her business—already shaky because of the new, cheap searches available on the Internet—collapsing altogether.

She'd wind up on a freeway exit, holding up a cardboard sign, "will sleuth for food," all because Marlena couldn't or wouldn't think.

"This isn't an investigation in the sense that we aren't looking for facts about the crime." Emma was positive she'd said this already. "We're preparing Gavin's defense, and in order to present a clearer picture of who he was, we need to find out more than we know." Scratch Marlena, even if the girl could prove she had a pulse. Emma had to wind this down, beat a quick and efficient retreat. "Maybe something you say will lead to someone else who knows something."

In whose dreams? When a mentally-challenged young man is found with a murdered friend, her blood all over him, it's "only" circumstantial, but how much more would a jury want? You didn't need a motive when the accused was considered less than normal.

If the accused's parents hadn't been wealthy, the case would be over by now, open and shut, and Emma wouldn't be cultivating germs in a nondescript moving company's office, squeezed beside a desk, her chair banked by flattened cardboard boxes. She wouldn't be the day's entertainment for apathetic Marlena, and for a co-worker who was trying not to snoop too obviously as she counted inventory a few steps away.

If Gavin's family hadn't been swathed in assets, Emma also wouldn't be listening to her own stomach growl as she watched Marlena pick at a fragrant take-out burger with still more fragrant fries. Was it feed a cold and starve a fever or the other way around? And what was it for the flu or the aches and pains of middle age?

"Couldn't go to lunch today," Marlena said sullenly. "Because of you."

A real charmer, this girl. Emma put on her Granny Em face, which she wore only as needed as a form of makeup, or disguise.

Emma was indeed a grandmother, but not a Granny Em, that harmless, soft, ignorable, fluffy-minded sweet old thing. This was the face people expected, the acceptable middle-aged woman. The un-crone. The not-possibly-a-witch old lady. Powerless. "There's nothing you can say that's wrong, and no reason I should make you nervous," she said sweetly.

Apparently, Granny Em worked even on Marlena. Her brow uncrinkled, and she smiled back tentatively. When she spoke, it was more gently than before, and even a shade less sullenly. But it was still without the hint of an operating intelligence. "Gavin Riddock killed Tracy, didn't he? I mean I read the papers. So what's to ask?"

"Help him get the best possible defense." Emma skirted the question. Innocent till proven, she silently repeated, even when there's blood on the hands. Not as if he'd confessed. The pathetic boy-man couldn't really say if he'd done it or not. Emma tried a different path. "Did you know Tracy Lester?" she asked.

"*Know* her?" Marlena shook the pale blond hair again. "I *met* her. She was in here now and then—worked across the street at the travel agency. We talked. So I couldn't say I *knew* her, but I knew who she was. We were in a group together for a little while, that's pretty much it. You get the difference, right?"

It amused Emma how idiots always assumed their listeners were as stupid as they were, thereby proving they were idiots. "What brought her over here?" Emma asked.

Marlena shrugged. "She was moving, I think. Is that right, Heather?"

The other girl in the office looked startled, then nodded.

"Moving herself. People do that, you know. People who are moving themselves still need boxes and the supermarkets, they cut them right up for recycling. Used to be you could get them there, but not anymore."

Emma made note of this overlooked modern heartache. "Was that the only time she was over here?"

She shook her head, then flicked the wave of platinum hair that nearly obscured one eye. "She knew my boss, Mr. Vincent. Came over to talk to him a couple times. That's how I knew her. Her and me, we said hello and all. Enough to give me the creeps when I read about her." She shuddered. "Right in Blackie's Pasture, by the horse statue. I mean jeez! There's always kids around there, joggers, bikers . . ."

Tracy Lester's bludgeoned body had been found at dawn near the Tiburon bike path, on public land named for a swaybacked horse whose pasture it once had been. Blackie's neatly fenced-in gravesite was nearby, and a statue of the saggy horse was in the center of the field. Gavin Riddock found Tracy Lester at Blackie's base just after dawn on a winter morning and the bloodstained Gavin was found in turn by a jogger. The murder weapon, however, had never been found and probably wouldn't. The theory was that it had been a rock, later tossed into Richardson Bay, a few steps away.

Tracy Lester's murder was the second in the history of the quiet town of Tiburon, and the first had been an open-and-shut family dispute. This one seemed equally obvious, but this time, unlike the first murder, in which a son had killed his father, the accused had money. Therefore, Emma was fully employed.

"All the same, I don't want to get involved," Marlena said. "I mean, a murder, uck!" She shuddered dramatically, excessively. "I could *not* be a witness."

"Oh, please," Emma said. "This isn't a gangland hit. You aren't in danger. I'm asking for what you know about Gavin Riddock, human being."

"Nothing. That's what I know. I don't even know why you're here. Did he give you my name?" Marlena glanced at Heather, the other girl in the office, her eyes wide, her jaw slightly open, making sure her incredulity was acknowledged. She was playing this interview like a bad actress auditioning for a role.

"Tell me about Gavin." Emma wondered whether the lawyer on the case had checked out the names his client had given him.

"What's to say? He came here once to get cartons. Come to think of it, it was around when Tracy was moving, so maybe he was helping her. I don't know. We talked a little so one thing I know is that it isn't easy talking to him. But business was slow that day so I wasn't in any rush."

As if business was ever not slow here. As if troops of people suddenly wanted to move their households with the help of a significantly unimpressive looking organization when there were so many other options nearby. Emma considered the stacks of flattened packing cases. The other girl, still pretending to be busy, turned away. "You worked together against animal testing, didn't you?" she asked, after double-checking her notes.

Gavin had, in fact, listed Marlena as a friend, someone who knew him. This, even more than Gavin's blighted life, made Emma sorry for him.

Emma needed specifics. It mattered whether Gavin Riddock had belonged to a radical animal rights group, or even whether he'd participated in a violent demonstration. She had to unearth whatever was there before the prosecution did.

Marlena blinked, chewed a fry, examined her manicure—the

appearance of her ring-fingernail seemed to trouble her—and finally answered, sounding as if speech exhausted her. "Not work together exactly. We just both belonged. Well, I belonged awhile. Tracy said CoXistence was cool. New people to meet." Marlena shrugged with world-weariness. "Then, like she dropped out. So did I. Didn't meet anybody and it was boring."

"What did that group do?"

She shrugged. " 'All things animal.' That's their motto. Anything bad for any animals—except humans—they do something about it. Gavin likes animals. Likes them better than people, he said."

"Did he say why?"

Did Emma care why? She liked most animals better than most people, too. Give her a comfy dog any day over Marlena. Dogs didn't dawdle and put you into afternoon commute hell, like slow Marlena was doing. Emma's pulse accelerated at the thought of sitting in exhaust fumes for the better part of an hour, with nothing to show for her day except multiplying flu microbes.

"Animals weren't afraid of Gavin." Marlena waved at the air, red nails physically searching for words. "That's why he liked them."

Amazing. She'd just said something semi-insightful.

"People," the girl said. "Well, he's different. That can be scary. He isn't scary, I don't think. But, like, people think he is because sometimes the things he says—they're weird. But it's not like he does bad things or didn't, until now. But animals don't worry about words that way."

Had his parents, or at least his mother, not been both protective and enormously wealthy, Gavin might be living on the streets now. Instead, he lived in a "cottage" in Belvedere—a million-and-a-half dollars worth of small shingled home on the bay—and he lived there alone, with daily companionship from a woman who was half house-keeper and half nurse.

Gavin kept a low profile. He had no records of any association with violence.

"Animals trust him," Marlena said. "He volunteers, or he did, at the place in the hills where they rescue seals and all?"

"The Marine Mammal Center?"

Marlena shrugged and nodded at the same time. Emma wondered if she voted, if she ever made a clear choice. "Those are wild animals," Marlena said, "And they trust him, too."

"Maybe cause they're sick," the girl with the boxes suddenly said.

Marlena glared at her. She in turn twisted her face away so vigorously, her hair billowed, as if in a wind.

Marlena settled back down, picked up another fry, bit it, and sighed. "That's all I know. Now you know it, too. I went to one meeting, I swear, and it was a nothing and that was it for me."

"Was Tracy Lester at that meeting, too?"

Marlena did her shoulder-and-head shimmy. Maybe yes, maybe no. "Gavin brought her in. He was the animal lover. She was like, kind of a fake, all excited suddenly about doing something. That's what she said, she had to 'do something.' So, like I had to do something too, like join that stupid group. And then she quit." Marlena rolled her eyes to over-express her disdain for the dead girl's fleeting enthusiasms.

"All I can sanely hope for is to throw a little sand in the jury's eyes," Gavin's lawyer, Michael Specht, had said. "Create doubt. Demonsterize people who are different just because they're different. The guy's a gentle creature, but it's hard finding somebody who believes that. You have to find that person. And if you stumble across anybody else with any kind of motive against Tracy Lester, then blessings on your head."

So with Emma's help, they would counterbalance the newspapers, which were behaving as if Gavin and others whose IQs and personalities weren't smack dab in the middle of the norm were time bombs planted all over Marin County.

Hercules' job description sounded easier to her.

Marlena ate the last of her french fries, then slowly folded the grease-stained paper that had cradled them before putting the resulting square in her wastepaper basket. She glanced at the clock, then picked at the hamburger's roll. One of Emma's kids had gone through a phase like that, eating in sequence. All of one food group gone, then the next begun. But Emma's kid was over that phase by age nine.

"Boring," Marlena said.

"Excuse me?" Emma was boring the world's most boring young woman?

"The meeting was boring. I didn't go back."

Perhaps Gavin hadn't given them Marlena's name at all. Emma hoped that was the case, that instead, Michael Specht had copied a list of all the people CoXistence claimed as members and sent Emma chasing after them.

Marlena stared at Emma with barely a flicker of life in her eyes. Emma didn't even know what the girl did in this pitiable office. Surely nobody had hired her to interact with customers.

She felt sick. And sick and tired of this. She wanted to go home and take aspirin and drink brandy until she killed all the flu bugs while she watched the most stupid TV show she could find.

"It's like this," Marlena said. She might have meant her tone to be civil, but she wasn't good at it.

Emma thought with envy of her trainee, Billie August, sitting in comfort in front of the computer, conducting lovely on-line background searches while she, poor Emma, endured this idiot. From now on, Billie could do the Riddock interviews and Emma could sit in peace with a cup of good coffee—and food when she was hungry—letting the computer do the legwork. No traffic snarls, no tedious young women.

It would be good practice for Billie, anyway. She hadn't gone out on interviews of this sort yet. Emma had wanted to give her more time, let her get her legs. She'd only been at the agency a few months.

Now, Emma felt that a few months were quite enough. Surely Billie—surely anybody—was quite capable of talking to people who said nothing back in return.

"It's like what?" Emma prompted.

"I only meant," Marlena said, rolling her eyes. "Isn't it obvious? I don't know anything."

It was obvious. She knew nothing and neither had the five others before her. From now on, let Billie face the know-nothings. They'd be a good match.

Two

Zachary Park hung up the phone as Billie entered the office and pulled off her raincoat. He turned and smiled, raising one eyebrow. "Is that a Lego tower in your pocket or are you just glad to see me?" he asked.

Billie patted her hip pockets. Empty.

"The blouse," Zack whispered, shielding his mouth as if they were conspirators.

Damn. She had felt relatively together today, too, liked how she looked in the bronze silk blouse and forest green wool slacks, her blond hair falling decently for once.

She pulled a red and white stack of plastic bricks out of her breast pocket. "The colors don't go with the blouse, either," she said dolefully. "Another fashion victim, but Jesse's such a . . . you could break your . . ." She shrugged. Who cared why? Bits and pieces of her various lives stuck to her as she moved from one point to the other, and that's how it was.

She went into her cubicle. After three months in the often frustrating job—working with Emma Howe was an exercise in learning patience—she nonetheless was delighted with this small space and its promise of a solid career.

The photo on her desk of her son reminded her of the Legos, which she put into her briefcase before she settled in at the computer. And then she remembered she needed coffee and returned to the small reception area where Zachary, office manager and all-around whatever-was-needed maintained a relatively fresh pot as self-defense against Emma's foul brew.

Billie filled her cup and gestured toward the closed door of Emma's office. "She in?"

"*She?* You talking about our employer, missy?"

Billie smiled. "Did your mother do that, too? You couldn't refer to her as 'she'?"

He nodded.

"Why do you suppose that is?"

"Beats me. But *she* is not in. She is home. Either getting sick, or being sick."

Billie's live-in sitter and entire support system, Ivan, had been showing signs of the flu this morning, too. The idea of what a sick sitter would mean made her feel ill herself.

"She's nonetheless dragging herself in shortly."

"Don't let her in. People shouldn't be allowed to spread their germs."

"You're so harsh!" Zack mimed horror. "She's not that bad, not really."

"Easy for you to say. She likes you. She has a thing for handsome men."

"We have that in common. And more relevantly, we both have a thing for Emma's son, whom she also loves."

"So where does that leave me? Do you and Nathaniel want to make it a ménage à trois, so I, too, can enjoy her approval? Or make that a ménage à quatre—I'd have to bring my son the Lego-builder."

Zachary shrugged. "Give her a decade or so, you'll see. You'll stop being afraid of her."

"I'm not afraid! I'm . . ." Afraid. Or at least wary, with cause. Her employer was unpredictable and rough-edged, perpetually exasperated, as if Billie were the unpleasant by-product of a repugnant but necessary process.

"The two of you have different styles, is all," Zack said. "She's no-nonsense, and you're—"

"Obviously, if you put it that way, then I'm nonsense."

"Nonsense."

"You talkin' to me?"

Zack lifted the fishbowl from his desk. It contained, as usual, nothing aqueous, but instead, a variety of candies. "Eat chocolate." The universal healing agent, he claimed.

"Too early."

"Then you're having a better day than I am." He carefully unwrapped a miniature Snickers bar, and once again, Billie wondered how he avoided becoming blimp-sized, but when she'd asked, he'd said it was "a guy thing." "By the way," he said as he chewed candy, "what happened with the cowboy?"

Zachary complained that once he transmitted information he got over the phone to Billie or Emma, neither remembered to tell him the rest of the story. This was not a valid complaint, since he constantly requested—and received—updates.

"It's my mother," the client had told Zachary. "She's seventy-eight and engaged to a man she's never met, a man she calls 'a diamond in the rough' when she isn't calling him her 'soul mate.' She met him on the Internet, and she will not listen to reason. I think she's already sent him money."

The betrothed mother found out what her son was up to and phoned. At that point, Billie spoke with her. "At first, I was furious with his meddling," the woman said. "But I've changed my mind. I accept the challenge. I'll show my suspicious son how wrong he is. I didn't raise him to be heartless, but look how he's turned out. Just because he believes old people can't be in love, doesn't mean it's so. And I have the right to send gifts to whomever I like. It's my money."

13

She was right about the money and possibly right about her son, but what Billie actually heard was a searing, hard-core terror behind her forced jolliness, and a need to have her Internet lover be precisely who he said he was.

And she was wrong about "Potter," as he called himself. It was, he said, his middle name, his mother's maiden name. James Potter Redbranch, sixty, retired Texas Panhandle rancher, "but not one of the big ones, mind you," he'd told mama. "Sheep, not cattle." But big enough. "Took care of me and my family and as long as I watch it now, I'll be okay." A widower with one son who was off in the Peace Corps in Africa. Interests: golf, travel in his RV, and computers.

The woman called again. "He might think I'm a bit younger than I actually am," she said. "I didn't have a brand-new photo around, you understand."

By then, Billie had understood too much. "A complete fake," she now told Zack. "Con man. No Redbranch—he's James Potter, age forty-seven. He must juggle his age to be whatever his correspondent wants. And of course in this case, his correspondent dropped seventeen years from her age. The man never had a ranch or a son in the Peace Corps, no dead wife, but five ex-wives. If they're all ex. Been in jail twice for extortion, once for auto theft." She waved her hand in the air, brushing away all the James Potters and the pathetic women who were so desperate to find love that they ignored all danger signs and all logic. "He's always temporarily short of liquid assets because of a deal that's pending. He can't visit them without a short-term loan. He can't complete the deal without a cash infusion. That sort of thing."

"I wonder how long he could have kept it up—this long-distance extraction of funds," Zack said.

"Doesn't have to be that long if he's got a big enough stable," Billie said. "New people always come on-line and he can have dozens and dozens at all times. But guess what the grand finale was."

"The newly disengaged mama is tracking Potter down and accusing him of extortion."

"Wrong. Try again."

"She's apologized to her son for being a fool?"

"Wrong once more," Billie said. "Mama's no longer speaking to her son."

Zachary shrugged. "I knew it all along. The basic truth of life is: Steal anything except my illusions."

"Anyway, that's done. I'm on another check and this one's fine, as far as I can see. Is honesty as boring as it seems?"

"You want boring? That last caller would not shut up. Somebody's been bothering her. Obscene phone calls. Actually, 'kind of obscene' calls, whatever that means. A month and a half ago. She meant to call sooner, but she was too upset. Then she thought the phone company would catch the person, but they didn't read her mind. It's making her too nervous to live, just about—even though the calls have stopped. Still wondering who they were from, and on and on and then on some more. Didn't matter that I told her the calls were over, she should perhaps talk to somebody about her anxiety, and that there wasn't much we could do after all this time."

Zachary was great with those people. Billie had heard him field crazies and cranks and this last and most difficult group, the hysterical "*Do Somethings!*" as they privately called them. There was nothing to be done in most cases, nothing that would help or change the situation or ease anyone's mind, but these people didn't care.

Emma had instituted a new fee category which was filed under PA, as in "Permanent Acquisitions," people who didn't know what they wanted, but were going to keep on wanting it forever. Most clients were given an estimated fee, usually a few hundred dollars for a routine search, such as the one for the imaginary suitor. But the PAs were assured that there was little to be done, and then if they persisted, were asked to pay a thousand dollars up front for the non-service. It helped weed some out, though not all. Mostly, the firm relied on Zachary to sound sympathetic and compassionate while simultaneously keeping the vaguely needy at bay.

Billie took her coffee back to her cubicle and directed her attention to the screen, searching for liens or judgments against the client's anticipated partner. She thought again of the furious woman who'd been suckered by a false fiancé. Nothing was as hard as an on-line search for love.

Except, perhaps, an off-line search.

She called it quits and decided to check the health status of her household when she heard the outer office door open and the somewhat hoarse voice asking Zachary about calls. Even through its scratchiness, Emma sounded softer-edged when she spoke to Zachary Park. Billie envied that tolerance, that bemused acceptance, despite what Zachary himself called his "time out for bad behavior."

She accepted the idea that Emma was incapable of being the friendly mentor Billie had fantasized, and that in fact, Emma would choke if forced to say the word "mentor." Billie had tried to convince herself that Emma had become how she was through working in a man's world for too long, except that most men were more gracious than Emma Howe, and her brusque, battering approach seemed inborn.

But Emma was fair, in her fashion. Ethical in a profession where ethics were as fluid and unpredictable as mercury, so working for her more or less balanced itself out. It was a job with a paycheck and relatively flexible hours, and Billie was doing well enough. Not that the woman said so, but after three months of the Emma Experience, Billie interpreted a declining rate of criticism as her employer's equivalent of praise.

"Not leaving, are you?" Emma said as Billie emerged from her cubicle.

"I thought . . . actually, I . . ." Billie paused, furious with herself for not simply saying "Yes I am" with equal force.

16

She reminded herself that she was not afraid of the older woman. "I have to be home early today," she said firmly. Much better.

"I want you to take over the Riddock interviews for a while," Emma said.

As if Billie's answer had been nothing more than static. White noise.

"Michael Specht's case," Emma said. "We're gathering whatever nondamaging information we can. Also damaging, if it comes to that. Character witnesses, anything that can help Michael's case."

Billie waited for more instructions, even though she'd learned not to expect anything resembling adequate explanation from Emma. She wasn't surprised when Emma simply handed her a list of names. Six had check marks beside them. People she'd already interviewed? Check marks for special interest? People she meant to interview? Names supplied by whom? Any background Billie should know?

"Feel free to add anybody else you think is related or relevant, too," Emma said. "The budget is considerable. I mean, you'll talk to Michael, of course. Don't go off without cause, but you don't have to be in a panic about time. The family wallet is bigger than God's."

Was Emma suggesting that Billie could use her own brain following leads? That would be a quantum leap forward from anything else she'd worked on. A leap of faith on Emma's part, too.

Billie knew that the Gavin Riddock case was stratospherically high profile. It was also important to Michael Specht's career and reputation as the hotshot criminal lawyer du jour and therefore very important to the PIs Michael Specht hired.

"I'll oversee it," Emma said. "Maybe do one or two. This is for now, and we'll see. Keep me informed, as well as Michael. You know the drill, right? You report to him in person."

Billie nodded. Not that Emma had deigned to mention it; Zachary had explained it to her. Investigators' reports were given verbally, to keep them out of the prosecution's discovery process. Nothing written, nothing to subpoena.

Billie felt reanimated; she was tired of staring at the computer. She craved the drama of a quick glimpse into another life. Plus the acting—playing a role herself.

Emma was handing her a major case. Maybe that meant, in Emma-speak, that Billie was truly doing well. In fact, it had to mean that. Why else?

"I did these," Emma said, pointing to the names with check marks. "My notes are attached. Nothing, really. A gum-snapper with ten hoops in one ear; a woman who lectured on our polluted Earth and what it was doing to the animals; a guy who couldn't remember ever meeting Gavin; a movie starlet named Marlena; and two others so boring I can't even remember what was boring about them. Nobody knew a thing worth knowing. But . . ." She looked at the list with something like affection and definitely with interest, and Billie feared that she was reconsidering her decision to entrust it to her. And then once again, Emma nodded, giving the transfer her stamp of approval. "Start in the morning. Maybe go see Michael Specht first, introduce yourself and get a handle on what he wants at this point." She cleared her throat. "Make it clear I'm having you take over because—"

Billie tried not to smile, although the joy of validation so filled her, it wanted out. She mentally completed Emma's sentence: Because:

—you're such a quick study.

—I've been so impressed by your instincts, your style, your diligence, your wisdom, your learning curve, your . . .

—you've shown you can handle anything I toss your way . . .

—I've seen how your natural talents make you able to blend into a variety of situations and . . .

—in three short months, you've—

Emma blew her nose, then began again. "Because," she repeated,

"I feel like hell and these interviews are meaningless time-fillers. The kid murdered the girl and the only reason we're doing this is because his parents have too much money and we don't. I don't want to waste my time and health, but I can't afford to turn this case down or hand it back, and I'm afraid if I have to listen to one more idiot, I'm going to say all this to Michael Specht himself and lose an important client."

So the answer was: none of the above. The answer was: You're doing this, Billie, because it's a stupid waste of time and energy that nonetheless earns me money.

Emma coughed. "Tell Michael I'm under the weather and you're subbing."

Not the script Billie would have written but she could live with that.

In fact, she *would* live with that.

What choice did she have?

Three

Gavin didn't want to talk to Mr. Specht anymore. He didn't like him.

But he was supposed to talk to him and to like him. Mother said Mr. Specht was here to help him get out of this mess. Mother was paying Mr. Specht to do that. She'd said so. Mr. Specht had to help him. He promised to. It was his job, and he was the best, she said.

But he didn't like him. Didn't believe him.

His mother wasn't right about everything. She told him things that were wrong. She said people meant well, didn't know any better than to call names.

His vision grew watery as he thought about how in school it was worse being called "dummy" than being punched.

Tracy had understood. Tracy had known the truth of how people were. She wasn't like the other people, but she understood them and she never lied about how it was.

Nobody punched him anymore. He was too big now, and he was strong from the running and the weights, and Tracy had said to do that, too, and that was good. But his mother said people didn't hate him, and she was wrong. They didn't know better, she said. But Gavin was sure that somebody had told them that calling names was wrong, that it hurt, too. And even if nobody had, couldn't they see for themselves?

His mother didn't understand that, but he didn't want to make her sad, so he'd stopped telling her she was wrong, that people knew what they were saying and that they didn't like him. Nobody called people they liked those names, threw those names like rocks at his head, but mother wouldn't hear about it. Didn't like him to talk about "sad things."

Didn't like that he was different or that he couldn't remember so much all the time right away. She said if he tried his best, he'd see how well he could do, but that wasn't true, either. He did try his best but things felt hard that other people didn't complain about. He thought it was different for him, but his mother said he was wrong.

Tracy understood. She knew what was true.

Mother said people didn't mean to hurt him. They were ignorant, she said. That meant they didn't know better.

He couldn't understand why their mothers hadn't told them. His mother had told him not to be mean to other children even though she didn't believe other children were mean to him.

His mother said he was as good as anybody. That he had a learning disability. An accident had happened when he was getting born, so some things were hard for him, she said. She made it sound like not much. She said she was a taxpayer and the schools were public and that he partly owned them, too, so he should just ask the teacher to repeat herself if he didn't understand. But when he did, the rest of the class got angry. Sometimes the teacher got angry, too.

His mother said it didn't matter. Not the accident when he was born or the way he had to go slower than other people in school. "Slow and steady wins the race," she said, but he never won. Except in real races. When he ran.

It didn't matter to her, maybe, but it mattered to him. And it mattered to other people. They didn't like him in their class and they didn't like him at their parties. They didn't like him anywhere. Sometimes, he didn't have to do anything—not say a word or make one move—and they still looked angry that he was there.

That he was.

His father was like that, but he didn't see his father much, so that wasn't so bad.

He thought that was all over when he was out of school and in his own house not bothering anybody. But now, look. A jail cell and people hated him more than ever.

He couldn't tell his mother how it had been, how it was. She was already too sad.

He told animals. It didn't matter to them. And they had no words to call him. But there were no animals here and he wasn't allowed to go where they were. And Tracy was dead and there was nobody to talk to.

Not Michael Specht, for sure. Maybe the lawyer was ignorant, because he looked like those people his mother said were ignorant. He talked too fast, and he wanted Gavin to answer too fast and his mouth curled when Gavin couldn't, or when he was thinking, or said the thing Mr. Specht didn't want him to say even though he wouldn't tell Gavin what would have been the right thing to say. He said that was illegal. His voice changed, his lips got little and curled like they were starting to say something—something Gavin knew would be angry or mean. He never said it, though. There was a big space in the air where he wanted to say it.

He acted as if Gavin were a dumb kid. Gavin couldn't answer as fast as Mr. Specht wanted, but that did not make him a dumb kid. He was a man, but he didn't talk fast enough to explain that to the lawyer.

A lawyer who thought he was a dumb kid was not, no matter what Mother said, going to help him.

Gavin Riddock sat in his holding cell, his hands folded on his lap, head bowed. He looked as if he might be praying, but he seldom did. Instead, he was thinking about how much he hated being here, locked away from everything on earth he liked. From his dog and his cats and the animals that weren't his and the people he liked.

They said he killed Tracy. Banged her against the horse statue or maybe hit her with a rock, he wasn't sure.

They said maybe he was in love with her. Mr. Specht said that maybe Gavin loved Tracy. Maybe he tried to kiss her. Maybe do it, everything, with Tracy.

Those words made him feel sick low in his stomach and in his throat.

Maybe, Mr. Specht said, she was so pretty and nice but she didn't love him back the same way? Was that the trouble?

Gavin didn't know how he was supposed to know what Tracy felt. Tracy was beautiful and he liked looking at her and he did love her and he said so. He had loved her since fifth grade when she told everybody she was his friend, and the kids teasing him backed off. There wasn't any trouble the way Mr. Specht said.

Tracy was kind, Tracy was his friend. But she married Robby a long time ago, so everybody knew Gavin wasn't her boyfriend. It was dumb to think that if Gavin loved Tracy, he'd kill her. It didn't make sense, but Gavin didn't think he was supposed to tell the best defense attorney in the entire Bay Area when he was wrong. His mother would be angry if she heard he was rude to the lawyer. Getting out of line, she'd say.

Mr. Specht said maybe Tracy said something mean.

Mr. Specht got angry when Gavin said she wasn't mean and shook his head fast, the angry way. Wrong answer, dummy. "I didn't mean she was mean all the time, Gavin."

Mean, mean. Confusing.

Gavin didn't understand why Mr. Specht made Tracy sound angry, the way he was. "She was *kind*. She was my friend. She ran with me. She said she could tell me things. Could trust me. She made me tapes."

"Of what?"

"Music. To listen to. To run to."

The lawyer sighed. Wrong again, even though it was true. "She was *scared*," Gavin said. "Not angry."

"Scared of what?"

"I don't know." She said he could maybe help her, but he thought she didn't say how, except now he didn't know whether maybe she had said, and he didn't listen right. Sometimes he only listened to the wind, or the air. Maybe then, and maybe that's why she was dead, his fault.

"Why do you say she was scared?"

"Because she was." Words jumbled between his lips and Mr. Specht's ears. "But she was going to make it better."

"What was 'it'?"

"The thing that scared her. I was supposed to help."

"How?"

"I don't know."

Mr. Specht took a deep breath. "Let's go back to when Tracy died. Did the two of you . . . were there angry words between you? I'm not saying you were there when she actually was killed, let's let go of that for now, but maybe at some point the night before she died."

"No."

"Meaning what? No angry words?"

Gavin's head got swimmy because the pieces of what they already said were gone and he couldn't look back and find them again and Mr. Specht acted like Gavin hadn't been trying.

Gavin wanted to ask what was wrong, why Mr. Specht was so angry, and if he was supposed to help Gavin the way Mother promised, why didn't he?

Mr. Specht leaned close, and when he spoke, every word came out as if it was all alone. "Okay. That. Morning. The. Night Before. Whenever. Did. Anything. Unusual. Happen?"

"What *happened* was Tracy *died*," Gavin said. "*That* was unusual."

"I'm here to help you," Mr. Specht said. "But if you don't try, Gavin, then I don't know how much I can do for you."

Do not cry, Gavin told himself. It was another thing he did that made people angry. Made them make fun of him, call him a baby. Do not cry. Do not.

Mr. Specht sighed, but more softly. "Without your help, my hands are tied. You're vague on where you were, with whom, and Gavin, there is that blood. Tracy's blood."

Gavin nodded. "On me. On my hands."

Mr. Specht looked sad. "Yes," he said softly. "And on your warm-up, too. You do remember, don't you?"

For once, Gavin knew exactly what Mr. Specht meant. "I remember that."

"Can you tell me how it got there?"

That was harder. When he remembered that part, his head squeezed tight until there was no light and nothing to see. When he tried to remember that part, because his mother or Mr. Specht asked him to, it hurt, gave him that sick feeling, and what he saw behind his eyes was swimmy and confusing. She was there, Tracy, and so was he, and it was dark, the sun coming up behind the fog. He saw himself running in the cold dawn, heard the foghorns, saw the heron on the edge of Richardson Bay. He stopped to watch the way it walked on its long legs. Then he saw Tracy over at the statue, and the rest went black.

"You touched Tracy?"

"If you say so."

"I didn't say so. I won't want to put words in your mouth, so tell me. Tell me about Tracy and you. That morning."

"She didn't come to my house."

"Did she usually?"

"Not always. Sometimes she couldn't run, so I went out by myself."

"And?"

"So . . . I went to run by myself. And then . . ." In between his house and Tracy, still clear in that morning mist. The bird walking slowly, and then he ran straight into fog. "I couldn't see much. Had to get close. I . . . she was there. I was surprised."

"Why?"

Now who was dumb? Wouldn't anybody be surprised to find a girl out before the sun came up, sitting on the wet ground in Blackie's Pasture where people weren't allowed to stay at night? "Because she never was there before when she didn't come to my house."

"Oh, Gavin . . . I meant . . ." He closed his eyes. Gavin knew that kind of look, like the person couldn't go away like they wanted to, so they just didn't look at him. The lawyer shook his head again and opened his eyes. "What was she doing when you saw her."

"Sitting, kind of."

"Was she alive then?" His voice was low, purry, like he was Gavin's friend. Like he did want to help him. "Gavin?"

He was trying, that's what was taking long. He was trying to look back through time, to before they put him in this place, to exactly what had happened before he started running and shouting—or was it before? Had he been running first? He did run there, early, when he could see his breath puff in the air that was still mostly nighttime.

It hurt to think about it.

Hard to breathe slowly and his eyes getting wet again, and he shook his head and tried not to cry in front of Mr. Specht.

"Gavin?" Mr. Specht said from far away, behind a wall or inside a cavern.

"I don't remember." Gavin closed his eyes, didn't want to see the curled mouth. He heard a small snap. Mr. Specht broke his pencil tip again, the skinny lead in a mechanical pencil, because he pressed too hard with it. He broke the tips of pencils every time Gavin hadn't answered the way he was supposed to.

"I want to help you," Mr. Specht's voice came from farther and farther away.

"I was running," Gavin said. "There was blood."

"Let me . . ." He was a foghorn, thick and indistinct and low. "You . . ." Sound, not words. Gavin shook his head and waved at the air, brushing away the sound, the foghorn in the cell. "Leemmmmmmmeeeeeeeee . . . youuuuuuuuu . . ." It was low, a moan, it bounced off the walls, in through his head.

"No words," Gavin said. "No more words." He put his hands over his ears and closed his eyes.

Four

"Do whatever you can. Ask around, see who you can find. We're going to have to do it for him because he's . . ." Michael Specht, who seemed a man never at a loss for words, faltered. "He's not helping his case," he said, his lips tight.

He was very much Prestigious Lawyer, tailored to perfection, fingers with manicured nails clasped in a pose of utter sincerity as he explained the situation to Billie.

"There's a lot of bad history about the Riddocks in Marin," Specht said. "The father, you know . . ."

Billie didn't know. "I've only lived here four years."

"Emma didn't fill you in?" He frowned, then erased it. "She must really be down with that flu."

Emma wasn't all that sick. Billie wished she knew if Emma "forgot" so many things because she wanted Billie to look inept, because she had a dreadful memory, or because she was the worst instructor on earth.

"Gavin Senior?" Michael Specht said. "An early high-tech zillionaire. Biotech in his case. Made a pile and from that day on, behaved as if he'd bought the county and all its inhabitants. There was the malpractice business after his son was born. Then he wanted to build a house about the size of San Francisco City Hall on the ridge top. It broke every Tiburon zoning rule and the town turned him down. So he sued. Turned down again. Sued again. He boasted that his legal budget was larger than the town's which was true, and he vowed to bleed the town treasury dry if necessary to get his house. He might have done it—this went on for years—except he lost interest. Met a new woman, got divorced, remarried, bought a Belvedere mansion and then repeated the cycle—new woman, new house, this time in Ross. But the Riddock name came to stand for the arrogance of extreme wealth. I still hear echoes of it, put-downs, as soon as I mention Gavin's name. So the kid's got two strikes against him from the get-go: his oddness and his family's reputation. It's tough finding friendly witnesses. It's tough even finding neutral ones."

"I'll do my best," Billie said. "I have your list as starters, and I'll see where it takes me."

"All anybody can ask."

His smile surprised her by its ability to change him completely. Humanized him and made him undeniably attractive.

"Now the budget here is large, the divorce left Mrs. Riddock an exceedingly wealthy woman and her mission in life is to insist that her son is perfectly normal, whatever it costs to say so. So feel free to follow up on good-sounding leads and don't overworry about that aspect, long as you keep me up to speed."

"Fine. Should I phone you?"

"Better in person. Call and we'll find a mutually good time." His hands were now clasped, and he leaned forward, his flat abdomen up against his sweep of blond wood desk.

"No problem," Billie said, amused by the obvious change in the lawyer's attitude toward her. When she'd phoned for this meeting, he'd been audibly peeved by Emma's defection, pointing out the significance and urgency of this case, and why it required an experienced pro, the woman he'd originally hired.

But his demeanor changed the instant she entered his office. She saw herself mirrored back, not as a possibly incompetent PI trainee, but as an attractive woman, and she watched with amusement—and interest—as Michael Specht tried to disguise his interest in her non-PI self.

Billie could stand being reminded that she was twenty-eight years old, and that despite the exhausting logistics of her life with a job, a child, not enough money, and no real support system, she hadn't yet been sanded down to sexlessness.

"The Speck" they called him behind his back, but he was anything but a microscopic bit of nothingness. He was a somethingness indeed. And no wedding band, although that didn't necessarily mean much. Was it unethical if something were to happen between an investigator and a lawyer?

She caught herself up short. She was here in a professional capacity. The Speck was trying to keep it that way and so should she. Shape up, pay attention, and ignore the signals the man across from her was trying to muffle. "Do you think my talking to Mrs. Riddock would be worth anything?" she asked.

"He's not married." Michael Specht realized his mistake, and covered quickly. "Oh, Zandra. His mother." He considered this. "Maybe. Maybe she'll remember somebody, something more. Maybe a woman . . . I'd thought Emma, more her age, although the two are nothing whatsoever alike. Wait till you meet her."

"Why? What is she like?"

He rocked back in his chair, his fingers laced, and a small smile played over his features. He had a fine, expressive face and he knew it. "Somewhat mythic," he said after a short pause. "The scary myths. She's the sort who'd eat her own young if it would upset her former husband. She got more money in the split than she can ever spend, but she lost her status, her ranking as 'wife of' and is she ever still mad about it."

Billie grimaced. "Something to look forward to."

His expression grew more serious. "That's part of why she's so unintentionally hard on Gavin. She won't allow him to be brain-damaged. She pushes, which would seem good, except she pushes him into situations where he's doomed to lose. But I think it had to do with the father, with this war between them."

"Must be difficult." An inane thing to say, but also true. Hard enough raising a child with all capabilities intact.

"It's about reputation, to her. The same way her divorce was. Gavin has been a drain on her social status instead of adding to it, the way proper privileged children should. Let's face it, we live in a pampered corner of the world and the Riddocks are close to the most pampered of all. Except that they aren't getting full perks. Their son hasn't accomplished anything and can't. People like Gavin—to the manor born—they're supposed to *shine*, to be envied and emulated. What's the point of all that wealth if nobody looks up to you?

"Sorry to sound cynical, but that's my take. And for good or for bad, her money is able to keep up the pretense that he is normal. She can cocoon him in that so-called cottage, provide a housekeeper-guardian who watches out for him, sustain the pretense of his eventually going to college."

"She probably thinks it's helping him. Making him feel ordinary."

"It's had precisely the opposite effect. At least from my viewpoint. He's . . . frustrating." Michael Specht raked his fingers through the side of his hair. He'd done that earlier in their meeting as a holding action while he thought about what he was saying. Billie thought that it was lucky he had such thick and springy hair, or he'd end each day looking like a cartoon's mad scientist. "Either he won't think," he finally said, "or he can't think. I'm not sure. Either way, it isn't helping him. Or me."

"Well, I'll try my best to," Billie said.

And after a few comments on the list of places and people compiled so far, the interview was over.

She turned on the ignition and put on a tape she'd made of different artists singing Gershwin and allowed herself to think about the law-

31

yer, and her life's impacted romantic side. It's nonexistent romantic side.

She didn't usually let herself dwell on that because there was no point except self-pity, but now, she felt a wash of longing for all the details and grand gestures of falling in love—and not with someone you gave birth to.

And then she realized her background music was her own self on the piano, backing up her son. "Elephants do not forget," he piped in his little boy voice.

Jesse's Greatest Hits. They'd made the tape one recent rainy Sunday. She wanted to save his baby-boy voice in all its sweetness. The tape didn't belong in the car, but Jesse adored being a recorded star, and he tended to bring it along when they went out.

And there you have it, she thought. Raped by reality again. Yearn all you like for Gershwin, but you're dancing to *Jesse's Greatest Hits,* girl. So symbolic, one could puke from it.

Though Emma hadn't given it any importance, Billie had noticed that an interviewee mentioned Gavin's volunteering at the Marine Mammal Center. What better place, she thought, to find positive impressions of the accused?

But she definitely didn't need to continue wearing her blue-gray knit silk sweater, or short navy skirt, or any of her Impress the Speck outfit. Sea lions did not enforce a rigorous dress code and their windswept convalescent home was out of doors, above the Pacific.

She pulled up to her house and wondered for a moment what the Riddocks, who called Gavin's Tiburon bayside home a "cottage," would call the diminutive clapboard building tucked at the back of a long narrow lot. A shack? A blight on the neighborhood?

It was possible Billie's own neighbors called it a blight. Her house, built years ago as an unheated escape from San Francisco's summer fog, remained true to its roots while all around it Gerstle Park remodeled and gussied itself up.

She liked to believe that the long front garden, ragged-assed as it was, made the house look more substantial. Still, she really ought to plant flowers, as soon as these rains ended, spiff up the yard. Also, paint the house.

Contemplating what needed to be done exhausted her. But she had to take care of the two by-products of her otherwise ill-fated marriage. Jesse and this house were her only assets. Her luck had been to buy the latter before the local real-estate market spiraled from merely grossly overpriced to its current insanity. She had to hold onto it.

She paused at her front door for another look back at the shabby garden and noticed Ivan's car parked across the street. This did not bode well. He should have been at college, and although Ivan was flaky about women, he was dead serious about his schooling and, to her relief, his duties as a baby-sitter.

As soon as she was inside, she heard loud coughing. Thin walls were part of her house's dubious charms.

She knocked and went into his room. He looked as if an alien had taken him over but hadn't gotten the form and face quite right. He was tall, six-three, and fit, but now he looked gangly and shrunken.

"Flu," he croaked. The physician on campus had told him so, even though he knew it anyway. "I have medicine." He waved a finger in the direction of his night table.

Billie was his only real family. She should be bringing him liquids and checking his temperature. "I'll get you juice," she said. And that would be the limits of her Florence Nightingale stint because she had to work. Had to, or Ivan, along with Jesse and Billie, would have no roof under which to be sick.

He was flushed, his blond hair rumpled.

Ivan's mother, Tatiana, had emigrated from Russia with him, but she wasn't on call for TLC. She lived upstate where she worked as a seamstress, and she wasn't a well woman. "Something with the lungs" was all Ivan had presented as a diagnosis. Plus, she spoke almost no English and didn't drive.

No point thinking about Tatiana.

No point in Billie's instinctive guilt and nurturing impulses, either. She reminded herself that Ivan was twenty-one years old. A strapping young man. He'd survived eighteen Russian winters, hadn't he? He'd be fine and meantime, the real problem was hers, code name: Jesse.

"Did you call your friends?" she asked. In negotiating their arrangement—child-care in exchange for room and board, Ivan had devised a Byzantine system of backups, fellow Sonoma State students with different class schedules.

He shook his head.

"They can't? None of them?"

"I mean, I did not call. Yet. I am just home."

She went into the kitchen to phone. The response was predictable, and not unexpected. She'd feared this would happen since the plan was presented, but she'd had no real options. Three separate perky female voices said she should leave a message and they'd get back when they could. What they were actually saying was that they had a life so why would they be in their rooms at midday?

An emergency plan wasn't much help if it ignored the fact that emergencies by definition did not give advance warnings.

Screwed.

"I take care of Jesse. Is all right," Ivan croaked as she returned to his room. "I wear mask, see?" He pointed at a package. And then he coughed, wrackingly, and lay back, exhausted. She touched her wrist to his forehead. Burning up. She popped the thermometer that was by the bed into his mouth.

"What a mess!" she said, mostly to herself. "I'm so tired of all the—He'll be sick soon, too, not from you, from what's going around at preschool, he's already sneezing and I have this big assignment—*finally* something interesting and important, and I cannot screw up by staying home. I just *knew* that deal with your friends wouldn't work, was too *pat* to be true—all that careful schedule-checking—what the hell was I thinking? And even *Emma* has the flu so then I'll get it, too, and *then* what?"

Ivan removed the thermometer. "Spill milk," he said, wheezing before and after each word.

"It is not!" The thermometer verified her first impression. One hundred and two.

"I think yes. Is what you teach me. Should not cry from spill milk."

"Your English stinks, and I am not crying over spilled milk. The expression means it's stupid being upset about something that's already happened." She heard herself. "You're right. I mean you're wrong, and we're going to have to work on idioms a lot more, but . . . I was even more stupid, crying about something that hasn't happened yet. Might not happen, and which I can't prevent from happening in any case."

Ivan wisely, or out of fatigue, said nothing for a while. Then, after blowing his nose, he said, "What Emma say?"

She shook her head. "Not in the mood."

Sometimes, after Jesse was asleep and the house cleaned up, she and Ivan had tea and talked. He was only seven years younger than she, but he'd turned Billie into a combination of mother-confessor and Ultimate Expert on the ways of American women. So most of the talk, most of the time, was about Ivan's adventures in his adopted homeland.

But sometimes Billie spoke about her life, which was to say her job, and her uncomfortable relationship with Emma Howe. Once, when she'd imitated Emma's brusque delivery, Ivan had applauded as if he'd just seen the best of Broadway. Since then, "doing Emma" had become a dramatic highlight of late-evening talks.

Although she lacked the energy to perform it, Billie could almost hear what Emma would say—or shout. "Ms. August," in that tone that felt like a battering ram, "this is precisely and exactly why I had to be insane to hire you. Your life is an incoherent disaster and absolutely no concern of mine. This isn't about *sisterhood*. We are not *sisters*. This is not some *cause* we're in, this is a business. I should have had my head examined before I hired you. Look at you! A preschooler, no funds, no family, just a sex-crazed Russian part-time college student babysitter! And besides that, you're an idiot!"

"Go work," Ivan said. "I be . . . Jesse be—"

"—Will be, Ivan," she said. "You've got to get a handle on the future tense. Things that are not happening now. They are going to happen later on."

"Not worry about things not happen now. Maybe won't happen ever," he said. "Jesse fine. I pick him up at party."

Double damn! "I forgot—whose party again?"

"Max in Kentfield. Address in kitchen. I pick him up."

Admirable Ivan, mouth-breathing, eyes wet with fever. She shook her head. "You stay here and work at getting well." She didn't trust him behind a wheel.

But he was right. There was no point in worrying over a future that was out of her control. She checked her watch. Time enough to check out the Marine Mammal Center and still pick up her son. Nothing was impossible, at least today. Then they'd have a quiet evening together while she made chicken soup from scratch for Ivan. It would be pleasant.

And who knew? Maybe Ivan would feel better by the next afternoon after day care, or his friends would have called back and be ready to step in. "I'll get him," she said. "No problem."

His eyes half closed, Ivan looked silently grateful. "I'll . . ." he said after a moment.

"You'll what?"

"I'll. That is how you say it. Is the tense future."

She went to change into her jeans. He'd gotten that much right; the future was tense indeed.

Five

"I'm Heather Wilson," the young woman said. She was a pale, shy girl; her posture and clothing subdued and designed to be unnoticed. Emma thought she looked familiar, but couldn't place her.

"This is——" Heather Wilson faltered, gestured toward the older woman standing ramrod straight next to her.

The woman flicked a glance Emma couldn't interpret at the now-silent Heather. "Kay Wilson," she said. "I'm her *mother*." Her lips clamped into a grim line.

Emma gestured for them to be seated. Zack had given her a cryptic description. Daughter the client, mother not happy about this. Refused to say what she—or they—wanted.

"I saw you," Heather Wilson said as she settled into the chair on the other side of Emma's desk.

Emma always found silence most efficient when in the company of a person not making sense. What was the point of talking into the wind? She waited and tried not to think about how stiff and sore her shoulder muscles felt. She wanted to blame it on that flu she thought she was getting, but she didn't feel as sick today. It was a head cold, and not much of one, and she now blamed her aches on a weekend spent hauling household junk to the curb for the township's large-object pickup.

The girl wasn't Emma's image of a "Heather." Too plain for her name, although God knew there were so many Heathers in her age group, it was foolish to have any idea of what one of them would look like.

This one looked in her early twenties and not overly affluent. Dressed conservatively, she looked ready for a political rally, perhaps, in a navy skirt with a white blouse and red cardigan. Above the neck, she was less methodically put together, with chewed off lipstick and brown hair insufficiently held back by barrettes so that wisps and pieces hung by her ears.

Her mother had similar taste in clothing, but her grooming was meticulous. She did not look happy.

"I saw you day before yesterday," Heather said. "You were at work—my work, remember?"

Emma did not. "And that was . . ."

"You were talking to Marlena."

"Ah." Emma nodded. Right. This was the lurker, she who'd been counting inventory at a glacial rate in order to eavesdrop.

"You told Marlena you were an investigator."

"So I did," Emma said. "And in fact, I am." On the telephone, Heather had said her problem was too personal for a man, even for a man hired to acquire such information. Zack had therefore put her into the Cranks-R-Us Permanent Acquisition category, which meant she was paying for this time, putting up a thousand dollars against her bill.

"So I thought to myself . . . I thought . . ." She nodded agreement with whatever she was about to say.

Emma pulled a tissue out of the box on her desk and caught her sneeze in time. Then she leaned toward the two women. It eased the tightness between her shoulder blades and made her look as if she were actually interested. "I assume, since you heard what I was discussing with Marlena, you've come in because you have information about Gavin Riddock." She didn't truly assume that. She merely wanted to get this girl unstalled. It would be shocking if imparting information about Gavin Riddock was her mission. Unlikely that she'd refuse to say so to Zack, and more than improbable that she'd pay to do so.

"Who?"

"Gav—"

"That murderer?" Heather shook her head and waved away the air in front of her. "No way. He's . . . nope. I never met him and never hope to!"

"Then I don't understand."

"It made me realize, your being there. I need something investigated."

Her mother looked around the room, as if trapped.

"And?" Emma asked. Was this interview going to be done syllable by syllable?

"Someone." Heather's glance fluttered from the bookshelves to the carpet to the window and finally rested down on her fingers. "I need to find someone." She picked at a cuticle. "My mother," she finally said, still looking down.

Emma glanced at Kay Wilson, whose hands were so tightly clasped the knuckles were white as she looked wistfully at Heather, who finally met Emma's eyes and spoke with a veneer of defiance. "My actual mother. The one who gave birth to me."

It was now Kay Wilson's turn to keep her eyes anywhere but on the other people in the room.

"You being a woman detective," Heather continued. "I wasn't sure there were such things, except on TV and all, but I'd rather be with a woman because I think you'll be more . . . more sympathetic." She flashed a quick, angry look at her adoptive mother.

"Tell me what you have in mind." Emma kept her voice neutral. She was not particularly sympathetic to unearthing long-buried things unless necessary. Searches such as this girl's were not shelved in Emma's "necessary" category.

"I want to find my birth mother. I found out I was adopted six months ago, but I can't find—"

Kay Wilson's hands were clenched and her eyes on fire.

"There are registries," Emma said. "You can enter your name and if your birth mother also wants to find you, she'll enter her name, and you'll be a match."

The young woman concentrated on her cuticle again. "I tried a place on-line. They said they could find anybody, but they didn't. And I don't know how to find things out on my own," Heather said. "You do."

"Please tell her." Kay Wilson's voice was soft. Emma almost felt as if she had to strain to hear the woman. "Please make her understand that sometimes people do not want to be found. She has a perfectly good life and shouldn't be squandering her emotions and money this way."

"Heather," Emma said, "explain it to me. Why do you want to find her?"

"Because I do, that's all. Because I want—I need—to know who I am."

"You already know that. And you already know who your real mother is: the woman who's raised you all these years. You said you found out about the adoption recently. Can't you think yourself back to before that time, to who you were? Because you're still her."

Kay Wilson sat back a bit, her lips tight. Vindicated, her posture and expression said, but that hardly made her happier. The tip of her nose glowed pink. She was a crier, Emma suspected. She hoped the woman continued to hold it in.

Heather did her air-brushing again, ridding the atmosphere of the words that had been said. "I know that. But I can't go back. Don't you do this kind of thing? Why are you being negative?"

"I'm trying to warn you because yes, I do this sort of thing and too often it ends sadly. Sometimes, it's best to let things be."

Heather tensed her mouth, looking remarkably like a young edition of her adoptive mother, and said nothing, holding her ground.

Emma considered the grim duo. "It's unusual for an adoptive parent to come along for something like this," she said. "You seem so unhappy about Heather's decision, so may I ask what . . . why . . ."

"I don't approve and I'm still hoping she sees that it's a waste of time and energy and money, but if she stays determined, then . . : she's my daughter. I want her happiness, so I'll help however I can, although I don't have much information at all." Kay Wilson dabbed at her eyes with a tissue.

Emma wished that people would ask her the best approach to their problems. And listen to what she said, understand that her years at this job had given her perspective and some measure of wisdom.

In this case, without even hearing specifics, she'd tell the girl to lay off. Respect the privacy desires of a woman who'd probably been younger than she now was. Let go of the phantom idea of mother and look at the real woman whose love and sweat and energy had gone into making her. Because odds were, in the end, the girl would be angry or disappointed, or both, when Emma handed her the truth. Emma loved the truth, believed in it, swore by it, made her living by unearthing it, but most people, no matter what they said, preferred illusions.

Emma's own daughter was a prime example, and their latest quarrel had been over precisely that. Caroline had twisted Emma's desire to never lie to her children into the reason she, Caroline, could not sustain a good relationship with a man.

"I never needed to know those things about Daddy!" she'd screamed. "I didn't need to know he died in a motel, with another woman. I didn't need to know about the gambling! You poisoned me with that stuff."

So there they had the current explanation for Caroline's divorce and recent breakup with another man. Soon that—or another offense of Emma's—would explain why she couldn't settle on a career.

"You like lies? You like mothers lying to their children? You think that helps children grow up?" Emma had asked, knowing that had she lied, those lies would be the subject of Caroline's lament. "I don't lie," she'd said. "I never lie and I'm proud of it. Besides, why should your father's ways ruin your chances with men? I'm the one he cheated on and I'm the one whose money he gambled away so if anybody should be afraid, it's me, but I have a perfectly fine relationship with a man."

This girl here, this Heather, had a Caroline-like look of wanting to find the single reason—outside herself—for whatever she lacked. Now, she'd undoubtedly decided that her birth mother was someone wonderful and exceptional who could transfer her secrets of perpetual joy to the daughter she'd given up long ago.

But the sign outside Emma's office didn't say "God." Didn't even say "Goddamned Psychologist." It said "Private Investigations."

Emma wouldn't take a case if she thought it was for purposes of stalking, harassing, or endangering somebody. Otherwise, here she was, legwoman for all the sad searchers who had the cash to hire her.

And, frankly, Emma had enough problems. Why discourage business when those Internet searchers were pulling enough away from her already? That was it, she wasn't saying another negative word. On with the search, and in with the money.

"I don't know anything about myself," Heather wailed. "My—she—won't say. Make her tell me!"

"Now you know that's not how it works," Emma said.

Kay Wilson breathed raggedly and pressed her handkerchief against her eyes, holding it there. "I don't want her to be hurt," she said. "That's all. I don't want her to be hurt." She breathed deeply, and put her hands and the handkerchief back in her lap. "I wish . . . I wish she'd think of me as her mother—or *call* me her mother the way she always did. But I don't know enough to be very helpful and she's just going to get angry again about it." She fiddled with the strap of her purse, which sat on her lap.

"Since we're apparently going to give it a try," Emma said, "let's see what information you do have." She pulled a clipboard holding a tablet and pen closer and nodded at the other woman.

"But it's next to . . . okay. My husband—my late husband Nowell—arranged for this through a physician, a Dr. Smith. You see? That was his name and I don't know his first name, either. I was ill right around then. We wanted a child and nothing was happening, and then this opportunity arose, very quickly, very hush-hush. Somebody told somebody else who told Nowell. A girl baby had been born and whoever was supposed to adopt it didn't want her. Wanted a boy instead."

They hadn't even begun yet, Emma thought, and Heather was already getting bad news. Rejected at birth because she was female.

"I didn't ask for information," Kay Wilson said. "We knew the mother was healthy, that was all, and that was enough. Perhaps I didn't want to know. I wanted this to be our baby. Period." She looked quickly at her daughter, and then at Emma, head held high with dignity, despite her bright red nose and watery eyes.

"Were you in California at the time?" Emma asked.

Kay nodded. "In Berkeley."

"Did the adoption take place there, too?"

Kay Wilson shook her head. "We moved a whole lot. I can't remember where."

"I guess I have to ask: Do you know the birth mother or father's name?" She knew what the response would be, but just in case.

Kay Wilson again shook her head.

"How did you discover that you were adopted?" Emma asked Heather. "How did all this come about?"

"She slipped up," Heather said. "She was really angry with me about . . . well, doesn't matter."

Emma watched Kay Wilson while her daughter spoke. The woman looked fragile, as if one tap from her daughter would shatter her. Emma did not like getting emotionally involved with clients, but this mother's sorrow was getting to her. She cleared her throat and pushed down the emotion. •

"She never drinks," Heather said. "Not in a way that would make you say she drinks. But that day, she had bronchitis and she had brandy because it helped her. And I—we—we don't always get along, but this time she found out that I hadn't been going to school." She shrugged after she said it, still diffusing the seriousness her mother had seen in the act.

"She's supposed to be at community college," Kay Wilson said. "And then, she could transfer to a four-year."

Heather shrugged. "I had my reasons, but she didn't ask them, and then there was all this about my boyfriend. Because I'd loaned him money."

"He had a record. Drugs, and—"

Heather glared at her mother, then went back to her normal voice. "This is stupid. We're not together anymore, but we were then, and she hated him."

Was this girl an idiot? Any mother who cared would hate a lout like that.

"And she got all red and started crying and said I was no good and never would be, and she should have known it all along, given what I'd come from."

Kay Wilson was openly crying now, shaking her head, as if attempting to rewind time itself, take back whatever she'd said to her daughter.

"And I said something about how I'd come from her so why was she talking that way about her own self, and she looked so—" Heather stopped, and cleared her throat. "She didn't know what to say. She got all . . . and I knew. Like that, I knew, that what she'd meant was that I hadn't come from her. I said who gave birth to me, then, and she got that look on her again. Frozen or something. Then she said I was crazy and it was just an expression and she hadn't meant it, but I knew. So eventually, she said I was right. So now, I need to know. It's my right to know."

Now, Emma felt a rush of pity for the girl. She was annoying and not overly bright, but by her own measure, she had been gravely wounded, cut afloat from humanity by her mother's accidental revelation. The pity was for the futility of her quest, for the mooring and connection she expected to find despite the odds.

"I thought I was doing the right thing," Kay Wilson said in a teary voice. "I thought . . ." She shook her head and looked too tired to say any more.

"I realize you don't have much information, but whatever you have, I'll need," Emma said. "Perhaps you can think of some things that could help, Mrs. Wilson. Things like what city your husband visited in order to get the baby, or canceled checks to a physician, anything that might narrow the search." Narrow was an understatement indeed. Given so little, the search was as wide as all outdoors. Or at least as large as California, for she hadn't said he went out of state, thank God. So it was now tightly narrowed to everyone who'd been in the state—or come to it perhaps to secretly deliver a child—twenty years ago. Super. "And you need to understand that the odds . . .".

"I understand." Heather's hands were fisted, holding tight.

Emma knew she did not understand at all. She didn't understand how futile this probably would be, and how expensive both monetarily and emotionally. And most of all, she did not understand that in all probability what she was asking for was trouble and heartache.

"Then it's a go," Emma said. "Let's see where we are."

Six

Five seconds off the freeway, Billie felt in another world as she drove into the headlands rising out of San Francisco Bay.

She waited for the light to signal her turn in the one-way tunnel that burrowed through the side of the mountain. A five-minute wait, they said, but it always felt much longer. Finally she was in and through the narrow gray passageway and out into the post-rain fluorescent green hills.

She drove on Bunker Road, its name the heritage of the military bases that had been at each "corner" of the Golden Gate during WW II. The abandoned Nike missile sites added a melancholy historic punctuation to the landscape, and in fact, the rescue center itself was on a former missile site.

A nice bit of recycling, Billie thought.

The center was set in a bowl of hills from which Billie, parking her car, could see the ocean but the patients behind the fencing could not. She wondered if they smelled it, heard it, and sensed it still. Surely, they were homesick for it.

She paused at an information booth and picked up a leaflet, walked by the large "FROM RESCUE TO RELEASE" posters near the entry, glancing at their explanations of what the center did, and moved to where visitors could observe the front row of holding pens. Each cement-floored space held a ramped round tub in its center, a tiny above-ground swimming pool for two or three sea mammals. Whiteboards on the surrounding fence gave each patient's name, condition, and where he was found.

She stood in front of a pen containing elephant seals that had been, according to the notes on its whiteboard, emaciated when rescued. Now they looked plump and were vociferous, filling the air with a hoarse sound, combining a bark and a crow. Their flippers fascinated her; each ended with five nails, as if a hand were slipping out of a flipper-shaped glove. Next pen over, a sea lion had a healing slash mark around his throat—"harassed by humans," his sign said.

A young woman in rubber boots, yellow gloves, and a flannel shirt-jacket hosed down a pen, silently regarding the sea lions who had clustered inside the pool when she approached. Finished, she backed out and locked up.

She waved acknowledgement at Billie, who was the only visitor at the moment. One of the sea lions descended the ramp and barked in her direction.

"Some asshole shot him," the woman said. "It makes me crazy, even thinking of the kind of person who'd . . . You volunteering?"

"Visiting," Billie said.

"Shame—you just missed a release. It's a trip watching the guys get put on a truck."

"Where are they taking them?"

"This group was going down the coast, I think. Where there's a colony." She smiled at Billie and half turned away. "Look around, enjoy yourself. I've got to get back to a mentally ill harbor seal. I call him Huck Finned."

"How do you know if a harbor seal's crazy?"

"Well, let's say he's not sick but he's one confused fellow. He was found at the freeway entrance in Greenbrae, sitting on the on-ramp. Apparently, he ran away to see the world. He must have gone for a long swim through the waterways and then the tide went out and he was stranded in the middle of a housing development.

But he's got guts. Hauled himself up onto dry land and started out for wherever. Which was ultimately the freeway entrance."

"Lucky he wasn't killed."

The volunteer nodded. "Or that a lot of people weren't, too, in a pileup—few things make you slam your brakes like seeing a sea lion on the freeway. We talk about sharing this space, but we assume wild animals understand the laws of human civilization and will keep behind the lines we've drawn."

"And what happens next?"

"Once we're sure he's fine, he'll be taken out to Point Reyes where his mother will send him to his room and make him promise to never do it again. And," her voice grew more solemn, "hope his sense of direction isn't screwed up. Remember Humphrey the whale? We had to get him out of San Francisco Bay twice." She pulled off a yellow glove. "By the way, I'm Sarah. I volunteer here."

Billie introduced herself. "Actually, I'm looking for information about a volunteer. Do you have a minute?"

Sarah laughed. "Last I heard, there were eight hundred of us. We're here twenty-four–seven, you understand. This is a hospital."

"His name is Gavin Riddock." Billie hoped that somehow Sarah had not picked up a newspaper or turned on the TV news in the past month.

"Sounds familiar." Sarah moved her head as if to get a new view of Billie. "Can I ask why you're looking for information?"

"I'm working with an attorney who needs the information."

"You're a lawyer?"

"An investigator."

"Doing legwork for a lawyer *here?*" Sarah's brow creased and she was silent, her expression one of deep concentration. Then she looked up. "Gavin Riddock! The guy who killed—"

"Who's accused of killing—"

"Of course." Sarah's voice had lost its animation. "I don't know him. You might ask the woman in the visitor's center out there.

She's been here a long while, and knows lots more people than I do. Or knows who would know."

She pointed toward the exit. That was indeed where the visitors center was, but Sarah's gesture also suggested that Billie should get the hell out.

Billie wanted to spend more time watching, but she reminded herself she had a different purpose. "Thanks," she said.

Sarah, en route to the bank of pens behind the ones Billie could see, turned around. "I have to ask. I know it's a job and I know about everyone's right to the best defense, but don't you feel bad about what you're doing?"

"Me?" Billie pointed at her chest, knowing how stupidly she was behaving. The girl wasn't addressing the animals.

"Working to defend somebody like that."

"Somebody like what?"

"Like a murderer!"

"He's accused," Billie said. "We don't know if he actually—"

"Oh, please. The Riddocks." She shook her head, puffed air out of her mouth. "Do whatever you feel like and to hell with the peons."

"I don't think this— He's entitled to the best possible—"

"I know that. And I guess I even believe it, but it kills me to think that you'd— I'm mean I'm one of eight hundred people trying to save animals. From us, because we shoot them, or we murder them if parts of them seem valuable. Or we pull them out of their habitat and collect them if we think they're rare or precious or pretty. Or we trap them in our garbage. What is wrong with people? How can you expect me to sympathize with—" She put a yellow-gloved hand up. "Sorry. I didn't mean to . . . but you can't spend all your time trying to heal victims—human or otherwise— and then get misty-eyed about somebody who bashes in a woman's head!"

Billie wasn't sure how they'd leaped from sea lions on the freeway to Gavin Riddock. "Really," she said. "You aren't giving him a fair—"

"All this legwork and energy and money for what? To try and save a mess who obviously has no sense of right and wrong. Like the person who shot that sea lion—you'd find ways to defend him." She shrugged. "Well, hell. It's your job." With another shake of her head and arm, shaking off Billie it appeared, she turned and went back to work, lifting and tossing a hose into an enclosure.

Billie went to the visitors center. The door was open and a middle-aged woman with cropped gray hair sat in its small space, playing solitaire on a computer. She looked up, smiling, when Billie said "Hello," then stood and came outside. "How can I help you? Have you toured the facility yet? Can I tell you anything about us?"

Billie paused a moment, afraid of another outburst. Then in the most efficient and unemotional voice she could summon, she introduced herself and repeated her mission. "I realize you have lots of volunteers, but if you know this person, or could tell me who might, it would be a help. His name is Gavin Riddock." The muscles of her upper back and neck pulled tight.

The woman's mouth tightened. "The one who killed Tracy Lester."

"Who is *accused* of—"

The woman's posture changed subtly, and Billie was reminded of animals poised to fight or flee. "Naturally, when we heard . . . people talked about it, about him. Horrifying. And he seemed . . . not normal, but not violent."

"He has no history of violence," Billie said softly.

"Until now, maybe," the woman snapped. "Murder's sufficiently violent. He's written himself a new history. You know, Tracy Lester was here, too. Came with Gavin one day when I was here. I spoke with her. Such a nice young woman, but very emotional. She cried when she saw a sea lion humans had hurt. She said she had only just then realized how horribly people treated animals. And that it mattered."

"About Gavin Riddock," Billie prompted.

"Well, of course, when we heard . . ." She leaned against the wall of the small white structure. "People talked, went back and checked about him . . ."

"He did work here, didn't he? I mean volunteer?"

"For a while." She put her hand up to the side of her face, her little finger pressed against her lips. As if she were silencing herself, Billie thought.

Below them, in the distance, the Pacific glinted in the clear winter sunshine. Behind them, a patient barked.

The volunteer's expression softened. "He was asked to leave. It's rather sad."

"How so?" Being booted out sounded bad, not sad.

"He didn't truly get it that those are wild animals. And even more important, they have to stay wild. This isn't a petting zoo, it's a rehab center. We don't talk to them. We don't touch them, except as medically needed. We keep them with others of their kind, so that they socialize with them, not with us. The goal is to get them back to sea, with their own species, in their real lives, as nature intended. We're only a way station."

"And Gavin?" Billie prompted.

"Oh, yes. Sorry. I was lecturing, wasn't I? Force of habit. What people said was that Gavin couldn't resist befriending the patients. He got it that petting them was dangerous—they are wild animals and they bite. But he couldn't resist talking to them, hanging out near their pens. We had a volunteer back then, Veronica Napoles. She'd gotten him to come up here, and she tried to work with him, but, well . . ."

"Does she still volunteer?" If she'd brought him here, she must think well of him, Billie decided. Or had. Even if he didn't make the cut because of over-affection.

"Not anymore," the woman said. "She's a rancher now out in West Marin. Raising llamas. A bit of a trek to get here, I suppose."

"Could I—Is there some way I could speak with her, then?" Why wasn't she on the list of contacts?

So far, no one had had much good to say about the accused, not even in the standard media way of neighbors insisting that the killer "seemed like a nice ordinary guy." Gavin had never been ordinary, had never blended into his surroundings. Maybe this woman would turn the tide.

"I'd like her permission before I give her number out," the volunteer said. "If you'd wait a minute or so . . ." She punched in numbers, then listened to the receiver for a long time before saying hello. To Billie's relief, her mission was described as "investigating Tracy Lester's death," instead of "helping that murderous Riddock boy," or some variation on that latter theme.

The volunteer handed the phone over to Billie.

"If you're not police," a determined voice on the other end said, "I'll talk to you. I have already talked to them until I was out of breath and look what a big nothing that produced. Gavin did not kill Tracy."

Billie scarcely knew what to say. "When?" was all she came up with.

Veronica suggested the next day, and gave directions.

"In case," Billie said, spelling out her name, and giving both her home and cell phone numbers. And then, with a final thank-you, she hung up, feeling as if she might have lucked into something.

After thanking the volunteer and gladly leaving a donation, Billie headed for the car, filled with new optimism. She tried not to be overly excited, but Veronica Napoles sounded like an actual character witness.

She stood for a moment at her car door and looked out to sea, which stretched flat and deceptively calm-looking out to infinity, hiding its nets, sharks, and secrets, revealing nothing. How sad for Gavin, who'd wanted to love the animals. He increasingly seemed a creature out of place, as vulnerable against mankind as these land-locked sea animals were.

Seven

Emma left the Wilsons in her office. She had to get out because she felt as if she were following a now-disappeared trail of crumbs. "It's fairy-tale time in there," she muttered.

"What's that?" Zack handed her the day's mail, which looked predictably boring. "Did I hear you snarl about fairies?" He waited. "My mistake." He gave a mock salute and turned his attention back to his desk.

Handsome Zachary Park. She'd always been a sucker for good-looking charmers and age didn't change that. Zachary made her smile, but she didn't feel like smiling right now. She blew her nose instead. Fairies, indeed. "Those women are driving me insane," she said. "Girl wants to find her birth mother. What she wants of her, I don't know. But okay, it's a job—except there's nothing. I know we charged her a big fee, and promised nothing, but the fact is I find running in circles annoying as hell."

"She's looking for her mother because she's human," he whispered. "I've heard something about some kind of bond? Mother and . . . how did it go? Mother and stranger? Mother and dog? Wait, I have it. Mother and child. Heard of it?"

"Nitwit. I understand the urge, but she has a bond and it's with that mother in there. She's a fool to waste her money this way."

"Emma." A smile played just below the surface of his skin. "Emma, you're not worried about the money. You're worried that you will find the mother, and it'll be another horrible non-reunion. Another rejection. That this girl, stupid or not, is about to be hurt."

"Don't be ridiculous!"

He held his ground. "It's not a crime to have emotions—no, make that to *show* them—even if only now and then. Say, once a fiscal quarter, maybe."

"Time to go back into the arena." She toyed with the idea of giving this futile search to him. He'd been making sounds about training to be an investigator. But she knew he didn't mean it. He was supposed to run the office using only one piece of his brain power and flex time to audition for theater and commercials and local film work. She didn't know what had kept him back so far, whether drugs had caused the failures or failures, the drugs.

He didn't talk about it while he was here, on his day job. Not even with Billie—despite her having been a drama major in college—did he discuss what in less formal moments and settings, he called his "real life." At least he didn't within Emma's hearing.

In any case, he was clean, he was happy, he was optimistic again, and she wouldn't mess with it. Besides, when he'd been gone from the office, there'd been constant chaos and nothing was where it was supposed to be.

The outer door opened. Billie was back from wherever, waving, pointing at her watch, then darting into her cubicle as if in a dreadful rush when Emma was sure her actions were designed solely to avoid any interaction. For unfathomable reasons, the girl seemed uneasy around her.

She returned to her own office, feeling condemned. The Wilsons looked grim and she wondered what, if anything, they'd said while she was gone. She looked at the mostly empty form on her desk. It wasn't going to do much good for anyone. Almost every blank was still pristine. And that was after she'd asked and asked questions.

She settled back down to work. And again faced the nothing. What did she have?

No name.

No city of birth.

No birth certificate.

No adoption papers.

Lots of damp-eyed murmurs and memory failures.

And two facts: A name—not the birth name, but a name. Heather Wilson. And a birth date. August 5, 1979.

But she'd taken the money, and she was an honorable woman. Futile as this was, she would search.

"How is it that you don't know where the baby was or where she'd been born?" Emma asked Kay Wilson, not sure whether she'd asked it that way before.

The woman incessantly realigned herself in minute increments— head shifting slightly to the side, as if her neck cricked, back straightening or arching, legs crossing. She was visibly and perpetually uncomfortable. "I wasn't there," Kay Wilson finally said. "I was ill, and Nowell said Dr. Smith had a baby for us, months before we'd expected, and so he had to go get her on his own. Dr. Smith understood. I don't remember details. I had a fever and it was a . . . confusing time."

"He drove off? Flew away? What?" Emma asked.

"Drove."

"And did he say how far, how long?"

Kay Wilson's hands clasped and unclasped.

"How old was Heather when he brought her home?" Emma asked. She didn't like this story, not at all. Didn't sound right, a father-to-be driving off solo to bring back a newborn.

"Just . . ." Kay Wilson shook her head again, and pulled a tissue out of a box on Emma's desk. "Only . . . a few days. Whenever they let her out of the hospital."

"Did your husband stay with anybody while he was gone? That might help us locate the hospital."

Kay Wilson shook her head. "He didn't stay. He wasn't gone."

"You're saying he went wherever and returned the same day?"

"He came back home," Kay Wilson said, then she frowned. "I was sick and he didn't want to leave me in the first place, so I'm sure he came back home with the baby."

Heather slumped and looked sullen. Emma hardly blamed her. There could not be a less loving, interested, or excited retelling of how Kay Wilson came to be a mother. She'd shown not an iota of joy, excitement, or even nostalgia. But Emma wasn't sure if it was from an absence of emotion or a desperate attempt to control an excess of emotion. After all, the girl she'd mothered since she was a few days old now referred to her as her "step-mother."

"Let's try to be sure," Emma said. "You were ill. So think: were you alone overnight? Did somebody come in to help you, make sure you were all right?"

The woman's eyes overflowed again. She looked around as if someone had called, then back at Emma again. "Nobody came to see if I was all right. Nowell was there."

"If you were so sick," Heather said, spitting out each word, "how could you let a little new baby in your house? Didn't you even care about making it sick? Making *me* sick?"

Her mother swiped at her eyes. "I—I didn't hold you that night. I didn't want to make you sick. I—I had things ready."

"What sort of illness was it, do you know?" Emma asked.

"A . . . I felt . . . it was probably a sort of flu," Kay said. "It's hard to remember now. Fever is all I remember. A bad fever."

Emma suspected the malady had been depression, one that was still going on. She wondered if this woman had wanted a child at all, if Nowell had browbeaten her into it. Or had fathered a child she then had to raise.

"Heather," the woman whispered. "This isn't a good idea."

"Let me decide that." Heather's voice was close to a growl.

"This won't make you happy."

"I'm an adult. This is money I earned, and I can decide what will or won't—"

"It won't. I know how you are, always up and down and—"

"See? There's the entire problem right there," Heather said, first looking pointedly at Emma, then glowering at her mother. "You don't know me at all!"

Emma had seen this particular roundelay. Had, in fact, been one half of it during Caroline's adolescence. Well, hell, past that, too. They'd never moved beyond that. Those same words, just about, spit out, shrieked, said coldly, used as shield and defense. You don't know me at all. Translation: There are no connections between us. None. And Emma was convinced that, just as was true for Caroline, nothing would make Heather happy or would stop either one of them from insisting that whatever quest caught her eye was the trick, the thing that would work.

Emma cleared her throat. "Nowell, your husband—his name was Nowell Wilson, correct?"

That terrified, about to run amok expression, then a nod.

"Middle name?"

"He didn't have one." The stern and tired face returned.

"And from what part of California was he originally?"

She swallowed again. "He wasn't. He was born in New York City. He didn't settle here till he was in his twenties. And I don't mean here—I mean, in California. After Vietnam."

"He served?"

She nodded.

"Then moved to California, to the Bay Area?"

She shook her head. "In . . . San Luis Obispo first, I think he said. Moved a lot."

Can you think of a way to make this more impossible? Emma wondered. But all she said out loud was, "Mrs. Wilson, when did you go to court, file the papers for the adoption?"

"I didn't. Nowell—The lawyer, actually, the lawyer did all of that. It was private, you see. Closed, if that's the word. We didn't know the natural mother, she didn't know us, wasn't supposed to. That's how it was. This kind of thing"—she waved at the room, at Emma, at her daughter—"wasn't supposed to ever happen."

"Did you know about her, however? Anything?"

She tilted her head from side to side, as if literally rolling an idea back and forth across the base of her skull. "I feel so bad that I know so little, but somehow—you have to believe me—it seemed natural back then. Like we were the family, and we were all there was. It felt . . . right."

Emma nodded. "I understand. Did you know anything about the natural mother?"

"Only that she was healthy. She had finished high school and some college. And she was a . . . a nice person. From a good family. That's what we were told." She cleared her throat. "Nowell, that is. That's what he was told."

Kay Wilson didn't sound convinced of it. Not even two decades later.

"Then why'd you tell me I came from scum?" Heather demanded. "Which is true? What you told me or what you're telling her?"

"Please, dear," Kay Wilson said. "Please." She shook her head, back and forth and back and forth, but offered no explanation.

"Fine," Emma said. "Let's get back to the house you lived in then. Where was it?"

"Why do you need all these things I can't remember? Can you remember every place you've rented? I can describe how it looked inside, but how does anybody remember every address or phone number? I wish Nowell were still alive—he'd remember." She looked ready to sob again.

"I know it was across the bay," she continued. "In Berkeley. Does that help? If you need the address, though, I can't . . . I don't . . . a little house. Green. Near . . . a dry cleaners. And a bookstore. I know I should remember, but I'm not good with names." She looked down at her lap, where her hands still twisted the life out of the shoulder straps of her purse.

Every bit of this situation was a grueling, overwhelming exam for this woman, who so feared flunking it. "That's all right," Emma said. "I just wanted the name of the town, that's all. And whether you owned the house."

"We rented."

No records there, then. She'd check the phone books for that year, see if that yielded up an address, although at the moment, she couldn't think what she'd do with it.

But that seemed it, all the information she'd been able to retrieve. That, and the birthdate of the baby who'd become Heather Wilson.

She bid them adieu. Kay Wilson repeatedly apologized for her faulty memory and Emma reassured her that it didn't matter, although of course it did.

After they'd left, Emma calculated the round-trip distance a sane driver might make from Berkeley and back again, including a break along the way in which to acquire a family.

A max of three hours each way? An exhausting day, a newborn to tend to en route—surely that was pushing it about as far as someone would go without sleeping over. She took out a ruler, arbitrarily declared a sixty mile per hour speed limit, averaged it out for the return trip with the infant, and made a circle on the map at about two hundred miles from San Francisco.

Bless the Pacific for filling half the circle, because what was left was sufficiently daunting. From Mendocino north, east to the Nevada border, south to San Luis Obispo.

Nowell Wilson had lived in San Luis Obispo. He'd have known people there, including the mysterious Dr. Smith. She'd search there first.

But just to be sure, she would check all the births in the three-hour-drive area on that date Kay Wilson had given her.

It wasn't as bad as it could have been. What if he'd flown? Or stayed overnight? At least this way, she could exclude Los Angeles and San Diego Counties. And all the boys born on that date.

She nonetheless wished she'd never accepted a cent from Heather Wilson. It was not only a bad case, a frustrating one, and a probably doomed one, but it was going to be a boring one to boot. She almost wished she felt sicker, really had the flu, so that she could ignore it while she was bedridden.

Just her luck to be so damn healthy.

Her mood, already low, sank into a sub-basement, and she turned to face her computer.

"Excuse me?"

That sweet voice that sounded as if it couldn't utter a negative word set Emma's inner ear aquiver. "What!" she said, swivelling around.

"Sorry, didn't mean to interrupt," Billie said. "I'm leaving now. I—"

"Is there a problem?" Emma snapped. *She* couldn't leave. She had to pay the bills and maintain this place and work with the helpless, hopeless Wilsons on this godawful fruitless search.

"No," Billie said, backing up. "I just thought—"

"Don't!" Oh, Christ, she hadn't meant to be that loud. "I mean don't for a minute think you have to tell me about every breath you take!"

Billie almost seemed ready to say something, but she didn't. She nodded, backed up and turned, waved to Zack, and left, closing the outer door more forcibly than was necessary.

"I only meant," Emma muttered as she tapped Heather's birth date into the computer, "I only meant nobody has to report in to me every movement. This isn't kindergarten. I *trust* her. How would it be if people had to tell me everything? It would be *demeaning* . . . but of course she won't understand that. Too immature. Too sensitive. Too . . . she'll think it means . . . something else."

Emma looked at the list of babies born in California on August

5, 1979. It was an effective argument for birth control and family planning.

Who could blame her for being impatient with an employee now and then? Wouldn't anybody be that way, faced with this?

Eight

She had no right to talk to her that way!

It was a good thing Billie was en route to pick up Jesse, because only the reminder of children, and children at play, kept her from driving the enraged way she wanted to.

This wasn't road rage, it was Emma rage.

What the hell was wrong with her? Billie surely hadn't done anything warranting that head-chewing response. She had stopped to explain that she was leaving early because of Ivan and the flu, and if she'd gotten to say it, that might have infuriated Emma, or seemed unprofessional. But she hadn't been given a chance. It didn't seem to matter. Emma was perpetually pissed at her, or the world. Or both.

She'd wanted to tell her about the Marine Mammal Center, and about the potential friend of Gavin's. You'd think Emma would want to know. Would, in fact, have asked on her own. After all, it was Emma's ass on the line with Michael Specht more than it was Billie's, and it was Emma who had specifically asked to be kept informed.

Near the party house, SUVs studded the curb like grommets on a seam. Billie always felt endangered near them, insufficiently protected from the behemoths by her aging Honda Civic.

She parked as close as she could get to where balloons floated above a mailbox, and made her way into the entryway of the house; a spacious, skylighted expanse of terra-cotta tile, soaring ceilings, and bedlam as farewells and peace treaties were made. Despite the presence of a disheveled clown slumping toward a car, Billie gathered that the usual miseries had taken place. The first clue was the missing birthday boy who'd been sent to his room for punching his guests, one of whom still looked red-eyed.

People thought birthing a child was the hard part, when it was nothing compared to the annual agony of celebrating the event.

"Hi, I'm Julia, Max's mother." A tired-looking woman extended her hand.

"My sympathies," Billie said. "Although you look to be holding up well." She turned to urge Jesse to gather his goody bag and get going.

"Wait, Mommy—come look. Max's mother said we could. Max has birds. Can I have one, too? Can we?" Jesse was starved for another small breathing thing—a dog, a cat, a pony, a hamster, a lizard, a snake, a baby brother or sister—anything. He requested one or the other on a daily basis. This was his first bird request.

Max's mother looked amused. She was obviously a resilient type, to have a sense of humor after hosting a preschool birthday party.

"Oh, don't bother," Billie said. "You're swamped here, and we can—"

"It'll give me a moment off," Julia said. "This way." Billie and Jesse followed her through several spacious rooms into a sunny plant-filled room off a swath of garden and then, beyond that, into a two-story caged expanse. An aviary larger than Billie's house was filled with brilliantly colored birds perched on a tall tree like so many dazzling ornaments.

"Spectacular," Billie said, meaning it.

"My husband's passion, though I've grown fond of them, too."

"I've never seen— What are they? That one?" She pointed to an intensely blue bird whose eyes and beak were outlined in bright yellow.

"A hyacinth macaw." Julia pointed. "He looks like a parrot, doesn't he, Jesse? And he's smart in addition to being gorgeous. That one over there is a black palm cockatoo—" The bird was blue-black, with red splashes on its cheek and wild plumage like a B-movie Indian's headdress.

"Amazing," Billie murmured. "Where on earth do you find such creatures?"

"People breed them. There's a whole network of collectors and my husband's pretty plugged into it so he hears when somebody's bred a great specimen. That's an African gray." Julia pointed. "Not glamorous, but the smartest of the smart. He has quite a vocabulary, when he feels like talking. Imitates all of us, laughs just like Max . . ." She smiled up at the bird.

Somebody called out for her and Julia charmingly made it clear that the show was over.

Jesse was not quite as tuned in to the subtleties of etiquette. "I want one," he said. "Can we have one, Mom? Just one?"

Billie rolled her eyes and Julia smiled. Kids.

Still, every time Jesse yearned for a pet, which was every moment he wasn't yearning for a sibling, Billie felt a throb of irrational guilt. He had no father to speak of, a distracted, tense mother, a somewhat nutty Russian as his nanny, and no pets.

So a bird might be a possibility. "I'll think about it, okay?" There was a store not far away. Maybe she'd take him over there this weekend. No, she'd go alone and surprise him.

Good intentions in place, she felt virtuous and guilt-free.

Jesse watched her the entire road home, as if monitoring her thoughts and making sure that birds stayed in them.

Ivan was in the living room, trying to look normal, at least until a cough that sounded as if it ripped out his intestines reduced him to a gasping wraith. He raised a hand in what probably was intended as a wave of greeting, but looked more like surrender.

"Look what I got, Ivan." Jesse dumped his goody bag onto the puke-green carpet—the very first thing Billie had vowed to replace if she ever had discretionary funds.

"Go rest," she told Ivan. "I'll bring you soup and tea. I'm here for the evening, so you don't have to do anything. Any messages?"

He stood up in slow increments, like an arthritic old man, and shook his head before shuffling to his room.

She sat on the sofa, her coat still on. Things would work out. Jesse looked hale. He'd be in extended day care tomorrow, too, and her appointment with the llama lady was for the morning. She could work in at least one additional interview and still pick him up in time. She let her muscles relax one by one and found herself staring at the TV as if it were an aquarium. She had no idea when Jesse had flicked cartoons on, but the swirl and flicker of moving shapes was soothing, made even more so when Jesse snuggled in next to her. She didn't even mind his playing the shrill plastic kazoo that had been in his goody bag. At least, she didn't mind much and in fact felt an unfamiliar rush of peace. Of contentment. "This is nice," she said, after a long while, her arm around her son. "I like being with you. Tonight we'll play whatever game you choose. Right now, it's time for me to take off my coat and go make our dinner."

Fifteen minutes later, the phone on the kitchen wall rang precisely as the pasta water surged up and over the lip of the pan. With her left hand, Billie poured oil on the troubled waters, and with her right, grabbed the receiver.

"I'm sorry to have to say this." She didn't recognize the voice. "I can't make it tomorrow." She paused for a fraction, then said, "Oh! I'm sorry even more; I didn't identify myself. This is Veronica. We have a meeting scheduled out here in the morning, but I won't be here."

Billie controlled a rush of irritation. Ranchers didn't up and chug off to— Where in hell would she be going?

The angel-hair pasta was about to leave the al dente stage for the mush stage. She braced the phone under her chin, removed the pot and headed for the sink.

From the tiny back room, she heard a choked cough. "Let's reschedule," she said. "When will you be back?"

"That's just it. I'm not sure."

Billie tossed the drained strands with another dollop of olive oil. "Thanks for telling me, then. When you do get back, why don't you give me a call—or—" Behind her, the tomato sauce hit the critical temperature and popped itself onto the wall behind the range. She put down the pasta, turned the burner to its lowest setting and covered the pot. "Easier still, could you talk to me now? I just wanted a handle on Gav—"

"I know and I want to talk to you." And then talk she did, in a great rush. "But—listen, I . . . well, is it humanly possible for you to get out here tonight? I'm thirty minutes away, max, and I know it's an imposition, but it's because of this emergency. My brother-in-law just called. My sister started labor. They have a three-year-old and a two-year-old and right now a neighbor's watching them, but I promised I'd— This turned into a high-risk pregnancy and she isn't due for another month, so I don't know how long I'll be—"

"Then it'd be a major help if you'd talk to me now. There is time pressure." Billie turned off the burner. She could reheat the pasta and sauce. The more the end product sogged into canned-variety taste, the more Jesse would enjoy it.

"The thing is, I was going to worm the llamas tomorrow, except I have to do it right now. The woman who'll feed them and all while I'm gone, she won't do worming. In fact, I'm halfway through. I was rushing around like crazy when I remembered you were coming tomorrow, and I'm really trying to get to them before it's too dark, you see?"

"Want me to come up to your sister's, then?"

"She's in Santa Rosa and I'll be in and out, back and forth—and those kids—it'd be really hard to tell you precisely when. I don't even know the drill yet."

Billie realized she was nodding. That surprised her because the rest of her felt too weary and put upon to move a muscle. It was nearly dark already. "How about I call you back in an hour and a half? You'll be done then, and—"

"To be honest, I'd rather do this in person. No offense, but the thing is I don't want to talk till I see you. Have a sense of you, okay?"

Not really at all okay, but understandable. "At your place, then. Tonight." Damn and double damn.

"I'll try to be all packed and everything before you get here so you don't waste your time. You still have the directions?"

She did, and she said so, and then she took a deep breath and went back to Ivan's room. The TV could babysit Jesse, much as Billie disapproved. Wouldn't hurt for one night, a few hours while Ivan vegetated in the wingback chair. No harm done.

Sickness was palpable in Ivan's room, the air thick with it. "Ivan?" she whispered in the dusky light. She could hear the moisture in his lungs with each inhalation. "Ivan?"

Nothing but the rattly, deep sucks of air. He was out cold, anesthetized with antihistamines and fever, and there was no way he could be responsible for so much as his own toes. She closed the door behind her.

She was going to look like an incompetent fool with a pre-schooler tagging behind her, either shyly lurking behind her legs or launching into hyperactive magno-destructo mode. Either way, not good.

If her fairy godmother ever showed her face and offered her three wishes, high on the list would be the appearance of competency. It seemed enormously important, maybe more important than competency itself. She wanted it so much she could taste it. She wanted Emma to slap her forehead and say how incredibly wrong she'd been about Billie August.

Tonight was not going to advance that goal.

"Jess," she said while they ate their overcooked pasta. "How'd you like to take a ride with me in the dark. You can stay up late, too."

He looked pleased by the idea, then he changed his mind. "You promised we'd play."

"We'll play 'take a trip in the car.' "

"That isn't a game. You said I could pick the game."

"Here's the thing," she said. "I have to work. I didn't think I would, but guess what? I do."

"No!" he shouted, then he put his head down onto the table, his hands cupping his ears. Hear no evil, ride no cars.

Well, great. Tonight she could disappoint everybody, all at once. She imagined Emma's expression when——if——she heard about her investigator taking a kid along with her. And Veronica's when she saw a three-year-old arrive along with Billie. And Jesse shouting "No!" the whole time.

Then to hell with it. Billie would behave as if this were the most natural thing. Of course I brought my son along. What would you expect when you screw up our appointment? It's your fault.

She could almost begin to understand Emma's approach to life, and see its appeal.

She cleared the dishes and prepared for the trip with her hostile three-year-old passenger. Obviously, her fairy godmother had put her name at the end of the wish-granting list, and this was how it was. A whiny kid, a frustrating interview with a woman who didn't like phones, and an employer who'd be angry at the idea of Jesse's doing a ride-along for an interview.

But Emma would be angry no matter what. Billie had to remember that.

She stood straighter and dried her hands with the kitchen towel.

Since she couldn't possibly please Emma, why the hell worry about displeasing her?

The only thing left to worry about was why it had taken her this long to realize that.

except she hadn't invisible please remove along the ballpoint faint explanation key?

like with him if not to it were should you give it had y you say that, to walk - that.

Nine

The ride might have been pleasant had they been able to see the countryside, a stretch of nearly virgin California landscape, except for the strip of blacktop cutting through it. But the night had become misty and heavy with clouds, and visibility was limited, and her son had obviously memorized the kid-script that made him whine, "Are we there yet?" at five-second intervals.

Once they arrived at Whynot Farm, things eased. Billie pushed the button in front of the gate, heard a voice shout, "Be right there," and waited as a tall slender woman in her thirties—close to Billie's own age, she estimated—walked from an unpretentious home toward them, and swung open the gate.

"I'm Veronica," she said, hand outstretched as Billie got out of the car. "Glad to meet you, and thanks, really, for switching your schedule around."

"Mom!" from the back seat.

Veronica Napoles looked at the car, then at Billie.

"I . . . my baby-sitter . . . I . . ." Billie shrugged. She was through with apologizing, even mentally, for how her life worked.

"So we both had child-related emergencies," Veronica said. "No problem." Her dark hair was pulled back and held with a large clasp, and her fine features looked scrubbed. No makeup, no ornaments. The word "wholesome" came to Billie's mind.

"Come with me," she said to both of them. "I need one last checkup, to make sure they're okay. They all just got shots." Jesse moved closer to Billie. "Needle shots," Veronica said. "Not guns."

"I don't like needles, either," Jesse whispered to Billie.

"I like the name of this place," Billie said. "Funny—or am I making a faux pas and 'Whynot' is a family name or something?"

Veronica shook her head. "It's an answer. My answer. I was a programmer. Good at it, but I had a small problem: I hated it. Still, when I inherited a little from my grandparents, and I decided to chuck the day job and grow organic vegetables and raise llamas, there was a general hue and cry as if I'd gone insane. If one more person said 'Why on earth are you doing that?' I'd have gone bonkers. Instead, I had cards made up with the name, and just handed them to them. Shut them right up."

The llamas didn't seem concerned about the logic behind their lives in West Marin. They regarded their nighttime visitors with mild curiosity. Veronica explained that this was the bachelor herd, kept segregated from the females and babies for the sake of population control. "The boys," she called them.

"Lemme *see*," Jesse said, and Billie lifted him so he could stand on a rung of the fence. Sometimes he loomed so large in her mind, dominated so much of her being, that she forgot how small he actually was.

"Don't my boys look beautiful?" Veronica sounded serious. "They've all been brushed, so they're at their best—although I'm half-dead. Do you like having your hair brushed, Jesse? My boys— and my girls, too—aren't keen on it, but we've got to keep that fiber in shape for shearing come spring, so people can weave with it later."

Jesse looked at her as if waiting for the point. Billie didn't blame him. Veronica was babbling in the nervous, overly animated voice of someone who'd forgotten that she, too, was once a kid.

"I can't see," Jesse whined. "It's too dark."

Billie knew he could see but dimly, as she did. The moon was blocked by cloud cover and the llamas seemed ghostly deeper dark shapes against the already dark background. Billie had to serve as intergenerational interpreter. "Veronica was saying that later on, when the animals get their hair cut, people knit sweaters and things out of their hair."

"I don't like getting my hair cut, either," Jesse said.

"I'm going to have a hard time talking to my sister's kids, aren't I?" Veronica murmured.

"It's a business, then? Selling their coats?"

"Struggling, but getting there. These have fine fiber." She waved at the herd in front of them. "And they're used as, well, watchdogs—guards—for sheep, against foxes, so I'm considering that, too, along with their becoming caddies."

"Excuse me?" Billie pictured a llama in a golf cap.

"Really. There's a golf course here that wants to use them as caddies, but I'm not so sure about that."

The world grew ever stranger, Billie thought, imagining these South American mountain creatures hauling clubs around a course, and wondering what the hell they'd be thinking as they watched humans tee off.

"Can I touch one?" Jesse whispered. At least he wasn't asking if he could have one, Billie thought. At least not yet.

The llamas were not near the fence, and Veronica took some while to answer. "Better not," she said. "They're way over there, and humming. It's a tired sounding hum, 'cause they've been through a lot—brushing and those needles, you see."

"Just look at them, sweetie," Billie whispered. "Aren't they interesting animals?"

"Don't want to annoy them because they're even more interesting when they spit stinky green stomach contents. Which is what I'd like to avoid by not making them come over."

Keeping her distance, Billie studied the creatures. Interesting— or strange was more like it. Not beautiful, except to Veronica, they looked hastily invented, like an assortment of mismatched parts and colors: rabbit-faced heads on thick, long necks, barrel-shaped torsos on spindle legs, fleece a crazy quilt of browns, whites, tans, and black in any and every combination and all hanging raggedly as if they'd borrowed their heavy coats from larger friends.

"Makes gorgeous fiber," Veronica said.

Billie had to take it on faith; some alchemy obviously transpired between beast and loom.

"They look fine," Veronica said after inspecting her small herd. "And, not that you asked, but I'll tell you anyway—not a single one of my llamas is named Dolly." She grinned. Jesse stared at her, stone-faced. "Now we'll let them sleep."

Jesse jumped off the rail.

"Can he watch TV?" she asked Billie. "I have some Disney on video from when my sister's kids were here."

Jesse, with a backward glance at the animals, now opted for his shy routine, which was fine with Billie. "Stay with me," he whispered. Luckily, Veronica's house turned out to be mostly one room, the TV at one corner, the kitchen table at the other. Things were going to work out.

The room was furnished with solid, worn pieces sitting on weathered planks partially covered by a faded Oriental rug. "Welcome to Flea Market Central," Veronica said. "I invested my capital elsewhere." She waved with both hands toward the great outdoors.

She brought a pot of herbal tea to the formica-topped table, and looked over at Jesse's back, where he'd seated himself in front of the TV. Beyond his silhouetted body, technicolor cartoon figures cavorted. "Tracy bought that video, for my niece and nephew," she said softly. "She was like that. Thoughtful. It saved the day then, too, but I wouldn't have thought of anything like it till way too late."

"You knew Tracy, then?" Billie said.

Veronica's eyes widened. Then she frowned. "I assumed that's why you called me."

Billie shook her head. "It was actually Gavin . . . the woman at the Marine Mammal Center said you were Gavin's friend."

"I knew him, but through Tracy. I tried to help involve him in some activities I thought he'd enjoy. Tracy thought it would be good for him. Tracy was really his friend. I wasn't, not that way."

"And you don't think he killed her."

Veronica shook her head. "Why would he? He's odd, I'll give you that. But there's a stunned kind of sweetness under his oddness. He gets muddled, fearful, and mixes signals. Not that I'm a shrink or any kind of mental-problems expert, but that's what I've observed. I might worry that he'd misunderstand something, or make a foolish choice—or even defend himself inappropriately—but never be the instigator, the mean one. That's why I suggested he volunteer up at the Marine Mammal Center. He loved animals and he was gentle with them. And Tracy was suddenly hot to do something with animals, so they could do it together."

Billie sighed. Nothing you could bring into a court of law. Gavin was erratic and not quite normal, but nice to animals.

"Gavin isn't the kind to make phone calls, either," Veronica said.

"Meaning what?"

Veronica leaned forward into the table, lowering her voice. "I'd get phone calls here. Wouldn't hear a thing. Not heavy breathing, not talk, not a hang-up. Dead silence until I hung up."

"Any idea of who'd want to do that to you?"

She nodded. "Tracy was staying here by then. She'd wanted to leave Robby for a long time, but she was always strapped for cash. Liked living well, better than she could afford. And every time she thought she had enough cash to make the break, something came up, like her car would die, but then she said she finally 'felt able' to make the break. I assumed that meant she'd saved money, 'cause breaking with him wasn't a matter of big emotional scenes on her part. Her feelings for him had ended a long time before."

74

"For how long did you get these calls?" Billie wanted to move on. Silent calls were the absence of anything. Sure, someone might be trying to frighten Tracy or Veronica, more likely. But if the person was clever—or stupid—enough to do nothing that was actually terrifying or threatening, how could that help Gavin Riddock?

"Every day for two weeks—the two weeks before she was killed."

"You told the police?"

Veronica sighed, and looked across the room to where Jesse sat mesmerized. "Yes. But only after . . . not right away. Not then. Tracy was . . . I don't know. Afraid of making Robby angrier, maybe. We told the police after about a week."

"And?"

"Silent calls don't make for major drama and that's all I got. The thing is, I think that when Tracy answered, when I wasn't around, he spoke to her, because twice I came in and she was on the phone, flushed and angry, telling him to leave her alone."

"Him?"

Veronica nodded. "She said so."

"And leave *her* alone? Not leave *us* alone? Or leave *you* alone? I mean it's your house."

"My point exactly. Those calls were for her, against her, frightening, and threatening to her."

"Did you try to—"

"Have them traced? We were going to. The next night, we weren't going to hang up, no matter how long it took, and I was going to call the cops on my cell phone and see if they could trace them but instead, well . . . there wasn't any next night."

"Despite what you heard, could the calls have been for you?"

Veronica's expression soured with annoyance. "Of course they *could* have been, but does that make sense? I never got one till the night after she came here."

"Peace," Billie said. "I'm trying to think of whatever . . . Any ideas about who it was?"

"Isn't it obvious? Her husband Robby. A piece of . . ." She shook her head and dabbed at the side of her right eye.

"We're still talking about these phone calls, aren't we?"

Veronica took a deep breath, tilted her head and looked at Billie appraisingly. "Robby Lester is the human example of Berserk Male Syndrome."

She said that too patly, with too much practice, and Billie suspected it was not the first time she'd described someone that way. "Okay, I bite," Billie said. "What the hell is that?"

"When a llama—practically always a male—is insane. He's abnormally socialized to people. Too much of humans, not enough of his own kind. Too little discipline when he's small and misbehaving. Eventually, he goes berserk. Territorial and aggressive, way beyond the norm. Dangerous. You can't unteach this, or send the llama to a shrink. What you do . . ." She paused again, tapped her short nails on the flecked formica. "You euthanize them," she said in a voice so cold it was in itself a death sentence.

Billie waited a moment. "Tracy talked to the caller, right?"

"She told him to leave her alone. When I asked, she said it wasn't Robby. Why she'd protect him, I don't know. She said it was a wrong number which was ridiculous because I heard her, and that isn't how you talk to a wrong number."

"And you told the police."

"They made note of it but then, when she was . . . when she died, it didn't matter. Robby Lester has an alibi," Veronica said. "He has friends." She waved at the air, almost fighting off invisible presences who were getting too close. "Of course they'd cover for him. It's too ridiculous. Dare I say that the Tiburon police force—they're nice people and I'm sure they mean well, and they're admittedly great at ticketing speeders, but before now, they've had to deal with exactly one open-and-shut homicide case in the last millennium."

Billie couldn't think of a counterargument.

"They're over their heads on this. Gavin touched the body, possibly even moved her a little and she'd been out there, against a metal statue for a while. It was dawn. So Robby claims to have been in bed, as would normal people. Only thing is, he's berserk, but how do I prove that?"

"I gather he wasn't happy about this divorce."

"Separation. They hadn't gotten to the next step. And no, he was definitely not happy about it."

It had only been a matter of weeks since Tracy had relocated from her marriage to Veronica's ranch. "Robby," she prompted. "How did he show his anger?"

Veronica shrugged. "I'm sure he was making those phone calls, listening, like he was bugging her. And I said what I think. Robby Lester is a male gone berserk. He was always a brawler if he thought he was provoked, a 'real man,' you know? The kind who says he doesn't 'take crap.' But it was all like the llamas—male against male. Protecting his turf, until Tracy walked out and became fair game." She shook her head. "Look, I'll give you the name of somebody else who knew Tracy and Gavin, too. Go see my friend Lizzie, she'll tell you how they were and why it's insane to think Gavin Riddock killed his best friend." She pulled a drawer out of the old-fashioned kitchen table, found a tablet and pen and wrote a number on it.

Billie put the paper into her purse. "Did her husband do anything physical?" she asked. "Anything to her? I mean before she was killed."

"You mean is there something that would impress the cops? Proof? No. She was banged up once after she told him she was leaving. She said she'd been in a fender-bender, but I couldn't see evidence of it on her car. She insisted it wasn't him, but I'm sure she was protecting him. She felt bad about making him feel bad by leaving."

"So she didn't bring charges," Billie said.

Veronica shook her head.

"Or take out a restraining order."

Another head shake. "After she was dead, I told the police about the black-and-blue marks and the cut and they said it was hearsay. I'm sure it wasn't the only time, either. Robby's that kind of man."

Billie remembered a WW II poster her parents had acquired, with a stern person demanding, in the era of gas rationing: "IS THIS TRIP NECESSARY?"

It had been a joking byword in their house—while they were still a household and while they still made jokes—the password that allowed the car keys to be handed over, and she'd always been able to defend the utter necessity of any outing she desired.

This trip had not been necessary. Veronica had yielded nothing but speculation, prejudice, skewed intuition, and llama analogies.

There was this good thing about children: they provided an excuse to leave. "You know, it's getting late for Jesse, and you're probably starting out early, so unless there's something else you wanted to say, we'd better be—"

"If you're trying to help Gavin Riddock, get somebody to think about Robby Lester."

It was traditional good form to exaggerate the onerousness of your friend's ex, but Veronica was pushing too hard and pushing nothing more than air. She *thought* he'd made those phone calls, she *felt it in her heart* he'd hurt his estranged wife that one time and others, despite Tracy's denials, she *felt it in her gut* that he'd killed her.

No wonder the police ignored her.

Veronica looked hunched, her elbows on her knees. "Gavin's finding Tracy was the luckiest thing that ever happened to the murderer. But anybody who knew that they ran together—and Robby surely knew—would have been able to predict that. Whenever she didn't show up at his house, he went out on his own. So anybody would know that, and how to get Tracy as she was going to Gavin's house. Anybody with half a brain and a major grudge could have planned the entire scenario."

"I'll see what I can do," Billie said. It was a fine sentence, promising absolutely nothing, which was, she thought, about what she could do.

Ten

Emma watched Billie sidle past her open door and into her own portion of the office. The girl behaved as if she didn't know Emma was there. Not a snub precisely, but definitely an avoidance. She'd heard her greet Zack when she arrived.

She was being punished by Ms. Sensitive.

Emma knew she probably should say something. Smooth the water. Obviously, the delicate child was in a huff, feeling injured.

Ridiculous. Emma hadn't said anything bad. Just . . . maybe she'd said whatever it was a little too . . . It wasn't as if she'd cursed at the girl or chewed her out or personally attacked her, for God's sake. Couldn't Billie understand that even Emma had bad days, didn't feel so hot, got irritable, was *human*?

This was the real world. The girl couldn't behave like a conservatory orchid and do this job, and that's all Emma was trying to do—toughen her up, make her able to handle this life. So what if her tone of voice wasn't always angelic, what was the big deal?

The girl was a fool and an irritant and Emma would be damned before she'd grovel or beg forgiveness. For anything.

Instead, she poured herself another cup of the burned-tasting brew in her coffee pot and returned attention to her desk. She flicked her index finger at a small pile of mail. Catalogs. A book on self-marketing, something she knew she had to do for the company and herself, although at the moment she couldn't bring herself to open the book. Three unanswered phone messages, one from Heather Wilson who was showing signs of being a world-class pain in the butt. One day into her search and she wanted to know how come the riddle of her ancestry hadn't been solved yet.

It surely hadn't. Emma was combing through the statewide birth index records for Heather's birthday, give or take a day. Adopted or not, she was born, so where was the listing?

She looked for asterisks, the state's indication that this was a second birth certificate, an amended one that followed the adoption and replaced the original one. Then she could search for the same certificate number elsewhere, and with some luck, find the original certificate.

Asterisks there were, four of them: two were boys, one was a child named Mei Chang, and the fourth, a girl now named Margarita Amelia Romero. But nothing showed up when she tried the list by name. No Heather Wilson born August 5, 1979 in California. Or the day before, or the day after. Or, in fact, that week.

Emma didn't even want to consider neighboring states; a baby born in Nevada, or flown in from Georgia or Alaska. It was possible, but close to futile to ascertain, so she was going to ignore that idea for now.

She double-checked for the possibility of clerical error, though she doubted it. She reformatted the list so that it read county by county. She eliminated children from the far north and south of California. Of course, Nowell Wilson could have been a maniacal driver capable of going farther than the radius Emma had drawn. And the entire story of Heather's arrival could be a lie to make sure that Emma didn't track her origin.

She simply couldn't deal with those ideas right now. They'd have to wait for the total desperation phase.

Kay Wilson hovered in Emma's mind. Smiling, pleasant, and as vague as an organism claiming to be human could be. Yet the woman had a good job at Macy's. She couldn't be as passive and forgetful as she appeared to be.

Emma couldn't blame her for disliking this search, but in that case, she might as well have said so and told Heather to do it herself if she felt it was important.

So many babies, Emma thought, going through the list. She wondered idly how many of them were still around, two decades later. How many had moved, fallen fatally ill, been gunned down in stupid rivalries. How many were in jail. How many were parents themselves.

She wondered what Heather's story was, who she was, aside from a listless creature with a boring and menial job. She wondered what the woman who'd given her up for adoption truly represented to her. Sometimes Emma wished people had to answer all her questions, not only the ones on the form. And then send in follow-up reports. *Dear Ms. Howe, This is how I used the information you found. Yes, I'm glad you confirmed my husband's affair.* Or *no, nothing's better now and I wish I had listened to your advice.* Or *we've fired those people you caught spying and now, here's what they're doing . . .*

But most of the time, she kept her attention on the here and now and her job. Her own life was hers. These bits and pieces of others were work, sufficient and complete unto itself, not stories to be unraveled, not blanks to be filled in.

She'd gone through the entire week's births twice now and nothing. She brought back on screen the counties she'd eliminated because they were too much for a one-day round-trip drive. Maybe Kay had been wrong about that. Maybe the child had been brought to a collection spot, a lawyer's office away from the birth site.

Nothing there, either. She'd known there wouldn't be; there hadn't been anything when she did it by name, statewide.

Heather Wilson's birth date was a lie and this wasn't vagueness. This was a deliberate lie. And since Heather hadn't contradicted

Kay, this lie was long-standing. For twenty years, the girl had celebrated an imagined birth date.

Emma stood up in frustrated anger, pushed back her chair and paced her office. What was it with Kay Wilson? She realized she was shaking her head with irritation at the woman's deceptions and ruses. Confused and walking in circles, precisely the way Kay wanted her to.

Kay Wilson had been so damnably vague about where she'd lived at any given time. "North of here around then. Not Mendocino or anything, but above Santa Rosa. We moved quite often. Rented. We lived in, oh, a grandmother unit in Berkeley. I guess it wasn't legal, exactly, but you know how those things work. Things were hard."

Had Kay been on drugs back then? Was that the big secret of her dimness, her murky memories? Had she been shut away some place she didn't want to identify? And if so, who'd have given her a baby to adopt?

If any of this was close to the truth.

She sat back down, sighed, muttered a few choice phrases to Kay Wilson, wherever she was, then, finally, did a global search—any day, any county—just tell me if a Heather Wilson got herself born, ever, that year.

And there she was. Not in August, but in December. Four months later. An enormous difference in a newborn—nobody could confuse the two ages. Could this really be the same child?

She was going to find out. Get the birth certificate and see the mother's name.

December, in Monterey County.

She imagined a young, single woman, twenty years ago, alone and unhappy in the beautiful surrounds of Monterey. Maybe her parents tossed her out, maybe she felt she couldn't face them. Maybe they were dead.

So what had she done? Had she found the mysterious Dr. Smith?

Found Nowell Wilson and sold him her baby? Or given her to him. Was Nowell possibly the father? There was no asterisk on the birth record, no indication that this was an adoption and there was therefore no corresponding certificate number for the original birth. This was disturbing whether it was a clerical error or, more probably, another, mystifying lie on Kay Wilson's part.

All Emma asked of humanity was a modicum of honesty. Be straight with her, refuse to cooperate if you're set against it, but don't lie. Kay Wilson's hypocrisy was infuriating.

"Okay, lady," she said out loud, standing up, "now this is about us, between you and me, and you are going to lose. Emma is on your trail."

She'd drive down to Monterey, get the amended birth certificate—she didn't want to wait for them to mail her one—and once she had that, see what she could dig up in the archives of the local papers. Sometimes—rarely, but sometimes—the paper fouled up and printed the name of the birth mother.

She checked the time. Tomorrow she'd do all that. Today, she'd go home, relax, have a drink, watch bad TV. She couldn't remember if George was coming over or not. She thought maybe not, so she'd cook herself something heavy on the garlic and spices. Everything he couldn't eat.

She had one sleeve of her raincoat on when Billie materialized in her doorway looking wary, as if Emma bit, for God's sake.

"*Yes?*" Emma hadn't meant to say it that loudly. The girl flinched. Too goddamned sensitive! Emma was tired of trying so hard with her. Plus Billie could surely see that Emma was about to leave, her arm was still stuck in that sleeve, for God's sake, and she was getting hot, and what did this pesky— "*Yes?*" She pulled off the raincoat and tossed it on her chair. Missed. It crumpled onto the floor. She left it there. "Yes?" The girl swallowed hard before she spoke.

"I was wondering when I'm supposed to check in with Michael Specht. Did he have a schedule with you? A regular time? You didn't say."

Emma picked up and pulled her coat back on as she spoke. "Talk to him when you have something to say. Do you?"

Billie hesitated, as if she were debating the answer to that simple question.

This was all an act. She wasn't retarded or mentally handicapped or whatever they called it these days, so it had to be that her artsy-fartsy background had ruined her. She had to make the grand entrance, had to make every statement a pronouncement, infuse every gesture with enormous meaning. She either had something to tell Specht or she didn't. Was that so difficult to decide? If she couldn't tell the difference between knowing something or not knowing anything, how the hell was she going to be an investigator?

"I was out at this place in West Marin. It's called 'Whynot Farm.' "

She paused. Emma suspected she was supposed to smile at the name, maybe even crack up, slap her knee, salute Billie for discovering such a witty pun of a farm name, but Emma didn't like that kind of fey cuteness, and that wasn't information, anyway. She thought bitterly of how close to home and a drink she'd already be if this girl expressed herself like a normal human being.

Instead of pointing at her watch, which is what she wanted to do, she waved Billie into the chair on the other side of her desk, and pulled her coat off yet again. Billie took her seat with an expression so grateful, you'd think she'd expected Emma to make her stand at attention while she reported in.

"The woman who runs it," she began, "was Gavin Riddock's friend, at least to the extent that she's the one who sent him to the Marine Mammal Center. She was also Tracy Lester's friend—in fact, Tracy was staying with her when she was killed. And she—Veronica— is convinced that Tracy's husband—she was separated—had beaten her up at least once and was harassing her with phone calls. He'd hang up if Veronica answered, and she's sure he killed her."

This was good stuff. Michael would be very pleased. "What else do you have?"

Billie looked blank.

"To back it up."

"See, that's the thing. Nothing real enough." Billie looked down at her hands, then up at Emma again. "That's why I don't know what to do."

"What about the violence?"

Billie shook her head. "No records. No police reports."

Emma's wavelet of optimism evaporated into the sand. Feelings again. Oh, but they must have been sympatico, Ms. August and the Whynot Farmer, emotions pouring forth. Emma was glad she hadn't been anywhere near them.

"Somebody phoned and stayed silent every night for two weeks," Billie said. "Except two times when Tracy spoke with the caller. She said it wasn't Robby, only a wrong number, but it didn't sound like a wrong number. She was heard telling the caller to leave her alone. She was killed before they tried a trace."

Stupid to have thought Ms. August would come up with anything you could put your hands on. This rancher had a crank caller. A silent caller, so who even knew if the harassment—if that's what it was—was for Tracy? Billie had precisely nothing except the words of an upset woman and a few wrong numbers.

"A pissed off husband is always a good suspect," Emma said, "but the police must have had reasons for not agreeing."

"This Veronica has a major hate on for Robby Lester and I'm not totally sure why."

"It's hard to warm up to a person you're sure murdered your friend."

Dim girl looked as if she wasn't sure if Emma was making a joke, mild though it was. As if Emma never joked!

"I meant . . ." Billie said, then she looked at Emma appraisingly, and grinned. "You're right. I've never cared for the people who murdered my friends."

"Can you talk to Mr. Lester?"

"Why would he want to help the defense of his wife's accused murderer?"

"Offhand, I can't think of a single reason, but I'm sure I could, if pressed. As could you. But if you go there as yourself—in case he really is dangerous—we should go together." She looked away as she spoke, focused on the Victorian hat rack that held two Giants' baseball caps, a scarf, and three coffee mugs.

"Really? Oh, that'd be—tha—" Sweet Jesus, there it was, just as feared. A complete overreaction. But then, Emma could almost hear Billie pull on the brakes, come to a shuddering, screechy halt. "Good idea," Billie finally said in a clipped, neutral voice.

Emma stood up. "And now," she said, leaving unsaid the rest of her directive: get out, leave me alone, get on with your work.

Billie also stood, but she wasn't ready to let go. Once again, she looked like the slow learner at the back of the class. "Then— what do I—should I even mention—I'm talking about Michael Specht. About telling him whatever, about this man." She moved behind Emma, and slowly the two of them left the room, until they were barely past the reception area, where Zack looked up for a moment, then returned to whatever he was studying on the computer screen.

Zack had said it wouldn't kill Emma to acknowledge human emotions once a fiscal quarter. But why? Every mess Emma was called upon to investigate had an overflow of human emotions as its root cause. It was idiotic to think there should be still more, and more show about them.

"I mean, is this worth telling him?" Billie stuttered out. "Michael Specht, I mean."

How many times in one sentence did the girl have to tell Emma that she meant what she meant? "Of course it is. Tell him whatever you found out. Let him take it from there."

"Now? When?"

"Well . . . what did you have in mind to do next?" Emma would take book that the answer was "not a damn thing" said politely, in the style taught the privileged few at private school.

"I thought I should talk to Gavin Riddock," Billie said promptly. "We don't really have much in the way of contacts, people who know him. How was the list drawn up? Who provided names? Why wasn't Veronica on it?"

"Gavin," Emma said. "In his fashion and for what it's worth. He's understandably stunned, disoriented, and less than normally articulate, which wasn't ever much. Less aware than he'd normally be. His mother helped a little, and the schools he attended."

"It's obviously not very comprehensive. I thought maybe Gavin would be calmer now, and be able to think of more names. People who know him, could speak up for him, who Mr. Specht doesn't know about."

She looked rabbity when she got this way, as if her face were pushing forward at its center, her nose all but twitching. "Help me!" Little Timid's expression said. How could she toughen up Rabbit Girl?

Zachary coughed. Little Timid glanced over at him. Then she squared her shoulders and raised her eyebrows and stood up straighter.

Something in the air shifted. Emma could almost feel it pass by her face, but she didn't know what it was. "Interview Gavin?" she murmured, repeating Billie's idea. "I don't know . . . you could be right."

Another look darted between Zachary and Billie. What the hell was going on?

Then: *"Right?"* Billie said. "I could be *right?*" Her face took on a positively beatific expression of joy. "You guess I could be right? Oh, Emma, *thanks!*" Her voice sounded like bright colored foil, light sparking off it. "It's *great* to be given positive reinforcement! Makes an *enormous* difference to a raw green recruit like me. All the difference in the world! I feel so much better now!"

"What did I—?"

Behind Billie, Zack smiled broadly, even when Emma glared at him.

Billie's own smile grew even wider, more brilliant. "What did you do? You did everything and just when I so desperately needed it, too!" She sounded like one of those motivational leaders Emma had seen on late night TV. "It probably doesn't register because it comes so naturally to you. All the same, I should have told you sooner how much it means to me. But trust me—I'll justify your faith in me. I will! I promise!" And she turned and all but skipped back to her cubicle.

Zack had his head at a ridiculous angle, so that she couldn't see his face. She could have sworn she heard something akin to a snort.

"Don't you dare say a word," she warned him. "Not a single, solitary word."

He looked at her, his lips held tightly together but curling up at the corners, his eyes dancing, "Not a single," he announced, "a whole lot. And they are: First, behold, the worm turneth. Second, and high time, too. And third, bet you can't drive this one away, Emma. She's tougher than you want to see."

Emma winked at him and left the office. Billie was more interesting than she'd suspected.

All the same, Emma was glad Billie had retreated to her cubicle before she'd seen Emma smile.

Eleven

Heather Wilson lifted the phone. The detective hadn't returned her call. Maybe she hadn't gotten the message. The guy on the phone hadn't sounded interested, so who knew what he'd done with it? And Heather wanted—needed—the detective to tell her how her case was going.

Her case. She liked the sound of that.

Liked having somebody work for her instead of always being the person who worked for somebody else. Liked being able to pick up the phone and demand a little attention, a little respect. The customer is always right. Right?

But just her luck, in came the boss, and she quietly replaced the receiver in its cradle. Mr. Vincent got royally pissed when you made personal calls on what he always called *his* time. His time. As if she lived in some parallel universe and the clock on the wall didn't apply to her. Actually, Mr. Vincent made her feel that way about herself, too. As soon as she got this all straightened out about her mother, she was going to find something else. Her ex-boyfriend had gotten her this job, and it had seemed like it would be okay, but there had to be something better to do than filing invoices and her nails day after day. She would have quit sooner, but she needed to save enough money to hire a PI, plus she didn't want to give her mother—her stepmother—the satisfaction of saying "I told you so."

She was always on her case about this job. It wasn't "good enough" it didn't "use her to full capacity." She was right, but she made Heather so mad with that whole business of what was proper and what a person should do. You would think she was the Queen of England, she had so many rules about how people had to act. Rules that nobody else Heather knew had to follow.

But the fact was, it had been a mistake since day one, leaving school and taking this job. The only saving grace was that now it could pay for the private investigator and she could find out who she really was. She was pretty much trapped here until she'd paid Emma Howe whatever it took, as long as it took.

"Hi, girls," Mr. Vincent said.

She didn't much like that, either, the way Marlena and she were "girls" while he was Mr. Vincent, and the accountant was Mr. Poulus, and even the guy who drew the ads was a mister. The truck drivers had first names, but they weren't "the boys" or anything like that.

" 'Lo." Heather said without taking her eyes off the estimate form on the computer screen.

"Hey, there, Mr. V!" Marlena said, as if his arrival were the biggest, best thing she could imagine.

She was always that way. A suck-up of the first degree, and a stupid suck-up because where had it gotten her? So she was the one who talked to people coming in to this dump and Heather didn't. Big major deal. Who wanted to, anyway? Half of them just wanted packing boxes. People moving called in most of the time, or Mr. Vincent made the deal himself without either of them, and she answered the phone, just like Marlena did. Without sucking up to Mr. V.

Marlena hinted that she had something going with Mr. V, but Heather was almost 100 percent sure that was just talk. Marlena thought she was gorgeous, when she was just a lot of bright colors, most of them fake.

"Long time no see!" Marlena said to their boss. Or to his back.

He'd gone into his own office, ignoring her, but that didn't stop her from talking to him, acting like they were having a conversation. Bet she thought that was original, that "long time no see." Or what she was always saying, it was "retro." She'd been saying crap like that a whole lot lately. Wearing clothing from the thrift store, looking like those women in late-night movies. The most stupid ones. Hopelessly out of style. But Marlena called it "retro chic," those weird dresses with the full skirts, or worse, the ones she called "sheaths" that were tight all over. She looked ridiculous in them and the hair that hung over one eye.

Mr. V reemerged from his office. Checking up on them now.

"You'll never guess who was here while you were away on business." Marlena's voice was trilly. Heather tried to think of who she could mean, but Mr. V frowned. He looked up from the pile of mail he held. Heather knew it was mostly junk because she was in charge of putting it in his in-box. Like a doggie with the morning paper, she figured. If she'd ever had a doggie. If Kay would have ever allowed pets who made messes and shed into their house.

Mr. V's mail was as boring as what they got at home. It was Heather's opinion that a boss's mail should be more impressive, with real correspondence, letters written on heavy embossed paper.

"If I'd never guess it, don't make me try." He sounded bored. He tossed a green flyer into the wastepaper basket next to Marlena's desk. "Who was here?"

He looked at Marlena differently than he looked at Heather, so maybe it was true that they had a thing going, the way Marlena said. He was twice her age and married and a father, but that didn't seem to stop people even if Heather's mother—if Kay, the Church Lady, the Queen of England—acted as if things like that were unthinkable.

"The law! That's who!" Marlena put her hand up to her mouth to cover her giggle.

Mr. V did not look amused. "Who? Why? What happened? We were robbed? There was a break-in? Nobody tells me a damn—"

Marlena was too busy being thrilled with herself to notice how annoyed, even angry, he looked.

"No," Heather began, but he wasn't paying attention. "It wasn't—"

"Jesus, Marlena, get a damn grip on yourself. What the hell happened and why wasn't I informed?" He looked ready to strangle her, and personally Heather thought she deserved it. So full of herself she didn't notice a single other human being.

"So easy to get your goat, Mr. V!" Marlena said. "Hold onto your hat, I'm *joking*. It wasn't about us. It was an investigator."

"A woman," Heather said softly. That seemed important, something that would make him less agitated, but he looked at her with surprise. As if he forgot that she worked there, too.

"Why? Who?" he said. "Investigating what?"

Marlena shrugged. "Gavin Riddock."

His expression was blank.

"The guy who killed Tracy Lester. You remember her. The girl who worked at the travel agency?"

He frowned, then nodded. "Forgot her name, but sure—that girl."

"She was killed last week, before you left town. You must know about it. Killed over in Blackie's Pasture. It was all over the TV and the papers."

"Okay sure, I remember, but I'm still confused. What did this—this woman—this investigator— What did she want with us?"

"Information," Marlena said.

Mr. V spoke low and slowly. "I figured that much out myself, Marlena. What kind of information? I assume she didn't want information about moving her piano, her pets or the like—so what?"

"Oh, just what I knew about Gavin. Like what kind of guy he was. He'd given them my name. I was surprised, because I barely knew him."

"What did you say to this detective?" Mr. V's voice had eased up a little and so did the tension Heather felt. The office was even

93

less fun when somebody or something pissed him off, and it wasn't hard to piss him off in the first place. That was another reason Heather was going to move on as soon as she could.

Marlena shrugged and gestured. One look at those red nails and you knew how super-slow she was on the keyboard to avoid getting them caught between the keys. "Not much. Like I said, I didn't know enough."

"This woman investigator—she's from the Sausalito police?" he asked.

Marlena shook her head. "She's not police at all. A PI. I have her card somewhere."

Heather could have told them her name and her office address and even her phone number, but she didn't see the point of letting them know she'd paid attention. She didn't see the point of telling anybody here about her own search, either. Too easy to let Marlena broadcast her personal life to the world. No way.

Mr. V seemed deep in thought. "Let me get this straight, then. A PI came around to ask you questions about the murderer, not about, um, Tracy, the girl who was killed. Am I right so far?"

"Correct you are, Mr. V!" Marlena had this movie star she liked, somebody who'd been big when Heather's grandparents—whoever they were, really—must have been young. Rosalind Russell, the woman was, and Marlena considered herself a blond version. Which was rich, because Marlena was no more that white-blond color of her hair than Heather was. Almost nobody was except an albino, so who did she think she was fooling? But Marlena watched Rosalind Russell movies and she tried to sound like her too. Called herself a "girl Friday" and started calling Mr. Vincent "Mr. V." Just like in the movies she watched. Heather had watched a few of them, too. They came on late at night, and then she could see who Marlena was imitating. Only Rosalind Russell said funny things, and Marlena just got the sound of the voice, the way she spoke, without anything smart coming out of her mouth.

"That means," Mr. V said slowly, "that she's working for the defense. For Gavin Riddock."

Marlena shrugged. Heather kept doing nothing, being invisible.

"So what did you tell her?"

"Like I said, there was nothing to tell. I barely knew him, and I knew Tracy even less."

"What did she ask?"

Heather could tell that Marlena was tired of the whole topic. She had the attention span of a gnat.

Heather was sorry for having that thought. Those weren't her words. She wasn't even sure what a gnat was, except not attentive. Those were her mother's—Kay's—and they were hurled at Heather too often. In fact, those words had started the whole quarrel with Kay that ended with being told in so many words that she was adopted. Because Heather said her classes bored her and Kay said she had the attention span of a gnat. And when Heather said she was sick and tired of hearing that stupid saying, that pushed more buttons, more and more until blammo!, out came the thing about being like what she came from.

But Marlena really didn't have much of an attention span. Now, she shrugged and looked at her manicure. "About . . . jeez, I don't know. Nothing specific. Like what was he like. And about . . . the Marine Center. How he volunteered there."

Mr. V looked confused. "Why the hell does that matter?" Then he shook his head. "Is she coming back?"

"I don't know. I doubt it. She gave me her card, in case I—"

"I don't ever, ever want to hear that you talked to her—or any of them—again, you get that?"

Marlena nodded. "But why?"

"Because I say so. Because I've got pride and so should you. I can't believe it doesn't make you as mad as it makes me." He waited. Heather couldn't imagine what he meant, but he wasn't looking at her, anyway.

"Don't you feel insulted?" he demanded. He even looked at Heather now, too.

Heather was ready to feel insulted, but she couldn't think why. She waited to hear his reason. Marlena looked worried and waiting, too.

"Acting like she can barge in, Miss High and Mighty, whenever she wants to waste your time. Like your job doesn't count, only hers does. Doesn't that make you angry? Like we don't matter here at all! Like we don't work! And"—he pounded a fist against the door frame near him—"and you know who's paying her? That rich brat! If he wasn't a Riddock, you think there'd be people investigating what doesn't need investigating? People like him who don't have to lift a finger their whole life make me sick. And so do the people they hire— And then to do it on my dime! In my offices! I resent that."

"You mean the investigator?" stupid Marlena asked.

Mr. V ignored her question. "Whole family stinks, including the kid. Thinks he can buy anything, including you girls, don't you see? Like a prince, he thinks he is. He can afford to hire whoever he wants, to find out whatever might help him, no matter what it costs. You going to fall for something like that?"

Marlena's eyes were wide. "I . . . I never thought about it that way."

"That's your whole problem right there. Start thinking from now on—think about it the only way it makes sense! We don't count to rich bastards like Riddock. Only they count. I'm not having my office and my business interfered with, you understand? I'm not laying down and letting rich bastards run right over me. You get that?"

Marlena nodded. "Yessir," she said meekly. So, Heather thought, the girl had actually noticed how angry she'd made him. If she'd kept her mouth shut in the first place, none of this would have had to happen.

"I don't want you cooperating with somebody taking advantage of you and of me that way, so if she gets in touch with you, you tell her to go to hell."

"She won't—I don't know anything else to—"

"You hear me? Tell her to go to hell."

"Yessir," Marlena said in a voice so crushed and flat Heather's heart expanded with joy.

"That's my girl," he said in a brand new, soothing voice. Marlena beamed up at him, and he smiled down at her.

Heather's heart returned to its normal state.

God but she hated this job.

Twelve

"Thanks for seeing me," Billie said.

"My pleasure." Michael Specht helped her into an upholstered chair at a small conference table, managing to make the gesture one of hospitality, as if she were a fragile, cherished guest, and not his hireling. She felt as if their script had been edited while she was elsewhere. Last time, he'd gone from frosty to awkward appreciation. Today, his expressions and gestures suggested that in her absence, they'd become close friends or, in fact, something more than friends.

"What's up?" he asked as he settled in next to her. The distance between them was precisely on the line between businesslike and intimate.

Billie spoke from behind that line. "It's not that I've accumulated a terrific amount of anything. But I did find people who knew him, who were friendly with him, who think highly of him—or at least say that he wouldn't have hurt anyone deliberately, ever."

"Good!"

His smile was more than encouraging, and encouraging more than business alone.

She didn't mind at all.

Her pheromones had been dormant for many seasons, but obviously more things than riding a bike came right back after a long hiatus. Somewhere inside a chronic tension eased as she remembered how much fun this particular game could be.

She kept her voice businesslike, hid the glee that wanted to creep in. "I'm troubled that neither of these people was on the list of contacts. Apparently, there's likely to be other animal-involved people with whom Gavin associated, to one degree or another. People who knew him as a decent, good person and dedicated worker. But they weren't on the list. Emma's notes from an interview made mention of the Marine Mammal Center, just in passing, and that's where I got the information about Veronica Napoles."

"The llama lady?"

So he knew about her.

"We had to rely on Gavin at first for names, and he hasn't been totally comprehensible since he found Tracy's body, or perhaps before then, too. We got other sources from his mother, who doesn't really know him. That's harsh, but she truly has invented a different person than the one she gave birth to. So I'd hoped Emma—and you—would be able to either find these names helpful, or find new names. And you did. Good."

She felt overly praised. Teacher's pet. Not a totally comfortable sensation. She pushed on. "Animals accept Gavin for who and what he is," Billie said. "People who saw him around animals saw a sweet and gentle young man, and I thought that if I could speak to more of them maybe we'd find a good character witness. Maybe several."

"Good idea."

"Also, we don't know enough about Tracy, including whether there was someone who'd want to murder her. Were there other suspects?"

"Sounds as if you have someone in mind."

"Veronica said Tracy's estranged husband made anonymous phone calls, harassing Tracy—Tracy was staying with her. Veronica said his alibi for the time of her death was weak. Besides, the spouse—the significant other—is always the prime suspect, isn't he? For logical reasons, because half the time he is the murderer."

The lawyer looked at his fingernails, and then at her. His lips curled into the hint of a smile. "Your statistics are accurate, but there are several things to consider. One is that everybody except nocturnal animals is likely to have a weak alibi for the predawn hours. Many, many people sleep alone," he said, pausing to let her consider what he might have meant by adding that, aside from the logic of weak alibis. "Also," he finally continued, "it's wise not to read too much into whatever Veronica Napoles has to say about Robby Lester. I've heard her claims to the police and they're unfortunately based on bile. I wish they seemed useful, something I could use in court, but they aren't. She's on the defensive with a mile-wide chip on her shoulder against Robby Lester and . . ." He shook his head.

"What?" Veronica had struck Billie as a level-headed sort. And what was his smile-smirk about? Anti-female bullshit coming up? But that couldn't be, or why would he hire female investigators?

He leaned closer to her. "First of all on a general level, an anonymous phone call by definition can't be from any one named person. That's supposition, an allegation with zero to back it up. Second, the beatings: fact is, she *was* in a small accident around that time. There's a police report, an insurance report. Her car wasn't bad, but she did some damage to the other car and to herself—she wasn't wearing a seat belt. And third, Robby Lester is not that woman's favorite person, and she is not even close to objective about him. And the feeling's mutual. It is true that he's an angry guy right now—and angry at her."

"Why?"

"Because Tracy left Robby for Veronica."

"You mean . . . romantically?"

"You got it."

She felt his eyes on her, checking her reaction, which was one of surprise shot through with an unexpected surge of anger. She tried to show no expression, although she was frantically sorting backward, through her conversation with Veronica, looking to see if the woman had deliberately misled or conned her.

But replaying the conversations in her head, she didn't think Veronica had lied. She'd said that Tracy stayed there, that was all, and why should she have said anything beyond that?

"Anybody who winds up odd man out—no pun intended—in a love triangle is understandably upset," Specht said. "But for a guy like Robby, who's pretty much what's called a 'man's man,' Veronica was a successful rival—at least that's how he sees it—and that was a double-whammy blow to the side of the head."

"Enough to kill Tracy over?"

Specht exhaled loudly, sounding as if he'd just sprinted across the room. "For my client's sake, I would like that, but he was checked out and, apparently, there were no links, nothing tangible to put him at the scene, no evidence of threats before or after she left him. With the single exception of the llama lady's allegations. That's why she wasn't on your list. She's old, unfortunately useless, news." He shrugged, and then his mood shifted again, lightened up. "You said you wanted to do some things. Such as?"

"I'd like to talk to Gavin Riddock. Maybe I can do better than his mother at getting names. Maybe he's less confused now."

"Locked in a cell? I doubt that, but sure, go ahead. I'll arrange it, no problem. You have a different approach and style than the rest of us—maybe he'll open up, remember things for you."

"And to follow up on some of these other friends of his."

"The animal folks?"

"Primarily."

"Then don't wear your mink to the interviews, you hear? The paint splats are permanent."

"I planned to wear the leopard skin. It's already spotted."

He walked her to the door of the office. "How about we touch base again in a few days? Best for me would be late afternoon, early evening. Could you make a detour in your home commute and take a few minutes over a drink somewhere?"

Had they just moved into stage two: open flirtation—or was this in fact only what he said, an easier way to meet?

Anxiety coexisted with—or amped up—the pleasurable buzz he produced in her. It was one thing to speculate and secretly fantasize about, but messing with an employer was bad business practice.

She could almost see Emma in the background, hands on hips, saying, "How stupid do you have to be? How stupid *can* you be?"

"Where and when?" She'd keep it businesslike. And play dumb. Being blond had advantages and she was happy to play to people's prejudices. She'd pretend she hadn't noticed any subtext to this business meeting. See what happened.

"Come in, come in," Lizzie Tomkins said, standing to the side of her doorway. "It's chilly out there. Awful, isn't it? This whole business, just awful." Billie estimated her to be in her early forties, a woman who seemed at ease with herself, but wary of Billie. She wore denim overalls, a white turtleneck, clogs, and a nervous smile. "I was heartsick for her, of course," she said, leading Billie into a small living room furnished in greens and tans. California colors. Live oaks and summertime hills. The sofa had needlepoint throw cushions; one with an elephant on it, one with a whale. "And for Gavin, too," she added emphatically. "An all-around tragedy."

She shooed a cat off the sofa, offered a seat, which Billie accepted, went to the back of the house and shouted, "Keep it down, guys!" into the backyard, and then returned, offering coffee that Billie declined. Finally, after marking her place in a book that had been facedown on her chair, Lizzie settled in. "Veronica called and told me you wanted to talk about Tracy's murder. What is it you want to know about Gavin? Or is it about Tracy? I wasn't clear on that."

"You knew them both."

"Still do know Gavin, one could say," Lizzie said mildly.

"Sorry, I didn't mean . . ."

Lizzie's smile widened. "Nor was I implying! Nor do I know him much, to be honest. Or Tracy—didn't know her that well. We met in the gym I belong to, saw her there now and then, and then she showed up for a while in a group I belong to. And Gavin was part of it, too."

"Which one was that?"

The smile looked as if it must ache at its edges. "I'd have to think about that. I'm pretty much in all the local ones. Whatever people who aren't overfond of us call 'animal activist groups.' I don't like that classification, do you?"

Billie shrugged. "I've never had cause to think about it much," she said softly. "What bothers you about it?"

"Makes us sound . . . pushy. Nobody calls other similar groups 'activists.' Besides, we're activist people, not animals. I think there must be a less objectionable term, myself. Call us 'not-for-profit lobbyists on behalf of animals.' That sounds all-American enough. And that's all we're doing, speaking up for creatures who can't speak for themselves. None of the groups are the crazies you read about in the papers, if that's what you're afraid of."

Her smile slowly faded. Billie realized that Lizzie Tomkins was on high alert, scanning the airwaves for hostility. She was afraid Billie might label and disparage her activities, might say that these groups had led Gavin astray. Whatever Lizzie feared, Billie tried to dispel through smiles and nods. "Sounds good to me, but could you give me a for instance? I ask because we aren't clear on what groups and possible contacts Gavin Riddock actually has. Something specific in which he was involved?"

"Poor darling. He does get confused, doesn't he? I think some of what makes him seem odd sometimes is pure fear—*his*. Of not knowing what to say or do. Of things rushing past him. And I imagine being in jail might push him over the edge—for fearful confusion, I mean."

"A group?" Billie prompted. "A project?"

"Oh—forgive me! Well, he was there for the wetlands protests, I think. You remember, the condos were going in, destroying natural habitat."

Billie didn't remember, at least not which project Lizzie meant. There seemed to be an endless ongoing clash between animal and human habitats.

"I remember him there. I think he had a special fondness for birds and like all of us, was quite in awe of the great white herons who lived—and thanks to us, still live—there."

"Was Tracy also involved?"

Lizzie's brow crinkled and she was silent for some time. "Tell the truth, I can't remember. Sometimes, I blur the memories of cases I worked on personally versus group projects we all were on, and then, it's hard remembering who worked writing letters, or picketing, or whatever on which thing. Tracy . . . I don't actually remember her much. Not there. No. Was she active? Now Gavin, I know he was involved in the dog-park fracas— In all of these, he couldn't make policy or anything, but he'd mail flyers, things like that. And I remember him at a meeting about the leghold-trap issue. About the red foxes that are eating the eggs of—"

"Excuse me for interrupting, but what did you mean about your cases? Did these groups go to court, or what?"

Lizzie laughed. "I meant my job. I'm a pet mediator."

Billie had an image of a tabby cat and a donkey seated at a conference table, Lizzie Tomkins between them. Good for *Alice in Wonderland*, but not as a character witness testifying to anybody else's stability. "I'm not sure I completely understand," she said slowly.

"I mediate disputes when people are having problems that concern pets. You know, the neighbor's dog barking all night, or a cat that invaded a neighbor's aviary."

Billie immediately thought of Max's parents' aviary, which in turn reminded her of Jesse the Petless. Maybe she'd stop off at the bird store today.

"I get involved in everything from poop disputes to— Well right now, I'm involved in a divorce custody case of a Great Dane. Trust me, there are cases aplenty."

"I've never heard of such a profession. Are you the only person in the world doing this?"

"Not by a long shot. Not even the only person hereabouts. There's one on salary from the county. Me, I freelance. Work all over this part of California. People hear about me and call, or sometimes police call because they're sick of the repeated complaints, and then people pay what they can. It's not a princely sum, but I'm okay. My husband has a normal job. The bills get paid."

"Amazing," Billie said. "Truly. I have a million questions, but I suppose I should get back to—"

"Gavin. Right. Nice boy. A man, actually, isn't he? But he always seemed so boyish."

"Do you recall any incidents, anything he said or did that you'd think characterized him? That shows that he was nonaggressive."

"Everything says it! He loved those animals. He looked stricken when he saw what a leghold trap does to a fox. I never saw him raise a hand or his voice to anybody. To anything! But you want something specific, an incident . . ." She stared into space.

"And Tracy?" Billie prompted. "You don't remember her?"

"Only a bit. I know they were old friends. It was an odd combo and, frankly, I always thought she must have been using him. In the sense of his being useful—not in a bad way—like a sympathetic ear. Somebody who wouldn't tell. That's what I assumed, anyway."

This woman didn't know anything and Billie wondered why Veronica had suggested talking to her. "Did Gavin ever phone you?" Billie asked.

Lizzie looked surprised by the question. "Why would he?" Her curly salt-and-pepper hair was cut in a loose short style, and it bounced and jumped with each emphatic head shake. "He never was the person organizing anything. That's who might call. Or a telephone tree, but . . . no."

It had been a thought. If he had a telephone habit, then maybe he'd been the one phoning Tracy each night at Veronica's.

"Wait, I just thought of something that showed what Gavin was like," Lizzie said. "When the oil washed up at Point Reyes, remember?"

Billie wasn't sure she did. She didn't pay enough attention, she thought. To anything. And she had the sense of oil washing up on beaches with appalling regularity and no sense of what good it would do for her to pay attention to all of it. Still, she nodded, lest she discourage a concrete fact.

"A while back, remember? Oil globs, tar balls all over the beach. Killed hundreds of murres, I think they were. Little black-and-white seabirds. Gavin came to the beach—it was open to everybody— and cried. The survivors were taken to the East Bay, the bird rescue center there and he helped throughout. He wasn't trained in removing tar, but there were things he was able to do and he did whatever they wanted. Swept the floor, prepared beakers of solution. Didn't matter, he so wanted to save the birds. He was tireless and an incredible help. 'They never hurt anybody,' was what he kept saying. Now I ask you, does that sound like a killer?"

"Thanks," Billie said, making notes. "That's great." The first actual first-hand—She stopped herself in mid-thought. "You saw all this, right? You were there."

Lizzie shook her head. "Actually, I'm ashamed to say I wasn't. I wish I could have been, but I was out of town at the time. Otherwise, I would have been there, of course. Those poor birds."

Billie's momentary joy had drowned with the oily birds. "Do you recall who told you this story?" Maybe she could still find that person.

Lizzie looked stricken. "No," she said quietly, "but I know it's true."

Billie wrote "hearsay" next to the lovely quote about poor little things that never hurt anybody.

"Was there anybody, in any of the groups you and Gavin and Tracy—"

"You know it isn't fair to make it sound that way, as if we three—or even Gavin and Tracy—were a constant presence. She only was interested, actively, for a little bit. She came to CoXistence with Gavin. But almost right after—a very short time after—she said she was putting her efforts somewhere else and that was that. I never got to know her well."

" 'Putting her efforts elsewhere,' " Billie repeated. "Those were her words?"

Lizzie nodded. "She said that to me. That time, I was there." Her smile brimmed with hope.

"Can you think of anyone who might have been her enemy?"

"We aren't that sort. You don't think somebody goes all out to save animals and then clobbers a human to death, do you? Or do you think all animal defenders are crazed, foaming at the mouth lunatics? We're trying to get people to share this planet, is all." She shook her head again, this time mildly, sorrowfully.

"It's bewildering. Nobody who knew Gavin seems to believe he's capable of this crime, and yet he's in jail. So we look around to see if there's somebody, something we've missed . . ."

"Gavin was—is—gentle and sweet and good. But he's not normal. Nobody's going to say that. Who's to say what he might have done if provoked?"

"Provoked how?"

Another head shake, this time with a different emphasis and meaning. This time, it was close to dismissal, and her voice, when she spoke, sounded weary. "I don't know, Ms. August. I thought I knew Gavin. But in truth, I didn't. Gavin—well, we'd make small talk, or work on a poster together. And Tracy? When Gavin brought her in, she was so enthusiastic, and we liked each other from the get-go, but she acted like we disappointed her in some way. As if she expected something more of us, although I don't know what it was. And then she quit. In hindsight, I suppose the restlessness or disappointment was about her marriage falling apart—that has to be it—but in any case, I didn't really know her. Gavin, poor boy. Poor both of them."

Billie thanked her for her time and left, with no more than she'd had going in. Except the knowledge that there were animal mediators and the wish that small black-and-white tarred bird survivors could testify in court.

Thirteen

"So sorry," the pregnant clerk said. "I'm here all alone. Flu's going around and I swear, half of Monterey's out sick, plus Doris is on her lunch break and . . ."

Behind those health reports, and her hands waving toward unseen messages on her desk, the clerk was saying that she was not going to be able to find Heather Wilson's birth certificate for a while.

Emma could not bring herself to hassle or hurry the girl who looked minutes away from delivering quadruplets. She debated how best to organize her time. "I'll be back in an hour," she said. "Would that help?"

The pregnant girl looked almost teary-eyed with gratitude. Again, Emma was astounded. Possibly the first bureaucrat she'd ever encountered who was upset at not giving instant, superior service. It had to be those pregnancy hormones. Nothing else explained it.

She thanked the girl again and left, deciding to check out the newspaper.

She was also required to wait at the *Herald*'s offices, although nobody seemed upset about delaying her. Finally, she was given access to their archives to check the date the girl called Heather Wilson was born. And to whom.

She found nothing in a week's worth of newspapers, and in fact, nothing in three weeks' worth, just in case. But it had been a long shot, anyway that the hospital clerk would foul up and put the birth mother's name in the papers before the newborn was adopted.

No great loss. She wasn't going to grieve over it. She had an early lunch by herself, two cups of coffee, then ambled back to the court house.

This time, the clerk's office door was closed, with a handwritten note. "Emergency."

She's gone into labor, Emma thought. And Doris, back from lunch, had to go with her. Just my luck.

Then the handwritten note on the door registered. "Back by 3 P.M." Something besides labor, then, unless this place was staffed by amazons. Emma fleetingly hoped that nothing had happened about the pregnancy. Nothing bad about anything, but then having given the unknown that much, she allowed herself a flare of irritation. Day wasted for nothing. It had taken over two hours to drive down and would take more than that in afternoon traffic to get home.

She knew that her irritation was less about the clerk's emergency than about herself, because she knew what she should do with the waiting time. Knew, in fact, why she hadn't stayed home and waited for the certificate to be mailed to her.

This trip put her in the neighborhood, more or less, and it was past time that she visited him. She always needed an outside excuse.

"Hi, Dad," she said, loudly, as she knocked at the doorway. Didn't want to startle him, tax his worn-down heart, even as her own accelerated in tempo and intensity. Seeing her father did this to her; a fear she never named that possessed her before each visit.

No response. He sat in a wheelchair angled so he could see out the window, onto the hazy, gray-blue day. She panicked until she noticed the plug in his ear. Not his hearing-aid ear. He was listening to something, couldn't hear her.

While she stood wondering how to alert him to her presence without so shocking him that his heart stopped, he must have become aware of motion, because his head swiveled, and he pulled the plug out of his ear.

Her father's eyesight had been disappearing from the center outward so that now he could only see at the very edges of his vision. She watched him angle his head until he could see her somewhat. She waved. "Hi, Dad," she said again. "I was in the neighborhood, so . . ."

"Emma!" His voice was gnarled, like his fingers. Sometimes it sounded knotted thick and sometimes close to worn through. "I was listening"—he pointed a twisted and swollen index finger at the Walkman—"I was listening to a book about a PI—a woman, just like you. I was thinking about you."

She sat down across from him. "And worrying whether I was in trouble the way that PI you're listening to was, right? Gunfights and chases. Things like that, right?" She spoke loudly. Even the hearing aids weren't enough anymore, and he could no longer read lips. Although the attempts were now close to futile, his face still had the slightly pinched expression of somebody straining to hear and see.

Emma's heart raced with inescapable sorrow. It wasn't fair, this shutting down and closing up, this being slowly pushed out of life. "Real life is much more boring than make-believe, Dad," she said. "I'm down here going through old newspapers and waiting for a clerk to pull a birth record. Wouldn't make much of a listening adventure."

"How are you?" he asked.

She squeezed his hand. She was fine, but she couldn't bear his cockeyed, sideways scrutiny. Couldn't watch this slow disintegration, worse by increments every time she saw him, which wasn't often enough. Her sister was better about it, but then her sister had always been the good one in the family.

Maybe Celia was the brave one, too. She and Emma never talked about whether the present sorrows and future implications of their father's slide terrified Celia as much as it did Emma.

Instead, they talked about medical progress, what the doctors or nurses said, the mechanics and economics and logistics of managing the inevitable. Of making it as bearable—for him—as possible.

A whole lot of talk, but no touchy-feely crap. They weren't that laughable California stereotype—people who "shared," except for food and chores, clothing when possible and money when needed. They got on with their lives.

It wasn't their way to talk and Emma wouldn't have known how to say that it physically hurt to see him progressively enfeebled, imploding as his eyes and his ears and his legs failed him, pushing him further and further inward toward an already weakened heart.

His voice was the only reaching-out instrument that had lasted, but he'd never been one for words, and he wasn't now, either.

She wondered what he thought about, whether he was frightened. Whether he felt satisfied about the life he'd led or if there'd been dreams he still held. Whether he missed his dead wife, or even thought about her. How he felt about being here, a place of no happy escape.

What he thought of Emma. Whether he had advice, had learned something in his long, hard life she should know. For years, she'd heard these questions every time she saw him. They rolled on the walls of her mind, clattering, incessant. It was hard work ignoring them, leaving them alone, as they should be. Because this felt different, this wasn't like the rest of life. This wasn't life.

This was a mystery and she hated unsolved puzzles and things that didn't make sense.

But it would have to stay this way, and that was undoubtedly for the best. This way, you didn't get as hurt. Ignorance was probably bliss, and it would only upset him—and her—to try being other than who they were.

They held hands in the pale afternoon light. Touch lasted. She offered to get him something to drink. He declined. She asked if he were warm enough, cold enough, if there was anything he wanted. He looked at her with blind eyes and said he was fine. She asked if there was anything she could get him or send him. She promised to send him more books on tape even though he said he had enough. He asked how her children were, and the grandchildren, and she said they were all fine and told whatever good things she knew about them. No need to trouble him at this point, or ever, with ongoing spats or misunderstandings.

When an hour had passed, she stood. She hated this part even more, not knowing whether this was a true good-bye or not. The top of his skull looked polished. She bent and kissed it, then stayed close to his ear so that he could hear. "I'll be back soon, Dad, I promise. Won't be as long this next time."

He was only a few hours from home, as her sister reminded her too often. Emma didn't think twice about driving down here to retrieve a birth certificate, but she thought an agonizingly long time before coming to see him, and always then with a racing heart.

She could never explain it, even to herself. But then, they weren't an explaining kind of family.

The other clerk, Doris, was now in the office. "She's having her twins," she told Emma. "A little early. Husband's out of town." She fanned herself. "Never thought I'd feel so nervous driving some-body—like a cartoon character. But we made it. And she'd gotten this for you." She handed over a copy of Heather Wilson's birth certificate.

Emma thanked her, and felt a flare of excitement. This had the original mother's name: Megan.

The flash lasted less than a second, because the last name was, indeed, Wilson. And the middle name, Kay.

Anger replaced excitement again. This was an amended birth

certificate, and the adopted mother's name was Megan Kay Wilson. The woman could have mentioned that she used her middle name. But of course, that might have made matters less confusing.

But why did it say "unknown" under "Father's Name." Where was Nowell Wilson, the man who'd driven to pick up the newborn girl?

"Everything okay?" the clerk asked.

"Fine," Emma said, still staring at the certificate. Given that there was no named father, maybe the big bad secret was that Heather Wilson had been born, in fact, to Megan Kay Wilson, unmarried woman.

But that didn't make sense, either. It wasn't as if Kay Wilson had tried to cover the illegitimacy of a daughter she'd produced by saying she'd adopted her. Instead, she claimed her as her own until recently, when she tripped up. For twenty years she'd said that Heather was her own. Was that a truth that she made sound like a lie, to cover up having had a child while not married? It sounded so baroque, so convoluted, and so very unlike the straitlaced Mrs. Wilson, that Emma's head hurt.

She had started with nothing and now she had less than nothing.

Heather's birth date had been months off. Kay Wilson turned out to have a different name. And Nowell Wilson, the supposed father, wasn't on the amended birth certificate at all.

Curiouser and curiouser.

Fourteen

The jail had been carefully designed to be nearly invisible so as not to remind Marinites that while they might be justifiably proud of their Frank Lloyd Wright—designed Civic Center, there was more to the business of running a county than atriums and airy offices. People were locked out of sight, in a jail built into the hillside, another bunker of sorts. Our dirty secrets, Billie thought.

She'd done a fine job of seeming sure of her direction, of believing—or behaving—as if she alone could get information from Gavin. A brilliant audition and she had gotten the role, and now she had stage fright.

She told herself she was being ridiculous. Nothing to fear. But she saw through that argument. A great deal was at stake: her still unborn career, the rest of her life, and whatever was gestating with Michael Specht. And she knew nothing. She had never interviewed a prisoner or even known one, and she had to do it right.

She couldn't have said how she'd expected Gavin Riddock to be, but it hadn't been this disarmingly ordinary looking young man. There were no outward signs of whatever emotional or mental problems he suffered, and he was fit and healthy-looking. A runner, she reminded herself, a weight-lifter.

He smiled tentatively as she sat down across from him.

"I'm pleased to meet you," she said. "My name's Billie August."

"Pleased to meet you, too." His speech was slow, but as if he carefully considered each word, not as if he had difficulty with them. His smile shifted from tentative to authentic.

"I'm working with your lawyer, with Michael Specht."

His expression blanked out, as if he'd clicked off an internal light so that she'd be less visible and so that she couldn't see him clearly, either. He acknowledged her words with a slow silent nod.

She had estranged him before she'd asked a single question. Her jitteriness escalated. Maybe it was her voice. Maybe she'd been so busy fighting stage fright that she'd come across as aggressive.

"I'm here because we believe you're innocent," she said gently. She hoped Gavin, who kept his eyes on his folded hands, didn't know that the word "we" wasn't a complete truth.

Michael Specht hadn't said his client was guilty, not in so many words. He instead had said in passing that "nobody is ever guilty, don't you know that? And they all are, except in the movies." It was clear what he felt about Gavin. Her mandate, after all, was simply to gather sand to toss in the jury's eyes. Confusion and doubt were the most the lawyer hoped for, not vindication.

"Why?" Gavin asked.

"Why? Why what?"

"Why do you think I'm innocent?"

"Because . . . because you are, aren't you?"

He looked at her with slatey eyes. "Why am I locked up? If you believe it, why don't the people who locked me up believe it?"

"Because the law . . . because we're unable to . . ." She sounded like an asshole. A pedant. Like every authority must have sounded as he stumbled and hobbled through school. "I believe you're innocent because everything I hear says you are a gentle person who wouldn't hurt your friend."

Now she sounded . . . flabby. Stupid. "You're locked up, Gavin, because I'm not the boss of the world."

He smiled. Sincerely, and quickly erased, but she'd seen it and

116

the first spark defrosting whatever had made him freeze up. "People say you like animals," Billie said.

Gavin nodded, his eyes focused on his folded hands.

"Want to tell me why you're fond of them?"

He looked up. "Aren't you?"

"Me? Of course, I—but—"

"Everybody likes animals except the people who hurt them, and they're bad people."

"But you maybe more than just everybody? I mean I heard that you don't just like them, you care for them, help them, do things for them. Not just for your pets, either."

"It's my job."

That made sense. In fact, he made more sense than she'd anticipated. "Okay. I know, for example, that you worked at the Marine Mammal Center."

"No. They didn't let me stay."

"Only because you loved those animals more than it was going to be good for them. They were afraid they'd love you back and not be able to return to the wild."

"They didn't let me stay."

"How about other places like CoXistence when they were protesting—" With every word, she worried about what he did and didn't understand, and suddenly resented not being more prepared. Surely, if Michael believed something tangible would come from this he should have given her a handle on Gavin's abilities, told her how best to speak to him. But he'd sent her out unprepared, patronized her.

Or, she realized with a small start, perhaps she was the one being patronizing, to Gavin. Maybe there wasn't anything for which to be prepared. She'd speak normally and to hell with such worries. "When they protested certain animal traps, and a condo that would occupy wetlands, and pretty much anything that might harm animals. Is that right?"

She waited, then watched the obligatory nod.

"Those people you worked with have a high opinion of you, a good opinion of you. But we don't have enough of their names, so let's think of all the names of whatever groups you recall and, still better, the people you liked in them."

His expression was sorrowful and direct. "I liked Tracy."

"You were in the groups first though, right?"

He nodded. "I like animals."

She took a deep breath. "I understand. You and Tracy were friends for a long time."

"Since fifth grade."

It was an amazing and unusual relationship, but Billie could understand its strength and evolution. First, Tracy had provided protection for the social misfit, and then, perhaps, Gavin had provided a listening ear, a protector, a trustworthy confidant.

"Maybe there were other people in the groups who knew you, too."

He blinked, looked about to speak, then simply, silently, looked worried.

His disability wasn't visible, but it was audible. Something blocked his words, dammed them up. "Who were your friends?"

He shrugged. "Friendly people, not friends. Except for Tracy."

No more patronizing from this camp, she decided. He knew the score. "Did you have any favorite times at these groups?"

"I liked the meetings. Sometimes we had parties, even at my house."

Gavin must have been an easy mark. Or was she being cynical now that she'd given up being patronizing? "Who came to the parties?" She felt ever less confident about her ability to fish for answers. Why had she expected that Gavin Riddock would reveal, for her ears only, information that would make all the difference? She was embarrassed on her own behalf.

"Different people."

No more names for her list, then. "Did Tracy come?"

118

"Once. When she belonged. Not before. She had a good job," he said.

And animal rights and caretaking, as he'd said, was his job. "Tell me about it." Billie had applied for a travel agency job when she was in search of a way to make a living, and it sounded mostly like sitting at the computer, checking fares and space availability, handling complaints, and living in terror of how much of the information people bought from her could now be found for free on the Internet.

The shrug again. "She got to go places for free." That had been the perk the owner of the agency dangled, but as a single mother, Billie wasn't going to be able to use it to much advantage. "Once," he continued, "on a ship to, um . . ." He sighed and scratched at the back of his neck, then his expression brightened. "South America." This sigh was one of relief. "Mexico, too. She went there."

"That must have been wonderful," Billie said automatically.

"She saw things," Gavin said softly. "Monkeys and parrots in the trees. And, um . . ." He scratched at the back of his neck again and looked distressed. "An animal that hangs from a tree."

"A snake?"

He shook his head. "She showed me a picture. She said I should think of slow. A sloth!" He pronounced it as "slowth."

Hadn't Gavin's wealthy family taken him anywhere? They could have shown him that sloth and those parrots, but instead, they kept his world cottage-sized, as if he were an unattractive accessory, better left home.

"She worked too hard," Gavin said with more energy than he'd shown so far. "She was going to find a new job."

"So I guess maybe those free trips weren't good enough," Billie said, but Gavin didn't seem to get her meaning this time. "Did her husband ever come to your house?" she asked.

"One time."

"For a party?"

"Her car broke. He came to get her. Robby didn't like me."

"Did Tracy tell you that?"

He shook his head.

"Did you like him?"

"He didn't like me," he repeated, as if that were an answer and, possibly, it was.

"Did Tracy talk about him?"

He looked surprised and amused, as if this was a silly question. "We talked about everything. She said everything. Except . . . the bad thing."

"What's that?"

He clasped his hands and looked near tears. "She said she'd tell me what to do, but she didn't. I would have done it."

She could hear him swallow hard, and she thought she'd come back to this when he was calmer. "I know you would have," she said softly. "So . . . what kinds of things did Tracy say about her husband?"

Another of his shrugs. Open-ended questions didn't work. Only specific ones did. "Did Tracy ever say Robby hurt her?"

"One time her arm was black-and-blue. She said he grabbed her."

That wasn't the fender-bender. Maybe Veronica was right. Or maybe, in the heat of their splitting up, Robby Lester had simply grabbed his wife's arm with too much pressure.

"She was afraid," Gavin said.

"Of him?"

"I guess."

"Why do you say she was afraid?"

"*Tracy* said that."

"When?"

"When we were running."

"I meant . . ." She tried a new tack. "Did she say anything more about being afraid?"

He put his hand back in the remembering gesture at his neck. "She said she did something bad, made somebody angry."

"Was that around when she had those black-and-blue marks?"

He looked upset. Didn't bother to scratch his neck. "I don't know."

"Okay, then was it only that time she talked about being scared?"

He swallowed hard, and folded his hands on the countertop, his thumbnails flicking one against the other while he watched them. When he spoke, his voice was low and almost inaudible. Billie leaned closer to the glass. "She said I could help her." He stopped studying his fingernails and looked up at Billie. "I didn't hear her right. I listen to the air sometimes when I run. I didn't hear her. She said I would know what to do but I didn't. I didn't help her and then she was dead."

"Remember when she said that?"

"We were running. It wasn't raining."

"And you hadn't run in a while because of the rains?"

"Then we could, and I said I would help her, but I didn't." He looked near tears.

"But you couldn't, if she didn't tell you how, and that doesn't mean you hurt her," Billie said gently.

His expression grew distant again. He didn't believe that. He believed that by not doing what he might have, he'd killed her, or at least was responsible for her death.

"Did you run every day with Tracy?"

"It rained a lot."

It had indeed, for ten days in a row until two days before Tracy died. Billie remembered it because of Jesse and cabin fever. But it meant that Tracy was talking about being fearful right before she was killed, because only then could they run together.

"Tracy went to the gym, too," Gavin said. "But we were . . . she was training. Run for the animals. And it was dark before she went to work, so she liked to run with me."

"So all those winter mornings—when you were with her—you were sort of protecting her," Billie said.

He nodded and looked down at his knuckles. "I brought a flashlight, too. Then she would shower and change at my house and make coffee and then go to work."

"Is that why you went to Blackie's that morning?" Billie asked.

"It wasn't raining, but Tracy didn't come to my house, so I went to run."

The police had made much of the entire relationship, of the odd couple, a quick-witted, attractive woman spending much too much time with a sweet but slow companion. They didn't believe it couldn't be sexual, if not for Tracy, then surely for Gavin.

He thought that by not understanding what Tracy meant him to do, by not saving her, he'd caused her to die. What muddled words had he used to express that belief when questioned and how much of what the police now believed had grown in the spaces between Gavin's words?

He looked at Billie now, his eyes a soft gray-green. "I loved her," he said.

It made no sense to assume that Gavin Riddock killed Tracy Lester. Not one person accused him of violence. Or believed him capable of doing conscious harm. He was too easy a target: arriving at the scene of the crime by force of habit, then bloodstained because of concern for his friend lying there. Given that, Gavin the runner literally raced into position as the prime suspect. And if he needed any more bad luck, it was there in the form of his disabilities plus a community that had been angry with his family for a long time.

"Gavin," she said, leaning close to the glass that separated them. "Tell me. You can tell me. Did you hurt Tracy?"

He looked at her for too long, barely blinking, then he nodded. "I didn't help her." She saw the glint of pooled tears at his bottom lid.

"That isn't the same thing. You didn't hurt her," Billie whispered.

The gray-green grew deeper. "Are you sure?" He touched the glass lightly with his fingertips, and she felt it on her flesh.

She took a deep breath. "I'm sure." The truth of it welled inside her, pushing aside the anxious, self-centered person who'd entered this place.

This wasn't about her and her reactions to a jailhouse or her pressures to succeed. This was about this ill-equipped man in a fight for possession of his life. A man who, she was sure, did not belong in prison.

"Let's see what I can do to find other people who are sure of that, too," she said. "Is that all right with you?"

He pursed his lips and frowned, then nodded. "All right," he said.

"I'll see you again, Gavin." She could promise that much.

Fifteen

Marlena Pugh loved the idea. She tapped a long fingernail—hot pink today—on her cell phone.

"Don't," her friend Paige said. "Don't even think about it."

"Too late. I'm already thinking about it," Marlena said. "That's why I told you about it. And I'm thinking it's a pretty fine idea. You have to seize the moment, you know? Like I told you how that PI was in?"

"The one asking about the murder?"

Marlena nodded. "It made me think—I mean look at Tracy Lester. Did you know I met her? She was in the office a few times. It gives me the creeps to think of that, then think of her dead. Over, like that. Life is going on one day and you're wasting time, waiting for things to happen and then"—she snapped her fingers—"you never know. So there's no point waiting for things to happen to you. You have to make them happen. Follow your star, your dream."

"Jesus H. Christ, you're not talking about some dream, you're talking about screwing your boss." Paige lowered her voice and hissed the last word.

"So?" Marlena said. "And don't make it sound cheap. It's not about sex, it's about love."

"Right." Paige finished her beer.

"People marry their bosses, you know. It isn't going to make the *Guinness Book of Records*. I know he's interested in me. A girl can feel it. He can pretend and bluster and do whatever he wants to, but I know what he really means. Like he asks me about my 'wild' weekends, what I did. I don't say, I let him think they're pretty hot. But I know why he wants to imagine it."

"Has he done anything whatsoever about it? Maybe he's a pervert. Somebody who likes to watch, or be told about it."

"He's probably afraid. Thinks I'm too young, or that I'd sue him for harassment—it's a problem for executives, you know? I read an article. So it's up to me. He needs a push, is all." She smiled again, partly to make Paige go nuts. She was so easy.

But the other part was the thought of giving that push. She was sure it wouldn't take much and then David Vincent would be free. She knew he wanted her, felt his eyes on her bottom, on her boobs whenever he thought she wasn't looking. "His marriage stinks," she said after signaling the bartender that they both needed new beers. She wished she could have a cigarette, but the damn laws forbade it even in a bar, which struck Marlena as ridiculous. You could drink yourself to death, but smoking was too unhealthy to be allowed. She didn't want to go outside where it was raining again. Even the weather was against her and made everything harder on her.

"How do you know so much about his personal life?" Paige asked. "Like you're suddenly his shrink or something?"

Marlena wasn't always sure why she hung around with Paige. Paige wasn't smart about much, and was definitely dumb about men. But she was convenient. Most of the girls Marlena knew worked in the city or down in Silicon Valley, and the few who were still in the county worked at high-tech places or the malls, and their hours were unpredictable and long. But Paige worked at the T-shirt store on Bridgeway, and her fiancé worked nights, so she was always available for a drink after work. Not that this bar did much with TGIF or anything, but there were snacks, and sometimes interesting people—not just tourists—came in. It would feel too weird sitting at the bar alone, anyway. Looked cheap. Paige came in handy.

"Listen," Marlena said as patiently as she could manage, because she hated explaining. She'd been in such a great mood, but it was fading fast. "First of all, I answer the phone, and all I can say is that his wife sounds like a bitch. Lots of time, he'll take the call, then close the door to his office, and I can hear—not the words, but the tone. Trust me, they aren't lovebirds."

Their fresh beers arrived.

"I don't think that's much," Paige said. She thought she knew everything about men because she was engaged. "They might have been talking about something a kid did," she continued, "or why he didn't bring home milk like she asked him. Besides, married people don't talk to each other like dating people do."

"My husband will," Marlena said. "You have to establish standards, is all."

"Did she ever come in?" Paige asked.

Marlena nodded. "She's . . . nothing. Letting herself go. Her stomach pooches out."

"She's had kids. That happens."

"Not if you take care of yourself," Marlena snapped. "And her hair didn't look good and there's no excuse for that. And she was in a rush and all impatient with me. I didn't like her attitude."

"What's second?" Paige asked.

"What?"

"What is the second thing? You said first of all you answer the phone. So if there's a first, what's the second?"

Marlena couldn't remember what she'd meant.

"Because, frankly, so far, that isn't much," Paige said. "And I don't know why you aren't happy with guys your own age. They're more . . . appropriate, you know?"

"They're children." Like Paige's fiancé Jason, the dinner manager at a burger palace, was the definition of a grown-up.

"It's about money, isn't it?"

Marlena wouldn't dignify Paige's attitude with an answer. What if she liked men who proved they could be successes? Paige was going to wind up in a trailer. All she cared about was how buff Jason was, and she had no idea there could be more to life than that.

"You still haven't said what the second thing is."

Marlena ate a handful of the trail mix out on the bar. The nachos were too far away, and she didn't want to ask the guy near them to pass the bowl because he'd think she was starting something.

She remembered the second thing. "It's that I'm sure he already plays around. So that proves about his marriage, anyway."

"And about him. He'd play around on you, too, is what my mother says."

Marlena waved the comment away.

"Besides, how do you know? Is he such a creep that he has you make his love nest reservations?"

"He goes on these trips—not long ones—and they can't be far. It's not like he packs a big suitcase or anything. He has a clean shirt and underwear and a toothbrush and razor in his briefcase. He says it's for business, but it isn't like he comes back with work for me to do, and wouldn't he, if it really was business? Besides, how much out-of-town, face-to-face business does a moving company do? Me or Heather takes the orders over the phone or in person, and sure, somebody has to go out to give the estimate and look the stuff over, but that isn't an overnight. And if it's really out of town, then somebody in that town checks them out. We don't travel for that."

"All the same," Paige said after an overlong pause—she was incredibly slow, and it was a real shame she was all there was at this hour in this town. "All the same, what you're talking about is wrong. Immoral."

"You've never, ever been with a guy who was going with somebody else?"

"Not married—and with kids!"

"Like they say, all's fair in love and war."

Paige shook her head. She looked like she knew what was going on. Dressed great, but inside that head, nothing. "It's wrong. I thought you had all these big plans about having your own business someday. Marlena Designs, wasn't that it? I thought you said you were working there to learn the ropes, find out how business worked."

"And I am. And I did, and all I can say is you must be an imbecile, or still in kindergarten. How do you think the women you read about in the papers got their studios and their contacts and things like that? They married guys with the bucks, guys who could help them. Check out *People*. Check out *Entertainment Weekly*. How you going to learn anything if you don't read?"

Paige's bottom lip was puckered and tight. She sulked too much.

"I'm not ending up like my mother," Marlena said. "My dad was nice enough, and then what? When he died, there wasn't anything, and she has to work her whole life. Not for me. No way."

Paige continued her silence.

"Be angry if you want to be," Marlena said. "The truth's the truth."

"David Vincent isn't even rich," Paige said. "That is a second-rate nowhere moving company."

"He's rich enough. You notice the ring he wears? That's a genuine ruby. And his SUV? Plus the Lexus? And he's bought presents for that awful wife. I saw a diamond tennis bracelet he gave her. Trust me, he's rich enough."

"Do whatever you want, but I still think it's stupid and wrong."

Marlena flipped her cell phone open and pushed numbers.

"It's too noisy in here," Paige said. "You won't hear right."

"She'll hear. I want it to sound like what it is, a bar." She waited while the phone rang in his house. She knew he wasn't there. He was working late, he'd said. Probably out on a date. And she was there, at home, Friday night, with the kids.

"Hello?" The voice was wary, ready to be angry. Well, it was telemarketing time, Marlena realized. She should be heading home herself, or at least calling her mother.

"Hi," Marlena said. "Can I talk to Davey?"

"Davey?" There was a pause. "May I ask who's calling?"

"Well, if he's not there, then I guess . . ." Marlena paused before she spoke again. "Sorry for all the noise in this place, but I've been waiting for him and I thought, maybe there was a problem. He's usually so prompt. So listen, to whom am I speaking? You must be his sister."

"His sister? Where did you get that idea?"

"From him! He said he was staying with her . . . Oh, what do I know. I have such a bad memory! But listen, I'm at a pay phone and I'm going to run out of change in about a half a minute, so could I speak with him?" She heard somebody shout in the background. A kid's voice, an angry kid's voice.

"David isn't here," Mrs. Vincent said.

"Did he leave a message for me?"

"Not for anybody. Do you want to leave him a message? I'm guessing you don't, am I right?"

"I guess not. If he doesn't show, then I guess . . . he isn't showing. Kind of rude, don't you think? But no. No thanks. Damn," she said with the phone away from her face, but loudly enough for Jeannie Vincent to hear. "Where the hell could he be?" And then she clicked the phone shut.

Paige had that sleepy face she got when she'd had a few.

"Don't look at me like that," Marlena said. "Like I'm a criminal or something. I didn't do anything illegal. I didn't do anything that anybody else wouldn't have done—you, too—if you were smart enough to think of it. If you were a *passionate* person, the way I am. A person with deep *feelings*." She really, really wanted a cigarette.

"Yeah, right. Feelings like wanting to wreck somebody's marriage. Feelings like wanting his money. Feelings like making trouble."

"That is totally the point," Marlena said. "That's what you don't understand. Trouble can be exciting, and I'm somebody who needs excitement in my life."

"Yeah, right. The passionate one, I heard you."

Marlena was off her bar stool and on her way for a cigarette, no matter the weather. She patted the phone in her pocket as if it were a lucky stone or charm.

She'd started it, then. Started it happening. Taken it into her own hands. She couldn't control the grin on her face, and why should she?

Sixteen

Billie studied herself, deciding whether she'd dressed for the part. According to Veronica, Robby Lester was a nightly patron of a bar that was an anomaly in Marin, seemingly left over from an era before the word "yuppie" was invented. It was, if not wild west, then at least mild west.

Since she couldn't think of a single reason Robby would want to talk to her if he knew who she was, she'd decided to check him out anonymously. She didn't want to accept Emma's offer right now. She needed to act on her own. Besides, she wasn't going to meet him as herself.

She'd put on her tightest jeans—which were, alas, tighter than she remembered them being—boots, and a sweater that had seen better days, but not a better fit.

She stood at the full-length mirror, and declared herself sufficiently "low class," to borrow her mother's vocabulary. Funny how after all these long years, and all their estrangement and physical distance, her mother's voice still criticized her. Her mother with her pretensions and airs, her aristocrat-in-exile persona after Billie's father walked out on them all.

Drunk, depressed, and deteriorating herself, her mother would nonetheless have looked at her now and declared her as bringing shame upon the family. As if they were a dynasty with all eyes upon them. As if her mother didn't have a glass with melting cubes and an inch of golden liquid in it as she stumbled over the word "appearances."

"Cheap" she would say if she could see Billie. That was perfect. The last thing she wanted to look was expensive. She worked on her hair, ratting a bit for height, spraying and gooping it into a deliberately rumpled style. Then she applied makeup with a heavy hand.

Ivan, snuffling into tissues, eyes so watery she was surprised they could see, gaped as she walked into the living room. Or perhaps he was simply mouth-breathing. Jesse had been invited to a Saturday night sleepover at his friend Max's, which was why Billie had chosen this opportunity to stalk Robby Lester.

"Halloween again, maybe?" Ivan asked.

"I'm going to work," she said. "At a bar."

"You are fired?"

"Work undercover."

His eyebrows raised. "Under covers?"

"An idiom. It means . . . secretly. Like in spy movies."

"At bar? Is safe to go there alone like that? I go with."

It was sweet of Ivan, but ridiculous. She imagined him as her bodyguard, an enormous, sniffling, snuffling, glassy-eyed Russian in a bathrobe. "No thanks," she said. "And it's 'I'll,' remember? *I'llllllll* . . . the tense future?"

He nodded. Grammar wasn't interesting him at the moment. She considered the fact that he was just about the same age as Gavin Riddock. Ivan's life was filled with difficulties, but how much better his bag of troubles was than Gavin's.

"You see this?" he demanded. "In paper? A man is in hospital here—in coma, maybe dying—from spider bite."

"That isn't what's wrong with you." Make that bodyguard an enormous, sniffling, snuffling, glassy-eyed Russian hypochondriac in a bathrobe. "You're going to live."

"Is huge spider bit him. So big—eats birds! Is Australian animal."

'I don't think spiders are animals."

"This man, he collects spiders," Ivan said with a shudder and a grimace.

"Serves him right, along with the people who think pythons make neat pets," she said. "I'll be back in a few hours. Have some more tea and go to sleep."

"I not sleep. I only dream of spiders," he said darkly. "Watch TV instead. Wait up for you."

"Do me a favor, okay?" she said. "Don't tell Jesse about that spider."

"He have nightmares, too?"

She shook her head. "Nope. He'll want one of his own."

Sleeping over at Max's wonderful home would only intensify Jesse's desire for a pet. Billie sat in front of the store—a detour she'd planned—suddenly shy about going inside in her cheap girl duds.

She decided that this was no more than another delaying tactic. No time like the present. She zipped up her ancient leather jacket and went in.

The birds were beautiful and noisy, although the sight of them in their cages caused an echo of the emotions she'd had in the jail that afternoon. Much, much lovelier to see them in an aviary, as they were at Max's. Or was that just a larger prison?

"Any questions I can answer?" She caught the clerk staring at her jeans. She had to watch her diet for a while. They were entirely too tight.

She surveyed the array of cages, with their yellow and green, scarlet and blue inhabitants, bright eyes studying her right back. They were amazing, living art. She didn't see the one for which she lusted. Surely, she could order one, pay it off over time.

"Actually," she said, "I saw a bird—fell in love with it—but I don't see anything here like it."

"Can you describe it?"

"A macaw, but not any of these. Not that they aren't beautiful, too." Which they were, but compared to the bird in her memory, they were too splashy, too gaudy. "He was purpley blue and his beak looked almost pale lavender, and he had yellow rings around his eyes and here." She drew lines down from the corners of her mouth. "Bright yellow. I remember the owner told me its name— the name of a flower. A blue flower, but I . . ."

"Not hyacinth," he said.

"Yes, that's it!"

"You saw a hyacinth macaw?" He made an airy whooshing sound and opened his eyes overwide in a broad pantomime of being both shocked and impressed.

"Why so surprised?"

He looked amused by the question, then he shook his head. "Listen, the reason you don't see one here is that they're so endangered there's barely any left in the wild. Maybe a few thousand at most. So they are totally illegal to import. Do not tell me where you saw it, either, or I'd probably have to do something about it."

"These are really nice people, they wouldn't do anything illegal. I mean don't parrots live a long time? Maybe this one came into the country before they were endangered."

He raised an eyebrow and shrugged again.

"And don't people raise them here?" she asked.

"Possibly," he said, looking as if he doubted it. "And the fact is, your friends were probably told their bird was hand-raised from birds already here. But odds are it was black market. And, incidentally, somebody probably paid around $20,000."

"For a bird?"

He grinned.

"I thought it might be pricey, but . . ." She shook her head. "Nothing like that."

"The more rare, the higher the price, and, unfortunately, the rarer it becomes because . . . well . . ."

"People steal them in the wild?"

He shrugged.

She stood in the middle of the noisy shop, wondering about that aviary's inhabitants. "I suppose people sell their own birds to other people sometimes." That must be how Max's family had gotten theirs.

"People sell everything." He raised his eyebrows slightly. "The question would be, how did the person he bought it from get it, and how did that person get it. By the time the buyer here gets one of the few survivors, it's impossible to track it down to a village in Indonesia or Thailand or Africa. You look shocked. You weren't aware of what goes on?"

"Not about this, no."

"So you're wondering about this friend with the bird, right?"

She didn't say anything, least of all say how many birds there had been in that enormous aviary. She thought of the one with the plumes and the pinky coral cheeks and was glad she couldn't remember its name.

"It's big business, the animal trade, especially in this country. Right behind drugs in profitability. People get rich, they want fancy toys. A rare fancy toy is even better. And a living rare fancy toy— it's the best. Of course, these aren't toys . . ." He raised his eyebrows and shrugged. "None of which means your friend knew he was involved in a criminal thing. If he was. But however he got it, from whomever, one thing is sure. He paid through the nose."

"I can't imagine how anybody could smuggle an enormous, noisy bird like—"

"They come in as eggs," he said. "Neatly packaged. But most of them—forty-nine out of fifty—die in the process."

"This is too depressing." She wasn't going to think about Max's aviary or what those survivors meant.

"How about something definitely not endangered, definitely raised right here, and still colorful."

"Such as?"

"A parakeet."

She considered it for a moment, but knew it wasn't going to

work. "Nothing against parakeets," she said, "but . . ." Jesse wanted a something. A big showy bird that could learn to talk to him, to interact would have worked, but parakeets would not. They were too insignificant, like party favors or garnishes. "Thanks anyway."

She thanked him again and returned to her car, letting go of her technicolor vision and seeing a fur-colored, four-footed something in her future. At least the Humane Society's creatures didn't come with twenty-thousand-dollar price tags, and they were legal.

Seventeen

Veronica wanted a drink.

No, "want" was too weak a word. She might want a chocolate chip cookie, or new shoes, or something good to watch on TV. This was different, the tug of gravity, a force of nature, pulling, pulling.

"Want" was an ice cube. She had an iceberg.

She sat on her faded sofa, arms wrapped around herself in the silent house and ached and yearned.

She wouldn't.

She couldn't.

There was nothing in the house. Tracy had been so good about it, no matter that she didn't have a problem with the stuff and liked a drink before dinner. She'd insisted there be nothing. No temptation.

So getting to the stuff required a goodly drive to the nearest bar or twenty-four-hour market, but if she sat here, stayed here—didn't even pretend she was going out to recheck the llamas, or getting up to turn on the TV, or check the door locks—just sat here, she couldn't get into trouble.

It had been so much better with Tracy in the house. Company, the sound of another animal's breath against the night. It had been so good, like calming down after a lifetime of being jumpy, that she should have known. She'd tried to warn Tracy. Told her she shouldn't move in because she, Veronica, was unlucky. Things simply did not work out for her.

"That is a crock," Tracy had said, and even now, even in this terrible wanting, Veronica felt a faint smile move her face as she remembered Tracy posing, feisty, wagging a finger at her. "Unlucky is ridiculous. But feeling sorry for yourself? Wallowing in it? Making up stupid superstitions like you're a doomed person—that's disgusting. Makes me want to find a two-by-four and hit you upside the head!"

Self-pity. A drunk's specialty. "This is a zero wallowing tolerance zone," Tracy said. Tracy hadn't believed in luck. She'd believed in herself, in making things change into what she wanted. And Veronica had believed in Tracy. And then, Tracy was dead.

God, but Veronica missed her. "Talk about it," Tracy would have said. She was a big one for getting things out of your system. Saying them, shouting them—it didn't matter—you got rid of the poison. "Then you see, most times, how stupid or illogical it all is."

Or, if you were really cooking, you saw the solution.

Veronica didn't like keeping notes or writing things down. She didn't even particularly like explanations and confrontations. That was one of the reasons she'd quit the corporate world, where too much information had to constantly be turned over to another person.

The process never had solved much for her. And right now, there was no one to talk to, and if she unclenched her fists enough to hold a pen, her hands would shake. Besides, what would she write? I miss Tracy. I do not know how to get on with my life.

And in any case, call it superstition or not, Veronica had been right. She had no luck. That short happy calm time with Tracy had been a lull, the exception to the rule.

This pain, this all-consuming wanting was the rule. This loneliness, this sense that the landscape had gone empty. As if now, she couldn't see the trees, the wild grasses, the vegetable garden, the hills, or the llamas—she saw only the empty spaces between them.

Tracy would hate these thoughts.

Which she wouldn't have if Tracy were here to know about them.

She missed Tracy all the time, but this was different. Worse.

Saturday night, she thought. Ridiculous. Why should Saturday night be particularly painful? She was long since past "date night" ideas, and it wasn't as if she went to an office Monday through Friday and had only the weekends free. Every day could be Saturday, so what was this abandoned feeling that filled her bone marrow? What was this Saturday-night craziness?

She clenched her fists, resisting the only idea in her brain, that if she didn't find a drink, she couldn't get through Saturday night. That she had no other alternative. That this was it, her only option.

No. She could drink herself to oblivion, and Tracy would still be dead, and her lousy husband still wandering free, as if he'd done nothing. And everybody assuming that poor, dumb Gavin Riddock did it because that was easy, and besides, nobody liked his family. The sins of his father indeed. She felt a tremor of rage against Robby and her muscles twinged, wanting to get him. Do something, anything.

But Tracy would still be dead.

She had to call her sponsor, talk this through, get through the night. This wouldn't last, she told herself. She'd been okay for so long. This would go away. She tried to remember how it was not to feel like this, but she couldn't. The wanting had clogged every pore and there was no space for anything else.

She stood and took a deep breath, and then another, and finally, dialed a number. "Clare?" she asked as soon as she heard a voice. "It's Veronica. I need—" But it was the answering machine. A message. A promise to get back within minutes. Which she had in the past, Veronica reminded herself. She had, even though that had been a long time ago. A year. More.

"It's Veronica," she repeated numbly, her voice flat. And she hung up, sat back down with the phone next to her, and waited, clutching her knees, taking deep breaths, trying to remember what she used to see outside and inside. What used to make up a day and a night.

The phone rang and she nearly wept with relief. "Clare?" she said. "Oh, God, Clare, I'm—" But she stopped, aware of some wrong quality on the other end. No breath, no consoling sounds, no rushed assurances that she was no longer alone, that help was there for however long she needed it.

Nothing except silence, and then a throat-clearing.

"It's you," Veronica said. Her free hand trembled. "It's you again. I thought— What do you want?"

The silence threatened again.

"Say something!" she screamed. "Stop doing this, she's dead! You killed her, what more do you want? You want to kill me, too? Why? I didn't do anything, it was her decision!"

She thought she heard him clear his throat or cough. Him. Robby Lester. Murderer. Playing with her because he could, because he was loose, on the streets, a free man and a sadist.

Because Tracy had chosen her, loved her, Veronica, and not him.

"Stop it!" she screamed. "Stop it right now and don't ever—"

He said something, his voice so muffled and distorted she couldn't make out the word.

"I can't understand you!"

"Wannit."

"Want it? Want what? What is this? Who is this?"

"You know. Proof!"

She felt as if she were going crazy, being toyed with by a gigantic catlike creature. His words sounded partial, as if he were speaking through a rug and only parts of his sentences were coming through. "I don't care!" she screamed into the receiver. "Stop these calls, stop it!"

"Coming for it."

"Don't you come anywhere near me!"

"Soon."

"*I know who you are you murdering son of a bitch! I know what you did. We talked about everything, I know all about you!*"

"Have it ready so you won't get hurt."

She would not cry. She would not let Robby Lester the son of a bitch hear her cry, know how he terrified her with his threats. "*Go to hell—just go to hell and leave me alone!*" She slammed down the phone. She wouldn't answer it ever again, wouldn't let him into her life, wouldn't let him get to her.

Had to leave, though. What if he came tonight?

What did he mean about getting hurt? Rape? Murder her, too? What proof?

He didn't know about her sister. She could get someone to feed the animals. A day or so. Then she'd think of something else.

The phone rang again.

She recoiled, as if it had reached out for her. "No," she said, staring at it, and now she trembled all over. "Noooo!"

But Clare—What if it was Clare?

But what if it wasn't, if it was him, again—

She let it ring, watching it, rocking back and forth, sat there, arms wrapped around herself, holding on for dear life.

Eighteen

Billie admired funky Fairfax for sticking to its guns. It had enjoyed the sixties and intended to remain there, no matter how gentrified and smoothed down its home county became.

And 19 Broadway, Robby's default spot, she'd been told, looked as if nobody'd touched, polished, or replaced one splinter, and possibly not one customer, for at least four decades.

Billie felt instantly like the stranger in town. Her getup had lost its humor, and she didn't feel comfortable tarted up—to use another of her mother's expressions.

She stood uncertainly in the front section, the bar, checking the small tables, the bar stools. She peered through the window at a covered area where smokers congregated.

Then she moved toward the back section. A quartet of Hawaiian-shirted musicians were backing up a woman holding a glass and singing "Angel Eyes." Her enthusiasm far exceeded her talent, but a group of middle-aged women in pastel pantsuits nodded, hummed along, and lifted glasses to her.

Billie turned back to the serious-drinking section of the place, searching for Robby Lester. She'd seen the newspaper photo of the grieving husband. And she'd seen him on the local news, vowing revenge on Gavin Riddock and all the "crazies roaming our streets."

He was a beefy, attractive-enough guy who looked like he might have played football in high school and watched sports since then. A beer drinker. A solid citizen with cemented-down opinions.

She didn't see him yet, so she sat down at the bar. "Anchor Steam," she said when asked. She didn't particularly like beer, but this was not a place to ask to sample the wine cellar.

She'd barely taken her first sip when Robby Lester walked out of the back room, from the men's room or pay phones, she assumed. He wasn't staggering, but he looked less than sober.

A drinker, she thought, wondering why nobody had mentioned it.

He seated himself a few bar stools away. She glanced at him, then away, gave him time for his beer to arrive, all the while looking at him in brief quizzical glances. Then, when he was drinking his beer, trying to look as if he wasn't looking back at her, she spoke.

"Forgive me if I'm wrong, or if I'm intruding," she said, "but you're Robby Lester, aren't you?"

He looked wary, then he nodded, grudgingly.

"Remember me?" She smiled.

He let the chip on his shoulder slide a bit and looked at her with less of a scowl.

"Audrey!" she said. "Audrey Miller, from high school. Drake, right?" The newspaper had quoted a "former Drake High School classmate" of both Robby and Tracy's. She smiled again, and when he said nothing, cleared her throat and said, "Sorry. Guess I was mistaken, although you look so much like him. Forgive me." She waved, erasing the air in front of her. "Won't interrupt any more."

He moved a bar stool closer. "No. Sorry. I thought—People have been recognizing me for the wrong reasons lately. I thought . . . Audrey Miller . . . ?"

Dear, nondescript Audrey Miller from a high school thousands of miles away. Forgettable Audrey Miller whose face Billie herself couldn't recall. Personality like a pillow, too. She didn't understand why Audrey always came to mind when she needed to put on a mask or adopt an alias, but she knew Audrey wouldn't mind a personality infusion. "I was a cheerleader," Billie said. "That help?"

"Oh, yeah. Sure."

He hadn't said that he was on the team, so she left it at that. "So you obviously still live in the neighborhood," she said. "Could practically walk to Drake from here."

"Pretty long walk," he chuckled as if vastly amused. "But yeah," he said. "Still in the old neighborhood. I like it. Haven't see you here before, though."

"I just moved back. I've been in LA since high school."

"Movies?"

She shrugged. "In my dreams. More like waiting tables. Lots of auditions, one commercial, a walk-on in a sitcom. So . . . here I am, again."

"What'll you do now?"

"Wait more tables, probably. I might have to move away, to where I have a chance of paying the rent. Can't stay with my mom forever, and I have a son." The best way to lie is to tell as much truth as possible, somebody had told her. It'll sound real because it is, and you won't get tangled up wondering what you'd said.

She wondered who had given her the advice. Surely not Emma, who never bothered to tell her anything that would actually be helpful.

"You married, then?" Robby asked with studied casualness while he signaled for two more beers.

She put her hand on top of her glass. "I'm fine," she said. "And no. Not married, not anymore. I don't even know where the bastard is." God, but the truth stunk.

He shook his head in sad agreement with the sorry state of the world.

"And you?" she asked. "What do you do?"

"Contractor."

"Things must be good for you. Wherever I look, if a house isn't for sale, then it's being remodeled."

For the first time he grinned as he nodded. "Can't complain about business. Believe it or not, I'm working on a million-dollar teardown, and not my first one. This buyer paid one million three to level the place."

"Dot com guy?"

"Dot com gal." He fiddled with the napkin that had arrived with his new beer.

"I told you about me," she said playfully. "So how about you since high school?"

"Told you. I'm a contractor."

"C'mon. You have more of a life than that." She winked at him. "Hey, I'm trying to find out . . . well, about you. Are you married? Have kids?"

He looked at her quickly, then away. "I was married. No kids."

"Well, judging by my experience, that'd make the divorce easier," Billie said. "No kids, I mean. Less complicated."

"No. It wasn't like that. My wife . . . died."

"I'm so sorry!"

"Killed." He looked teary- or glassy-eyed. Billie couldn't decide whether he was reacting from grief or from alcohol.

"My God! That's so—"

"I can tell you're just back, or you'd know. It was in all the papers, and the TV . . ."

"Oh, my God—the girl in Tiburon?"

He nodded, his attention completely focused on the glass in front of him.

"My mother told me, but I don't think she said her name or I didn't recognize it and . . ." She reached over and touched his arm. "I'm so sorry I brought up something so painful."

"S'all right. You didn't mean to. Besides, it's not like it's a secret, or that I forget about it."

"Terrible." Billie could feel his eyes on her, studying her as she stared at her half-full beer glass. Maybe he was still trying to figure out who she was. "What a horrible shock to you, too. What a loss."

When he didn't say anything, she went on. "But at least they caught the guy. That must be a relief."

He still said nothing.

"Isn't it? I mean, I'm thinking, by your silence, you're saying it isn't. Or am I out of line here?"

"What was she doing with a retard?" he said. "Why'd she spend so much time with him? It wasn't just about the running. Besides, we belonged to a gym. Why?" he said. "That's what I can't stop asking. Why him for a friend? You don't know them, the people we marry. You think you do, but you don't. Or they change."

"Don't I know," Billie said, although her ex hadn't actually changed. He'd just grown to be more so. And most unfortunately, the parts that grew exponentially were the same traits that initially attracted her to him. Those differences, the parts that felt exotic, necessary to fill in her spaces, morphed into unbearable problems. A wild sense of adventure became irresponsibility; his joie de vivre, unreliability; delightful irreverence, callousness. And so forth and so on.

"An' I'm not saying it just because we were going through a . . . rough spot when . . . the thing happened. It wasn't because of Gavin, except she didn't need him as her friend. She could have told me whatever . . . she could have talked to me."

"Um," Billie murmured, encouraging him on.

He sighed and drank deeply of his beer. "Do you believe in separate vacations for married people?" he asked.

Billie believed in anything that worked for anybody, but doubted that Robby did. So she tried to look puzzled and generally doubtful, with room for approval, if that turned out to be what Robby felt. "Never had to think about it," she said. "My marriage being one long separate non-vacation, that is."

"I don't," he said. "But her goddamn job . . . I told her she didn't even have to work. I'm doing good." He shook his head, then signaled for another beer.

The backroom boys and their singer were doing "Georgia" which, till now, had been one of Billie's favorite tunes.

"I don't care if she had to know about the cruises and the places so's she could sell them better," Robby said abruptly. "It wasn't a good idea."

"Why's that?"

"Nothing was the same when she came back from that cruise. That damn job ruined my marriage. And now, there's no chance to make anything better." He pulled a bandana out of his pocket and blew his nose, then cleared his throat.

Interesting what theories we make up, Billie thought. We are such a pathetic species. Anything to explain how it was possible for somebody to stop loving us.

He drank half his beer before he turned to her with an intense and serious expression, about to reveal ultimate truths. "It was all about money." He nodded in agreement with himself and drained the rest of his beer.

She couldn't believe he could still sit upright. Or at the very least, wasn't charging back to the men's room. She hadn't needed to dress this way, or any way. Robby wasn't looking at anything except beer and his sad story. "Why money?" she asked. "What about it?"

"That's what she always wanted. Bottom line: she was up for the bucks. I'm doing real good, but not good enough for her. She loved clothing, jewelry, living big. Those cruises she booked? Told me she wanted to live like she was always on one of them. She had new clothes after that trip, and she acted different. Talked different."

Billie still couldn't figure him. Was he sincere? If so, then where was the bully Veronica described? Even drunk, or borderline, he seemed pathetic more than aggressive. But then, she wasn't challenging him or leaving him. "What do you think changed her?" she asked softly.

"Money," he repeated. "Some guy on that cruise. And my fault. I was finishing a big job, I couldn't go. She had to, anyway."

"So she went alone."

"I blame myself for the whole thing. The ship, the guy and . . . what happened. I was too emotional about everything."

"About——She told you about this other person?"

He drank some, then exhaled loudly. "Didn't have to. Married long enough, you don't have to spell things out."

Billie imagined his thoughts like pale moths in a dark place, bumping around, looking for the light, going nowhere directly.

"I heard her once," he said. "On the phone. I heard her say she couldn't anymore. She felt too *guilty*. It was too *risky*."

His voice was taking on a lurching quality, as if he was stepping carefully from idea to idea.

"She said his name. Jimmy. 'I can't do it anymore, Jimmy.' " He wiped at his eyes. A drunk's tears, Billie decided.

"Then," he said, "she tells me it's a telephone solicitor, a guy selling credit card insurance." He shook his head. "Jesus. How dumb did she think . . ."

"Then you think this Jimmy did it, then?" she asked. "Killed Tracy?"

He looked mildly surprised, as surprised as a man pickling himself in alcohol can be. "The retard did it."

"Then why did you say you blame yourself about what happened to her?"

He sighed heavily. The waiter, without being asked, placed a fresh beer in front of him. She hoped his house was in walking distance. "I was mad at her. Maybe too mad. That's gotta be why she told her secrets to the retard. I . . . I drove her away. I wanted to meet her, do right by her, that was all. Talk. Make things better. She wouldn't come."

"Meet you here? You mean like after work?" He seemed oblivious of his wife's new partner, of her living arrangements—unless of course, Michael Specht was the one who was off-base.

Robby drew a circle in the condensation on the bar top. "We weren't living together then. She . . . moved out a while after the cruise."

"Oh, man," Billie said, hoping it sounded sincere. "I know how that is."

He nodded. "I can tell you do."

"So did she move in with that—Jimmy?"

"With a girlfriend. A goddamned farmer."

"So you wanted to meet Tracy here. The night before . . ."

He nodded. "She said there wasn't anything to talk about. And the next day . . . gone. I said something about Jimmy, and she kept crying and saying I didn't understand her or anything, so see, I drove her to him. I think she went and told the retard about falling in love with Jimmy and that made the retard flip out."

"Gavin Riddock? Why?"

"He was in love with her. You could see it on his face; he isn't good at hiding how he feels. I thought it was funny, nothing to worry about, but look how wrong I was."

She patted his arm again. "Don't blame yourself," she said. "Sometimes fate . . ."

"Screw fate," he said, and she could suddenly see a different kind of drunk. A belligerent, dark, aggressive drunk. A murderous drunk?

"I want Gavin Riddock to fry," he said. "I want to be there to watch his execution at Quentin. Jimmy, too. And whoever else—her crazy farmer friend who helped her leave me, her, too—everybody who made this happen to Tracy. I want to see every one of them dead."

Nineteen

Emma reread the letter. Better than coffee to jolt one into a new work week.

Whenever she thought nothing could surprise her, up went the ante and did. And here it was, a letter from an entertainment company that wanted PIs to help with a new "reality" show about "actual cases of adultery and infidelity." Folks caught in the act. Cinema verité. The letter wanted to know if she would be part of their referral base and/or had leads she'd like to offer.

Incredible. Didn't people come to her because of the word "private" in her job title? She could imagine saying to a client, "By the way, let's put Claude's cheating on national television! There's a penny or two for you and me, too, and doesn't that make it inviting?"

Had these producers ever witnessed the emotional fallout from these discoveries? She in fact discouraged such surveillance. The person hiring her inevitably already knew what was going on and hired Emma for confirmation, which was nothing short of masochistic. Or vengeful. And neither of those options was meant for national syndication.

Nonetheless, she made note of the show's name. She'd have to watch, at least once, and see how the hell they did it. She hoped, just as there'd been with that insane marry-for-money show, that there'd be dramatic and horrible fallout for the producers.

She heard Billie greet Zack. From her desk, she could almost see them both. She had her door open because the heating system worked better that way, and it was a chilly, damp day.

She considered her suite's four rooms. One was empty, but if she were wise, three would be. Or would be filled with tenants, not employees. What with computers these days, she didn't need this much space—or people—but she was stuck with the luxurious overabundance. She'd gotten her long-term lease when real estate was down, and San Rafael was scrabbling for tenants, and older buildings, such as hers, were in particular distress. Nowadays, it would cost her more to downscale than to stay in place, so here she was. Maybe she still could sublet one or two of the other rooms.

Or sublet those two people out there and get workers who didn't chat and laugh on her dime. He was regaling her with the same news story he'd shared with Emma that morning, the one about the new county ban on keeping wild animals near people's homes. It was incredible there hadn't been such a ban earlier, but it was even more incredible that people wanted to live with monitor lizards and wildcats. And they obviously did, since the clampdown had been triggered by a Bengal tiger showing up in an otherwise tame neighborhood.

More giggling, and murmuring. Something about a bird—a blue bird. Of happiness?

And then a loud sigh and something about exhaustion.

". . . partying?" Zachary asked Billie.

Emma heard a soft sound, somewhere between a laugh and a cry. "Wish," Billie said. ". . . babysitter has the flu."

Emma heard what seemed to involve taking the boy somewhere with her, and now he was sick and she was . . . screwed? Was that what she said? And she'd found somebody for tonight's appointments, but . . .

151

Emma tuned out. She wasn't unsympathetic to the conflicting demands on Billie's time. She'd felt familiar tugs in her own stomach, memories of just such times of insoluble conflict between work and home. But sympathy didn't help a thing. Either you did your work and could bill the hours or you didn't, and Billie was going to have to find her way because that's how it was. Maybe not a good way, but reality. And whether or not Billie's sitter and son were sick, Emma had to pay the rent and utilities and workers' comp and buy computers and databases and gasoline. Zack could offer chocolates as the universal cure for woes, but try and give them to a bill collector.

Emma returned to the business at hand. She had a workers' comp case she should think about and a woman looking for her lost college love. People were enraptured with the elusive or lost. That way, the illusions persisted, glowing through time.

Worst thing that could happen was you fell in love and stayed together. That way, next thing you knew, you were having your infidelities televised.

Sooner than she'd have liked, Billie appeared in her doorway, knocking on the frame. "Don't want to bother you, but I have this idea," she said.

Emma waved her in. "Help yourself." She pointed at the coffee machine.

"No thanks."

"Be honest," Emma said. "Is it that you don't like coffee, or you don't like this coffee?"

She immediately knew the answer as sickeningly polite Billie August silently struggled with how best to respond. Emma had known, anyway, ever since Zack brought in his own machine and beans. "To save the back and forth," he'd lied.

"I'm not always up to the challenge of your coffee," Billie finally said.

Not bad at all. An interesting approach to honesty, although neither she nor Zack understood what real coffee was. "And now—you had an idea about something?"

"I spoke with Tracy Lester's husband. Her widower, I suppose is more accurate. He thinks there was another man. Michael Specht of course, thinks—or knows—there was another woman. The husband says she met a guy named Jimmy on a cruise she took. One of those freebies for travel agents. The place she works for specializes in booking cruises. So I thought I'd go there, pretend to be interested in a trip. Maybe somebody there—gossip on the job stuff—will give me a handle on this mystery man."

"Why do that?"

"Because maybe there's a whole other motive for murder. A love gone wrong. A brush-off."

"I thought she was living with the woman she loved."

"So did I, but apparently . . ."

Emma shrugged. "What the hell, Specht could be wrong. It's worth a few questions, although realistically, what's the chance of finding out who her shipboard love was. I mean you could check the entire ship's register for a Jimmy . . ." She paused, considering how much work getting access to that list would be. "Then, of course, we'd have to track him down, and I'm not sure for what, exactly. So what if she had a fling? Where is it we're going with this?"

"I'm not sure. Of course, I should say that Robby Lester thinks finding out about Jimmy drove Gavin to murder Tracy."

"Great. That's really great."

"Robby says Gavin was in love with her. He does admittedly love her—but he's loved her forever—including when she married Robby. He didn't kill her then, or show anger or jealousy anybody knows of, so why would he now? It doesn't make sense, but Robby didn't make all that much sense, either, so all of this is subject to doubt. I will say the man can drink. His mind was sliding sideways, but he wasn't, and I have no idea how many beers I saw him down, let alone the ones before I got there."

"You're right. Go ahead and check it out."

Emma had always heard about people's faces lighting up, and had thought it a particularly stupid expression, but there it was. Billie's tired face suddenly looked as if she'd switched a bulb on inside. "And please," Emma added, "you can skip the 'thank you Emma, you said I'm right!' dance of joy this time."

Billie grinned, but didn't look ready to leave. Emma watched, sure there was more and sure that it involved her. Billie looked as haggard as a beautiful woman in her twenties could. Circles under the eyes and an unravelled air about her. Sunday with the sick sitter and son must have been rough. But all Emma said was, "More?"

"I thought I'd wear my black wrap and dark glasses. Look rich, like a person booking a cruise. Kind of Audrey Hepburn as rich girl look? What do you think?"

What Emma thought about was Billie's sniffling son, and that Russian lummox felled with the flu and probably complaining like crazy, if Russian men were like their American counterparts. "You know," Emma said. "I'm sure you'd be good, but . . ."

"A problem?"

"Yes."

Billie didn't look worried enough. Being told she had a problem should have made her quiver. For God's sake, half the time she girl looked terrified when there was nothing, so this lack of fear was frightening.

Emma couldn't decide if she was being exquisitely manipulated, set up, or whether giving the girl a hand was her own idea. "Nothing you can help, no matter how well-trained an actress you are." Emma watched as her apprentice's eyes opened wide, the brow above them easing into a slight frown.

Okay, good. She looked scared again, so this was Emma's own idea, not something the girl had planned. Or was she such a good actress that she'd scripted her entire performance, playing Emma's emotions all the while? "Your age," Emma said. "That's the problem."

"Twenty-eight is a problem?"

"You're too young. Cruise people aren't in their twenties. People in their twenties go to the beach. Show off their bodies. Frolic."

Billie laughed. "I haven't frolicked in a long time."

"Then you're wasting time. Me, I'm past beach frolics," Emma said. "I sit discreetly back, as wrapped up as the temperature allows. But the thing is, cruise people—let's be honest. Old farts."

"Well . . . thanks, but you aren't exactly . . ." Sanely, she let go of the sentence and the attempt.

Emma herself still didn't feel old or sedentary enough for that kind of travel, but she fit the stats more than Billie did. "Where's this place, then?" she asked, re-segmenting her day. Not that she had to go today, but pretending to be a wealthy vacationer sounded like more fun than anything else on her desk. Not that she'd say so to Billie. Or acknowledge that this allowed Billie to get home sooner, to the germ-ridden masses awaiting her care.

"Sausalito. Right off Bridgeway."

Close enough to drop in on Heather Wilson and tell her how she'd failed to find out a single usable thing, and that she should stop phoning every five minutes. All roads lead to Sausalito? Pity it was too cold a day for a good hike up on the headlands while she was in the neighborhood. But then, a cruise kind of woman wouldn't be dressed for hiking. "Sure," she said. "I'll do it."

"You want my wrap?"

"I'll pass. It'd make you look rich. It's likely to make me look like a street person wearing an old bedspread and asking for cash. My age, you need jewelry and surgery to do the rich thing. I'll figure something out."

Billie nodded. "I'll touch base with you later today, okay? I'm meeting with Michael Specht at seven, and maybe we'll have come up with something real to tell him."

So that was the appointment. At seven. Interesting choice of time. When it was Emma, it was always during the day. With Billie, after work, over drinks. Maybe Billie's long frolic-less time was about to end. Not an overly great idea, though. "Make sure . . . isn't always great to mix—"

"Drinks?"

"That, too."

"Got you," Billie said as she made her exit. But she stopped at the door and turned. "Thanks," she said. "Thanks for doing the travel agency. I'm sure you heard me telling Zack I've got a sick kid home. And the sitter's been sick for a week. This really helps. Kind of you." She ducked out.

Double-damn. Played for a sucker. She'd made sure Emma overheard and she'd known that good-hearted Emma would offer, and Emma would do her a favor.

And she'd *thanked* her for it.

The girl sure knew how to take the fun out of things.

Twenty

      Emma dawdled at the parking lot, watching as a ferry disgorged people dressed in inappropriately lightweight clothes. It was March, and the sky was a chilly winter blue, a washed out, grayed-over blue. But "Sunny California," they'd insisted, packing short-shorts and sleeveless cotton dresses. They all looked surprised and uncomfortable.

      The travel agency across the street and down a piece seemed small, squashed in between more substantial storefronts. Set among shops geared toward visitors—from T-shirts to expensive jewelry—it seemed an odd marketing ploy to suggest there were other, better, places to be.

      The small size would make this easy enough. How many people could work there? And all she had to do was mention Tracy. She envisioned another young woman, an easy talk and some hint as to the existence or nonexistence of this Jimmy. A husband plus lovers of both sexes. Tracy Lester hadn't had a long-enough life, but she certainly had lived before she died.

      Emma felt properly cruise-oriented in her blazer, slacks, white tailored blouse, and a never worn printed silk scarf Caroline had given her. Caroline had also shown her how to toss it over her shoulder this way. Emma looked almost nautical and surely financially able to book a good berth on a cruise ship to . . . South America. Always wanted to go there anyway. She pushed the door open.

Revolving racks with brochures in front of an unattended counter and behind it, two desks. Emma fiddled with pamphlets, pulling off one blazing the word "Caracas." A gorgeous crackling word, bursting with life, and she didn't feel she was play-acting anymore. She really wanted to go there, though never by ship. The thought of being trapped in the middle of the sea with hundreds of happy, vacationing strangers was unbearable.

A head, and then a slender male body rose from behind the counter. "Sorry!" he said. "Didn't realize anyone was here. I was tidying these . . ."

"No problem at all."

"Can I help you, then?"

She nodded and came closer. "I'm interested in a cruise. Never have gone on one before, but my friends say—"

"I'm sure they say it's the *perfect* way to travel. Because it is. A floating hotel, you know. No need to pack and unpack. Luxury all the way."

She nodded. "And . . . safe," she said. "A woman, alone."

"*Absolutely*. Do you have a specific cruise line or destination in mind?"

"No specific ship," she said. "I'm a novice at this. Friends say this and that, but . . ."

"No problem. That's what I'm here for, to help you decide among them."

"I want to go to South America."

He nodded vigorously. "Wonderful choice." He beamed as he walked to a computer on his desk. "Let's see who we have going there, and when, and what the differences might be." He waved her over. "Take a seat at my desk and let's look at the options. What time of year?"

"I don't know, I guess whenever the weather's good. I mean their seasons are backward, right?"

"They don't think so!" He winked at her.

"This is my first—I mean I'm not sure I'm ready to sign up right away. I need to gather information."

"Of course." He continued tapping keys while he checked the screen.

"But the thing is, I came here because I met this young woman who works here, and she was so sweet, I thought—Well, frankly, this is awkward, but I promised to ask for her."

She could almost watch his thermostat drop and the warmth leave him. "Her name is Tracy," she said. "Tracy Lester."

A curious stew of expressions filtered across his face. Surprise, concern—both of which seemed appropriate. Worry, which also seemed right. This was a place for only happy thoughts, so how awkward to tell the client Tracy was dead. And then something like apprehension and a backing away, hands off the topic, that seemed less comprehensible.

"I'm really sorry," he said. "Tracy isn't here."

True, she thought, although a surprisingly inadequate way of putting it. "I appreciate the help you've shown me, but maybe I should come back on a day she is. I promised, after all. Do you know her schedule?"

"Um, I'm sorry, Ms. . . . I didn't ask your name."

"Beane, with a final 'e.' Margaret Beane. I live up in Santa Rosa, but I'm down here a lot. That's how I met Tracy. And it's 'Missus,' even though I am widowed."

"Of course. Well, Mrs. Beane, I have rather sad news. Tracy isn't with us anymore."

"She switched firms?"

"No. I meant that in the . . . Mrs. Beane, Tracy died. You probably saw it in the papers. Or maybe not, in Santa Rosa. Tracy was . . . killed."

"Oh, my . . ." Emma put her hands to her mouth. She assumed that's what a cruise-buyer would do. "Terrible. Dreadful. I never read those horrible stories. Turn off the TV, too. She was such a sweet girl!"

"Yes," he said. "We miss her very much."

"My condolences. It must be hard on you, working so closely every day and then . . ." She shook her head again and took a few breaths before speaking. "You know, she's the one who suggested I get away. My husband died a while ago, and I'd never traveled on my own, and . . . well, she was so helpful."

He looked grave and sad. And then he seemed to make a connection. "She's probably who suggested Caracas, too," he said. "If I may guess."

Emma pretended to think, and then she nodded. "Possibly, but how did you know that?"

"Because she went on a cruise there last year and she was quite enthusiastic about it."

Emma nodded.

"I was on that same cruise," he said. "Spent a lot of time with Tracy and saw most of the same things. So although I realize I'm a substitute, and for such tragic reasons, perhaps I could be of assistance after all. When, of course, you feel ready to talk about it again."

"You were on the ship with her?"

"At the same time as, but not . . . *with* her, in that sense, you understand. I was traveling with a friend."

Well of course Emma understood. The young man was obviously gay and communicating that. And whether Tracy had been gay or straight, a gay man seemed an unlikely contender for a romantic idyll. Emma could almost hear her son and Zack tsk-tsking her unquestioned labeling, and she knew that sexual orientation wasn't a visible trait, but people, straight and gay, had the option of codes, mannerisms, and dress styles that signaled clearly. That were in fact designed to signal. This man was signaling.

160

But he'd still probably know about shipboard romances—if he was willing to talk. She leaned closer. "I hear . . . Tracy said that interesting things happen in those exotic places."

He angled his head, the skin around his eyes tightening. "What kind of things?"

"The truth is . . . one reason I thought it would be easier to talk to a woman . . . I'm a widow, and meeting men is really difficult at my age, and Tracy, poor soul, said . . ."

"Ah." He nodded and looked relieved. "A good place to meet people."

"Shipboard romances," Emma said softly. "I wonder if Tracy had one, the poor dear. If that's why she was so . . . why she talked that way, mentioned it."

"She was married, you know. Separated, but her husband wasn't on the trip. That's how I got to go with her. It was a ticket for two."

"Oh! So you . . . well, anyway."

He grinned. "We were friends. Platonic friends. But they found a second cabin for me. It was a double, so my friend decided to go. Paid his way, of course. We send a lot of business to the cruise line. We may look small, but most of it is done over the phone."

They'd lost the thread somewhere there in the analysis of who slept where. "So she went without her husband."

He shrugged. "But that doesn't mean she had a shipboard romance. She didn't. I would have known. Not that it doesn't happen, and happen frequently," he added.

"It doesn't actually matter," Emma said. "But to find someone to perhaps have a drink with me, or a dance, that would be nice."

"And you surely will. Now if you like, we can compare the different ships and routes and departure times. Each line has its own personality and of course, different classes of travel."

She let him speak on, nodding every so often to show she was being attentive, actually listening now and then as he spoke of the various ports en route. But mostly she pondered the idea of Tracy's affair—or Tracy's husband's conviction that there'd been an affair—versus the travel agent's denial of any cruise-ship romance.

The travel spiel seemed to be running down. He looked to her for a reaction and input. Her turn now to ask questions, suggest a budget, although there was no point to that. "You make it sound just the way I'd hoped," she said. "And please don't hate me if I ask you to give me brochures, or an estimate—something I can study at a slower pace before I make my decision. But I promise I will book through you when I do."

"No problem at all." He pulled out a form, filling in dollar signs and numbers and names and dates, signed it and handed it to her. "Whenever you're ready. Give a call. Here's my number, and my card."

She looked at the sheet. The prices were staggering but she nodded and tried to look interested. "Thank you," she said, standing up. "You've been exceptionally helpful"—She scanned the business card he'd attached to the sheet: Lawrence Erroll St. James—"Lawrence," she said, putting out her hand. "Or are you a Larry?"

He was also on his feet now, and he took her hand and shook it. "Been a pleasure meeting you, Mrs. Beane. And it's neither, actually. I should have other cards made up, though it wouldn't seem businesslike, would it, if I used the name everybody calls me? It's that last name, you see, that St. James that did it. People started calling me Saint Jimmy, but it's just plain Jimmy nowadays."

"Jimmy," she murmured as she walked outside.

A few steps up the pavement's gentle rise en route to the parking lot, she stopped to catch her metaphorical breath, as if walking interrupted the flow of logic.

Standing still didn't help. The gay young man in the travel agency was still Jimmy with whom, perhaps, Tracy had clandestine, guilt-laden conversations. Or maybe Robby Lester imagined that, too.

And maybe none of it mattered. Whenever you started looking further and further from the heart of things, the picture grew more dense, less sharply edged as each new person's story was woven into the web.

And at the heart of this one, maybe it was as simple as the DA felt. Maybe Gavin Riddock in a fit of whatever mood possessed him at that moment killed Tracy Lester, who still loved somebody else. Not Robby anymore, but not Gavin, either. And that was that.

Emma's felt nauseated. Seasick, perhaps. She tossed the fistful of brochures and all thought of shipboard romances into the nearest basket and was, miraculously, cured.

Twenty-
o n e

"It sounds like interesting stuff, but . . ." Michael Specht smiled wryly and shook his head. "In the end, it's still only stuff." The bar at Savanna Grill was crammed with people. Billie was somewhat amazed that so many people were free for after-work drinks in Corte Madera. They looked as if they had all the time in the world. She tried to imagine a life without perpetual deadlines, and couldn't.

The lawyer leaned across the high small table. "Suspicions with nothing to back them up. Look at it: Her lover—"

"Are we sure of that?" Billie asked. "Are we sure Veronica wasn't a friend? People run for shelter with friends all the time, including when they're running out of a marriage. Why not here?"

Michael—he'd asked her to call him just that, to end the formality—frowned. "Somebody . . . something. I can't remember, but I didn't invent it out of the blue."

"Maybe it's irrelevant."

"Except that Veronica thinks Robby Lester killed his departing wife. Because of her, right?"

"Right," she said. "Except Robby Lester thinks Gavin did it because of this Jimmy fellow."

"Makes you wonder what Jimmy's thinking, doesn't it? Probably if you asked, he'd introduce a whole other villain."

"According to Emma, who met him this afternoon, Jimmy wouldn't be a likely love candidate for Tracy or any other female. And she said Jimmy would be the first to tell you that."

"What happens between men and women makes one dizzy in the contemplation." Once again, he flashed the smile that crinkled the skin around his eyes. And once again, he—deliberately?—blurred the clarity of their topic. Of course he could be—undoubtedly was—referring to the dead young woman's life. But he made it sound as if contemplating what could be between Billie and him was what made him dizzy.

Danger, danger, danger! flashed across her brain in hot neon.

She clicked off the switch. Where, really, was the danger? They were peers. That's what he'd said by way of getting rid of the "mister stuff." "Stuff" was apparently one of his favorite words when he wasn't being the brilliant courtroom orator.

He was attractive and dynamic and it was flattering to be admired. She hadn't felt it for a good half of her marriage, and she surely hadn't felt it since.

There wasn't time in her life for much that wasn't immediately practical, but a man could be damn practical. At least now and then. She was too young to feel this ancient and rusty.

Billie sipped white wine and Michael a single-malt scotch and she cooled herself down by looking out the window. Book Passage, the bookstore across the paved walkway, was filling with people. Printed banners announced that a retired captain of industry would read from his autobiography this evening. She found herself thinking it would be fun to go with Michael, to hear his opinions, to have somebody with whom to talk about what she'd heard.

She shook herself back to the moment, tried to pay attention, to filter out the voice around them along with the questioning voice within her.

"—I think it's great you're tracking them," he was saying. "Because it can help the case. Enough of these loose ends—even if they don't connect—and how can the jury be without the shadow of a doubt? The fact that Gavin doesn't deny it—"

"Doesn't remember," she said. "Isn't sure."

"—and that he was there and had her blood on his—"

"He touched her. He was distraught."

"—at six A.M.—"

"People run at that hour. Earlier, too. It's not even unusual."

He put up a hand, like a crossing guard. "You don't think I'm sincere, do you?"

"About Gavin?"

"What else?"

She rushed, to cover her gaffe. "I'm just saying the obvious. What you'll say. It's all ambiguous, double-edged. That's why Gavin's in jail."

He looked weary. "Forget it. Listen, I'm interested in hearing about everything you've got. I'm talking about Gavin, of course."

So she hadn't rushed quickly enough. She let a beat go by, just so he'd know she'd caught it. "I wonder why Gavin said Tracy was afraid. He sounds . . . honest to me, doesn't he to you?"

"A limited, distorted kind of honesty. I guess he's reporting what he saw, but you don't get the feeling he pays much attention, or sees exactly what we do." Michael looked at his watch. "I'm starving. Any objections to seeing if we could get a table? Food's good and I'll be more coherent if I don't pass out from hunger."

She, too, checked the time. "I'd love to, but I can't stay that long. I didn't realize we'd . . . I mean I scheduled an appointment back to back with this one. Have to drive to West Marin in fact."

"About this case?"

She nodded. "Veronica Napoles."

"Again?"

Her wine was just about gone, so she twiddled with the stem of her glass, sorry this pleasant interlude was about to end. "She's had more phone calls and is freaked out and she says there's something about Tracy, something Tracy had and she needs to talk. I think it's more that she's desperately lonely, with only llamas to talk to. But I did say I'd come." In full truth, partly because she liked the woman and the idea of spending more time on the ranch. It was different there, peaceful.

Michael glanced wistfully over at the tables. "So," he said slowly, returning his attention to her. "Are you enjoying yourself so far?"

"Enjoying . . . ?" She smiled. This one wasn't ambiguous. "Very much," she said.

"Good. Because if you're not having fun, why do it? Nine to five is too big a chunk of life to spend in hell, and believe me, I know from experience how bad it can be."

"My job," she said. "We're talking about my job."

He laughed. "What else?"

She bit at her upper lip, then caught herself. "Despite its weird hours, like now, and even coping with Emma, I like it so far. I wish there was more money in it, but I like the autonomy and—" She was babbling.

"Old Emma's a toughie all right, but I admire her. She's for real."

"Hitler was for real, too."

He grinned. "She gets things done, and you can trust her. So it's a good 'for real.' Mostly, at least. She is also a for real pain in the butt. I've seen her trainees come and go—mostly go—so hang in there. She's a good teacher."

"Hah!"

"In her own fashion," he said before draining the last of his scotch. "West Marin, eh? Want company? It's a clear night, a pretty ride and maybe Veronica could talk to me, too. Or I can stay in the car and think bucolic thoughts. You can leave your car here. And afterwards, we can grab a bite."

"Are you sure you don't want—" She waved in the direction of the dining area.

"Trust me on this," he said. "I always know what I want. And do what I want, too."

And get what you want, she was willing to bet. And make other people want it as well.

He drove a Porsche. She should have known. Sleek, fast, appropriate. And a few years' worth of income for her. If he could afford this, he could pay his investigators more, she decided, and then she wondered how much he was paying Emma.

Emma could pay her more. She was going to ask. Demand.

Meanwhile, she snuggled into the passenger seat as if it were a catcher's mitt and she were the ball. She felt pampered, luxurious. On the edge of something good.

Michael turned all-business, so much so that she thought she'd misinterpreted him earlier in the evening. "What's her number?" he asked.

"Why?"

He didn't precisely roll his eyes, but somehow managed to give the impression of having done so. "To call her?" he said. "To make sure she's there before we're in the middle of nowhere?"

"I spoke to her earlier. She's been going back and forth to her sister's for a while. She's driving home from there right now, and she'll be there about when we are. Maybe a little before, but probably not quite yet."

He shrugged. "A nice night and a pretty drive even if she isn't, I guess."

"She will be. People who raise animals are good about appointments. Something has to be fed, or groomed, or led to shelter or I have no idea what. Last time, she'd just wormed them."

"Go no further. That is already more than I want to know about llama problems." The car slid through the night and he discussed, obliquely and without particulars, the difficulties of this case, the pressures Gavin's mother was putting on him. "You ought to talk with her," he said. "For the life experience."

168

"She doesn't seem to know him, from everything I've learned so far. Not a clue. How can she be of help?"

He said nothing, looking completely focused on the road, his headlights highlighting the edges of the canopy of trees and the occasional house. She, too, sat quietly and enjoyed herself as always, on the trip from the developed bay side of Marin through the winding roads to the rural ocean side of the county. Again, she felt the deep peace of the almost untouched hillsides and farms.

But it wasn't so peaceful that she could stop thinking about Gavin Riddock. "I feel sorry for him," she said after a while. "Even if he did it, I feel sorry for him."

"I get the sense that you don't think I share that feeling."

"Not really. I—"

"That because I'm a realist, that means that for me, it's all about and only about money. Oh, maybe notoriety, too. Fame. That if I do a good job, I'll get lots of other yummy murderers as clients. That I'm cynical and world-weary and had by the third year of law school lost any vestigial morals and emotions."

"I never—"

"Lawyers deserve to become a charity, to have their own publicly supported antidefamation league, if you ask me. But"—he looked over her way and flashed one of his win-the-jury's-heart grins—"nobody ever does ask me about that. Never would cross anybody's mind how unfair they're being."

"Point taken." Even though she knew he was undoubtedly billing this time, this ride, and even his cute little speech about his being maligned. She settled back to being his passenger, being his employee, and when thoughts of Gavin Riddock didn't intrude, she enjoyed the silhouetted hills, the smooth shot of the car low on the road, the ride for what it was.

She recognized a landmark tree that almost jutted into the road. "There," she said. "Around the bend. There's an arch over the gate. Can't miss it. It'll say 'Whynot Farm.'"

"Why not farm? I could give you a dozen answers to that question."

The road bore to the right, around the trunk of a live oak, the headlights finding pattern upon pattern as it swept through the leaves, over the blacktop—

"What in hell?" Michael shouted, swerving and downshifting as his headlights impaled the silhouetted image of a tall woman—Veronica—arms flailing, mouth open in a scream.

Twenty-
two

"Go to hell you son of a bitch!"

He wasn't even inside his house yet. The front door was still open and David Vincent stood on the threshold, keys in his hand. So okay, he didn't expect a sitcom-style greeting, but, still, this was ridiculous. Lately, he'd felt as if the house was mined and he'd better be careful wherever he stepped, because the least likely spot could contain explosives or snipers behind the staircase.

Or a lunatic wife carrying a grudge the size of Rhode Island and waiting, just waiting, for him to do something. Only he didn't know what it was.

He'd made the mistake before of asking if maybe she wasn't feeling well, if she had her period and—sweet Jesus!—she'd nearly killed him. He wasn't about to ask anything like that again.

"Gone all last night—"

"You knew I had to be in Sacramento for a—"

"And late today! Dinner's ruined, asshole. Leather. Eat your shoes; they'll taste the same. You think you can walk in here whenever you feel like it? Why'd you come home at all? To pick up fresh clothing?"

"What are you talking about? If you'd stop screaming and—" He had to be calm with her. Always calm, but it took more energy than he had. She was killing him.

"Don't you get all level-voiced and act like I'm insane. Don't you try to gaslight me!"

"Jeannie, for God's—"

"Don't 'Jeannie' me! I've been a fool long enough, but now—"

"Where are the kids? What are you doing with my kids—"

"*My* kids are at my mother's. I didn't feel up to giving them dinner. I'm a nervous wreck, and it's your fault."

To hell with this. This was *his* house. *His* money paid for it, for everything in it, and he'd walk into his house whenever and whatever time he pleased.

But he had to get out of this mess, this marriage, this hell. Had to play it smart. Who knew how much she knew, really? or what she'd do. Because she was crazy. He'd tried to believe it was just stress. People under stress freaked out sometimes. But not this much, not like the way she had.

"Take care of her. She isn't . . . strong," her own mother had said to him on their wedding day—like that was a good time to mention it—whatever she meant. He could never stop thinking about how she'd said it, then.

"I'm not sure she's altogether stable," his mother had said a few years later. They hadn't spoken for ten months after that, but then she apologized and now they were at least polite to one another. And now he knew she was right, and that's what Jeannie's mother meant by her not being "strong." And a man like him, in his position, he needed somebody strong, or at least normal.

He was under stress twenty-four hours a day. His life was one long stress test and he couldn't have a wife who added to it. But Jeannie didn't believe in divorce. Even the mention made her more insane. And he wasn't hot for the idea, either. Too much with examining the books, looking at every cent he'd ever made. Too dangerous.

He had to figure this out and he was working on whether she could be put somewhere. To rest, they could call it. To get away from him and his kids.

She might not be a strong person, but her voice sure was. It could saw through steel beams, but what the hell was this new fit about? He waited while she lit a cigarette and slammed things down on the kitchen counters like she was testing at what strength granite shatters. "Why don't you tell me what it is you're so—"

"Don't use that voice like you're talking to a raving lunatic! I'm not crazy, David! I'm just sick and tired of this life, of you!"

"Why?" He whispered, but not because he was afraid of annoying her, and not even to keep her calm. He whispered because if he let go of any part of himself—even his voice, his vocal cords—then he was likely to let go altogether and kill the screaming woman.

"Don't play dumb. I know about your lies. I know what you've been doing. You take me for a fool, don't you? You think I'm too stupid to pay attention and see what you're up to? *I know about you, David!*"

His heart stopped. For a minute he was dead. How could she? But better he didn't ask what she meant, didn't plant ideas.

Still, she kept doing this. Hinting, all-but-saying, driving him up the wall. And Marlena had mentioned that she'd been in the office while he was gone. Wanted to check an insurance policy, she said. Went into the files, for God's sake. Not that anything was there, but what did she want? What was she looking for? What did she know?

Nothing, he told himself. She knew nothing. All of it, her hints, the file cabinet, all of it was one long fishing expedition. Her sickness, her craziness, that was all it was.

But he was sick of this. "Tell me what's bothering you."

"Well, it isn't my period, if that's going to be your next sexist, stupid question," she snapped.

He nodded. And waited some more, finally seating himself on one of the tall stools at the kitchen counter. She paced, alternately sucking on the cigarette she held in one hand and the thick tumbler of red wine in the other until, finally, he'd had it. He stood up.

"So don't tell me, then," he said. "Throw a fit, then clam up so nobody knows what's going on or how to make it better. The truth is: I don't need this crap. I work myself to death to provide you with everything—look around you—everything! And then I come home to this? Well, no more. You can go to hell, Jeannie. I'm leaving. That should make you happy, finally."

She stared, her nose reddening, her eyes flooding, as if he'd attacked her, done something horrible to her. As if he'd done one single thing! "Who is she?" she asked in a raspy whisper.

She?

"Tell me! I deserve to know."

A woman? Another woman? That's what she thought?

There wasn't any other woman. Not in this time zone. He wasn't that stupid. Away from home, it was different. All rules off, but there was no way in hell Jeannie knew about one-night stands halfway around the world. "I don't know what you're talking about."

He looked at his house, this carefully put together glass-and-shingle cube she loved so much. Quiet, safe street, good schools. A swimming pool, a gas barbecue, a hot tub. How many people had such things? Tennis courts, golf links not far away. Everything she wanted, and then some, and she didn't lift a finger outside the house. If she had any sense, she'd shut up and be grateful.

"For starters," she said, pausing to light another cigarette and drag deeply on it. "I am sick," she said after she exhaled. "Physically sick from your lies about needing to travel."

"What lies? Business travel is not a lie." She was definitely insane. Maybe he could have her committed, for real. Or had they changed the laws about that, too. Did she have to agree to it?

"You travel for a moving company? A second-rate moving company?"

"What's wrong? You're not living well enough? Did I walk into somebody else's house just now? You don't like your bread and butter anymore? You'd rather live on the streets? Can the insults. My company is not second rate. We don't need a fancy front,

174

money wasted on a flashy office. We have a reputation, which I work to keep up. We're specialists!"

"You're changing the subject. People with moving companies don't have to travel for business, except the van drivers, and you aren't one of them."

"Listen to me, Jeannie Vincent, you don't know squat about business. You think I just sit in that office in Sausalito and people trot in and fill out forms for me? Well, I've got news for you. In the worlds I work for—art and music, international moves, special items moves, the things most moving companies don't touch—you have to publicize yourself. You have to go to conferences, to industry shows. Take booths, promote what you do. You have to sometimes go to somebody's out of town house or a museum or whatever to estimate the cost of the objects—"

"That isn't true. There are cooperating agents." She said it as if she'd memorized it. "I know that, because I called your office and pretended to be somebody else and I asked, you filthy liar."

"In general, right," he said. "If you called, you want to move an ordinary household, then that works that way, but what if you own—" Then he stopped? Why was he wasting breath? "What the hell are you doing making a call like that? Checking up on me? What kind of attitude is that? What kind of—"

"You're a liar! You sneak around, spend your nights in motels, and I'm supposed to take care of the kids and take it? What kind of way is that to treat me?"

"It's business!"

"Monkey business!"

He took a deep breath. "You are out of your mind."

Her hair looked lumpy, twisted, as if she'd forgotten to brush it today. "I'm not dumb, you know. I thought for a while it was that girl. Maybe it was, in fact. Probably was. The one before this one."

"I'll bet you think you're making sense."

"That girl who got killed. The one at Blackie's Pasture."

"Tracy Lester? Why her? Where do you get your—"

"Because I have eyes. I saw her go into your office for a very long time, and she wasn't ordering up a special moving job, was she?"

"She was probably hanging out with the other girls in my office. She worked across the street."

"No. She was in your private office."

His mind turned her words over, looked behind them, reread them. You couldn't see into his private office from the street, so where had she been? Or else she'd seen Tracy enter the outer office, then tracked her and saw that she was no longer visible. But in any case, Jeannie was tailing him, goddamn stalking him and for how long? She was crazier than he'd understood. "You still think I had a thing with Tracy? And you're mad now, so you think maybe I'm spending my nights in the coroner's office, still carrying on with her?"

"Don't talk that way about the dead."

"Then don't talk that way about me! Do you know how precisely and exactly stupid you are, sneaking around and checking up on me like a madman in a horror movie? You're so stupid I can't believe it, because Tracy, of all the people to pick, was gay. She left her husband for another woman."

"How would you know?"

"The papers. You know, they use code, like saying 'her partner.' "

"They didn't say that! They never said anything like that! I read every single word because—because—" She was working herself back up again, and he knew why she'd read the accounts. Because she was sure he was having a thing with Tracy. And probably with Queen Elizabeth, too.

"You knew her. You're making this up to cover up what you were doing."

He felt chilled, as if the air had dropped forty degrees. He calmed himself. "You're right," he said. "I didn't read it in the papers. I know it because she told me it herself. That's what she was doing in my office. She told me because she was afraid of what her boss would say."

Jeannie opened her mouth, then closed it with the slow-registering expression of a drunk. Then she shook her head, her wild black hair flopping back into more messiness. "You didn't come home *twice* last week!" she shouted.

Back to square one. He sighed. "I told you, I—"

"It's that girl in your office, isn't it?"

"Oh, my God, Jeannie, for Christ's sake, you just finished saying Tracy—"

"The one with the hair and the clothes from the fifties. The one who thinks she's Marilyn Monroe."

"It isn't *anybody,* Not in my office or any other place."

"Then where were you? Explain. Explain where you were and why you're late now, too. I called your office and you weren't there. Where were you?"

"Taking care of business," he said wearily. Jeannie could make him more exhausted than anybody or anything on earth. She changed the weather, made the air he breathed heavy, asphyxiating. He felt the tightness in his chest, and coughed.

"Why aren't you wearing the clothes you left in this morning!" She looked like that Greek myth, that lady with snakes for hair he remembered from school. She looked like she could kill.

"I worked out. Then I changed."

"Sure, you worked out at her place. You keep a wardrobe there? Her Marilyn Monroe stuff and your clothing, too! What do you call what you were doing?" she demanded.

He coughed again. "Business," he said when he caught his breath. It was always easier to tell the truth.

Twenty-
three

"Holy mother of Christ!" Michael shouted. "What the——I could have killed you!"

Billie got out of the car even while he continued to shout, working through his terror in his own fashion.

Veronica's face was tear-streaked and she visibly shook. Her hands, which she held up, were dark. "Blood!" she screamed.

Billie reached toward her. "We're here." She turned, Michael was out of the car, pale and stunned. "This is Michael Specht, the lawyer." She felt beyond a fool, making introductions while Veronica trembled and sobbed about blood, but she didn't want to further terrify her with an unknown man. "What is it?" she said, scanning Veronica up and down. "Where are you hurt?" Aside from the bloodied palms and fingers, there was no sign of injury.

"Me——it isn't——" Veronica shook her head from side to side, swallowed.

"Shhhh," Billie said. "It's going to be all right."

"No!"

"Veronica," Michael said in a theatrically calm voice. "What happened?"

She looked at him gratefully, as if only that question could have released what roiled inside her. "I got home——I just got home——" She shook her head again. That hadn't worked, either. "I can't——

You look. Look yourself." She motioned them to follow her, her posture almost tilting back and away even as she moved forward, her head shaking "no" all the while, uninventing whatever was ahead.

They reached the fence where Billie had stood with Jesse as he warily regarded the funny-looking animals. This time, there was a moon and she could see more clearly. This time, there were no llamas regarding her back, although she saw a cluster in the far distance.

"Look!" Veronica's voice was strangled. She pointed down.

Now Billie saw llamas. Close by. Three of them, their heads nearly severed from their shaggy bodies.

"My boys," Veronica whispered. "My babies. They never hurt a soul. They just . . . my boys . . ."

They lay sprawled and broken, their thick coats matted with dark bloodied patches.

"Who could? Why . . ." Veronica cried.

Billie's stomach, her entire insides, reversed and tried to undo, unsee, get rid of what was in front of her. She heard Michael Specht gag, and at the sound, had to run across the road, to find privacy to empty what little she'd had on her stomach. When she finally stopped heaving and had taken enough deep breaths to feel stable again, she crossed back again. Veronica still sobbed, and Michael stood back from the fence, where he could no longer see the corpses.

"You okay?" he asked softly as she approached.

She nodded, as long as he meant only that she was through throwing up.

"They were shot first," he said. "Then when they were dead or dying . . . it's awful. Their throats." He gestured, quietly, toward the Whynot Farm gate. A dripping red "X" was on one white side post in what Billie fervently hoped was paint. She wasn't sure why writing with their blood would make the murder worse, but it would.

"What do you think it means?" he asked quietly.

She didn't know. She thought of CoXistence, but couldn't imagine who could so hate the animal protectors and the animals themselves.

"I think it's 'X' as in 'marks the spot,' " Michael said. "Just in case the message wasn't clear that this handiwork belongs to him. Whoever X is."

They both looked back at Veronica, waited while she worked toward control, her back to them, and then Billie watched as Michael, in the gentlest, most caring and calming tone, spoke to her—about nothing, really, about everything, as he walked her toward her house. Billie's eyes welled again, though not from the same source, and not that she could explain it. Still, she paused and listened for a moment before following them into the house.

She heard them gasp and exclaim before she herself entered the pulled apart, upended room. Veronica pointed, waved, said nothing, then crumpled onto her pillowless sofa.

"Here," Michael said, putting pillows back on the frame and resettling her. "Here."

Billie envied his ability to do something, no matter what it was. While Veronica hiccuped, Billie visually checked the kitchen area. The small counter and the formica table at which she'd sat were littered with containers—cereal boxes, rice bags, popcorn jars—all, as far as she could see, with their contents spilled about, as if a hand had gone into each and every potential hiding place.

Looking for what?

All the drawers had been opened and were still pulled out to varying degrees. The cabinet doors stood open and empty plastic storage containers lay on the floor.

"Would I be disturbing the scene if I made tea?" she asked. It seemed a positive step forward, a first-aid emergency action.

Michael still hovered over Veronica. "Or something stronger?" he asked.

Veronica closed her eyes, took several deep breaths, her hands curled into fists. Then she shook her head and said, "Tea."

"I'll use the pot holder on the teapot and only touch the three mugs," Billie said.

Apparently, nobody had been interested in the cabinet holding Veronica's small dinnerware collection; the four mugs and four plates were intact. She noted that the place had been searched, not vandalized.

She put water on to boil and excused herself. She knew about not using the bathroom in case there were fingerprints on the seat or elsewhere, but she risked assuming the llama killers had not stopped to brush their teeth, although they had opened the medicine cabinet. She squeezed toothpaste onto her finger and swabbed her mouth. Then she checked the bedroom, in which the dresser drawers and closet door were open, contents pulled half out, and the bedding pulled off, the mattress pushed so that it sat at a tilt on the floor.

By the time she was back in the kitchen, the water had boiled, and Michael Specht was pouring it into the mugs.

They almost could have passed for normal people in an exceptionally messy home. "Can you talk about it yet?" Billie asked when they were all settled.

Veronica had gone from near hysteria to preternatural calm. Her skin blotched from emotion, she sat and stared directly ahead. Finally, she took a long, ragged-edged inhalation. "I came home and went right to check my . . . my . . ." She exhaled with a loud whoosh, shook her head and continued. "I didn't even come in. Didn't take my bag out of the car. It was dark, so at first, I didn't see. I was looking in the distance, looking for the bachelor boys. I nearly . . . I just about fell over . . ." She shook her head. "And then I'm not sure. I don't know what next."

"I think next you ran into the street, ready to flag down whoever came by, and that was us," Michael said. "Do you have any idea who could have done this?" Michael's voice was both consoling and in control. Billie wondered whether it was a voice he used often.

"Who would do anything like that except an insane person?" Her eyes were wild and the head-shaking resumed. "I can't stand it, I honestly cannot. It feels worse than . . . worse than anything."

They sat in silence punctuated only by the infrequent sound of a car passing in the night. "Shall I call the police now?" Michael asked.

"It's only animals, they'll say. They think I'm crazy. Only animals. I don't even think you can murder animals. You can kill them, but that isn't the same thing legally, is it?"

Michael cleared his throat. "There's a . . . did you notice the mark on the gate post?"

She looked confused. "I drove right in, I didn't . . ." And then she pushed back, deeper into her seat and half averted her face. "Why? What did—what writing? What did it say?"

He sighed. "It's an 'X,' that's all. Unless you know something that explains it, I'd say it's meaningless, except that I think you have to leave again for a while, be someplace that feels safer."

"It's him again. It's Robby. He's still calling and threatening."

"Threatening? I thought the calls were silent," Billie said.

She shook her head. "Now he talks, but I can't understand what he says. I didn't know he could be this insane. I mean with Tracy, at least, there was love once, there was . . . but my . . ."

"The phone calls," Billie said.

"They started again."

"But they're different, aren't they?" Billie asked. "You said he's talking now. Maybe it's not Rob—"

"He talked before, too. But only to Tracy. I only overheard— walked in and heard her saying she wouldn't, and she couldn't, and he should leave her alone." Veronica held onto her teacup and saucer with both hands, as if it were supporting her. "He killed her," she said bitterly, "so there's nobody left to talk to except me. And now"—She waved, weakly, toward the front of the house—"anybody who did that would have killed me, too."

It was hard to disagree. In fact, the llamas seemed a pitiable substitute—creatures at the wrong place at the wrong time when it turned out that whatever they were looking for, and Veronica herself, were missing.

"What does he say when he calls?" Michael asked.

She put the teacup and saucer that had been clattering softly in her trembling hand onto the trunk that served as a coffee table. "The last time he called, he—"

"When was that?"

She had to stop and count backward. "Saturday night."

"Wait, if this was the last time, then he'd done it before? I mean since Tracy?" Billie asked.

Veronica nodded. "The time before that—a few nights after I saw you—he said creepy things like 'I want what you have.' And I slammed down the phone. By Saturday, I'd had it, you understand? She didn't love him! Why act as if I—I screamed at him this time. He said something like that again, or maybe he wanted what Tracy had—I can't remember, honestly, he wanted proof, I don't know of what. It felt dirty, disgusting, like he wanted me, and I blew up. I told him I knew who he was and I was sick and tired of this and that I'd told people about him and he was going to jail."

"What time Saturday?" Billie had been with him for an hour, maybe two, that evening at the bar.

Veronica shook her head. "After dark."

"That's so early. Can you get any more precise?"

"I don't know. I was feeling so bad. But maybe eight o'clock. Not late. Because afterwards I left for my sister's. He scared me."

Before Billie had hooked up with him at the bar. But she remembered him coming out of the back. The men's room or the phone, she'd thought then.

"Did you call him 'Robby'?" Michael asked. "Use his name? Did he respond to it?"

Veronica reached for the teacup, changed her mind and sat,

hands clasped. Finally, she shook her head. "I don't think so. I hate his name. It's like a baby's. Cute, and he isn't. I'd remember if I'd said it because it's so stupid it hurts to say it!"

Billie watched Michael's subtle change of expression. He'd had hopes, she thought, of a solid witness in Veronica, but now he was dropping that idea. "Why would he do that?" Michael asked quietly, and indicated what "that" meant with a wave of his hand out toward the field. "What sense does it make?"

"He's the one who doesn't make sense. He's crazy. I told you, didn't I?" she said to Billie, who nodded. "He'd do it because"—she blinked furiously and when she spoke her voice sounded constricted and painful—"it hurts me more than anything could, except Tracy . . ."

"What about this?" Michael asked, gesturing to the trashed room.

She shook her head. Her expression was bleak. She'd lost so much, so quickly, Billie thought, and all she was seeing was the absence of what mattered. "The proof? He thought the proof—whatever that is—would be here? I hope they bit the hell out of him," she said in a drained voice. "Butted him and kicked him and I hope . . . maybe he'll be marked up. Evidence."

Billie nodded, but a man with a gun eliminates the need for close contact. The killer was probably mark-free. Except for their blood, she thought, and shuddered. "Do you have a place to stay?" Billie asked. "Do you feel as if you can drive? Can I call someone to pick you up?"

"It must have been because I wasn't here," Veronica said slowly. "So he killed them. It must have been that."

"Yes. I'm trying to say—"

Veronica nodded. "A friend I can . . . I'll call . . . she'll come. She has three sons and a husband. They can . . . they'll come with me when I have to come back. Until . . ."

"Yes," Billie said. "Until we're sure this is settled."

Veronica's features seemed to congeal, pull in on themselves.

"He has to be locked up," she said in a voice from deep within herself. "Forever."

They made the phone calls, then stayed with her until first her neighbors, and then the police arrived.

By the time they were back in the burgundy Porsche, Billie was numb with exhaustion. "I hope you have more energy than I do," she said. "Or this is going to be one slow ride. I can barely breathe, I'm so tired. But—I hope this isn't too personal—but I have to say how impressed I am with how you were with her."

He looked startled before he thanked her. They drove in silence.

She was struck by how lonely and isolated the landscape now looked. How vulnerable a solitary woman in a house out here must be. It had seemed so different on the ride out, so filled with peace. She hoped it hadn't changed permanently for Veronica, who deserved something strong and reliable left in her life.

Michael broke the silence. "It doesn't make sense, does it? Why would Robby Lester do that? I wonder if this is related to Tracy at all."

"Why wouldn't it be?"

"Because however sad it makes us, Gavin probably killed Tracy. Probably by accident, and we'll try to soften it up every way we can, but that's the likelihood. And he's locked up now and couldn't have done this. That's one. But more important, Veronica's admittedly an animal-rights advocate. She isn't part of the lunatic fringe, isn't one of the bombers, but she's out there, very public, picketing and protesting and holding petitions, and maybe it's hurting somebody's business."

"A pretty extreme response, don't you think? Unless we're talking about an insane person."

"We're talking, in any case, about a person with a great deal at stake. Most likely, money. So all I'm saying is maybe the animals weren't killed out of malicious spite because she was away. Maybe the animals were the signal, the connection, the point."

"X marks the spot?"

"X for an illiterate signature. Their mark?" He sighed again. "Maybe it's kids. Sicko kids, but a random, meaningless, horrible act. It happens."

"That's the least bearable idea of all." She noticed the time on the dashboard clock. "My God," she said. "I thought hours had passed. Didn't it feel like forever?"

He nodded. "But it is, in fact, still early. And I for one could use another drink. Or five. What a night! The tea was nice, but not enough. How about you? Care to join me?"

She looked at her watch, then remembered that she'd already seen the dashboard clock.

"I hope this doesn't show too gross an insensitivity on my part, or at least on my stomach's part," he said. "But I am also hungry. Besides, I'd . . . I'd like to get to know you more."

She was so upset and bone-weary, was it possible to be interested in the proposition, if it was one?

It was. The life force, one of her friends had labeled all such astounding impulses. The label reduced guilt by 90 percent.

"A quick meal," he said. "A drink. Absolutely no talk about Tracy or work or tonight, either."

"I really want to. Truly," she said. "But I can't."

"Oh, come on. It's early, we're single, we're adults. And even if it was late, if you come in later tomorrow, does anybody care? You're paid by the hour."

"It isn't that. It's my baby-sitter. I told her I'd be back by . . ."

She never finished the sentence because it didn't matter to Michael Specht what time she'd said she'd be back. His features had realigned at the sound of "baby-sitter." "I didn't know you had a child," he said in a new, politely sociable voice, as if they'd just met at a massive cocktail party. "Or is it children? How old? A girl, a boy? Both?"

"One boy. Jesse. Three and a half. I am that modern classic figure, a single parent."

"Ah," he said. "Well . . ."

"Normally, there's no problem. A college student lives with us, and he's terrific, but he has the flu, so I have a substitute and . . ." Michael was not interested in her domestic logistics. In fact, in an amazing instance of vaporization, he was no longer interested in her.

She hadn't known that the mere mention of a child could drive a grown man into hiding.

"A pity," Michael said. "But if you can't stave off starvation along with me, you can't. I'm sorry."

No protest, no alternate plan. She knew about take-out, including exquisitely prepared take-out, but apparently he had forgotten it.

And there she'd been, worrying about what the lawyer's interest meant, and whether it would be ethical or wise to date her employer, and she could have skipped the dithering because all along she was carrying a piece of baggage named Jesse that was a guaranteed Michael Specht repellent.

She wanted to say something, to tell him about life and priorities and values along with stupidities and blind spots and polished surfaces. She wanted to tell him that complicated didn't mean bad.

But she couldn't and didn't. Instead, she accepted the exchange for what it was: another goddamn learning experience. What she could never accept or understand was why they were never fun.

Twenty-
four

"Three," Billie said. "Shot. Hacked. Horrible."

Emma was speechless. Killing llamas. If ever animals looked innocuous, invented, like something out of *Doctor Doolittle*. Why? Surely not because of anything they were capable of doing. They weren't eating or destroying another rancher's crop or livestock. All they did was stand around, growing wool. Where was the harm in that?

"Do you see any link with Tracy Lester's death?" Billie asked.

"There's no logic I can think of," she finally said. "Which usually turns out to mean there's no logic, period. Not helpful, I know."

"It really bothered Michael. Well, just seeing those animals was enough to upset anybody, permanently."

Michael. Was Emma hearing the sound of something going on?

"The fact that she's still getting phone calls is bothersome. Seems to open different possibilities."

"What if they're two separate sets of phone calls, given that until Tracy died, Veronica never actually heard the caller's voice. She's assuming the conversations she overheard were the same caller, but what is there to support that idea? And how does all this affect us? What does Michael want now?" And what was it Michael had wanted last night that propelled him to drive to Veronica's ranch with the investigator he was paying to do just that? Not that Emma cared as long as it didn't interfere with the relationship she'd built up with the lawyer.

"More of the same," Billie said. "Widen the scope, see if we can find out about the calls, see if it could help Gavin's case. He wants me to talk to Gavin's mother, hope she says something this time that pushes us somewhere. I gather that despite her frantic phone calls and threats that Michael had better *do* something, she herself has offered amazingly little. I don't mean holding back, just having nothing to put on the table, as if her son was a . . . I don't know . . . pet. She made sure he had food and shelter, but she didn't even think to ask who his friends were, or how he spent his days."

"And you think you can miraculously make her think of things she doesn't know?" Emma asked. "Waste of time. She bought the lawyer for her son and that's about it. Gavin's sole job is not to bother her, and he screwed that up. Does not sound promising, but go ahead. It's her dime, and our income, after all."

Billie looked sadder still.

"Dress up. Look rich. Like you're playing at this business. I'm sure she's a gold-plated, small-minded snob, so pander to her. Let her think you're on her wavelength, and maybe something will come up. Although why she wouldn't have said it to the lawyer she hired to defend her son, I surely can't say."

Now Billie looked not only mournful but anxious. Emma knew the girl could do it—she was a goddamn trained actress, for crying out loud. And Emma hated stroking employees' egos, had a policy against it born out of experience. You did it once, twice and suddenly, they were Sam Spade demanding raises and then, having gotten them, they left to open their own agencies.

But this one required praise and bucking up the way normal people required oxygen. "You nervous about this?" Emma asked.

Billie didn't say; she looked preoccupied.

"Don't be. You'll be . . ." Damn, she hated to insist on future terrificness when who really knew? Praise inflation cheapened the whole thing. ". . . great," she reluctantly said. "Go be Grace Kelly. Or was she too long before your time?"

"I know who Grace Kelly was," Billie said. "I studied history." Touché.

"And thanks for the vote of confidence. But to be honest, I wasn't—I'm not nervous."

She had the unmitigated gall to smile. To look amused. She gave Emma heartburn.

"I was momentarily overwhelmed by how sad Gavin's life really has been," Billie said. "Privileged in every way except the most basic ones, and in those ways, really deprived. Like a kid in those English novels, the rich little orphan whose parents live in one of the far colonial outposts. Plus, I think he's smart enough to know he isn't smart enough. That has to be the worst, like being a prisoner of yourself in some way."

Emma waved away her words. There was no point in going wobbly and sentimental over each sad person along the way because there were too damn many of them and nothing to be done about it. You'd just break your own heart and join their ranks. "How about the housekeeper?" she asked.

The girl looked baffled, as if Emma had been speaking in tongues.

"The *housekeeper*. Gavin's."

"How about her?"

"She knows a hell of a lot more about Gavin than his mother ever did. Are you going to talk to her?"

"I . . . sure, I . . ."

Never thought of it. Typical. "The people nobody thinks about," Emma said. "You know: attendants and newspaper vendors and floor-washers, they notice a hell of a lot because nobody's noticing them." She had surely told Billie this simple, basic truth before. And not only one time. Surely.

"Of course. I was going to . . . his mother, the housekeeper. And I'm trying to get the names of the people in those animal-

190

activist groups. A lot of the groups Gavin was involved with were for one purpose and they dissolved afterwards, but those people move on, so I think I can find some who knew—know him."

"Don't wear the same clothing as you do for Zandra Riddock. For the housekeeper, I mean. She's probably keeping secrets, and not sure which secrets to keep—probably trying to protect Gavin. Or herself. Somebody. So don't look threatening."

"Well . . . sure."

Emma couldn't read the tone. She'd insulted the girl's intelligence, was that it? Screw that. Look how dense she'd been about the housekeeper. How was a person supposed to know which basic truth came naturally into that head and which had to be pounded in? "Keep track of whatever's going on with the llama lady. She going to be okay?"

Billie looked surprised. All but fell to the floor with shock that Emma could worry about somebody. "I think so," Billie said after a moment's hesitation. "Even last night, she was able to think of what to do. After the initial shock, she was . . . I think she's going to regroup and be fine."

"Okay, then," Emma said. "You've got your work cut out. A whole lot of people to find, looks like."

Billie nodded. "And if you . . . if you feel like . . . any of those people . . . you know, just . . ." Billie's voice drifted into the ionosphere.

What was it with the girl? One minute she had it all together, and the next, nothing. Zero, blank. They were paid by the hour, for God's sake, and time-wasting and dithering cost money. "*What?*" Emma snapped.

Billie swallowed. "About that long list of people. I mean . . . if you wanted to interview any of them, that is, of course. Not that you have to—I mean, I'm fine with it, but—"

"I'll let you know."

Two seconds after Billie swept out, Emma heard muffled laughter in the outer office. Zack, too.

She didn't know what so amused them and did not care. She returned to the month's reports that Zack had handed her that morning, sighed over the bottom line and wondered again what the future of her profession would be when anyone could search for people on-line, or pay an information broker who would simply check a few databases. She wasn't sure how she—and all her professional brothers and sisters—would survive. Working for lawyers was fine, but it didn't pay well. And meanwhile, she annoyed herself by going around in mental circles this way. Her form of dithering, she had to admit.

Which brought her back to Billie. Sometimes she wondered if she should just lay it all out for the girl. A reality check. After all, the girl was counting on making enough at this to live a decent life and raise a child, and Emma wasn't sure that was going to be possible. She'd hinted at it, grumbled about it, but couldn't bring herself to say it outright. George said she was being superstitious, acting as if saying the words made it so.

She yawned. She needed fresh air. The old building's heating system was creaky and out of her control, and whatever she was breathing right now smelled stale and slightly burned.

She needed to check fictitious name records at the Civic Center for a client considering a partnership. So far, his would-be business partner had been fine, but she needed to check his supposed past business deals. Might as well do it now and breathe fresh air in the bargain. She'd grab a few minutes by the lagoon first.

"Back soon," she told Zachary, who was no longer laughing with Billie at Emma's expense; she was sure she had somehow been the butt of their humor.

He nodded. "By the way, that Heather Wilson girl called again," he said.

Emma paused, with her hand on the doorknob. "She thinks it's like a TV show, all tightly wound up within an hour. And so far, I have nothing—less than nothing. I have lies and more lies."

"Lies are something," Zachary murmured.

Emma thought about that en route and even as she settled onto a bench at the lagoon. This was her favorite part of the Civic Center. No matter how many children raced wildly around, how many mothers or nannies called for them, how many lost-looking souls sat on other benches, Emma felt the world slide off her shoulders.

She was glad she'd brought the anorak. Not many people here today for a reason, and she had to admit she was less than comfortable, bundled as she was.

But she loved this place, the scale of it, the awkward blend of the nearby freeway, and the slow-motion life by her bench, punctuated by honks and quacks and splashes from avian takeoffs, landings, and skirmishes over who owned which bit of water.

She watched a man with a gray ponytail toss bread to the ducks, geese, and grebes in the water. Overhead, seagulls screamed and dived at the sight of each tossed chunk. Emma watched the tussle and felt a surge of sympathy. They were trying to stay alive, get their daily bread.

She was able to let go the whirligig in her mind. She considered the furious, frightened, battling seagulls and vowed to stop squawking about her own contest for food. She'd do what she had to for the agency and herself. She was lucky. She wouldn't wind up on the streets. She had options. She'd saved some, could cut back, sell her house, move. Or she could go on-line, too, although the idea made her claustrophobic, as if she'd have to crawl into a computer and be forever locked in there, scrunched in the fetal position.

Or maybe there was some entirely different line of work— something with animals, perhaps? She looked at the ducks' iridescent plumage, and though she knew the serenity they projected was undoubtedly an illusion, they at least had the attractive quality of being only what they seemed to be. No pretense, no mystery, no duplicity, nothing to figure out about them. Ducks didn't have royally screwed families like Heather Wilson's. Or, for that matter, Gavin Riddock's.

And possibly her own.

That's why there were no duck PIs. Animals were what they were: gloriously uncomplicated.

Emma felt hopeful. She watched as a duck made a feetfirst water landing. Maybe she could circumvent Kay Wilson's—aka Megan Wilson's—lies. Maybe Heather's adopted father, missing from the birth certificate, was somehow the key. Perhaps his death records would show a surprising secret beneficiary. Maybe he was indeed Heather's biological father. Maybe he had a second family elsewhere. Maybe . . . maybe . . . who knew? She was grabbing at straws that were fiber-optic thin, but she couldn't think of another route.

What did she know about Nowell? "Nowell because he was born on Christmas day," Kay had said. So Emma knew his birth date and that he was the child of bad spellers, though that latter fact wasn't overly helpful.

What else did she know? He was born in New York, hadn't gone to college, had served in Vietnam, worked for Safeway afterward, adopted a baby girl, then died when Heather was a toddler. Cause of death not stated, but Emma assumed an accident. Perhaps Kay had created that impression by saying he died "suddenly," or simply hadn't named a disease. Date of death not given. Kay didn't seem to have paid much attention to him. She didn't know his social security number by memory, had promised to find it. She had to know it if she was collecting death benefits, but, not surprisingly, she'd never contacted Emma with the number.

The one concrete fact that Kay had offered up about Nowell Wilson was that he was dead.

Except that Kay lied.

Maybe he'd left her instead. Maybe he'd never actually been married to her.

But somebody had turned a baby over to him. Or was that true?

An enormous goose stepped onto the pavement, looking up as the area around him suddenly shadowed. Emma followed the direction of his gaze and saw a jetliner high above.

The goose flapped his wings, then held them out, increasing his size as he honked skyward, his mate and goslings behind him as he fought off the shadow of the plane. Emma imagined his goose brain and the terror he must have been hiding at the sight of an enormous and unknown bird flying above him. She silently applauded his guts and bravado.

Every living thing had troubles. Time to take care of hers.

Twenty-five

She crossed the road toward the Civic Center, a source of civic pride since it was the only government building designed by Frank Lloyd Wright. Nearly forty years after its construction, it was still sufficiently futuristic looking to serve as a movie set for science-fiction extravaganzas.

Architectural pride, tourist destination or not, Emma had never decided if she liked the Civic Center at all. It lay low on the hilly land, echoing the terrain with its arches, and might have seemed a part of the natural character of the ground, as Wright had said buildings should be.

But why then paint it a gooey pink shade of tan? Or make the roof bright blue, as if that made it blend into the heavens? Or top it with a gold tower, the antithesis of blending in.

The striking interior was just as peculiar, long and narrow with oval atriums dividing the building's corridors. It made Emma feel as if she were in a fancy diner or a narrow spaceship, and as often as she went there, she wasn't sure she liked either sensation.

First, for the client considering the partnership, she checked the fictitious names record. She was amazed to find the prior business life of the proposed partner to be precisely as he'd said it was. The man was on the level. What a contrast with Kay Wilson.

Why, then, did Emma find his complete honesty mildly disappointing?

She checked her watch. Time to look at the death records, start figuring out Nowell Wilson.

She took the elevator up to the fourth floor to the county system's main library and controlled the urge to browse through the new acquisitions. Too busy, too many unread books at home.

She walked back to the California Room, where a special collection of books about state history was housed. The California state death records were stored in an oversized recipe box in a locked glass cabinet. Someday when she had more time, she wanted to check what else was behind those glass doors, but so far, she had never had the required time.

The librarian unlocked the case, and Emma settled in at the microfiche machine. The slips of film were stored by the decade, and Kay Wilson hadn't said precisely when Nowell died, except that Heather was a toddler. Roughly before age two, Emma assumed, which would make the cutoff mid-1980.

She began, therefore, with the seventies, and scanned, without success, all the Wilsons who had died in California. She felt the flutter of the chase again, of information waiting for her if she were just clever enough to figure out where it was curled and hiding. And so far, what seemed waiting was the idea that Nowell Wilson wasn't dead at all, just someone Kay didn't want Emma to encounter. Or someone who never existed.

She laid the "W"s for the eighties on the glass plate and pushed it into the machine, finding the Wilsons, and then . . . Nowell. So she'd been wrong. He had lived and now was dead as advertised. Dead in the late summer of 1980, close to Heather's false birth date, a few months before she actually turned two.

So much for that, then. Kay had told the truth, more or less. The only thing intriguing was that there were no death benefits to anybody, and that was odd. And Nowell had died in Butte County, one of the parts of Northern California that Kay hadn't mentioned when describing their wanderings. It could have been an outing, a vacation trip, a driving or sporting accident. Maybe that deserved looking into.

She drove back to her office.

Billie was out and about and there were no new phone messages. Was that good or bad news about no callers, Emma wondered. No further pestering by Heather Wilson but no new clients, either.

Time to clean up her desk and, while she sat there, thinking about Butte County and Nowell Wilson, she clicked her mouse onto the Internet icon and clicked a bookmarked site that took her to the social security death index, to double-check her Civic Center findings.

She typed in his first and last names and, as always, the site delighted her with its speedy and thorough response: there he was. Nowell Wilson, dead August 30, 1980 and again, Butte County, California was listed as his last residence.

His social security card had been issued in California. Kay had said he was from New York. That he only came to California after serving in Vietnam? Had he joined the army in California? Never worked in New York, even as a soda jerk? Most kids got a number by age fifteen.

And then for the first time, Emma paid attention to the math of the dates in the listing. Not Nowell Wilson's death this time, but his birth. She'd skimmed over it before, verifying that he had, indeed, been a Christmas baby. Born December twenty-fifth, indeed.

But in nineteen hundred and sixty-six.

Nowell Wilson had died at age fourteen.

Her office felt airless and overheated again. She stood up and opened its door, then returned to the computer to stare at the screen, make sure she'd seen that date. She had. Which would make him the only twelve-year-old to ever adopt a child, she'd bet. And talk about a young recruit. How old would that have made him in the service? Seven? Eight?

Kay Wilson became even more of a puzzle. Of all possible lies, why make a fourteen-year-old dead Butte County boy her imaginary dead husband?

If his name were any less unusual, if more than one match had come up, she would have assumed there was an error and she was confusing two men. She tried it out, typed in "Norman Wilson," and up came 295 options. She tried properly spelled "Noel Wilson" and found close to thirty. But when she typed in "Nowell Wilson" again, only that one Christmas baby came up.

She sat immobile, no longer even seeing the screen, which in any case she'd now learned by heart. She tried to see, instead, a place where all the dangling strings might join and make something coherent. But all she saw in the space between her and the computer was the shadow of Kay Wilson lying about herself, about Heather, about Heather's birth date, about Heather's adoptive father, and who knew what else.

And doing it so stupidly. Nowell, of all the dumb lies to pick. No wonder his name hadn't been on the amended birth certificate. He didn't exist.

How had Kay gotten Heather?

Or was there another Nowell Wilson who wasn't dead at all and therefore wasn't listed here? That was a possibility. But why then say he was dead? Why not say you'd been divorced. Why mention him at all?

It was all about blinding and hobbling Emma. About making this search impossible.

Emma shook her head, consumed with the image of Kay Wilson waiting for her to fall on her face. "I'll be damned if I do, you bitch," she muttered.

"How's that?" Zachary called over from his desk.

"Nothing," she said. "Talking to myself."

"Again?" he murmured.

Again. And for real. She'd be damned if that Wilson woman was going to get away with this. She said it to herself again, this time silently.

Twenty-
six

It was impossible to find a place to park in Belvedere. Nonresidents obviously weren't overly valued or welcomed. Back in the days when travel was by ferry, railroad, and horse, the island had been developed as a retreat for wealthy San Franciscans tired of the city's chilly summer fog, which didn't reach across the bay.

Now the former summer houses, rambling Victorian affairs, were joined to the rest of Marin with landfill, and the narrow hillside roads were hell for motorists who wanted to park their cars.

Lines were drawn on the blacktop delineating spaces where parking was allowed, and finally Billie found a niche in the uphill rockface. She was glad she drove a relatively small car or she'd have spent the entire day searching.

She walked slowly back down the hillside road toward Zandra Riddock's home, and if she hadn't called and set a time, she would have dawdled even more. She dreaded meeting a woman described as one who'd eat her own young if she thought it would advance her.

Plus, Emma's advice had presented a near-impossible challenge. Billie didn't feel capable of fitting in or looking as if she did. It was fine for Emma who wore the woven equivalent of paper bags to say she should dress accordingly, but how? Did Emma think Billie wore her old rags to work while her closets held secret stashes of designer togs?

She'd finally decided that her grandmother's cameo would serve as the signal that she, Billie, was a rich and comfortable PI, working for the larkiness of it and quite familiar with the finer things of life.

Shivering because she hadn't had a sufficiently rich coat to wear, she rang the bell with one hand while the other tucked and straightened her black slacks and matching sweater. It was more difficult guessing the economic status of black. She patted and smoothed in nervous gestures she resented making even as she compulsively did so.

"Hello," the woman said. "You must be . . ."

"Billie August." Zandra Riddock was cordial, more than Billie had hoped for. Gracious, though not to the point of actually remembering her visitor's name. And she answered the door herself, which was a nice surprise.

Billie shouldn't have worried so about her outfit because there was no way she'd blend in with the twig-thin woman's expensive costume. She was pulled tight in every direction, but too old, Billie thought, for the skintight leather pants, the flesh-toned tank, and the silky loose-knit sweater over it.

Zandra Riddock ushered Billie into a spacious living room where dark Victorian woods contrasted with pastel carpets, while the view of the bay and San Francisco beyond served as the art. When they were seated, and tea had been poured from a flowered pot, Zandra Riddock sat back, tapped a long, burnt sienna fingernail against her teacup, and smiled rather bitterly. "Not that I understand the purpose of this visit," she said without preamble. "I've spoken to Michael time and again and he knows what little I know. So why, in essence, am I paying you, through Michael's exorbitant rates, to repeat myself?"

"We've expanded the scope of the interviews," Billie said. "There seem to be aspects that the police haven't investigated adequately, things worth going over again, perhaps from a different angle. Sometimes something already said now fits into this additional information . . ." She hoped that made sense to Zandra Riddock, because it didn't particularly to her.

"What then, what?" Zandra was still tapping, now on the arm of her chair.

Billie took a moment to back off from the woman's imperial impatience, her wealth and comfort, her leather pants and the enormous emerald-cut diamond she wore on her right ring finger. "I'd like to talk about Tracy Lester," she said when she felt unsmothered again. "Michael asked you a great deal about Gavin, but not as much as now seems important about Tracy."

Zandra Riddock looked at if she were deciding whether to answer.

Billie was incredulous. The woman's only child's life was on the line and all anyone asked was her time and a few observations, yet she behaved as if it was a major imposition. No wonder Michael had described her so harshly.

"Mrs. Riddock?" Billie prompted.

"Zandra, please," the woman said. "It gets confusing with so many Mrs. Riddocks in town. His second discard lives here in Belvedere, too. And the third Mrs. R is in the county as well." She waved her hand as if pushing the other Mrs. Riddocks away. Tracy," Zandra said. "She—they—were friends since elementary school. A playground sort of thing that started when older children teased him. She defended him. Befriended him. That was fifth grade."

"And they were friends ever since, I gather."

"Yes." Zandra said the word as if it tasted bitter.

Billie waited.

"It made sense when they were young," Zandra Riddock said. "It was rather charming. Gavin was her . . . confidant. She could trust him to always be loyal, to keep her secrets. She could tell him anything. But when they were grown-up, these past few years . . ." She shook her head. Her hair was auburn, beautifully cut to cradle her face. She flicked a piece back from her forehead.

"What about these years?" Billie softly prompted.

Zandra leaned forward, put her teacup and saucer on the coffee table, and stood. She walked to the wall of glass at the back of the room and spent a moment considering the distant San Francisco skyline. "One has to wonder," she said, her back to the room and her voice so soft Billie had to strain to hear, "why she remained his friend. I mean . . . after all . . ."

She turned, slowly, and Billie felt as if she'd seen this movement, this entire play somewhere long ago.

"They're grown people," Zandra said. "I know they trained together. Gavin isn't quite as . . . quick mentally as some, but he's a natural athlete. Not so much in team sports, but he's a fine runner and he enjoys it. So they trained together, and that would be all right, except . . ." Another sigh and a shrug. "Mind if I smoke?" she asked.

"It's your house, Mrs.— Zandra. Go right ahead."

The standing woman went to a side table and opened a crystal box. This room, perhaps this house, increasingly felt like a stage set. Even the cigarette box. Who had such things anymore? Smokers were less tolerated than lepers and the accoutrements for it—cigarette holders and boxes and individual ashtrays for dinner parties— were historical artifacts. But here was Madam, displaying and using a large investment in crystal smoking props. Closing the box, lighting her cigarette with a heavy globe of cut crystal that sat on a side table, flicking ash into one of many crystal dishes around the room and drawing on the cigarette several times before she spoke again. "I wondered—I mean one would have to wonder—what Tracy really wanted of my son."

Billie cocked her head, but said nothing.

Zandra paced the large room, one hand holding her cigarette, the other, a small crystal ashtray. Billie thought the woman's happiness would probably be complete if cigarettes, too, were made of crystal.

"Gavin is, after all, unsophisticated in many ways and . . . he's—let's be honest—wealthy. Someone might consider him a catch."

"She was already married," Billie said softly.

The older woman shrugged, the gesture dismissing the idea that prior contracts were relevant. "The girl liked money. Ever since she was a child. She oohed and aahed about my rings or my new shoes or car. You know what I mean. And she and Gavin were entirely too close for entirely too long. A married woman and a . . . gentle, naive young man . . . it's wrong. She used his house as a gym locker and she used him . . ." She dramatically let go of the sentence and blew a smoke ring.

"She left things here. Years ago, like a dog marking its territory." Zandra Riddock pursed her mouth, then sighed and dragged on her cigarette again. "I had to ask her to stop. It was too much . . . closeness. As if she, too, lived here. A recipe for disaster."

Billie didn't want to ask her what she meant, if she were implying she believed that her son had bashed in the skull of his longtime friend, and that it had been Tracy's own fault for leaving things behind. "Did you—did you have the chance to speak with her recently, perhaps?" she asked instead. "To get a sense of what was up?"

Zandra shook her head. "I tried not to interfere in my son's life. He is an adult and deserves to be treated as such. I'd confer with the housekeeper, of course, and I kept track of how the money was being spent, but other than that . . ."

She ignored him as much as possible, is what she couldn't say. Didn't care, didn't bother. Probably didn't like him, either.

"Still a few years ago, I found her in the spare room there, with her hand in a dresser drawer. She said she was putting her things away. As if it were her home! I tried to come over once a week, to be sure all was well, and once I found a Sak's box in the trash, and another time, a shopping bag from Nordstrom's. I think she hid things at his house—things she didn't want her husband to know she'd bought."

This wasn't the sort of information Billie had hoped for, and the resentment and suspicion couldn't help Gavin any way she could figure. Billie wanted to believe what Gavin so obviously believed, that Tracy Lester had been his friend. In some large-hearted, giving way, Tracy had found solace and comfort in this gentle, handicapped boy-man. Billie didn't want Gavin's own mother twisting it into something mean-spirited.

Zandra Riddock stubbed out her cigarette and stood in front of Billie, uncomfortably close. "I know what you're thinking," she said abruptly. "You've heard I'm a terrible person. A witch. A bad mother. That I don't care about anything except myself. Haven't you?"

"No," Billie lied. "No. Why would you—"

"Because everybody says that. Including, I suspect, the lawyer I hired who then hired you. Because . . ." She backed off and sat down on the loveseat across from Billie. "Michael Specht lives in Marin. In Belvedere, in fact. I almost didn't want him because of that, because he's got preexisting ideas about me, and he doesn't see me, he sees my reputation, so anything I do is interpreted in the worst possible way."

"Well, I surely . . ." Billie put her hands out, palms up, to say she was at a loss for words.

"I'm not an ogre," Zandra Riddock said softly. "And neither was Gavin, at first."

"Gavin an ogre? Who could ever think such a—"

Zandra's eyes grew wide, her forehead furrowing above them. "Not my son!" she said. "My husband. My ex. He was an ordinary, sweet, dull boy who cared only for science. The 'mad scientist' my family called him, because he was almost a cliché. Incredibly brilliant, but he left things undone, forgot things, dressed sloppily— nothing mattered except his experiments. I expected to support him throughout our life. And then bingo, he got rich. He won awards. He sold his firm to an international group and had more money than God."

Gavin Senior had developed some piece of the new genetic engineering industry, Billie remembered from Michael Specht's notes. Something that led to vast pharmaceutical possibilities, and something he could and did patent.

"He changed," Zandra said. "Let me rephrase that. I don't think people change, they just allow themselves to be who they are. So it was as if this arrogant perfectionist had been hiding inside him all the while, ashamed to come out before he somehow 'earned' it. Back when he was just another scientist, he was arrogant only about his work. Maybe about his brain, too. But once he'd made it, the world was his and nothing was good enough for him. Everyone was his inferior. 'Nobodies,' he'd call them. 'Idiots.' I was still okay—his equal, perhaps—until I gave birth to Gavin Junior."

She paused, stood, extracted another cigarette and repeated the crystal-studded routine before continuing. "There was a problem during delivery," she said. "A mistake and the baby didn't get enough oxygen for a while, so he wasn't perfect. He wasn't the best that money could buy." She stared at Billie silently as if letting hot emotions cool down, before she could let them pass through her mouth. "He was not found acceptable. He was not a fit heir.

"His father sued everybody associated with the birth. He would have sued me, if he'd found an angle. Lots of headlines, accusations of incompetence, malpractice. My o.b. quit his practice and moved out of state. The entire hospital staff loathed our name, and I didn't blame them. And ultimately, what difference did any of it make—except to make us hated. Because Gavin was, is, still . . . different. Nothing changed, except for the worse.

"I couldn't handle how he felt about my child and how he handled how he felt, but I had this scary baby, so I stayed with him and Gavin decided to build a house suitable to his stature. So there were more lawsuits, more headlines. Now he was taking down an entire town, openly willing to bankrupt it, if necessary, to build his castle. Our name became a synonym for whatever was bad.

"And then he told me he was through with us."

She stubbed out the cigarette and folded her hands, although her two index fingers tapped and tapped against one another. "I asked him how he could slough us off, like dead skin, and he said 'because I can afford to.' And so it went. I'd seen my husband fight a hospital and a town, so I fought long and hard when we were divorced. More headlines. The company he'd started after the one he sold was in jeopardy because of me, they said. Their stock would fall. Well, screw them. Screw him. I was in jeopardy, too. My son was in jeopardy. I didn't play by their rules. I didn't quietly slink away, taking whatever he was willing to dole out to me and Gavin. I fought for what was ours. And then I compounded it by staying in town, not disappearing the way he wanted us to."

She stood up and moved slightly toward the entryway. Billie thought the interview, or whatever it had been, was probably over. She lifted another lid—this time, a box of inlaid woods. "I . . . I never knew what to do with Gavin, what would be right. And neither did anybody else." She lit another cigarette and waved at the smoke she was producing. "I did the best I could, but I'm still the villain of the piece. Whatever I did about or for my son was wrong—deliberately so. Isn't that how it goes?"

She sat back down across from Billie. "The thing is, I know that's what you heard and I know Michael Specht hates me, but I hired him anyway. Because he's good at what he does, and he'll find the way to save my son. And that's it. Did you find out anything new? Did you get what you came for?"

Billie stood. "I didn't have an agenda."

"I can't tell you anything, don't you understand? I—I don't know my son. It somehow feels a choice between hovering and treating him with a measure of contempt, needing to know and control, and backing off and letting him grow and become himself—and not knowing him, pretty much. But I did the best I could. Don't judge me until you've been in my shoes, until nobody anywhere can tell you what's wrong with your child or how to fix it.

Or where he belongs—with people slower than he is? Or people faster than he is. You do the best you can."

Billie nodded, and when she shook Zandra Riddock's hand, it wasn't the hand of the witch she'd heard about. She no longer had an easy label to put on the woman.

Gone the villainess. Here the middle ground, the not-all-bad and not-all-good.

Gone the clarity.

Gray was not Billie's favorite color. It was fog and smoke and limited visibility. She much preferred black and white, and mourned the loss of those solid hues.

Twenty-
seven

Emma was awake and staring at the ceiling. Beside her, George slept deeply. She listened to his breathing: a shallow snore like a soft metronome keeping time through the night.

What was this, though? Emma wasn't an insomniac—George was. He made fun of how she could sleep through everything and anything. She wasn't used to being up in the middle of the night and felt disoriented with fragments of a lost dream still floating in strips and threads around her. What had it been? Not precisely a nightmare, but not a good dream, either. More a nag, an annoyance. Frightening but not threatening . . .

A man, a face at a window, grabbing something.

And then she had it, and she sat up in bed and reached for her glasses and the notepad and pen that were always by the phone.

"What?" George asked in a half-asleep voice.

"Nothing," Emma whispered. "I'm awake is all. Go back to sleep." She saw the white outline of the notepad, and "Baby—78—check." That was it. That had to be it. The whole thing still stunk. Stank? Whatever the word, it did it.

While she slept, her mind had put it together, insisted that she pay attention, finally, to what the blind alleys and deliberate obfuscations meant.

George had not resumed his soft pre-snore. "Whazzit?" he asked again. "You don't wake up this way. What's wrong?"

She should have known she'd wake him up. A loud breeze could do it. But since he was up, she wanted to hear it said out loud. "Remember the girl who found out she was adopted?"

He yawned and blinked. "Work?" he said. "You're letting a client get to you to the point that it wakes you up?"

"It never made sense and still doesn't. The mother's playing games with me and her daughter. I'd decided to call Heather Wilson tomorrow and tell her sayonara. Except—something nagged at me."

George's yawns had deafened him in spots. She had to repeat herself and she listened again and was convinced that so far, she sounded logical.

"What about it?" George asked. "Adoptive parents probably all get nervous when their kids search. I would. I'd worry if they'd switch allegiances—I'd worry about a lot of things."

"That's not what it's about. I'm positive."

"The search fizzled out. Why let it get to you? Especially since you discourage people from this kind of thing. Why don't you marry me and retire? Let me make you an honest lady of leisure. We'll sell both our houses, find a new place and—"

"It's the middle of the night, George."

"What better time for a proposal?"

"You're out of your mind." She waved away his proposal just as she had the ten other times he'd made it.

"Thought maybe I'd catch you at a weak moment, when your mind wasn't working yet."

"Your mind, you mean." She shook her head in mock despair, and wondered what he'd do if she accepted. Probably faint. "It isn't that," she said out loud.

"Want tea? Milk? Something to help you get back to sleep?"

She shook her head. "I'm supposed to listen to me. That's what my dream was saying."

"Your dream? You're being directed by a dream? What's happening to you? Emma's gone woo-woo?"

She ignored him. "In my dream, I saw somebody in a mask—one of those silly raccoon masks, the kind the kids wear at Halloween. I saw him snatch something out of a window."

"A pie. That's what they're always stealing in cartoons. And where else would a robber announce his occupation by wearing that stupid mask?"

He was right. Those robbers were always snatching pies, but what did pies have to do with her? And who were those housewives balancing fresh baked goods on wobbly window sills? "I think the mask was so I'd know what was meant. It was all . . . symbolic. The mask and even the guy's outfit—striped long-sleeved T-shirt, you know the kind?"

He nodded. "You dream in comic strips."

"The mask and the stripe signaled 'Bad guy alert!' "

"So you dreamed about people stealing pies."

"A child, not a pie. I'm sure that's what the bundle they passed through was."

"Bundle, schmundle—who cares? It could have been the recycling. Or laundry. Or stolen goods. Oh, what am I talking about? It wasn't anything except a *dream*. Probably the revenge of something you ate."

"I've been trying to get past a nagging feeling about this business since it started. I was censoring it, but it broke through in my dream. That's what's behind the mother's fear of being discovered."

"Come on, Emma. Like I said, there are hundreds of reasons this search would scare her."

"They aren't her reasons."

"Have you asked?"

Emma swung her legs around so that they were on the floor. She shivered. The room was cold. She stood and got her robe. "I'm going to. But first"—she turned as she tied the belt of the robe—"I've got research to do."

"On comic books? The interpretation of dreams? It's the middle of the night."

"I can't sleep, George, and there's nothing I hate more than lying in bed wishing I were asleep. There must be stuff on the Net."

"What kind of stuff? You're making me nervous."

"Kidnaping stuff. Kids who disappeared roughly twenty years ago. It must be on there somewhere."

He groaned. An honest, up from the innards, groan. "Please. Tell me I'm misunderstanding."

"My gut's telling me that's the only thing that makes sense of this. That young woman was not legally adopted. There's something criminal in her background and that's why this mother has spun an entirely untrue story around it. Why she's trying to look cooperative, to allay suspicions and monitor me. But she's really trying to brick me up and shut me out. It's about fear."

"There must be a million other reasons for—"

"Go back to sleep. I'm sorry I woke you. I'm fine." She left the room and padded first into the kitchen, where she poured herself a glass of wine. It made her sleepy, but that was fine—she felt so on alert, it was going to take more than wine to get her back to sleep. And then she went into what was now called her study, but would always be, to her, Caroline's room, though no real traces of Caroline were left, except the god-awful pale lilac walls that Emma meant to repaint.

The computer was always on, and as soon as she saw the familiar screen saver, she stopped, horrified. There it was: little men in striped shirts and raccoon masks. She'd forgotten. She watched as they hurled bombs and climbed up ladders into windows, while men in fedoras and trench coats paralleled their every move, guns at the ready.

Was that all it was? Had she been dreaming of her screen saver?

She sipped wine and controlled the urge to look over her shoulder to check whether George was there to notice the incriminating screen saver. He wasn't, and she settled in.

She did a search under "kidnaping," and was first amazed, then daunted by the number and scope of sites that came up. The Lindbergh baby. The kidnaping of Aimee Semple McPherson. The saga of Elian Gonzales's long absence from Cuba. Sites on Uganda's, Mexico's, Chechnya's kidnappings. Business kidnappings. Political kidnappings. So many misplaced people. On protecting yourself from and what to do if. And then, missing children sites promisingly full of photos.

Most were recent.

So many missing children, primarily noncustodial parent snatches. She thought about Billie, about her first interview, her expression when she described her ex-husband kidnaping their son, and her search for the boy. She looked at other people's children, faces as they were ten or fifteen years ago, aged by computer to how they might look now, although Emma was skeptical about how accurate those artificially matured faces were. It had been her observation that huge noses flowered from baby's button noses, and silken white blond hair turned dark and curly, ears flapped, chins disappeared, teeth bucked, skin erupted. She wondered whether the computer was aware of these developmental surprises.

Or of people dyeing the child's hair—wasn't that what Billie's husband had done?

There were almost no listings going back to when Heather would have been born, except for a pitiful photo of an infant, nameless, who'd disappeared in 1947. The caption asked "Do you recognize this child?" Emma wondered who possibly could and who was still hopeful enough to have posted the picture.

She wasn't going to find her on a list like these and would probably have to go back and comb through newspapers of that time. It would have to be for the entire US, and Canada, too. An overwhelming task.

And what if Heather hadn't been kidnaped at all, but bought? Emma couldn't hope to trace that.

"Oh, Emma."

He was behind her. She could almost feel the air ripple from his head-shaking, and she watched his reflection on the screen. "Cut it out," she said without turning.

"You couldn't find the girl's natural mother, and that's that. There is no basis for this. There is no payment for this."

"I know." She leaned back into her battered desk chair and took a deep breath. "I know everything you're going to say and I also know you're saying it because you care about me."

"Oh, Emma," he said more softly.

"And I appreciate that."

"But you aren't going to listen to a word of it, are you?"

"Nope."

"It's the opposite of everything you've always preached. You're getting involved where you shouldn't and . . . and those faces— How can you sit and look at them. This . . . this is foolish."

"Don't you ever operate on gut feeling? On something you couldn't describe, but it's the sum total of all the years you've put into what you do know? Haven't you, ever?"

"Sure, but come on, Emma, what are you going to do? Check every unsolved child-abduction for the last twenty years and then do DNA testing? This is futile and doomed and there's no reason to do it in the first place."

She swiveled around so that she could see him directly. "First of all, we aren't talking two decades. The girl wasn't taken when she was twenty, or fifteen, or even five. I know the mother's lied about most things, but if she'd been taken, or bought at a later age, she'd probably remember something. She was an infant. It's a small window of a few years."

"Not necessarily. I've read about cases where older kids are taken and then, more or less brainwashed. Told their parents died, or didn't want them. They get confused, forget, buy into the fiction."

"Are you discouraging me or encouraging me to widen the search?"

His voice had no levity. "Discouraging. Emphatically. This way lies nothing good. Humiliation, maybe. Legal action. Wasted time. You pick. It's all bad."

She shrugged. She could feel the rows of children's faces behind her. Didn't George feel their glances, too?

"Isn't this what you've said an investigator should not do? Getting personally involved? Isn't that what you told me that new girl of yours—that—"

"Billie"

"Right, wasn't that a problem with her? Didn't we sit here over dinner the other night while you said how idiotic her behavior was in something or other, because she got personally involved?" He folded his hands over his chest, waiting.

"I am impressed with how much and well you listen, George. That is a rare talent in men."

"Complimenting me? I can tell you're having a breakdown. But tell me this: how can you say one thing, loudly, insistently, absolutely, all these years and now, suddenly, justify this wild-goose chase?"

"I like the truth. I believe in the truth. I want the truth. That's what this is about."

He shook his head. "This is about getting in over your head and my question remains: Why aren't you practicing what you preach?"

She put her hands up by her shoulders, palms up in a classic giving-up pose. "I guess . . . what I preached all those years was wrong."

His mouth opened and then he clamped it shut. "Wrong? You said you were wrong? Know what? Before, I was joking. Now I'm serious: You are not Emma Howe. You are an alien impersonating the woman I love, but you've given yourself away with that last sentence."

There was that, about George. He could be a pain, but he listened, and he made her laugh.

"Idiot," she said, waving him out of the lilac room. He could call it insanity or alien possession or whatever he wanted. She had work to do.

Twenty-eight

        She was back, this time in person. Heather Wilson's persistence might be attractive or useful elsewhere, but not here, not for Emma.

She wasn't ready to tell this girl that the only thing she knew was that Heather's mother—the one she knew—was a complete and total liar.

"I was in the neighborhood," Heather said. "Had to buy office supplies, so . . . I thought maybe you'd have some more to tell me?"

Some more? Emma had told her nothing except that the search was going poorly. Did that girl consider that something? Or was she painfully polite?

"It isn't going well," Emma said. "I might as well be honest with you. Adoption searches are the hardest. For better or for worse, people go to great lengths to cover up the actual facts, but I warned you about all that, didn't I?"

Heather looked stricken. She was pinning too much on this search, and Emma could see it in her face. She believed, for whatever reason, that the results would turn her life around on its axis, when in reality nothing would change for Heather. She wasn't going to become more effervescent, or clever, or ambitious, and her problems would still be there after she was given—*if she* was—a new history. Her parentage hadn't been a part of her consciousness till a matter of months ago, but when it arose, it became a convenient straw to grab as the explanation for whatever was lacking in her life. The problem was, a straw was too weak to be used the way Heather wanted to, as the centerpost holding up her world.

But Emma had not been hired to give that talk. "Heather," she said, "since you're here, and this is proving so hard, maybe you can think of something else that might help."

"Like what?"

Anything that had a relationship with the truth, Emma refrained from saying.

Emma was bleary and tired after last night's marathon of examining lost and missing children's faces, especially since nowhere among them had been the child who could have become Heather. And there was no site for children illegally bought from their natural parents. Or children snatched in foreign countries.

"I wondered if you remember places you vacationed in your childhood, for example?" Maybe there'd be friends or relatives who'd know something in such spots.

Heather shook her head. "We didn't go anywhere, except over the hill to the beach sometimes."

Maybe she didn't count family visits as vacations. "Relatives? Did you visit cousins or aunts or uncles or have them come visit you?"

Heather shook her head again.

"Never? How about friends up in Butte County?"

"Why? Did you find something there?"

"Nothing that makes sense yet. Do you remember going up there?"

Heather shook her head. She wouldn't remember—she was barely two when Nowell died there—but Emma had hoped there were contacts that had survived. Apparently not.

Heather's eyes matched her name, Emma realized. Bluish gray

and pretty. She studied the girl's face again. Nothing wrong with it and yet Heather managed to look half erased and slightly blurred. Emma wasn't sure why.

The pretty eyes opened wider. "I don't have aunts or uncles or cousins," she said softly, as if suddenly aware of and amazed by that fact. "My—Kay—was an only child and my adopted father, well, wherever his family was, after he died, it drifted apart. Never contacted us that I know of, and we didn't visit them or anything."

"Grandparents?"

She shook her head. "Mama told me that my grandfather died young, of cancer, and my grandmother was killed in a car crash when I was only six months old."

And the father's family—whoever he was, if he existed at all— was equally inaccessible, of course.

"Do you know where your mother went to high school? I realize I could ask her, and in fact, I will, but since you're here already . . ."

Heather looked stunned, as if the question were so beyond the pale of normal human discourse it paralyzed her tongue. Finally, she shook her head.

"Do you think it was around here? In the city, or here in Marin?"

"I don't think so . . . I think she would have said. I think she said Oregon. And her friends here, they aren't, like, from high school or way back, like I think she'd have."

"Does she have many friends?"

Heather nodded. "Pretty much. From work and church. But nobody who ever said they knew me when I was a baby. Nothing like that."

Nothing like anything, Emma thought. Just empty space between Heather and her origins.

"So what sort of person does that?" Emma asked rather rhetorically over their whole wheat pasta with nonfat tomato sauce. George's doctor had given him a short list of permitted foods. Emma found it sad that in order to live you had to half-live, but she was trying. She kept stashes of butter and chocolate and marbled meats for the nights she was alone. "Why," she continued, "make up a husband who, with some checking, turns out to have died at fourteen?"

"Unless the lie is that he's dead, Emma." George spoke softly. He, too, seemed mildly depressed by his blanded out meals. "Maybe he left her, and she doesn't want to say so. Maybe there's another Nowell Wilson."

"I already thought of that." She pulled a piece of her roll off and controlled a sigh of longing for butter. "Do you think she'd do this number to save face? I admit she is a very proper looking woman. A churchgoer. Straitlaced, but still . . ."

"Stranger things have happened," he murmured. "All of it could be true—the adoption, all of it—and then he ups and leaves her. And she didn't sound completely with it in the first place, the way you said she couldn't remember names, and she hadn't gone with him to get the baby. Maybe she's a flake."

"She's a competent woman. She raised that child on her own."

"What kind of life has she lived here? Does she seem like she's hiding a wild past?"

"Anything but. She looks conservative, dresses quietly. She's worked at Macy's for fourteen years."

"That's responsible. Upstanding."

"I know, but I can't help but think she's a fugitive of some kind."

"I've got it—she's part of the witness protection program."

It was always hard to tell when George was serious. "Miss Mousekin. Fun to imagine her with an automatic rifle, taking out a neighborhood, then turning state's evidence. Fun, but not easy."

"She could have been the wife of one of them. The girlfriend. Or the daughter."

"Would that have caused her to lie to her daughter about her birth?"

"Maybe different pieces of her story are different."

"I get it. She's the original bad-luck girl. A mafioso's daughter put into the witness protection plan along with her entire family. A family she never mentions to her daughter, never sees, never visits or is visited by, not under any name. And Miss Mafiaette marries a guy who leaves her, so she lies about that, too, and says he died not knowing that somebody with the same misspelled name and Christmas birthday had died at age fourteen. And then she lies to the adopted girl saying she's hers."

"Well, if you put it that way . . . is there any dessert?"

"Fresh fruit." She didn't look at him so she couldn't see his reaction.

"I'm thinking sometimes I'd rather die a little sooner," he said. "How many minutes would a slice of apple pie take off my expected life span?"

"About that woman . . ."

"Emma." His voice lost its playfulness. "She could be any number of things, including precisely what she says she is. But what she cannot be is profitable. What this means is that as of now she is literally none of your business. You searched. That's all you promised. Search is over. Give it up."

"She's putting me on, George. Deliberately putting me on."

"You've lost your focus. The question isn't about her—it's about that girl's birth mother."

"I cannot tell you how much it pisses me off—"

"You don't have to tell me. I know you."

"This is a goddamn mystery, and you know how I hate mysteries." She stood, and lifted their dinner plates. Neither had finished the pasta. "I hate liars."

As she heard herself say the words, she felt an echo of her daughter, angry Caroline berating her for being honest about Caroline's father, about how Harry had lived and died. Ridiculous to be angry about being told the truth. It was the basis of civilization, as far as Emma was concerned.

"She's going to explain herself, tell me her big fat secret," she said.

"And then?"

She was at the sink now, running water. "I'm not sure. Except that the truth will come out. That's my only goal, and I'll do it. You heard it here first."

Twenty-nine

      Billie detoured for a few moments after she parked her car. She walked from the lot to the Tiburon bike path—officially, a multipurpose path—along Richardson Bay.

She stepped aside to allow a woman the entire path for a private dance performed on in-line skates. The woman was middle-aged and somewhat lumpy, but her striped T-shirt and shorts and half-closed eyes and wide grin shouted that she was content with herself and life was good. Headphones in place, she wove back and forth, snapping her fingers to the rhythms only she heard.

The dancer contrasted sharply with the bird behind her, a long-legged egret making delicate and considered progress across the shallows.

And with the unchoreographed tumbling of a pack of children Jesse's age who performed their rough rotations through the swings and seesaw and climbing devices on the nearby tot lot, and raced in wild circles on the adjoining grassy space, their shrieks and calls joining those of the birds.

She watched their mothers or nannies or au pairs with envy, then caught herself. She'd briefly been a full time tot lot mother, with time to play and socialize and she had to remember the cons, too, of that life.

It was a pretty setting in which to take a break, and the other women looked happy enough, but she knew how exhausting and repetitive tot lot excursions actually were, how isolated the rest of the day.

She wondered whether they'd envy her, if she waved and said, "Have to run—I'm investigating a capital crime." The thought gave her a small rush.

She turned away and walked back up the path, past Blackie's Pasture and the statue of the swaybacked horse. The scene of the crime.

In a few moments, she'd reached the home the Riddocks had given their son, the place they referred to as "the cottage," a tiny home, backed up against the bay, surrounded by a small, well-tended, and colorful garden.

She pushed open the low gate that was the only part of the white fence not covered with creeping roses. Once again, the point was driven home: It was good to have money. Forget about the root of all evil. Money could also be the root of making sure your handicapped child was comfortable and safe—unless accused of murder.

She pressed the bell and took the moment to admire the plantings, wondering if Gavin worked in the garden and whether the green space around her own home would ever be this well maintained.

The inside of his house was even more of a contrast to her own "cottage." She followed the housekeeper, who identified herself as Ana, into a small, pleasantly furnished living room flooded with light and waited while Ana insisted on getting coffee for her. If she kept being offered drinks, she would soon be the county expert on bathroom decor.

A pair of tabby cats entered the room, eyed her, then wandered back out. A dog barked and was told to quiet down by Ana. Meanwhile, she admired the room, its deep-green furniture contrasting with bright white walls. One wall was half covered by shelves filled with videotapes, CDs, and audiotapes. She browsed the titles and labels, checking Gavin's taste in movies (comedy, slapstick, heroic historical epics) and music (all shades of rock and folk rock). As he'd said, some of the tapes were homemade with handwritten labels that said "Tracy's Rainy-Day Favorites" or "Wake up, Gavin!" Billie was halfway through the CD titles when Ana reentered the room.

Billie settled down, by invitation, on the green sofa, and Ana sat across from her on a matching loveseat on the other side of a slab of polished wood—cherry, perhaps—that served as a coffee table. The back of the room faced the bay and Sausalito, and bright light off the water reflected on the white walls.

Ana was short, somewhat stocky, and thoroughly protective of the man-boy she called "Mr. Gavin." "The police already asked all the questions," she said. "I don't know nothing about what happened." She folded her arms across her middle. "Except Mr. Gavin couldn't do something bad like that. Not to anybody, but for sure not to his best friend. And he didn't." With her last words, she pushed her head forward, pugnaciously, in a make-me-prove-it stance.

Unfortunately, Ana didn't arrive until nine each day, well past the hour when she could have provided an alibi for the morning Tracy Lester was murdered. "We don't think so, either. As I said, I'm working on Gavin's defense team with Gavin's lawyer."

Ana sniffed with disdain.

"This must be sad for you, too. Very," Billie said. "You must have known Tracy Lester, too."

Ana nodded. "Miss Tracy was like Mr. Gavin's sister. She saw the goodness in him. Many people could not. They were friends. They ran. The police, they want to make something dirty out of that, that's their business, but they're wrong. She lived in Fairfax, worked in Sausalito. This was on the way and it is a good place to run and company to run with. It would be stupid to go back home, and it would be sad for Gavin if she didn't run with him. So she takes shower, changes, has coffee, and goes to work. Is wrong to try to make that sound dirty."

Billie did not point out that Ana was never here during that innocent showering and changing time. She was undoubtedly correct—there did not seem to be anything but friendship between Gavin and Tracy—but that would still not make Ana's testimony work in court. "Did Tracy leave clothing here? Cosmetics? Shampoo? Her things?" In truth, Billie had seen the list of items. Sweats, warmups, running tights, and shorts and a few items that must have wandered into the closet through various visits—windbreakers, caps, spare socks. Nothing suggesting the police's "dirty" interpretation to which Ana referred.

"The police took it," Ana said.

"All of it? Every last bit?" She had a wild hope that something that would turn all attention away from Gavin was sitting in a closet, or in the pocket of a leftover pair of jeans.

Ana's expression blanked in a way that Billie was sure meant a decision was being made. Then Ana shrugged. "Miss Tracy, she's family. But I draw lines. Nothing personal because it could hurt Mr. Gavin."

"I'm sorry, I don't quite . . . what do you mean?"

"Miss Tracy's husband is not nice. She was sad all the time about him. A mean, jealous man. My heart hurts for her, but I said nothing personal in this house so that he doesn't come here and make big trouble, you understand? Miss Tracy, she making notes about him, I think. She said she would leave them here, these notes, but I said no. I feel sorry for her—my ex-husband was jealous and it's bad. But I said no. You understand why I was that way?"

Billie nodded. "Certainly. Gavin was your first responsibility."

"And me, I'm my responsibility, too. I don't want some husband hitting me or pushing me around. Or like happened to her. Not my own, not hers."

Billie nodded again. "So she didn't leave them here." She wondered what they could have been. A log of Robby's offenses? Why? That didn't sound probable. And she wondered what else was going to come after Ana's long, explanatory preamble.

Finally, Ana pursed her mouth and made a half-nod. "Two things. I have to get them from the kitchen. She left the room and returned with a folded black cardigan sweater and her pocketbook. "The police, they came and took most things of Miss Tracy's, but I was wearing this. She said I could wear her things. It was a cold day and I borrowed it."

Big deal, a black cardigan. "Thanks," Billie said.

"You give to the police—or keep it," Ana said. "What should they want with a sweater? It didn't do nothing bad to anybody."

"You want to keep it?"

Ana shook her head. "Bad luck, maybe." She pursed her mouth and took a breath. Now, Billie thought. Whatever had been pressing on her innards wanted out now.

"I don't want you think bad things about Miss Tracy," she began. "She worked hard, and I think maybe this year, she bought herself something nice, like her husband wouldn't buy her." She shook her head. "He no like her having things, spending money. My ex-husband was like that, so cheap. Took all the money I make. If I buy a lipstick, he shouted. Selfish, that's all.

"So this one time, when she explain could she leave her ring for a while and he didn't know nothing about it, I said okay. She knew she could trust me. When the police came, I wonder what will they do with it. Give it to her husband, is what I think, but she didn't want that mean husband to know she had it. What would he do with it? Give it to his woman?" As she spoke, she shook her head, answering her own questions.

"He had another woman?"

Ana rolled her eyes. "Those men, they're no good. My ex-husband he chased women, too, so I threw him out, but Miss Tracy, she was too nice. She wait and wait, and then she moved out herself. Dumb to give him the house that way. I say kick him out, instead."

A ring, Billie thought. And then Ana articulated her next thought.

"I say that if another man give it to her, she shouldn't leave it here," Ana said. "I don't want no trouble with the husband. Jealous sons of bitch like Mr. Robby no good. Dangerous. Not just for me, but for Miss Tracy, too. So I said get a box at the bank, but nothing here that will make trouble, but she said no, she bought it for herself and nobody knows about it and she thinks maybe she'll sell it in a little while. I think that means after she leaves her husband so he doesn't get any of that money, you see? I figured no trouble. You understand, I love them all, but no trouble, please?"

"Could I—Do you still have it? The gift she left here?"

"Sure is here. I carry it in my pocketbook every day, back and forth. I am not a thief."

Billie wondered why Tracy hadn't reclaimed her jewelry once she was settled in with Veronica. Maybe her ex was still causing her too much grief. Then she remembered that they weren't divorced yet.

But if it was worth that much hassle, if it was really valuable, then Ana might have had less innocent reasons for hiding it. Ana was shrewd and Ana loved Gavin. It wouldn't help Gavin's case if he was hoarding something valuable or refusing to return it to the dead woman.

"Here," Ana said before she was completely in the room. She carried a worn leather handbag. "Every day, I carry it home, then carry it back. Now maybe you take it." She extracted a small pouch and handed it to Billie. "Makes me too nervous."

Billie emptied the pouch into her palm and stared at the cocktail ring that landed on her hand. A good sized green stone set high in a sunburst of tiny diamonds—or at least, bright, clear stones. Billie couldn't imagine where a woman living Tracy's life would wear a ring this size or this valuable. It looked too old for her as well, designed for a dowager's hand.

Gem-quality emeralds were more expensive than diamonds, she'd been told. She couldn't tell if this was real, let alone its quality, but if it was . . . Thousands of dollars at the very least. An incredible souvenir of the shipboard romance that Jimmy said hadn't happened.

And the idea of a generous lover with gaudy but expensive taste was quite a stretch given that her lover supposedly had been the financially struggling Veronica the llama rancher. Billie put the ring back into its pouch.

Ana raised her shoulders and put her palms up. "Is all I know."

"What if we said you just this minute found this? In, say, a dresser you were cleaning out while I was here, talking with you?" Billie asked.

The housekeeper pursed her lips and rocked mildly on her heels, then she nodded.

"One other thing," Billie said. "Those notes she wanted to leave—that diary or whatever it was—has anybody found it?"

Ana shrugged. "I tell her don't bring that kind of problems into the house and she didn't. Notes, what are they? Secrets, right? And her husband so jealous." She shook her head. "Not here."

"Did she seem upset about not being able to keep it here?"

Ana shook her head. "Is nothing."

"Did she ever talk about anything like that before?"

"No. She never have a jerky nosy husband before, either. I know about bad husbands. That's why I'm single now. And forever."

Billie put out her hand, but in mid-shake, she paused. "Congratulations on getting rid of him. I must say your ex sounds awful."

"Which one?"

"Which . . . there were . . . may I ask . . . how many?"

Ana rolled her eyes and grinned. "Too many! Five!"

"You're certainly brave."

Ana giggled. "I keep thinking this one is different, and he is. He's bad in new way. You have a husband?"

"I used to."

Ana nodded. "You see that ring Miss Tracy had? She was smart.

Unlucky in the end, but smart then. Rings——they last, they stay the same. Men . . ." She shook her head, sighed, and having said her piece and then some, the interview was over, and she closed the door to the cottage by the bay.

Thirty

"I'm humiliated. The son of a bitch probably hasn't been faithful for a day of our marriage. I feel . . . used. And what kind of fool am I that I didn't realize it for years! Like a dumb stupid—" Jeannie Vincent, still in her tennis skirt, punctuated the air with jabs of her cigarette as she paced her living room.

"Jeannie, hon, you're burning the carpet," Adrienne said.

"Big deal. Serve him right if he has to buy new carpeting. Look what he's been doing to me! And he has money—he has more money then he lets on. I can tell by things he says, little things he drops. Things he buys me—to celebrate, he'll say. Disappears for three days, then buys me something. It's no celebration, it's a *bribe*! Don't notice, Jeannie. Don't put two and two together. Don't make a scene."

She stubbed her cigarette out but continued pacing. She'd spent a lot of time in this room today, wondering how it would feel to kick him out, wondering whether he'd hire some funny lawyer so that she'd wind up with nothing. How would she live? The thought sent her into new shudders.

"He's made me a laughingstock, alley-catting, ignoring me and the kids—and now, carrying on with that tramp that works for him."

"You don't know that for sure," Adrienne said.

Jeannie wheeled around. "Are you on his side?"

"I'm your friend! I just want you to remember that what you have are *suspicions,* not facts."

Adrienne was a good tennis player, but an idiot. Like there were other explanations for his disappearances. For that girl who'd phoned three separate times now. If there were good explanations, then why didn't he say them? "How about he says he went to the gym and that's why he's home late and in different clothing but he doesn't put workout clothes in the laundry. How about that?"

Adrienne shook her head. It was clear she didn't get it. No wonder Adrienne's husband was such a jerk, she was totally dense. Why waste breath on her?

"Don't be so hard on yourself," Adrienne said. "You're going through a bad time is all. Have you seen the doctor?"

"I'm not crazy!"

"Did I say? I meant you seem . . . jittery. Your game was off, too."

"Wouldn't yours be?"

Adrienne shrugged. "Something for your nerves wouldn't hurt."

Jeannie sat down across from Adrienne and tried to speak calmly. "That won't change a thing."

"It could make you feel a whole lot—"

"He's cheating on me with a teenaged tramp!"

"Men sometimes . . . you know, midlife crisis and—"

"Don't give me that crap! I don't want to hear about how men are. You may put up with that, Adrienne, but I refuse to!"

First Adrienne sulked, just the way Jeannie had known she would. Adrienne's husband was a jerk, not that anybody ever said so. He was a doctor over at Marin General, a man with status in the community, so nobody mentioned what an asshole he was and how he chased anything female. He'd come on to Jeannie, his wife's good friend, at a dinner party Adrienne had slaved over for days. A jerk. And the word was he'd been with practically every woman who worked at the hospital, or he'd tried to be. But it had never been clear whether Adrienne knew or cared, and that wasn't a discussion Jeannie wanted to start now. This was about her own situation and nobody else's.

"It could be something else," Adrienne said.

"What? What could be?"

"I saw this movie . . ."

"Don't give me movies—say what you meant. Something else like what?" With some difficulty——her hands were shaking on the outside now, too——she lit another cigarette. Now Adrienne was driving her crazy, too. As if she needed additional stress.

"Something else than another woman."

"*Women.*"

"Than sex. It could be a secret he has. Like this movie I saw—the man had these old parents he was ashamed of, and he never told his wife they were alive, but he'd go there to take care of them and—"

"Oh, for Christ's sake!" She stood and paced again, couldn't stay still. She itched under her skin all over. Out back, the rhododendron——the purple ones she loved so much——were in bloom. Did he want to make her give this up? Maybe that was his plan all along. "His parents are alive and fine and they live in Sebastopol. They aren't secrets."

"That was an *example*. It could be anything. All you know is he takes trips."

"And never invites me on them. Why shouldn't I go, too? You think he has aging parents all over the world?"

"An example. Only an example."

She turned from the vista of lavender rhododendrons and looked at her friend. Adrienne was tiny, the sort of person with every hair in place even when she was batting a tennis ball across the net. Adrienne made her entire life have every hair in place. She didn't look where it might be different. She didn't look at what her husband did. She didn't think about it, either, and she couldn't understand what this was like. "Okay," Jeannie demanded, "so give me another example. Another explanation. How about"—she could feel how tight her throat was becoming, pulling at its sides like she was screaming, even though she wasn't—"how about he comes home late, way late for dinner with those filthy shoes and no gym clothes again the other day, okay?"

"It could be a secret *gardening* project."

"I give up!" She put her hands up and ash fell on her forehead. "You're impossible! A garden? David?"

"Okay, but it's been raining off and on, so there are a million muddy—"

"Forget the shoes!"

"Okay, then," Adrienne said. "Don't get angry or anything but I saw this show"—she put her hand up—"don't tell me not to quote from shows, Jeannie. I learn things there about the world. Things you should think about."

"Such as?"

"You promise not to get angry?"

Jeannie closed her eyes and counted to ten. Then she opened them, took a deep breath and said "Promise." Of all the ridiculous things—how could she tell what she'd feel in advance?

"Maybe he's . . . with a man, not a woman. Maybe he has a secret life. It happens. I saw it on—"

"Gay? You think David's gay?" She wasn't sure if she'd screamed the words, but she was afraid maybe she had. Her throat felt tight in a dizzying way, and it hurt. As if she was screaming and laughing and crying, too, all at the same time.

"It happens." Adrienne looked at her watch and stood up. "I have to get my kids." She stopped near the door. "You don't think . . . don't get angry now—I'm thinking out loud—"

"Stop telling me not to get angry, okay? What now? He's a gay spy? Or what?" Thinking wasn't something Adrienne was good at, and Jeannie wasn't interested in her theories. All she'd ever wanted was sympathy, which seemed the last thing in the world Adrienne could provide.

"Is it possible—have you ever thought—that David could be . . . I mean like he accidentally got involved in something . . . maybe . . ."

"You're driving me up the wall and I have a car pool so what the hell are you trying to say!" She hadn't meant to be that loud, her voice pitched that high. But Adrienne didn't seem to notice, she was gulping and looking like she wanted to swallow whatever she'd said.

"Nothing. Forget it."

"Adrienne Pascali, you are not leaving here without saying whatever—"

"Illegal." She said the one word, then stood there, a tiny woman in a tennis outfit. "I'm not saying he is, just what if? Like maybe he's protecting you by keeping his secrets."

Jeannie's brain squeezed together. The top of her head prickled and she wondered if her hair was standing on end. David, a criminal? It was ridiculous, but still and all, she had wondered. The moving company didn't seem busy enough for how they lived. David said she just didn't understand enough, so how would she know how busy they were.

"David isn't a drug dealer," she said. "He doesn't touch drugs."

"I didn't say he was. But I know he has guns, for example. He must be worried about something."

"Everybody has guns. I have one for my protection, so what? Because he's away so much, which is what I'm saying!" She shook her head against all the poison Adrienne was spreading, but then she didn't want to stop shaking it, almost couldn't. Moving—motion—kept down the buzz inside, that loud itch, and now, her hands were shaking on their own, inside, where you couldn't see it, inside the blood vessels, they were shaking all the time now.

"I'm not—I didn't say David is a drug dealer—*you* said—you twist everything up!"

She touched the bracelet he'd given her, diamonds, and it felt, all of a sudden, on fire, burning her. He wasn't a drug dealer, he

236

was a cheat, screwing around, shaming her, disgracing her with teenaged tootsies. The bracelet was the bone he tossed her to keep her quiet. "He's playing around," she said. "That's what he's doing, that's why he's doing it. That's his secret so stop making a huge deal. Next, you'll call in the FBI. I can handle this myself. You watch."

"What are you . . ."

"I'm not taking crap anymore. I'm not a rug for him to walk all over. I'm going to—I'm going to—"

Adrienne put an arm on Jeannie's shoulder. "You're scaring me—you look so . . . what are you saying?"

Jeannie could barely hear her for the roaring in her head and the pulsing in her veins. "I'll show him," she finally whispered. "Show them."

"You aren't going to do anything scary, are you? Jeannie? Think about it. You haven't seen anything, you've only heard—Maybe a wrong number is all." She tightened her hand on Jeannie's shoulder, and shook her just a little. "Say something! What are you going to do?"

"Do?" She heard her voice as if it were coming from somewhere outside her head. "Do? Car pool, that's what I'll do." And then she laughed, that was so funny. Really, really funny. Maybe the funniest—

Adrienne squeezed her shoulder till it hurt.

"Hey!"

"You okay?"

Jeannie stopped laughing. Nothing was funny anymore.

Adrienne glanced at her watch, sighed and nodded, and together, the women walked out of the house, then separated, each into her SUV. Adrienne's was dark blue; Jeannie's, tan.

For a second, Adrienne paused, her car door open, one foot already up inside the car. "Jeannie?" she asked.

Jeannie didn't want to talk with her anymore. There was no point. The only thing on her mind was David. He didn't like it when she checked up on him, watched him. Tough. Adrienne thought this was all just ideas with no reality. Tough. She would prove she was right. She would make them understand what they were doing to her. And she wouldn't ever again try to tell another human being what was going on with her because nobody understood. But they would, after they'd see. They'd know exactly how bad all this felt. She'd show them all.

Thirty-
one

"Some sort of diary, or notes," Billie said. "The housekeeper didn't want them at Gavin's house; she was afraid of the jealous husband. She thought they were about the jealous husband, in fact. I don't think anybody's found them."

Emma tapped her index finger on the desk, then caught herself and pulled her hand down and onto her lap as she saw Billie watching it. "Haven't we wandered afield?" she asked.

She was quite proud of the diplomacy involved in using "we" instead of the more truthful, "you." "Aren't we forgetting the point of this all?"

"Isn't the point finding out whatever will help prove that Gavin Riddock's innocent of murder? Or okay—since even his own defense team thinks he's guilty—isn't the point finding whatever would help his case? Wouldn't finding out that Tracy was involved with someone dangerous, or someone jealous, someone quite possibly murderous—"

"And then what?"

Billie shook her head. "I don't know. But that ring . . ."

Emma wished Billie hadn't gone directly to Michael Specht with the jewelry, even though it was the appropriate thing to do. She wanted to have seen it herself, as if the stones would reveal their secrets to her. "Maybe it's enough to know there is that ring even if we don't know its origin. Of course, it could also be used against Gavin, to suggest he wanted it and killed for it." Emma wondered if Specht was handing over the ring to the police at all. He hadn't withheld evidence, the housekeeper had. And in fact, it was only hearsay that the ring had ever belonged to Tracy or when she'd gotten it or how it came to be with the housekeeper. Emma was sure it fell into a deep gray area that the lawyer could interpret however he liked.

"I thought of that." Billie looked like a chastised dog. It was an expression that particularly irked Emma, even when dogs did it. "But," she said, brightening somewhat, "I have these other interviews ahead, so maybe, somebody along the way will know about these notes, or a journal . . . ?" Her voice trailed upward, hesitantly, somebody contemplating a mountain she didn't want to scale.

Emma shrugged. "Do what you like. Just be careful about it. You don't even know what it is or whether it's relevant. But if there *is* whatever it is—which there probably isn't, and if it has any relevance to this case, which it almost definitely won't, but if it has and hasn't been destroyed already, which is highly, highly unlikely—then whoever has it and hasn't turned it over wants it for some important reason. And does not want you to have it. Which is simply to say they aren't going to be keen on your asking for it."

Billie had blinked rapidly during the riff, but now her features shifted to what Emma thought of as absolute zero. Annoying that Billie could do this. Vastly annoying to consider the idea that all her expressions were practiced and purposeful, including that you've-taken-the-joy-from-my-life hangdog one. That, in fact, she played Emma the way she would any audience, manipulated her for all she was worth.

The absolute zero face said Billie knew everything Emma was saying, had thought of it herself and did not need to hear it. Well, she was wrong, dammit. She was a trainee, and Emma had obligations to fulfill.

"Look," Emma said, "as long as Zandra Riddock is holding an open wallet up for Michael Specht, and as long as he approves of your whereabouts and fees, do whatever." She cleared her throat. She did not want to do this, but still . . . "One more thing"—there were things Emma knew and Billie did not—"Michael Specht is an attractive man with an interesting reputation. Likes women, but generally for short spells only. Told me once he loves complicated cases. Everything else, he likes to be as simple as possible. And I don't think he loves anything simple or straightforward. Anyway, in case he . . . if you . . . if he— If that in any way over-involves you in this case, then I'd advise against—"

"Not to worry," Billie said blandly. "No problem there."

So something was happening or had already happened between them. Not that Billie would say what, not even after Emma had extended herself, tried to help Billie avoid trouble.

Well, Emma wasn't going to ask, dammit. She had better things to do than wonder what it was. She wasn't going to beg for the salacious details.

" 'Bye," Billie said, halfway to the door.

"Did you ask the llama lady about the notes?" Emma said.

"What?"

"The llama lady—the one she lived with! Didn't you ask her about the diary, the notes, the whatever?"

"I didn't know about them until—"

"Well, for God's sake, woman, why not? Isn't it obvious she'd be your first go? Call her!" She waved her out, glaring at her back as she made her exit.

She did not care about Billie's personal life. It was none of her business, as George would have said. Her business was her business, so she had no choice but to look at the files on her desk, including the one she'd marked "closed." The one she now guiltily opened.

George had been right. She'd searched, done her best, and had come up with very little. Not the results she'd have liked, but results all the same.

Time to give it up. Emma plain and simply could not find Heather's birth mother.

An image flashed across Emma's brain. Timid, whispering, buttoned-up Kay, in a private, very unbuttoned, and wild victory dance. Kay triumphantly clutching her secrets.

Damn that woman! Damn everybody's secrets!

And damn if Emma was going down for the count without so much as a squawk, letting Kay Wilson think her lies had gone unrecognized.

She glanced at her watch. Not yet noon, plenty of time. The woman worked at Macy's, unless that was another lie.

But in the course of that first interview, she'd said that Heather had worked there briefly as well, and it was her dropping out of that job and then college that had started some of the mother-daughter fighting.

Where was that intake form? She retrieved the file and flipped through the pages until she found it. Macy's, she'd written, although not which one. There were three in Marin alone. Why the hell was Macy's chopped up that way with the clothing in Corte Madaras, the housewares in Terra Linda and the furniture store in Novato? So which one? She had a dim memory of Kay Wilson clucking disapproval because Heather had barely "sold a single wire whisk" before she quit, but she wasn't positive she'd actually heard those words, and even if so, she wasn't sure it might not have been some peculiar retailing expression.

Emma called information, then punched in a series of numbers until she reached Macy's personnel. She introduced herself, explained her line of work. "I'm investigating a motor accident case," she told the woman on the other end. "One of your employees was a witness to it. A good Samaritan—she stayed to help the police, but unfortunately, she just wrote down 'Macy's' as her employer, and I'm not sure which of the Marin stores she'd be at."

Please let it be Marin, she silently thought. Because if she had to drive elsewhere, she'd have to acknowledge what a fool's errand this entire confrontation was. "I need to confirm an item with her." Like why she is such a total liar.

"Kay Wilson?" the woman on the other end repeated, after Emma had given the name. "Let me take a look." Then, after a pause, "You sure of that name?"

No, she thought. Not again. Then she remembered the birth certificate. "Wait—no. It's *Megan* Wilson. Megan Kay Wilson. I'm sorry for the confusion."

"We don't have any employee with that name," the voice said, still pleasantly.

Had Emma actually believed it could be otherwise? But Emma wasn't ready to give up and let that woman do that victory dance yet. "She said something about selling whisks. Does that help? Kitchenware? It would be such a shame for the victim in this accident if we can't find Ms. Wilson."

"Housewares, you mean, then. Whisks," the woman said. "Let me double-check." The silence went on too long, and finally, the woman said, "Could you possibly mean *Caitlin* Wilson? If you give me a minute, I can pull up her record on the screen and see if there's a . . . yes, there it is. Kay could be a nickname for that, don't you think?"

Emma's pulse pounded in her neck, her esophagus, her fingertips. No one had ever uttered the name Caitlin. It wasn't on the birth certificate, either. "Thank you, that's probably her."

"Want me to connect you?"

"Yes—wait, no. If you'll just tell me what department she's—"

"You were absolutely correct. Housewares. The Terra Linda store."

"Thanks, I'll be in touch later." Emma sat and fumed before turning back to the computer's bookmarks and hitting the one for the social security death index. Apparently even Megan Kay Wilson did not exist. Emma had been working with ghosts. Had the woman who called herself Kay—or Caitlin—checked the obituaries and picked up the name of a dead woman her own age? It happened.

Or worse, she may have killed someone and taken her child and name.

She typed in Caitlin Wilson. No listing. Did that mean she actually was Caitlin? Then who was Kay? Or Megan, for that matter? She typed in that name: Megan Kay Wilson.

That woman had been dead for nearly two decades. November, 1980. Three months after Nowell Wilson's death, and also in Butte County. Nineteen years old.

Emma closed the screen. But then she had one last thought, and she returned to the site, finding several Heather Wilsons, but none whose identity this Heather could have taken as they'd died much too recently.

Heather was actually alive. Or at least not listed as dead. Emma was no longer sure that was the same thing.

The housewares section was busy and Emma watched women run their fingers adoringly over small appliances and glossy cookware, but Emma was interested in only one item, the mysterious Mrs.-Miss Megan Kay Caitlin Wilson.

And finally, she found her, explaining the pros and cons of two brands of ice-cream machines to a woman who cocked her head alertly, as if each word was of enormous import.

Emma waited until the sale was completed, which felt near to forever. Finally, Kay—or Megan, or Caitlin or whatever other person she'd turn out to be—turned with a happy-homemaker smile. When she saw Emma, her expression froze as if she'd put it in one of the machines she'd just sold.

"Ms. Wilson?" Emma said, "I'm sure you remember me. I know you're not my client and I assure you this is as unusual for me as it must be for you but for once I feel I really have to do this before I talk to Heather."

"What . . . what do you . . . ?"

"We have to talk."

"I'm working now."

"Break time."

"I've already told you whatever—"

"I mean the truth, this time."

"I'm not your client!" she snapped. "I don't have to—"

"I think you will, though, Kay," Emma said.

Kay Wilson held her head higher. "Leave me alone," she said. "I'm working."

"It must be really difficult to work," Emma said.

Kay's eyebrows pulled closer together. "I don't know what you mean," she said in a low voice.

"Don't you feel . . . dead tired? Dead on your feet? Or just plain dead?"

Kay's eyes darted left to right. A woman inspecting a juicer stopped to listen.

"People have been searching for the secret of eternal life forever," Emma said. "And here you are with an interesting spin on it. Who'd imagine that the afterlife consisted of selling kitchen appliances? Think of what this information's going to do to the world's religions."

"Please," Kay said.

Emma smiled. "How come you aren't asking me what I'm talking about?"

"Please. I'm working."

"Even the working dead are legally entitled to coffee breaks," Emma said. "I'll wait right here."

Thirty-
t w o

Billie drove reluctantly, as if her mind, not her hands, were on the wheel, and the conflicts raging in there caused the car to barely move.

It wasn't fair. She'd actually heard herself say those annoying and infantile words. As if anything in life were truly "fair."

As if Emma Howe was ever fair.

How could Emma assume those notes of Tracy's—notes Billie didn't know existed until the day before—would be something she'd have already asked Veronica about? Did she expect Billie to have said something like, "And do you have anywhere on the premises something that will later prove of possible importance? I don't know what it is I'm searching for but it might be significant in a way that I can't yet know, so do you have it?"

She and Michael had asked Veronica whether anything seemed missing from the tossed home, but Veronica hadn't been able to tell if anything was gone. Nor had she been able to think of anything anybody could want.

Now, in hindsight, it must have been the emerald ring that the llama-killer had been searching for. It was the only thing of value, although proof of what? The affair? Who wanted to keep that secret enough to kill?

But to act as if anybody knew anything then, to shout, out of the blue, "Call her, then!" To act as if Billie were an idiot for not having done so already . . .

And it was so odd, because before then Emma had been almost benign. Even almost cute, warning Billie about Michael Specht's womanizing or whatever.

And then—blammo! Back to Der Führer.

No one with a shred of humanity or sanity would have made that order. In the first place, it lacked logic. If Veronica hadn't mentioned notes, it meant either that they weren't in her house, or known to her to be there or there were notes she knew about, but she'd chosen not to mention them.

The most likely scenario was that there were no notes anywhere. That Ana the housekeeper, in trying to establish the fact that she set the rules, reacted to a casual sentence on Tracy's part. Perhaps something she thought she might begin. An idea, not an actual set of notes.

Using common sense, what was to be gained through a phone call?

Nonetheless, here she was, because aside from lacking logic, the idea lacked humanity, something Emma was incapable of understanding.

The last time Billie had seen Veronica, the woman had been distraught and in despair, her animals slaughtered, her lover dead, her house upended.

Billie didn't like the hit-and-run involvement with people that seemed a component of the job. Get information, leave people at their lowest moment and if they weren't of further use, never see them again. Phone in future questions.

Nonetheless, she had tried. She'd called Veronica and asked how she was doing, but the dead voice on the other end didn't actually have to respond. She was barely being.

There were things you did because you were a human being, things like visiting the sick, and it seemed time for a sick call. Billie lied, said she was going to be in the area, and would it be all right if she popped in for a few minutes to say hello. And Billie told the truth, said that she was concerned.

As soon as she saw Veronica, she knew somebody had better be concerned. She looked like photos taken during the Depression, like a woman weathered until there was no hope or joy left in her. The first time she'd met her, she'd been impressed by her un-adorned beauty, but it was growing sharp-edged and she was aging in fast-forward. "You look exhausted," she said. It was an under-statement. Veronica looked like the haggard older sister of the per-son Billie had first visited.

"I can't sleep."

"Have you seen a—"

"Doctor? Shrink? Yes, and I have medications. They don't work. Not enough." She stood still, looking awkward, as if she didn't know what to do with herself. "Look here," she said. "I'm planting seed-lings. The vegetable garden. Mind if I keep working? So much to get done. It helps, though. Gives me a place for my hands."

They walked around to the back of the house where a large square of ground was surrounded by high chickenwire. "Deer," Veronica said. She stood, hands on hips, regarding her vegetable plot with its neat raised rows of freshly tilled earth. But her stare went on too long, and Billie understood that she wasn't seeing anything.

"I brought you something," Billie said, handing Veronica Tracy's cardigan. "She left it at Gavin's and I thought you might like having it."

Veronica smiled and held it close. "Thanks," she whispered, and she put it on although the weather was mild, smoothing and holding it as if it were an embrace. "I can't stop wondering what's next," she said after a while. "And why, too. Mostly, why."

"Have there been more phone calls?" Billie asked gently.

Veronica's sigh was ragged-edged. She shook her head. "He made his point." She pulled at a frayed thread on her jeans. "Or maybe he realized she's dead for keeps and there is no point. Or backed off because he realized that somebody's going to think this through and know that he killed Tracy." The thread wouldn't loosen, and she picked at it, her expression concentrated and almost angry. And then she abruptly let go, as if she'd noticed how intent she'd been, and she shoved her hands into the deep pockets of the cardigan to keep them still, or at least out of sight. She looked at Billie, her expression bleak. "Or maybe he's going to kill me, too. I've given up on hiding at friends or relatives." She shrugged. What would be, would be, including her own murder.

"Time to get back to work." She pulled her hands out of the pockets. One held a crumple of paper. A tissue. A pack of matches. "Stuff," she said. "Trash." She unfolded a scrap of paper. "Tracy's trash. She made eights weirdly. Two separate circles. I used to make fun of how she wouldn't join them. Look." She handed Billie the scrap of paper and shoved the tissue back into the pocket.

"How can I be nostalgic about trash?" she said before lifting a flat with tiny green leaves poking through dark soil.

Billie looked at the scrap. An 800 number and the eight was, indeed, oddly made of two floating circles.

Veronica had walked a few paces and now knelt, carefully making small holes in the earth and putting an infant vegetable in each.

Billie waited until an entire row was planted. "I hate to bother you with more questions but I have to," she said. "Did you go through everything Tracy had here? I mean, so you'd know whatever that was?"

Veronica looked baffled. "I guess. Plus the police were here. They looked through her stuff, too. Took a few things, not all that much. I assume they did that everywhere, not that any of it matters."

"Why everywhere? Where else? I mean I knew she left things at Gavin's—"

"She left things all over the place. It was how she was. As if the world was her closet." Veronica sat back on her haunches, and pushed the visor up a bit, so that more of her face was visible. "We called her the 'Unpack Rat.' She'd leave things where she thought they'd come in handy instead of carrying them back and forth."

"I'd never know where anything was that way."

"But she did. She left things like this sweater, or running shoes or an umbrella. You know. Things the rest of us wish were with us, but never are when you need them."

"How about valuables? Did she leave them around, too?"

"She didn't have any. But I don't think she would have. Money was a problem. Money kept her from leaving Robby for a long time." She shook her head slowly. "Didn't own any jewelry, except for her wedding ring, and that was a plain gold band. Come to think of it, she left that with Robby, so I guess there was a valuable left somewhere else. Otherwise, no. Why?"

"No real reason." Maybe the emerald would turn out to be paste, left at Gavin's for the next Halloween party. "Okay if I ask a few more questions?"

"Do I have a choice?" Veronica pushed another wisp of a plant into a hole. "I germinated too many," she said. "I thought there would be a second person here. And they all flourished and I don't want to kill any, so if you want pole beans, or squash. . . ."

"Thanks, I'd turn them to dust. Maybe when they're actual veggies. But I have to ask whether notes were part of what the police took. A diary, maybe. A journal." She knew the answer to that. There hadn't been anything listed in the inventory that seemed remotely like a notebook or pages with writing.

"From here?" Veronica shook her head. "I don't even know that she ever kept anything like that. Notes about what?"

"I have no idea. Life. Her life."

"Why? Do you think she wrote something incriminating about him somewhere?"

"You mean Robby?"

"Who else? If so, he probably still has it. Or he's burned it."

She finished the row. "It isn't here. And I'll tell you what, I don't think there ever was one. Where'd you get that idea?"

"Gavin's housekeeper. Tracy asked if she could stash something Ana called 'notes,' but Ana didn't want it at Gavin's. According to her, Tracy didn't want it left at home. It would have made Robby jealous, the housekeeper thought, and she was afraid of his jealousy."

"If she didn't want to leave it here, either, then it must have been about me." Veronica straightened up.

"I have no idea what it was about. If it even *was*."

Veronica slumped back down. "There aren't any notes. I can't imagine Tracy keeping a diary. She was an action sort of woman. A runner, a biker, a hiker. It doesn't fit her. Besides, if she wanted to leave stuff at Gavin's, she wouldn't have asked Ana—or listened to her. She didn't like how Ana made rules for Gavin all the time, even if she meant well. Tracy called her 'Big Nurse' behind her back."

That left the emerald ring, an object Veronica obviously was unaware of. "Let me ask whether you think Tracy might have . . . did she have any . . . wealthy admirers?"

Veronica stood and brushed off her jeans, then removed her gardening gloves. She kept the cardigan on, even though Billie thought she was probably too warm. "Admirers?" she said in a high thin voice. "Admirers! You sound like Jane Austen." Her expression was intense and her voice back to normal. "You mean lover? A rich lover? And you're asking me?"

"Not because I think it's so, but if there was a third party you knew about, somebody she was involved with, that would be . . . well, you understand. Especially if she, say, dumped him for you, and—"

"Do you realize what you're implying? If she had another lover, a man—even another woman—somewhere, a rich lover, then what does that make me? A convenience?"

"Of course not! I never meant to—"

"The closest free bed? The closest sucker? Is that what you're saying? Whenever things seem as bad as they can be somebody like you comes to make things worse!"

"Please, Veronica, you're overwrought. Don't . . ."

"You're making it out to be trash. Making whatever I can still feel good about into nothing! Worse than nothing!"

"I'm not. I didn't say anything that—"

"She confided everything in me." Veronica tossed her gloves onto the ground and started back toward her house and Billie followed. "Maybe . . . maybe she wasn't an angel, who is? But she wasn't a calculating bitch, the way that makes her sound. She wasn't a user—she didn't use me and she wasn't seeing some sugar daddy on the side, either!"

"I never meant to suggest she did." It wasn't easy making a case while rushing behind a tall woman with a long stride. "I only know that some things don't fit."

Billie followed Veronica into the kitchen. The house had been straightened, and all drawers and cabinet doors shut tight. Veronica opened the refrigerator and took out chilled water and, without asking, poured two glasses.

"Thank you."

"I'm sorry. That was . . . I'm sorry. I don't seem able to take in anything—"

"It's completely understandable."

"I acted like an imbecile."

"No problem. Honest. Now, would you mind," Billie asked, "if I used your phone? It's a free call."

Veronica gestured toward the wall, and Billie punched in the number on the scrap of paper, explaining what she was doing. "In case it's relevant."

"I guess it isn't a sugar daddy with an 800 number."

"Not unless he's made it a business—" Billie stopped as a mechanical voice said she'd reached the U.S. Fish and Wildlife Service. She repeated the words to Veronica, whose response was "What?"

Options for various sub-services were being recited by the voice, so Billie hung up. "Can you think why Tracy had their number?" she asked.

"She didn't fish, if that's what they do. Maybe she was making a call for Gavin. Like for one of those groups he was in."

It did not seem a profitable path to pursue. Billie sipped ice water instead.

Veronica gestured her to sit down at the table. "Listen," she said once they were both seated. "What did you mean when you said that something didn't fit?"

"There was a piece of jewelry. Just found. Possibly expensive, although it hasn't been appraised yet. It might be fake. In any case, Tracy left it at Gavin's."

Veronica tapped a finger on the table. Her nails were cut short, the taps soft sounds. "Maybe he gave it to her," she said. "Gavin's the only person she knew with money."

"He didn't. She wanted it kept a secret from Robby. The housekeeper thought she was going to sell it and take the cash and that she didn't want it to be part of the divorce. Didn't want to divide its worth."

"I wonder if Ana's telling the truth." More soft taps of the pads of her fingers. Then she looked up, the skin at the corners of her eyes crinkled, her expression meditative and worried. "Maybe that's what it was. I've wondered."

"What?"

"The bad thing. That expression sounds childish, doesn't it? But that's the way she labeled whatever it was. She said she'd done a bad thing. Actually, she asked if I'd ever done anything so bad that I knew I'd feel guilty about it forever, because she had." Veronica sat back, her eyes closed, revisiting another time.

Billie waited. Veronica would get to it in her own time.

"Maybe it *was* a shipboard romance," she said. "Because after she went on that cruise, she was distracted and tense. Mostly, I thought—and think—because she'd finally decided to leave Robby.

She said she could now. Something or somebody on the trip convinced her. But she wouldn't talk about what it was. Maybe it was the ring. It meant money, and she wanted some security before she left him." She looked at her hands. "She didn't have to feel so guilty about it. I could have told her so. Those things happen. I wish she would have talked about it."

A shipboard romance, a ring, a decision to leave your husband and that degree of guilt? Billie wasn't as sure it tied up into such a neat package. "You never asked?"

"She didn't say, you could tell she didn't want to, and I thought it showed my faith in her not to ask. I thought she'd tell me when she . . . I thought we had a long time together ahead. I didn't say anything to you or anybody because it was private, a thing between us and because what's to say? I don't know what she meant, but I tried to think of what could have been so bad. After all, Tracy wasn't exactly a nun about things like sex or partying, so sex wouldn't be it. But the jewelry could. Especially if it was . . . payment, more or less. Her ticket out. Being mercenary. Money was her worst issue. Didn't have it, but really wanted it.

"Anyway, that cruise was before the two of us were on solid ground. So it isn't as if . . . besides, she said she'd thought of a way to make up for it." Veronica's voice lowered to a near whisper. "She probably meant being true from now on. Us. She moved in about a month after that." She looked down at her folded hands.

"I'm sure that's what it was," Billie said. "And I hope that having talked about it, you can set your mind at rest."

But Billie's mind was at anything but. The loose ends had multiplied, and all the way back to San Rafael, she counted them. A hidden ring. A guilty secret. Missing notes. A plan to make up for the guilty secret. Money lust. And to add to the confusion, the phone number of the U.S. Fish and Wildlife Service in her pocket.

None of it implicated Gavin Riddock.

All of it suggested a secret life. The life somebody had felt it necessary to end.

Thirty-three

It was better that they were on strictly business terms. Not that it had felt great when his interest plummeted the other night. But it had been for the best. There weren't even remnants of a subtext now. Just the job. "About the ring?" she said, "if the DA decides it's more proof against—"

"What ring?"

"The ring that . . . Oh." He hadn't given the ring over to the DA's office.

"It has no known relevance." He paced his office, gesticulating as he spoke, as if she were a jury he needed to convince. "The law has a little give here. There are alternative ways of looking at what has to be done with the ring. One is to let things remain as they are—not introduce a potentially damning and in any case inconclusive Trojan horse. That's my pick. We don't even know how and where the housekeeper came by it."

"Or, I guess, if it's worth anything in the first place," Billie said softly.

The lawyer stopped pacing and stood at his window, his back to her, as he regarded his view of sky. Then he half-turned and said over his shoulder, "That much we know. It's worth around thirty-five grand."

"Jesus. How did she get it?" Billie asked.

"An interesting question to discreetly pursue," Michael said. "But meanwhile, it is not my job to put my client into additional jeopardy. It's not as if this was deliberately withheld, certainly not by Gavin, and in the wrong hands, wrongly interpreted, it could play right into the prosecution's hands. Look here: a shiny bright thing he had to have."

"Gavin's nothing like that."

"We know that, but how do you prove he isn't? All anybody knows is that he's not normal. They'll believe just about anything. And he's so inarticulate, he'd make their case for them."

She couldn't think of a counterargument.

"Anyway, who's to say this ring was actually there at the time when the police searched? Maybe the housekeeper had removed it long before then. For whatever reason. Maybe it's evidence of nothing. Maybe it never belonged to Tracy. All kinds of maybes, so don't worry about it, okay?"

Okay, but there was no way to forget about it.

She took a deep breath and moved on. "When you went through the evidence box, did you find notes? A journal? A diary? Anything close to that? I'm assuming not, because I didn't see mention of it."

His expression was strained, as if he were translating, with serious difficulty, her words. "From whom? To whom?"

"From Tracy. By Tracy, actually. Anything?"

"Nothing like that in there. Nothing that meant much at all. Running gear. A paperback about how to be successful——"

"Did you riffle the pages?"

His silence was pointed.

"Something could be stuck between them," she said, regretting the words even as they exited her mouth.

"Like a notebook?"

She bit at her lips. "It might not have been a book."

"Where are you getting this from?"

"The housekeeper. She said Tracy wanted to leave notes there.

The housekeeper didn't allow it. She thought the notes would make Tracy's husband jealous. But maybe it wasn't about Tracy's love life. Maybe that was the housekeeper's misinterpretation."

"Man, but this housekeeper stirs up trouble. The suddenly discovered ring and now a secret notebook. Maybe she'll produce it, too, eventually."

She ignored that. "It could do with whatever Gavin meant about not helping Tracy. That she never told him what to do— Maybe that report, or diary, or note was what he was to do."

"Do when? Where? About what?"

"Maybe about Veronica's 'bad thing.' Maybe it matters."

He looked not at all pleased and about ready to say so, but then he stopped himself and made it clear he was doing so reluctantly. "Interesting theories you've got going," he said. "In any case, yes. I always riffle pages. Besides, I asked him about it again yesterday. I asked him what he thought Tracy had meant and how he was supposed to have helped her.

"He doesn't have any idea. He just cries and makes himself sound more and more guilty by saying things like he should have helped her and he didn't so it's his fault she's dead. I asked whether she'd given him hints as to what he could do. I asked him whether it had to do with the groups he belonged to, the way you suggested. I asked him what exactly that cockamamy group did—I didn't use that word—that CoXistence. I asked him a dozen questions and he didn't have a clear answer to one of them. Not even about what he'd said the first time, to you. You can't hang on to each of his words as if it deserved interpretation and commentary."

Gavin didn't like Michael Specht, and Billie couldn't blame him. Every "cockamamy" showed contempt for his client, however brilliant and clever his courtroom tactics would be.

He glanced at his watch. "I'm going to see him in twenty minutes. I'll ask about the ring, and I'll ask about the mysterious whatever it was again."

And a lot your kind of questioning will get you, she thought. Wasn't a definition of mental illness doing the same thing and expecting different results? Michael would push and bully and emit "you're guilty" rays and Gavin would back off and balk and grow ever more disoriented and fearful. "May I come along?" she asked. "I was going to ask to see him, but since you're—"

"Wouldn't you say that's overkill? How can I justify that to my client?"

"Gavin?"

He looked startled, then annoyed. "My client's mother. I stand corrected."

"Don't bill Mrs. Riddock for my time, then. This is on the house. Don't pay me for that hour."

He looked at her appraisingly. "Why?"

Was she supposed to say "Your client doesn't like you"? "He's more at ease with women. It makes sense. His dad walked out, he's lived with his mother, then this housekeeper, and then there was Tracy, his best—maybe his only—friend. I think he gets more muddled if he isn't at ease. As do most of us."

Michael Specht's facial muscles registered defensiveness, then belligerence, and finally, a chilly form of amusement. "You could be right," he said. "But all the same, I don't like waste or redundancy, and having both of us go is just that."

"But please, I—"

"So you go. And I will bill Mrs. R and pay you—if you get answers out of him. And only if. Not further theories. Not wispy, maybe leads. Answers. Because if you can't, then I'll still have to make the trip. Fair?"

For once, life was fair. Michael Specht was fair. He was also snide.

She wouldn't have liked him. It might have taken awhile, but ultimately, the snide part would have overshadowed that winning smile.

She felt as if she'd managed to leap, painlessly, to the far side of a potentially disastrous, ultimately wretched relationshp without scars. She was over and beyond him without having had to experience him.

A whole new reason to be grateful for the existence of her son: He saved her time.

Gavin had pulled in on himself. He seemed to be withdrawing into a form of solitary imprisonment that even the legal system couldn't impose.

It must be hell, she thought, for someone who ran every day to be cooped up this way. He seemed restless behind the glass. Fidgety.

"I was at your house," she said. "I met Ana and saw your cats and heard—"

"Ruffles," he said softly.

"Ana's taking good care of them."

"I miss them."

She wished she could put her hand on his shoulder, offer some human contact and comfort. He looked—he was—alone and isolated.

Perhaps a change of topic would help. "I saw your collection of movies and music, too," she said. "Quite impressive."

"They won't let me have my Walkman."

Not a great conversational gambit, then. "Well," she said briskly, "it will all be waiting for you when you're released. But tell me about your music. Who do you especially like?"

He named groups, none of which Billie knew, but he was able to summon a long list of names, and that surprised her. His memory was obviously selective. "And the tapes Tracy made," he said. "The mixes. They're good, too."

The mention of Tracy made it easier to ease into the purpose of the visit. "Did Tracy leave things at your house?"

He nodded. "Running stuff, I guess." His eyes wandered around the room even though his answers were polite, as if he were paying as much attention as he could. "Did you find them?" he asked. "Are you here because you found them?"

"Excuse me? You mean the things Tracy left?"

He shook his head. "People say things and then I never know."

"What's that? I'm not following . . ." She felt a stab of sorrow. He really was as confused as Michael Specht had said.

He leaned closer to the glass partition. "You said you were going to look for other people who were sure that I didn't hurt Tracy. Like you said you were sure. Did you find them?"

She stifled a smile. Who was the one with the feeble memory? "I'm working on it. And how about you? Have you remembered anything else?"

He shrugged slightly and shook his head.

"Then let me ask you a few things. You said Tracy was scared the last few times you ran with her."

"I already told you."

"But she never said of what?"

He shook his head.

"Not even a hint?"

He shook his head once more, then stopped himself, and wrinkled his brow. "She said . . . she said that she got in trouble and she couldn't get out."

The bad thing?

"But she did get out," he said. "She left Robby."

"Is that what she meant?"

"Isn't it?"

"So you think she was afraid of Robby?"

He nodded.

"But she told you she was afraid after she had left him, so do you think she was still afraid he'd come after her?"

Gavin looked worried. "She was still scared after she left him."

Billie nodded. The chair's configuration hurt her back, and she shifted her weight, wondering if these chairs were part of the process of punishment, even for visitors. "Did Tracy wear rings?"

"Her wedding ring."

"A fancy ring. Big, glittery thing."

He shook his head. "A wedding band, that was all. It said 'Forever T and R' inside. She showed me."

Gavin didn't seem to have the guile or instinct for self-preservation a lie would require. He hadn't known about the emerald and he surely hadn't lusted for it.

"Oh, wait," he said. "Wait."

Billie's heart fluttered. Maybe now a ray of memory, an illumination. She'd show that Michael Specht. She'd get to the heart of something.

"She didn't wear the wedding ring anymore after she left Robby," he said. "Even though she was still married."

That seemed that. No answers for Michael Specht, and both her vanity and wallet would be deservedly deflated. Unless . . . "Do you remember telling me that you were going to help Tracy some way, but she didn't get to tell you how?"

"I don't like to talk about that."

"It could help. It could help a lot."

"I would have helped her. She said I'd know how, but I didn't."

Maybe the notes would have told him.

"I don't know what I was supposed to do."

"It's not your fault," she murmured.

"Then she was dead and I was here and I still didn't know if she gave it to me like she said."

"Wait—did she say she gave it to you? Or that she was *going* to give it to you?"

His brow wrinkled again. Billie felt cruel putting him through this, but if Tracy had in fact left information for Gavin, and if it was about the "bad thing" for which she was going to make amends—and if that bad thing, or the making amends for it was why she was living in a state of fear—then Gavin had a chance.

A whole lot of ifs.

No wisps, no theories, Michael had said. He'd forgotten to say "no ifs." Maybe she could get away with a technicality.

Gavin scratched behind his ear. The gesture seemed a part of his thinking process. "Maybe she said she told me what to do. Or was going to tell me. Or maybe she said she gave me it. I wasn't listening right and I don't know where it is." His expression was bleak.

"That's all right," Billie said quickly. "How could you? She didn't tell you that, did she?"

"I don't know." He sounded pitifully young and miserable. "I don't know. I don't remember things good, and I should know—I think she did tell me, and I asked them to let me go look, but they didn't, and anyway, I don't know!"

"Don't worry about it, Gavin."

"It mattered to her," he said in a hoarse whisper. "She was my friend and I promised her. I promised to help her."

Billie nodded. "Then I'll find it," she said with resolution and conviction she didn't feel. "I'll find it and you'll feel better. How could you find it if they're keeping you here, anyway?"

She felt ashamed of herself as his face flooded with gratitude and relief. He believed her. He trusted her.

As if his life depended on it.

As it did.

Thirty-four

In Emma's entire life, she had never spent this much time contemplating housewares. Her kitchen equipment had been catch-as-catch-can, a realistic start, she thought, to her entire domestic life.

She considered herself a sufficiently good cook. Nobody starved or died of malnutrition around her. But she had neither the time nor the interest, and probably not the palate, to bother with whatever required this enormous range of apparatus. Obviously, she was in the minority. The place was crowded—almost all women, almost all in intense pursuit of the graters, slicers, mixers, grinders, and dicers that Emma had lived happily and well-fed without for a lifetime.

She was bored, but not enough to allow Kay Wilson out of her sight. She'd seen the woman's expression and it had been in search of an escape hatch. Emma was having none of that. For too long already, Megan Kay Caitlin had been on the run in a way Emma didn't yet understand. Without monitoring, there was nothing to stop her from slipping out a back door and disappearing, becoming someone else again.

So Emma waited, discreetly at a remove, but there. And finally, the mysterious Ms. Wilson had a break, and Emma moved closer. "Let's talk now," she said.

"I'm exhausted. I've been on my feet for—"

"We'll sit down. There must be a coffee shop around here."

Kay Wilson put up a hand, like the crossing guards Emma remembered. "I don't want to talk with you, Mrs. Howe. And I don't have to, I didn't hire you. Talk to Heather. I want no part of her craziness. I don't approve."

She wasn't the Milquetoast Emma had first thought her, but of course, the woman Emma had met was an invention. The real woman was a con artist, and slick. "You'd better talk to me," Emma said. "I'm giving you a chance to explain. Otherwise, I'll go directly to the police."

She blanched, put a hand to her mouth. "*Why?* Adopting a child is not a crime."

"There's too much wrong with your story. So much that I think abduction or black market child-selling is involved. Or murder."

"Oh, my God." Kay Wilson closed her eyes and shook her head. Her fists were clenched as she took a series of deep breaths. When she opened her eyes, they were moist.

But she followed Emma, her posture ramrod straight, Emma striding briskly and Kay Wilson, expression registering acute disapproval, more slowly, saying nothing as they stood at a counter, being served. Nothing, until they were at one of the small tables, facing each other. Out of a menu offering eleven coffee options in three sizes each, both had ordered plain coffee, regular size.

"What is it, then?" Kay Wilson's voice was sharp and lined with anger, but she herself looked defeated. Maybe it was only exhaustion. She'd been on her feet all day, hawking small appliances. But maybe not.

"Who are you?" Emma spoke softly, but even so, the woman across from her flinched.

"You can't have dragged me here to ask me a ridiculous question like that. You know who I am. I know who I am. It's Heather who is questioning her identity."

"I know who you say you are, but you aren't Kay Wilson. Or,

more precisely, Megan Kay Wilson, the name on Heather's amended—or not amended—birth certificate. You're not her, unless you're dead. And dead for a long time."

The other woman looked momentarily flustered, then she pushed her jaw forward, sat back in her chair and eyed Emma coldly. "I don't know what you're talking about."

She was good. But then, she'd had years to perfect this identity. "Megan Kay Wilson died nineteen years ago at age nineteen. A few months after your so-called husband Nowell Wilson died. You must have liked your men young. He died at age fourteen. But then, he must have been quite precocious to have served in the Vietnam War by then and to have had a job, not to mention being allowed to adopt a child at such a tender age.

"Furthermore, Heather wasn't born in August, as you told me. She was born the following December, and you'd have known it since the birth certificate was changed to show your—supposed—name. Why the lie? But interestingly, it does not show the name of your imaginary husband who was not raised in New York as you said. You came to my office to purposely cloud the picture, to set me off on false trails. Not a solitary so-called fact you gave me was the truth. I want to know why. And I especially want to know how you got that baby."

"Or you'll go to the police with your suspicions." Kay Wilson shredded her paper napkin into filaments. She didn't look at Emma as she spoke in a flat voice, but kept all her attention on the rapidly disappearing napkin. "I didn't do anything wrong."

Emma shrugged. "Prove it to me, or prove it to the police."

"You're going to destroy everything," the other woman said, her voice chilling because it was soft yet strangled. "Everything I've worked for and lived for. Things are better as they are. Don't tamper with them." She leaned closer to Emma. "You'll make everything worse, and for what?"

"For my mental health. For the rule of law. For my client. But most of all, for the truth. Nothing more, nothing less."

"You think the truth is the be-all and end-all. You're arrogant and you're wrong."

Emma shrugged.

The skin on Kay's cheeks had grown mottled with red and pale patches. She took a breath, then, her eyes still on her hands, she spoke in a rush. "We were trash. That's why it all happened." Her voice sounded as if it were coming out of constricted vocal cords. But her words smacked at Emma. She'd anticipated explanations and defenses, not this.

"My mother was sick. She had polio when she was a kid—a mild case, but she dragged a leg and was weak. Couldn't do much. She worked when she could, but that was barely ever. Dad was a mechanic. And a drunk. Mostly a drunk. Fired a lot, or quit. There were three of us: Megan, Caitlin, and Nowell, named for Christmas even though it wasn't spelled right. They thought this was more masculine."

She glared at Emma, who nodded acknowledgment. One small, but cryptic, piece of the puzzle in place. Origin of the names.

"Megan was the oldest, and wild. Getting in trouble for as long as I can remember. Nowell was too young still to really carry on, but he wasn't ever going to be that way. He was quieter, even shy, but a good-hearted boy. Then there was me, the one they called the 'good one.' They didn't mean it as a compliment. 'Smart' was what they liked. Not school smart, but smart like getting something over on somebody."

She was truly Caitlin Wilson, then. Megan was her sister and Nowell her brother. Both dead. "You lived in Butte County?" Emma asked.

Caitlin looked startled, then nodded. "When I was sixteen," she continued. "Megan was three years older and had a baby and a record for shoplifting. People talked about us, but when I was twelve, I'd joined the church and it had become my family. I loved the order, the respectability. I knew those people could help me be different than my real family. Them and my English teacher. Miss

Andrews told me I had abilities, that she'd help me find a scholarship. It felt like I'd been in a dark place and somebody picked up a lantern and said 'Look, there's a way out.' " Her cheeks puffed and she exhaled vigorously, poof, as if she'd just run a distance. "I probably don't have to say that Megan didn't take good care of Heather," she added quietly.

"Her baby was your Heather?"

Kay nodded. She was out of napkins, so she folded her hands, as if she were in school, as if Miss Andrews were still observing her.

"I'll get us more coffee." Emma couldn't explain it, but these words that so far explained nothing had diffused Emma's hostility and left her anxious instead.

When she came back, Kay had found another paper napkin, and was dabbing at her eyes with it.

"Sometimes Megan was just crazy about her baby," she said after she'd added sugar and milk to her cup. "She'd buy—or for all I know, steal—gorgeous clothes for her and go show her off, but to places you don't take a baby. Other times, she'd scream about 'the brat' and how tied down she was and she hated the baby so much I was afraid for Heather."

So it had been a benign kidnaping. Sister Caitlin foster mother to a child in need of saving. But that didn't explain the web of lies she'd woven around it.

"I was the baby-sitter and most times, it meant I had her all weekend, because Megan wouldn't come home at all and my mother, she was in bed sick, and you didn't want my dad baby-sitting. Daytimes, Megan was there. She didn't work much. But soon as I'd come home from school, Megan would pass the baby to me and out she'd go with her boyfriend. They were into serious drugs. Taking them, dealing them.

"I got a summer job through the church, watching a family's kids at the pool, and when I had to, I brought Heather along. And every night and all weekends, I was with her. She called me 'Kay,' couldn't say Caitlin, you see, but sometimes she called me 'Mommy' and . . . I let her."

Kay twirled the coffee stirrer between her thumb and middle finger and looked at the wall across from them until Emma felt obliged to clear her throat and get the woman's attention. "I hate doing this," Kay said.

Emma nodded. It was obvious from the halting speech, from the starts and stops, from her facial expression, but it didn't matter.

"It was the end of August, and hot, and I had all my summer earnings on me so I could buy clothes for school, but my dad, he said I should stay home. He had steaks. I don't know where he got them—traded something for it at work, but there they were. Thick steaks to barbecue for the four of us—mom and dad and Nowell and me. Heather was going to share a piece of mine, if she could chew it, and Megan wasn't home.

"What happened was before we got to the steaks, my dad drank too much beer and Heather fell and scraped her knee and she was whining, and he was shouting at her, making threats. So I asked my mother could I borrow the car, take the baby out. I knew she'd say yes. Dad was too drunk to drive, and my mother never drove. Besides, Heather was annoying them.

"I didn't feel like shopping. Too hot. I thought I'd drive to San Francisco. I'd never been there, it was too far. Three, four hours. But I dreamed about going there after college. I liked that it was so far away, that it was big, that the water was there. Of course I didn't make it all that way. It was too late in the day when we started. But we had a good time. We stopped at a fast-food place for hamburgers and I didn't miss that steak at all.

"On the way home, after dark, Heather sleeping in her car seat, I heard the news on the radio. My mother and father and Nowell were dead. Murdered."

Again, she glared at Emma, as if, somehow, this was her fault and for the slightest moment, Emma thought perhaps it was.

"Shot," Kay said. "The police were looking for Megan. The

neighbors had seen the whole thing, just about, and called the police. After I stopped shaking, I turned that car around and headed anywhere as long as it was away."

Kay stopped talking and looked at Emma. She lay her hands flat on the table. "That's it. That's who I am. It gives me a headache to think about it. I hope you're satisfied."

"I—" This was nothing like what Emma had imagined. In many ways it was the opposite of that. "I'm sorry for— That is a terrible story. But I'm not satisfied. I'm not clear what happened then."

Kay sighed. "Isn't it obvious? I couldn't go home. They said on the radio that I was not a suspect, that I'd left early in the day with—I swear, the radio called her my child. I heard it, that mistake. Maybe that gave me the idea. If I went home, they'd know that Heather was not my child, and they'd take her and put her in foster care. I was sixteen and still in high school, with no real job. They wouldn't let me have her. If I went back, she was doomed.

"I was too afraid to go to San Francisco just then. I don't know why, a little place seemed safer. Or easier. That night, we made it to the coast, around Fort Bragg, and we slept in a motel. The TV said my sister and her boyfriend had been captured in another shootout at the boyfriend's house. They weren't smart or sober enough to get away. Megan was injured badly, the news said. Her boyfriend was dead.

"It seems Megan and her boyfriend had barged in and gone berserk about the steaks. About how there weren't any for them. There was this fight and my father got his gun and told them to get out, but Megan's boyfriend jumped him and got the gun away and was beating the hell out of him and Megan took the gun and shot our mother and dad, and even Nowell, because he tried to grab the gun away."

She lowered her head and Emma heard her sniff, then look up again and clear her throat before she spoke. "Steaks. It was about steaks," she said. Her eyes were still moist nineteen years later.

Emma nodded, acknowledging the waste and stupidity of those deaths, along with their toll.

"We slept in cheap motels and a few times in the car, and we ate fast food. The big problem was Heather's diapers, but I bought the throwaway kind, and we made out all right. My money lasted us three weeks and by then, we were in Oregon. From there, I called the pastor. I told him we were safe. I didn't want them worrying—and I didn't want them searching for me, either. He promised to tell the authorities, but he said I should come back, that they were 'trying to find a place for both Heather and me.' I realized I would go into foster care, too, and I knew I couldn't go back. If he'd said they *had* a home for us both, I would have gone. I could have finished school. But who'd want a murderer's kid? Or her sister?

"He told me Megan was in a coma. Later, I read in the papers at the library that she'd died. It meant there wasn't a trial and that was the end of the story.

"I told the pastor that we were going to an aunt's up in Oregon, where we'd both live. I never was in touch again, of course. But Oregon felt safer, being in another state, in a little town that had never heard of the Wilsons or the Barbecued-Steak Massacre." She folded her hands and nodded, as if her story were completely done.

"But—why take your sister's name?" Emma asked. "Or lie about Heather's birth date?"

"I . . . sometimes I could show copies of Heather's birth certificate to get her into programs, and I changed the date so she'd be eligible. Just a few months, so she could be in play school sooner."

"And taking your sister's name?"

"I didn't have a plan. I didn't know what to do. You have to imagine yourself at sixteen, suddenly . . . I decided that the easiest way to be was to stick as close to the truth as I could, so that I wouldn't be caught. Heather already called me Kay. I got a copy of Megan's birth certificate, and used it when I applied for jobs. That way, I could lie, too, and say I was a high school graduate.

"I said I was a widow, that my husband—I said his name was Nowell, just in case I needed another birth certificate—was killed in an accident while I was pregnant. People felt sorry for me, or at least, they didn't say anything bad.

"First, I got a job tending an old lady in her house. A companion, they called it, but I was everything: cleaning lady, cook, entertainer, medicine giver. Whatever you call it. Heather and I shared a tiny 'in-law' apartment out back, and I got a small salary, just about enough for day care.

"Nobody came to find me. I got books out of the library and studied for my high school equivalent degree, and I got it, so I could apply for real jobs. When Heather was in the church's nursery school, I got a clerical job in an office, found us the smallest, cheapest decent apartment and that's where we lived for three more years. By then, my big story wasn't news anywhere else. Every place had its own massacres. I could go back to California, as long as it wasn't my hometown.

I finally came to San Francisco, just the way I dreamed. That was the thing I did for me. So I was there, even though it wasn't the way I'd hoped. We moved over here, to San Rafael because I found a place we could afford to rent here, and we made a life. A good, solid life. Heather was a regular little girl with a respectable history. She wouldn't be trash and nobody was going to talk about her that way. About us. We were—we are still—respectable.

"When I moved back and went to work here, I switched back to my real name and birth date. It didn't matter any more. I had a high school degree myself and I was old enough for any jobs. It's a clean, decent life. Nobody talks about us. Nobody. That's what I got. I never married. I barely ever had a date. I had a child to raise, and it wasn't easy supporting her, making sure she dressed like the other children, did her homework, had the advantages, that she could be proud of who she was.

271

"But it was worth it, until that day——" She shook her head and her face contorted bitterly. "I seldom drink; I'm the daughter of a drunk. But that day . . . Heather was acting up and I said it. She looks like Megan, and it was always on my mind, and there she was, throwing it all away. Quitting her job, quitting college. I worked so hard to give her that—I gave it up myself for her—and she was tossing it away, flushing it down the toilet. I couldn't believe anybody could waste what I'd wanted so much and never had a chance for and worked so hard to give her. I guess I was angry with her and feeling sorry for myself and I said it. 'You're just like your mother and you're going to turn out just as bad if you don't shape up.' "

A sound, half sigh, half sob, rolled through her, then she looked directly at Emma, her mouth tight. "I've tried to make her feel good about herself, make her proud. To protect her. How will she feel knowing she's the illegitimate daughter of a teenage drug addict who murdered her family? And that is the truth. Precisely what you wanted. Are you pleased? Is it still the measure of everything? What are you going to do now, Miss Howe?"

Thirty-five

Marlena had noticed the figure earlier, but by the time she tried to check it out, it was gone.

But here it—she—was again: Mrs. Vincent. Watching them, like a detective in a bad movie, leaning against the wall across the way. Marlena wondered when somebody was going to come out and ask her what she was doing. If she weren't so nicely dressed in her designer jeans and suede shirt-jacket, she'd have been picked up or questioned by now, for sure.

What did she want? What could she possibly get from watching where he worked?

Then Marlena understood and smiled to herself. David's wife was making sure. She wondered how she'd figured out that it was Marlena on the phone. The calls had been fun—little breathless stupid-me calls—but she hadn't identified herself.

Or maybe she didn't know, had no idea, but was waiting to follow her husband when he left the building. Because in the end, what she wanted, no matter who the girl turned out to be, was to see for herself. To be sure.

Across from her, Heather hunched over the account book. The girl was so drab, Marlena couldn't understand how she could tell if she was actually alive. And lately, she'd been even more silent, all pulled up and the doors locked shut. As if Marlena wanted to know

Heather Wilson's secrets. That'd be a laugh; that girl had the world's most boring life. She wondered if she'd ever had a date, let alone anything more than that with a man.

And Marlena surely wasn't telling Heather her own secrets. She could imagine Heather's expressions if she were to tell about the phone calls, about her life plan for Mr. David Vincent. The girl would alert the police, the church and Dear Abby.

Marlena did neck-stretching exercises. She had a painful crick from sitting too long, and that helped her decide what to do about that and about Mrs. Vincent across the street.

She lifted her cosmetics pouch out of her purse, stood, and went over to the window, pausing, posing, enjoying the knowledge that David Vincent's wife was watching her. Let Jeannie Vincent make sure. Life could use speeding up.

Marlena was glad she was wearing the lacy slip and the transparent chiffon candy-striped shirt she'd found at the thrift shop. Let her get an eyeful. Slowly, she powdered and patted her face, turning her head this way and that to get different angles in the mirror. More slowly still, she ran the lipstick across her upper lip and then, after a head-tilting self-examination in the mirror once again, repeated the process with her lower lip. And all the while, she arched her back, making sure Mrs. Vincent was aware of her enemy's ammunition.

Eat your heart out. The war was over even if nobody but Marlena knew it yet. She saw signs of it all the time. The way he looked at her, watched her when he thought she didn't know it. The way he touched her shoulder that day when she said she was upset about Tracy. Consoling her was just an excuse to touch her.

The way he was watching her now. Her back still to him, she snapped shut the mirrored compact that had shown her his office door opening, had shown her that he stopped in mid-stride to watch her. Really watch her.

She checked the other side of the street. Jeannie Vincent wasn't there anymore. By craning her neck, she found the woman all the way up at the corner, leaning against another wall, smoking.

"What's up, Marlena?"

He was very close. Surely closer than he used to get. Everything a signal, everything a sign.

"Oh!" she said, turning slightly. "I didn't hear you—"

"You seemed mesmerized."

She waved lazily at the window and sighed. "Thinking about Tracy again, I guess."

He followed the direction of her glance, across the street in the direction of the travel agency. "What about her?"

She shrugged. "I get sad thinking about her."

"It seems to me . . ." He looked at Marlena so intently it weirded her out.

What was this about? Did he think Marlena was a cold person? Without emotions? The fact was, she didn't care one way or the other about Tracy, but what did his questioning mean?

He'd explain or he wouldn't. She certainly wasn't going to say "I didn't mean that. I was actually watching your wife stalk you. She's nuts you know, and I've been helping her along, helping her realize it's about you and me now, not you and her."

"It seems to me you weren't close to Tracy when she was alive," he finally said. "But since . . . but now . . . you mention her pretty often. How is that?"

"I guess when somebody dies that way, somebody you've actually met and talked to, you think about them a whole lot."

He was still looking at her as if he was looking right inside of her, waiting for more. She had no idea what to say, but kept talking anyway. "It's called posttraumatic stress. I saw about it on TV. I didn't know her that well, but I liked her. She was friendly. She talked to me a couple of times. She was pretty interesting, actually. Told me things I didn't know anything about."

"Like what? What did Tracy Lester know?"

Was this a come-on? Did he think she was secretly close—that way—with Tracy? Or that gay Tracy taught her about sex for God's sake? Did he maybe think Marlena was also gay? "About *animals*," she said. "Things that happen to them." God, but she hoped that cleared things up for him.

It must have. He stopped looking at her that way, and now, Marlena thought maybe she was boring him. She glanced back at the street corner she faced but he did not. Jeannie Vincent was still there, grinding out her cigarette with her shoe and looking. She could see the window. She could see them. Marlena rearranged herself so that she was tilted toward David Vincent. Now, she put a hand—the window side hand so that Jeannie Vincent would surely see—on his shoulder. "Are you all right?" she asked. "You're so quiet. Have I done something wrong? Does it bother you that I mention Tracy?"

"Why would you say that? Why would it bother me to talk about her?"

He seemed angry, maybe because she was missing the point, that he just wanted to be close to her. That this was a man and woman thing, and not about some dead girl. "Did—did you not like her?" she asked.

"Like her? I didn't know her."

"Know her well, I guess you mean. I mean you *know* her, but maybe you didn't really *know* her."

"I meant what I said. I didn't know her at all."

"But . . ." She'd seen Tracy inside his office. She knew they knew each other, but probably only about business, tickets or something that was easier to hand-deliver than to mail across the street, and of course he'd forget who the messenger was.

Except Tracy had been in his office pretty long. Marlena noticed things like that. She'd thought Tracy was her competition until, of course, she found out that Tracy was moving in with a woman. But he wasn't saying anything about it and he must have his reasons.

Maybe Tracy had rejected him. Maybe it was a bitter memory. She let go of it, didn't contradict him.

Her hand was still on his shoulder and she slowly, reluctantly, dropped it, letting her fingers touch the cloth of his light sweater.

"You're feeling sad, is that it?" he said in a softer voice. "That's what this is about?"

His wife was walking back toward them again.

She nodded, and snuffled. "I can't help it," she said, holding her hands up to her face. "It was so awful, what happened to her and I think, well, it could happen to any of us, then. So alive, and then dead, like that. *Murdered*. I get so frightened!"

"Don't be." His voice was gentle, and he put his hands on her upper arms, holding her steady as if he was afraid she'd topple. She kept her head bowed, so he couldn't see that she wasn't managing to produce tears. "You'll be fine. There's no reason to think that anything bad is going to ever happen to you." And he moved one hand from her shoulder to under her chin, which he lifted gently, to reassure her. "Come on, now," he said. "Let me see a smile."

She couldn't help it, she glanced out the window again and he followed her glance, his hand still on her chin.

"Shit!" He dropped both hands.

"What did I do?"

He stared across the street, so she looked, too, and of course saw Jeannie Vincent, hands on her hips, staring back at them, her features bent and twisted.

She looked insane.

"My wife. She's across the street. She's . . . she's got some really wrong ideas about me, about what I do and just now I had my hand on your arm and under your chin—"

"It was completely innocent!" Marlena gazed at him. Let her see that. Unless she could lip-read through glass and across the street, let her think the love-words were still going on.

"I know it was innocent and you know it, but she—she's a

nervous woman, and . . ." He backed off, literally. Marlena watched, amused. What did he think, that he could rewind the film and do the scene again? Move them back to the point where he came out of his office and saw her by the window?

She was proud of how cleverly she'd scripted it, how perfectly it had played out.

Her talent was making things happen. You had to know what you wanted. And then you had to think through what it took to get it. She knew how to do that, even on the spot, even when she had to improvise, like just now.

And it had worked. The bait had been snapped up.

He could retreat all he wanted to. Something was going to happen because something already had.

Thirty-six

Billie sat in her car with the motor idling. She'd promised Gavin Riddock something it wasn't in her power to grant. Now what?

This was worse than a needle in a haystack. She didn't know where the haystack was and wasn't sure it was a needle she was after in the first place.

But she was convinced now that it—the letter, the journal, the diary, the note—was important and had to do with Tracy's death. Why else tell Gavin that if anything happened to her, there'd be something that explained, that would tell him how to help her?

The something had to be where he could find it. She'd probably told him where, but he hadn't heard. Hadn't listened. Had listened to his breath, only his breath while they ran. Maybe Tracy hadn't been aware of his inattention.

Except Tracy Lester knew Gavin Riddock better than anyone else on earth did. She would have anticipated his inattention, or his poor memory, and if he'd made it clear he didn't want to hear it, she would have been able to interpret his agitation and refusals, especially given her own fears.

She wouldn't have told him whatever it was. Too risky. What she would have told him was where those notes were. And they'd have to be where Gavin, with his limited experience and contacts, would find them. It had to be his house. His own house. She directed the car toward Tiburon.

There was a pledge drive on NPR and she had already pledged, so she pulled out a tape from the box in the console, saw that it had a handwritten label, and popped it in. She'd copied a friend's CD onto a tape. Vladimir Ashkenazy playing Chopin. Perfect.

"And the twinky bird sang in the high silly tree and the—"

What the hell? That goddamn *Jesse's Greatest Hits* again. She snapped the tape off.

The kid kept bringing it back to the car, afraid to be without "his" music or the headphones that would soon fuse to his ears. The way Gavin must have been. His Walkman was what he missed most, after his animals and, of course, Tracy.

She held the offending tape. No wonder she'd mixed them up. It also had a handwritten label—her handwriting.

And then, thoughts about music, Jesse, Gavin, and handwriting combined and sent prickles over her scalp, as if the idea that now possessed her literally blazed a path across her brain.

Ana was holding her purse when she answered the door and reluctantly let Billie enter. "I was leaving for a while," she said. "All done here and my grandson is waiting." Ruffles barked from the backyard. "Nothing left to do," Ana added.

And indeed, the little house sparkled, every millimeter in place and shiny without so much as a dust mote marring a surface. Billie wondered how Ana avoided having cat hair anywhere when the two cats seemed everywhere. One was asleep on the dark green sofa, and the other sitting in the hall, deciding whether Billie could pass.

"Please, I'll be quick," Billie said, and with a heavy sigh, Ana allowed her freedom of the house.

It looked the same. The view across the water to Sausalito, the sofas, the cats, the coffee table, TV, stereo, shelving filled with neatly arranged CDs and video- and audiotapes.

She had to proceed logically. First eliminate the idea of mail.

"Ana, tell me: Did Gavin receive any mail that he didn't get to see? Any personal mail?"

Ana retreated from the neck up, turtlelike.

"I didn't mean you kept it from him, but did any come around the time of his arrest? After his arrest? Or before, even, but he wasn't interested in reading it?"

"No mail."

"Bills?"

She shook her head. "Mrs. Zandra pays bills. They go to her place."

"Magazines?"

"Mr. Gavin, he doesn't get magazines. Catalogs, maybe. That's all, and ads, and things from the animal people. The group with the big 'X' in the name."

CoXistence. Tracy had briefly belonged as well. "Did he read what he got from them?"

"Nothing has come. I meant sometimes, when things come, that's what comes."

The dog, Ruffles, barked in the yard. Billie felt her excitement mount. The dog who didn't bark in the night, wasn't that it?

That dog was what made her finally realize there were no books on these shelves. No magazines on the table. Gavin could, but didn't, read and Tracy knew that. There was no diary, no notes, no journal.

"May I look through those tapes over there?" Billie said.

"It would take hours! My grandson waits for me."

"I don't want to look at the videotapes—I want to check the outsides of the music tapes. It won't even take a minute."

Ana nodded with a great show of sacrifice and resignation.

Billie felt older with each new title. She and Gavin weren't all that far apart in age—six years, she thought—but she didn't recognize most of the groups' names. She skimmed the printed labels, cassettes that Gavin had bought, and concentrated on the handwritten ones, praying that Tracy and Gavin hadn't developed a secret code so that "God's Wrath," which was written on one, didn't actually mean "Here's the information I told you about."

In tidy progression, she found group after group, collections of the songs of the eighties, one of whale music, even a sprinkling of classical music, handwriting that might be Tracy Lester's, but nothing that in any way could by any stretch be a message from her.

She was out of ideas.

"Something is wrong?" Ana asked.

"I thought . . . Gavin loves music so much . . ." She felt as if all the air and energy had been sucked out of her. She'd been positive a tape would be how Tracy could be sure he'd find her message, hear her out.

Ana nodded. "All the time, that boy. Music, music. And so loud! When he listens and I am here, I make him wear the earplug thing."

"And this is all of it? His music?"

Ana nodded. "I keep it nice. Everything he listen to."

How could she have been so wrong? She knew Ana was in a rush, wanted to go home, but she was reluctant to leave, to give it up, concede permanent defeat. And then, she either had it, or she was grabbing for her final straw. The tapes here were for listening inside the house. Ana tidied and refiled them each time in alphabetical order. But he'd said that one of the nice things about Tracy was that she'd made him mixes for running and he'd done the same for her and Billie hadn't seen labels of tapes like that here.

"Ana," she asked, "one last favor: music that Gavin ran to? Are those tapes somewhere else?"

She rolled her eyes to the heavens. "They are not for listening that way. Is for running."

"Yes, right. Can I see them?"

"In the little room," she said. "All his things." She led Billie to a small room with a treadmill and another TV, plus a stand holding free weights. "The police took his shoes he runs in," she said. "And Miss Billie, I have to leave. My grandson—"

"One second. I promise." Let it be obvious. Please. Let it be labeled in a way she understood.

The police hadn't been interested in the running cassettes tossed in a basket on top of the tiny chest, but Billie was. She pawed through the pile, almost feeling Ana's impatient breath at her back. Then she herself took a deep breath, reminded herself that this was important, and went through them systematically. "Run Mix—August '98." "Tracy's Run Mix—January '98." She saw their different handwritings now and Tracy's was easy to distinguish. She focused on the feminine script. "Tracy's Fave Rock Mix for Gavin," "Tracy's Fave Oldies for Gavin." Half a dozen in her hand—she must have spent her life making mixes and he as well, for there were just as many that began with "Gavin's" and ended with "for Tracy."

She nearly passed right over it because it looked so much like the rest. But Gavin would have found it. "Tracy for Gavin—February '99. Just that. It looked and sounded enough like the rest to hide in clear sight. Tracy, on tape.

"Ana, may I use the living room tape player?"

"Miss Billie, my grandson will be on the corner all alone if I don't—"

Billie nodded. "Sorry," she said. "I know how that is." And she in fact glanced at her wrist to check the time, even though Ivan, sufficiently recuperated, was picking up Jesse from school today. "I won't keep you any longer."

She put her hand back into the basket, as if to return the tape but palmed it instead and slipped it into her pocket. She wasn't sure if Ana noticed, whether Ana would care, but she wasn't taking any chances, and was glad the housekeeper was distracted and intent on getting Billie out of here.

She thanked Ana, and almost raced to her car, and once in it— the housekeeper, hands on hips watching from the front door— started the engine and put in the tape.

She realized she had gone the wrong way on Gavin's street, when she eventually reached a barrier—the "no entry" side of

Blackie's Pasture—from which she could see the statue of the horse, the spot where Tracy had died.

It seemed, accidentally or not, the right place to pause and listen, to hear Tracy Lester for the first time.

"Hi, Gav," a light, lively voice said. "I don't know if you noticed the new tape or not yet, or if I've called you because I got hung up and couldn't go to the meeting, because it might be that I have to go away for a while. But in any case, here goes. After you listen to this, would you just not do anything or tell anybody except take this to CoXistence and ask them to play it. You know how good they are at getting the newspapers interested. And you won't get in any trouble because of it.

"Know how I told you to never start anything you can't stop? Well . . . I was right, but I started something and stopping it is making a big mess. Don't be angry with me, Gav, but I did a very bad thing. And stopping it is really tough."

Someone tapped the windshield. Billie looked up, alarmed by the tape, then by the noise. "You can't park here," a runner said. "Fire lane. The police will tag you for a million bucks."

"Thanks." She stopped the tape, missed the last sentence or two and was disoriented. She turned the car around and parked twenty feet away, on the side of the road. She could no longer see the statue of the swaybacked horse, but that was just as well. Hearing the voice of the girl who'd died at Blackie's feet—and such an airborne voice—brought home the crime with horrible immediacy. Whatever she'd been preparing for, it wasn't murder.

"Remember my free trips and cruises? Well, I found out I could make a lot of money pretty easily on them, that other people I knew were doing it, by doing something I'm really ashamed of now. The travel company I work for and the moving company across the street are in this together—plus other people, too. They go to these foreign countries where they have contacts and they . . . they steal wild animals. Birds. Snakes. Lizards. Even insects. There are people who collect insects, Gav. Animals and animal parts, like skins or horns or the feet of elephants. They're all creatures that aren't allowed to be sold because they're endangered."

Tracy's voice had thickened. She cleared her throat before she went on.

"They do it a lot of ways, but the way I did was— Remember how one time I flew home? To save time, I said? Well, it was, but only so that all the parrot eggs I had in my clothing wouldn't hatch while I was traveling. It was special clothing with pockets hidden in the vest and the skirt. I looked like a tub, but you couldn't tell if you didn't know me, and it was winter, so a thick coat didn't look all that weird.

"If an egg had hatched, I was supposed to kill the chick. Thank goodness none of them did. I did that again, from Mexico. I'm ashamed, but I did it. And on the boat, there were turtles in the cargo, packed in a box like a row of books might be. They die. Most of the animals die.

"They call what I was being a 'mule.' Funny that it has an animal's name, isn't it? I did it four times, and then . . . Now I can't stop thinking about the animals, and what I did. I thought I needed money so I could leave Robby but . . . I didn't. I just liked . . . well, you know me.

"I bought a ring in South America with the money I'd made, so that Robby wouldn't know. I figured to sell it later on. And then you were talking about CoXistence, about saving things, and I knew what I'd done and I couldn't stand me anymore, so I joined, remember? I don't blame you if you hate me, Gav, but please try not to.

"Joining groups wasn't enough. Too slow. Too indirect to make up for what I did. The only thing is to stop those people, which means I have to confess what I did and tell what I know and maybe go to jail.

"These people act like once you've been a mule you're part of them forever. That's why I'm leaving my job. It got creepy when I said I wouldn't do it ever again. I promised to never say a word to anybody, but Jimmy . . . he's who got me involved first off. He's a nice guy even though he does those terrible things. He wants to stop, too, but he's too afraid of the boss, this man, David Vincent. Vincent owns Moving On and, I think, some of the travel company, too. That way he uses the trips and then his vans and everything to move these animals around and nobody suspects. I'm afraid of him, too. He made me come into his office one day and said if I didn't keep doing it, then they wouldn't trust me and if they didn't trust me, they'd have to take action.

"So I started something I can't stop, and I'm trapped, but I'd rather face jail than David Vincent's 'action,' so I called the Fish and Wildlife Agency. I'm going up to Sacramento to talk to their agents. If I'm not back in time to go myself, take this tape to the CoXistence meeting. This is my safety net, my insurance policy. I told David Vincent that I'd hidden proof of what they did somewhere, and it would go public if anything happened to me, so there's no point in his hurting me, but all the same, I might have to stay out of town for a while.

"And please, Gavin. Try not to hate me."

Billie sighed and put her finger on the rewind button, but heard Tracy's voice once again. "I forgot—there's another copy of this tape in your tuxedo shoes at the back of your closet. And one other thought: just in case—I mean nothing bad's going to happen, but just in case—Ana has the ring. Please give it to Veronica. She needs money for the ranch. But don't worry, nothing's going to happen to me. And thanks, buddy. I love you!"

It was horrible and sad and Tracy had been tragically wrong about being safe. But, everything now fell into place. The proof the caller wanted. The ring. The mysterious cruise. The groups she joined and quit. The fear.

The name of the killer.

Billie took out her phone and called the office. "Zack?" she asked. "Let me talk to Emma."

"Not here. Meeting that Wilson girl."

"Okay," she said. "I guess it can wait." But she wasn't sure she could. "Hang on! Where is the Wilson girl? I'm in Tiburon—isn't she around here?"

"Right next to you in Sausalito. You want the address?"

"Sure, I'm five minutes away."

She'd tell her in person. She couldn't wait to see Emma's expression.

She'd done it. Solved it. Found the evidence. Billie the kid had cracked the case.

God, but she felt brilliant. The old witch would have to be impressed. That's all Billie wanted. That one moment of recognition. Of amazement. Of admiration.

And then—Gavin. She'd kept her promise. To her amazement and delight, she'd found the person who knew that Gavin hadn't killed Tracy. The person who also knew who had, and why.

Ironic. In the end, Tracy would remain Gavin's best friend, and it would be her voice that testified on his behalf.

Billie looked at the address Zack had given her. She'd written it in a shaky, overexcited hand, but she made out the numbers and headed toward the freeway.

Thirty-seven

Mid-afternoon, Friday. Still time, and south-bound traffic wasn't bad at this hour. It was the return to San Rafael in the Friday escape-the-city rush that would do her in, but Emma wanted this over and done. The Wilsons made her head hurt and by the time she'd left Kay-Caitlin, she felt as if her muscles had dissolved and there was nothing left to hold up her bones.

"What will you do now?" the woman had demanded.

"See my client," Emma said. "I owe her what she came for. The truth."

She'd never take on another birth-mother search. Even when they weren't this filled with evasions, detours, and sad stories, they were too often futile and depressing. No more.

Right now, if she had her way, she'd never take another case or another client. The business of digging through lies had gone stale and ashy. Time to sit back and watch the world go by and not wonder at its motives or what it was hiding.

Traffic south was heavier than she'd anticipated and several times she decided to pull off the freeway and go home. Pour herself anything that would blur the edge of this feeling, a frightening feeling she couldn't remember having before. Aside from the waves of fatigue, a counter force—jittery, quivering anxiety—pulsed through her. And inexplicable anger, too.

Where was this coming from?

It had to be Kay Wilson, trying to make Emma feel guilty about doing the right thing. Sure, her story was sad, but sad didn't alter reality. It didn't matter why she'd lied. It didn't matter what excuses she had. It mattered that she'd wasted hours of Emma's life for her face-saving, so that nobody would know who she really was.

As if all of us were no more than rubber stamps of our family. Kay Wilson wasn't her mother or father or murderous sister. She was herself, the day-to-day woman she'd become, and nothing could change that. People weren't show dogs, with pedigrees that determined their worth. Why didn't she understand that?

Why obsess about what other people think of you when in fact, other people don't think about you in the first place?

What if people simply accepted the truth and lived with it? Look at the Riddocks, look at the misery and ill will Riddock Senior set up with his belligerent attempts to bend the truth, not be who he was, which was the father of a brain-damaged child. That was big-time lying, different only in scope and expense account. So he'd sued and driven doctors out of practice and so what? It didn't change one iota of reality except to make people recoil when they heard Gavin's name, make things worse for him.

Caitlin Wilson had taken a quieter, stealthier path, adopting new identities, changing her story as it evolved, living a long lie and passing it on to her niece, who would have been long since finished with the story had it only been given to her as truth, right away. But her mother, the woman who raised her, who still had to save face, had made her life harder and ultimately more painful because of lies.

And she'd made Emma's life more painful, too, because Emma, a woman not given to headaches, had a searing, screaming one. She had to find coffee before she faced Heather. Sit quietly, take aspirin, drink caffeine, and get her head back in shape.

She pulled off the freeway onto Bridgeway. The traffic was appreciably worse; stop and start along the road of restaurants, shops, and small hotels. Tourists no longer seemed to have a season, just a constant presence, she thought as she watched a ferryboat load of them pour out onto the sidewalks and streets, further slowing traffic while she waited, her head burning as if she were wearing a spike-lined helmet. Her brain alternated between pulses of pain and echoes of Kay Wilson's explanation, until the pain and her story mixed into one intolerable vise.

And then, as she stopped at a crosswalk filled with slow-moving outlanders, she registered her furious thoughts and was further confused. Why was she acting like an outraged ingenue because people didn't tell the truth? If Emma knew anything, she knew that. In fact, if human nature were to change and everyone became straightforward, Emma would be out of business. Her livelihood depended on the duplicity of strangers.

She wasn't angry because people lied, but because Kay Wilson, in her flat and undramatic way, had undermined everything that held Emma up, drilled holes in all of Emma's supports. She had somehow made it obvious that Emma Howe, missionary of truth-telling, was the worst kind of liar because she lied to herself.

"The *truth* is what's important," she'd insisted to her own daughter, although Caroline couldn't look real life in the face and insisted she was that way from an overdose of truth when softening its edges might have been both kinder and wiser.

Caroline's words pursued her, stuck to the back of her neck, bit at the sore places in her brain. "What would it have hurt if you'd spared us the details of what a bastard my father was?"

Which he was. A charming and lovable bastard, but one all the same. That was the truth. What she'd said was the truth.

Now she wasn't sure why it had felt vital to let her children know precisely how worthless he'd been, how he'd died bare-assed in a motel with a sleazy pickup. How he'd gambled away their money. How he had zero sense of responsibility, of his role as protector and provider for his children, as husband to his wife.

She'd wanted her children to be free of illusions and delusions. Wanted them to know how life was, so they could cope.

She'd told the truth.

Her head pounded.

But the real truth was that there were lots of truths and she'd only told the one that suited her then, the one she could see from her furious, hurt, and frightened position.

She hadn't mentioned Harry Howe's infinite charm, his cleverness, or how he played the guitar and sang, or how dizzy in love she'd been in the beginning.

She hadn't mentioned lots of truths about her dead husband.

Her headache enlarged, reddened. She was afraid she was having a stroke. Finally, her head seconds from detonating, she found a parking space, two blocks down and halfway up the steep hill above Bridgeway.

She had to regroup. Difficult enough facing Heather, but with this headache and worse, this thrumming anxious, angry exhaustion, it would be impossible.

Time out. Time to get back to herself, to be Emma again.

If she could find her. Because that Emma was dissolving into a fog with no hard edges, sometimes called the truth.

Thirty-
eight

"For my protection," Jeannie Vincent muttered, patting her pocketbook and pressing it to her heart. That's why she had it. He'd said so.

She'd come to see with her own eyes, to find out, and she'd seen, all right. But she had never, ever thought she'd see that much in the middle of a day on a street in Sausalito.

They were animals. Like they could do whatever they wanted to do wherever they wanted to. Right in front of the window for the world to see.

At least now she knew for sure. Wife knows last, wasn't that how it went? But now she could protect herself. She knew.

She'd seen that tramp with the hair preening at the window, sticking her boobs out. Guess his bimbos didn't have to work, as long as they stuck out their boobs. Because then he was there—holding her in public, in the window, for God's sake. They didn't care who knew, in broad daylight, her hand on him, his hand under her chin. Saying things to each other. Saying things that had nothing to do with business and everything to do with running a knife through her heart.

She had to calm down, but how could she? The arrogance of it! The contempt for her and her feelings and her children and the life they'd made.

The blood in her veins wasn't moving right. It jumped, it didn't flow.

The life she'd thought they'd made.

She'd had suspicions, but it wasn't the same. What she'd said to Adrienne, it hadn't been real, like this. That wasn't the same as seeing them, a nightmare acted out in front of her open eyes. The jumping blood filled the top of her head, the pressure building so that it might blow off.

She felt naked, skinned, exposed.

She reminded herself that she didn't have to feel this way. She could be in charge. She didn't have to be his victim.

He gave it to her for her protection. That's what he said. She patted her bag.

She couldn't hear her thoughts for the roaring in her head, the shouting, the screams. She was all noise—there was nothing left of her. He'd made her nothing, less than the dirt on the sidewalk.

She couldn't breathe.

The fact of him was killing her. She had to protect herself.

Emma had finished her coffee and the refill so long ago she was sure someone was going to ask her to leave, but this was a polite café and a slow hour, so she sat and allowed the aspirin and caffeine to kick in while she sandblasted the cornerstone of her life.

It amazed her that a decision made years ago by a teenager had caused an earthquake in Emma's personal landscape, heaving moss-grown fixtures every which way.

Heather had said she'd take her coffee break when Emma came around, and it was long since time to get this over with—although at this point, she'd skip the coffee part. But she'd start the weekend with a clear mind. She stood and paid her bill.

"You okay?" the cashier asked.

Emma touched her cheek, her hair. "Why?" she asked, "Is there something . . . odd about me?"

The cashier's cheeks colored. She looked about twelve, but then most of the population looked that way to Emma these days. "Sorry," the girl said. "I didn't mean to make you uncomfortable. I noticed you sitting there for some time, and then, right now, you looked worried and you were doing this thing—like now—like what you're doing."

Emma realized she was pulling in and biting down on her bottom lip, a nervous habit she thought she'd outgrown in junior high. She released the lip and tried to smile.

"Lots to think about, right?" the cashier murmured tactfully.

Emma felt her eyes stay with her, drill into her back as she walked away from the café, and when she turned, she saw that it wasn't her imagination. The cashier had been watching her, still wondering what was going on with Emma.

As Emma herself wondered.

Marlena honestly didn't hear the woman enter, she was working so hard. She hated this part of the job, these endless insurance forms with their lists of everything anybody owned, and how chipped or warped or frayed it was. She wasn't a particularly good typist and her neck felt as if she was going to need traction by the time she was done.

"Excuse me." Then a throat clearing.

And there she was. There was something about her that belonged in another time. Old-fashioned. Marlena could picture her in a black-and-white movie. A British black-and-white movie, the kind that bored her.

"Remember me? We spoke a little over a week ago."

Marlena nodded. "Sure. Um—"

"Emma Howe. I was here about Gavin Riddock and the Tracy Lester homicide."

"Oh, sure. I remember. So, ah . . ." Marlena checked David Vincent's door, as she remembered how upset he'd been by the idea of somebody butting in during the workday, using up his time with her questions. It was half open. "Is this more about that case? Because my boss—"

"No," Emma Howe said quickly. "No questions. This has nothing to do with that."

Fat chance. The woman was lying, because why else would she be here? And why had Marlena thought that a private investigator would be up-front with what she was doing? "See, the thing is," Marlena said, "Mr. Vincent is here this time, and he was really mad about having the day disrupted that way." She waited, but the old woman wasn't getting it. Maybe she was hard of hearing. "He doesn't want more visits like that," she said more loudly.

Emma Howe backed up a step, and frowned. "I'm here to see Heather Wilson."

"Heather?"

"She's expecting me. Would you buzz her or tell her I'm here?"

"Heather Wilson." The woman was definitely not telling the truth. She hadn't interviewed Heather last time. Besides, Heather Wilson hadn't known Tracy Lester or Gavin Riddock. Heather Wilson barely knew anyone. "Mrs. Howe," Marlena said, "I'm trying to tell you—this investigation stuff—this place is off-limits. Mr. Vincent doesn't want it going on during business hours."

"If you tell me where she is, I'll find her myself."

"One sec," Marlena said. "Let me do this one thing." She needed time to think. She found the right lines and typed in "spindle nicked," "front left leg paint chipped."

"This is not an investigation and it is not on your employer's time and I would appreciate it if you would find her for me. This is simply a matter of genealogical research."

Heather's ancestors? Of all the closed-mouthed bitches, that drab little Heather Wilson! There was only one reason people searched through the family tree that way: to find an inheritance. And not a peep out of her. Or maybe this woman found her because somebody else hired her to find an heir. Maybe this woman spotted her last week, while she was interviewing Marlena and dull Heather Wilson was eavesdropping.

Marlena had read about things like this, had dreamed about them, too. She scrunched her forehead. "Like, about a will? You one of those people who find missing heirs and stuff?"

Emma Howe's smile was tight. She thought she was hiding something, but she wasn't fooling Marlena. "Could be," she murmured. "Could you please buzz her? I don't mean to rush you, but I don't want to get stuck in Friday afternoon northbound traffic."

"Hold on a minute. I'll find out where she is." If Heather Wilson was inheriting money, she could wait a few minutes longer, the bitch. She wouldn't need this job then, but Marlena still would, and Marlena's only "inheritance" possibilities were behind that office door, which was half open anyway, so he'd probably already heard. She wasn't going to risk pissing him off by not telling him who was here.

At her boss's door, she turned and smiled at Emma Howe, who scowled back, as if she didn't approve. Marlena knocked smartly.

Billie paid the parking-lot attendant and walked toward the address Zack had given her. As eager as she was to tell Emma—to gloat, in truth—she'd wait nearby, or outside, until Emma was finished with the Wilson girl. She wasn't going to risk spoiling her moment by angering Emma. Again.

The address was across the street, she realized, and she looked for the nearest crosswalk, but as she scanned the opposite side, she caught the words "Moving On" and stopped. The place Tracy mentioned.

She checked the address again, and looked across at the big letters under the awning. Emma was already there. She'd found out before Billie had.

Billie's great, amazing discovery popped into nothingness, like a soap bubble.

And then she remembered that wasn't necessarily so. The girl in search of her birth mother had come to Emma because she'd seen her interviewing a co-worker about Gavin. This made Billie uneasy for a new reason, because it put Emma at a disadvantage. Ignorance was never bliss and less often safe. Dangerous to have no idea you're in the dark heart of what your agency is investigating. She reminded herself that Emma had been inside there before and nothing had happened, and there was no reason to think anything bad would happen today.

With less than the comfort level she'd anticipated, she leaned against the dusty pink clapboard of a dress shop, and waited for Emma to exit. She looked upward, watched and listened to the seagulls, knew she looked relaxed, but she couldn't make herself feel that way. Ten minutes ago, she'd rejoiced in the fact that she knew things Emma did not but now, the same idea caused anxiety instead of pleasure. Emma was suddenly an innocent, unaware of the true nature of her surroundings, of why or by whom Tracy Lester had been killed.

She filled the waiting time by studying pedestrians, deciding who was a native and who a visitor, even aside from the peaked hats or inappropriately light clothing for the season. And then slowly, she realized that one of them, a well-dressed woman in jeans and a suede jacket-shirt was behaving peculiarly. She pressed herself flat against the moving company's facade, standing beside the window, then tilting toward it until only her head bobbled in front of the window glass in quick back and forth motions. And after a series of peeks so quick she couldn't have seen anything but a blur, she'd press her pocketbook to her heart, then sidestep farther away from the window, her lips moving, as if in prayer.

Then she repeated her ritual.

Solo hide-and-seek? Another woman off her meds, Billie thought. But too well-dressed for the homeless.

After the third series of bobs and silent prayers—or curses, for all Billie could tell—the herky jerky woman, now past the window, faced the building, clutched her pocketbook to her chest and opened the door of Moving On.

Too much. This, and Emma in there unknowing. Billie couldn't stand out here, holding onto her news until Emma made her exit. Whether or not it made her look a fool, whether or not it cost her the job, whether or not the woman in the suede jacket was a danger or merely a pest, whether or not Billie could even explain this decision, she couldn't stand herself if she simply stood on the sidewalk, waiting.

"Come in, come in," Mr. Vincent—David—said immediately after she knocked. Like he'd been waiting to see if Marlena would come to him. Testing her. She was glad she'd made the right decision.

She closed the door behind her. He smiled and nodded. "You're looking cheerier than you were," he said. "Good for you."

"The detective's here," she whispered. "I knew you'd want to—"

"Who? What detective? What are you talking about?"

"Remember? You got all upset when I told you? The detective who was here last week, asking about Gavin Riddock and Tracy Lester."

And he got all upset again so she was really glad she'd told him.

"Why?" he asked. "Didn't you tell her? I thought I said I wouldn't allow—"

Before she could answer, he asked more questions, each in an angrier tone than the one before. She didn't like that one bit. She wasn't responsible for the old lady who'd come back, and she'd done her part by telling him, so what was this about? She backed closer to the doorway, unable to correct him, to get a word in edgewise to tell him about Heather and the inheritance.

Well then screw Heather. Let him talk all he wanted. What was the big rush? Heather would have to wait fifteen minutes longer to get her hands on the money.

David went on and on. "Did she ask you anything this time?

What did you tell her? Where is she? Did she say why she came back? What the hell did you tell her the first time? She has no right—"

"Listen," she said, "I tried." Before she could calm him down or answer a single one of his questions, he reached in front of her and flung the door open. It was like they were suddenly on stage, one next to the other.

"There she is." She pointed. "Her name is . . ." Marlena's voice dribbled off into silence, because Emma Howe looked odd, standing stiffly beside Marlena's desk, right where she'd been, but now her body was too straight, too still, and her expression peculiar, as if she wanted to speak but couldn't get the words out, as if—

As if she saw what Marlena suddenly saw, what David beside her saw because he made a strangled sound as a woman leaped into view.

Jeannie Vincent—mad eyes, suede jacket, wrinkled linen shirt. And gun.

Thirty-
nine

Billie snapped her phone shut and opened the door of the moving company.

And stopped, mid-stride.

Emma was oddly positioned, as if on alert, practically vibrating.

She glanced at Billie with short-lived surprise, then moved her head, directing Billie's glance toward an inner doorway where a man and a young woman with platinum hair looked sculpted into place.

Billie thought, irrationally, of a childhood game called "Statues." "Freeze!" someone would call and wherever you were and whatever you were doing, you stayed in that position.

The woman in the middle wasn't playing. The wild woman in jeans and the suede jacket shouted and gesticulated, her gestures emphasized by the addition of a gun in one hand. She waved with it, as if she'd forgotten it was there, as if it were an extra, familiar appendage.

Slightly behind Emma another young woman, this one with plain features and brown hair, had also resisted freezing, at least verbally. "What's happening? What's going on? What's happening?" she frantically repeated, punctuating her phrases with wails and sniffles.

"You!" the wild woman screamed at the paralyzed couple in the doorway. "You son of a bitch, I'll kill you! I know what you've been up to! I know now! I know what really goes on here."

The man in the doorway looked stricken, cornered, his glance sweeping the room, as if he expected to find an ally or rescue committee.

"Thought you could get away with it, didn't you? Thought nobody would know, but I do!"

"No," he said in a low voice. "Nothing's going on except the moving business, so calm down. Whatever you've heard—"

This madwoman had also found out?

"Adrienne thought you were smuggling drugs, but I knew better. I knew she was wrong." The veins on her neck looked ready to pop.

Emma made another jerky "look there!" gesture with her head. She wanted Billie to notice something. What? She could see very well that the woman had a gun. And Emma didn't begin to understand what Billie knew, what was going on there, and what this woman knew.

"Jeannie, I'm telling you to be quiet," the man said. He spoke in the overly calm voice adopted when animals foamed at the mouth or men thought women were likely to do so. Billie knew that a voice like that—patronizing and offensive—had never once calmed a woman down. She herself bristled at the sound, remembered her ex using it near the end when they understood that theirs was not going to be a friendly divorce. It was a tone that said, "I am sane and you are not," and was itself capable of driving people insane.

She listened to this man drone on in the pseudo-soothing way, telling the woman that she didn't know whatever she thought she knew.

Next to him, the blonde in the fifties getup had both her hands up to her mouth, eyes bugging out above her scarlet nails. She looked like a cartoon character.

"What's *wrong* with you?" the man said, dropping his I-am-sane-and-you-are-not bit. "You look like hell!"

That clinched it, he was definitely her husband.

"Go home," he said. "Get some sleep and you'll see things more like they actually are. This is a place of business."

"Monkey business!" she screamed.

He got that cornered look again, checking Emma and Billie and whoever the brown-haired girl was. Billie could almost see him controlling his breath. And no wonder. Monkeys as business was an unfortunately apt choice of idioms. Monkeys and parrots and lizards. Whatever slithered or jumped or fluttered and interested a collector.

She suddenly thought of Veronica and her llamas. She had to tell the woman what had happened and why. If she got out of here in one piece, she'd drive out there the next day with Jesse, make sure Veronica was going to be all right with it. She'd ask Michael about the ring before she mentioned it, but she was sure the tape would prove to be a valid will. Besides, the ring was in a limbo of nonexistence. A transfer seemed easy enough and Veronica could replace the lost llamas, for starters.

"We work here," the man was saying in that irritating voice. "Us, drivers, accountants, clients. That's all we do, and whatever terrible thing you imagine is in your mind, Jeannie."

"Don't Jeannie me! I have eyes. I have ears. I know about your women! I'm the one got the phone calls—"

"What?" He looked as if only now she had become unhinged. "What are you talking about?"

"Your women, David Vincent! Your lies and whoring, your—"

This was the smuggler himself? The murderer? He was so ordinary looking.

"I *saw* you!" Jeannie Vincent screamed. "I know what's going on! You"—she raised the gun and pointed it at the blonde—"you tramp!"

"Put down the gun," the man said. "You're making an enormous mistake. And you're driving away whatever business I have." His tone turned cajoling, as if to a child. "Look, Jeannie, look over there." His chin pointed toward Billie. "If you frighten customers away, where will we be?"

At the word "customer" Jeannie turned and looked where David Vincent pointed, at Billie. The gun, held absentmindedly in her hand swung with her. She stared at Billie as if she were a new life-form.

Billie smiled weakly and waved her hand in casual greeting. This was too ridiculous for words.

Jeannie Vincent's gun hand waved her away. "Out!" she said.

"Mrs. Vincent, please," the blond girl in the doorway said.

Jeannie Vincent pivoted back so she faced the girl. "That's right! *I'm* Mrs. Vincent! I'm his wife, so remember that and don't you *dare* speak to me you two-bit small-town Marilyn Monroe! Don't you——"

Cops said domestic disputes were the most dangerous situations on earth. The only thing to do, Billie decided, was nothing. Anything she'd do now would be likely to make things worse.

Hold on and wait.

Emma fumed. What the hell was wrong with them all? Why wasn't anybody doing something? How many signals did she have to send before Billie understood? If they banded together, worked in concert, they could take that little woman in two seconds flat. And they'd better, because she was beyond a talking cure. The woman didn't understand English anymore. She'd gone over the edge she'd been tottering on, left the land of logic far behind, and now anything, for any reason—or none—could happen. They were in big trouble if they didn't stop her now.

Emma had hoped David Vincent would calm his wife, had thought perhaps such displays were part of his marriage and that his god-awful super-calm tone had worked before, although personally, it drove Emma up the wall. But it hadn't worked and now, David

303

Vincent didn't look like he had a clue as to what to do and it didn't matter, because nothing save drugging her or knocking her unconscious would slow that woman down.

If the woman was sane, she'd take one look at that jerk of a girl, Marlena, and say "take him." They deserved each other. What was she except big boobs and a sly, dim intelligence? "Walk away," Emma wanted to tell his wife. Take him to the cleaners.

Only stop screaming. Even Emma couldn't think through that shrill knife-sound and, added to it, Heather Wilson's keening.

But if she and Billie, each on a side, rushed Jeannie Vincent, they could get her down before she remembered that gun she was carrying like a bunch of keys. They were behind her now, her attention elsewhere—she wouldn't have a chance to shoot before they got her down.

Dear God, she thought, hearing herself. She sounded like one of the characters in the books her father listened to. She wondered if he'd be proud—or horrified—if he knew the situation she was in, or what she wanted to do. They'd talk about it next visit. She'd visit soon. If she lived through this, she'd take Caroline and the grandkids, too. Make peace all around.

Admit her truth wasn't always the only truth.

If she lived.

She looked at Billie, sharply. Notice how we're positioned. Act on it. The girl was so dense!

Billie seemed to feel Emma's glance, and returned it. Emma nodded—the tiniest, most subtle of nods—toward Jeannie Vincent, then raised her eyebrows microscopically.

Billie looked from Emma to the screaming woman, then back, her brows contracted. She didn't get it.

Emma repeated the motions, more boldly. Surely, even if David Vincent saw them, he'd want them to go forward. She didn't have to be all that subtle.

And Billie shook her head, just barely, but nonetheless definitely. She held up her right index finger, signaling Emma to wait.

Emma couldn't believe it. Billie was saying "no."

No to the only sane option, the only quick end to this, the only hope.

No!

If they got out of this alive, Emma was firing Billie August this afternoon.

In fact, she was firing her even if she had to do it from the grave.

Marlena didn't know if people her age could have heart attacks, but she thought she was having one. She couldn't breathe right and she could hear her own heartbeats. "I'm sorry," she whimpered. "He isn't—we aren't—I didn't mean—"

"Shut up!" his crazy wife screamed. Squinting her eyes, she aimed her gun at Marlena's forehead.

Marlena could feel it. A hole waiting to happen, right above her nose. How could she have known his wife was crazy? It wasn't fair and she was going to *die* because she hadn't known. The spot between her eyebrows grew hot, a bull's-eye waiting to be blown away.

She'd thought Emma Howe was going to do something. Marlena had seen her scope out the room, saw her eyes, the way she really looked at stuff, figuring things out. But all the old woman did was look. She was too feeble and old to do anything more. She must be waiting too, for somebody—who?—to save them.

It wasn't going to be Heather, no surprise. She was as useless as always, bawling, as if this had anything to do with her! Even Mrs. Vincent couldn't think her husband would fool around with Heather.

And David was a coward, and stupid, too. He wasn't anything like what she'd thought, and she didn't love him anymore. She didn't even like him. Was he going to stand there until his wife shot Marlena dead?

Obviously, it was up to her to save herself. "Mrs. Vincent," she said in her calmest, telephone-answering voice. "This is all a big mis—"

"I don't want to hear it! I don't want to hear anything from your—"

"But you don't understand, I only—"

And she shut up because everybody was making noise at once while the old lady did this weird wobble-headed thing again, and the blonde shook her head, and David said they should talk this over, and Heather sobbed about not being able to stand this and what was going on anyway and through it Jeannie Vincent let out her loudest scream ever—noise, no words, a scream so big it covered them all as she raised the gun and held it out straight, for real now, and she waved it back and forth, from her husband to Marlena. Marlena felt the space between her eyebrows go from hot to icy as the gun aimed at it.

Back and forth—David, Marlena. Gun. "I'll kill you," Jeannie Vincent screamed, finding words again. "I'll kill you both! You ruined me, you lied to me, you shamed me and I'll—"

"YES!" The old lady shouted it at the top of her lungs and Marlena heard it as a gunshot and could barely breathe.

Nothing. They could have had her down and disarmed by now if Billie weren't an idiot! What the hell was inside that jerking head, what the hell was that finger business?

The madwoman had remembered her gun and what it could do and she was seconds from using it. They'd lost the moment and Emma had no partner, no nothing. She had to do it herself, then.

"You don't want to do this, Jeannie," David Vincent said. "You don't want to go to jail. What about the children?"

"Did you think about the children when you—"

"I never, I swear, it isn't—"

Emma shifted her muscles. She didn't want Jeannie Vincent noticing or hearing anything.

"No!" Billie whispered. "Wait one minute, I—"

"You son of a bitch I'll make us both dead and I'll see you in hell!"

"Are you out of your mind?" Emma screamed as she lunged.

And she realized that Billie, sputtering and still shaking her head, still saying "no!" had nonetheless mirrored her motions.

Jeannie Vincent fell, Emma on one side, Billie the other.

Emma had a partner.

"I wasn't talking to you, Billie," Emma lied. "Get the gun!"

Billie had banged her left elbow onto the ground. Pain rocketed up her arm.

Emma was half under Jeannie Vincent, struggling to get up and keep the woman down at the same time. Billie reached for the gun but missed as a weight dropped onto her back, forcing the air out of her lungs. David Vincent had hurled himself onto the pile.

"Get off—What are you—!" Emma shouted as Jeannie writhed and screamed from within the body sandwich.

God. Billie's arm was in agony and her back felt broken from the pressure of his knee, but she got hold of the woman's gun before he could get it, shifted her hip to lessen his weight and fell back again, deafened by a blast she felt in her fillings, in the back of her skull.

The weight on her back lifted.

Jeannie Vincent lay flat, groaning in a low, constant tone.

The girl at the back of the room finally stopped wailing and the sudden silence felt as if it might smother them. Billie could hear their breathing and hers, raspy, hard, fast.

The girl at the back of the room started up again. "He has a gun! He killed his wife!"

Emma and Billie let go of her at the same time. Blood covered half her linen shirt.

The platinum blonde stood at the doorway, screaming and pointing at Jeannie Vincent and pulling at her own hair.

"Stop him!" Emma shouted, with one quick glance at Billie.

David Vincent was crawling away from his wife's bleeding body, bracing himself to stand back up, the gun—his gun, because Billie had his wife's—in his hand.

"I had to—" he said, crouching. "You saw what she was going to— She would have—" Without a word or signal that Billie could have described, she knew, and she grabbed one of his legs while Emma grabbed the other and both pulled straight back.

David Vincent splatted down, onto his chin and chest, mid-explanation.

Billie beamed at Emma. They'd done it—something—the right thing.

Emma stomped on his hand until it released the gun. "Don't move," she said, sitting down on him.

The platinum blonde reanimated, leaping onto Emma and pummeling her. "Leave him alone! Didn't you just see? He saved my life! What's wrong with you? Leave him alone!"

Billie grabbed Jeannie's gun from where it had fallen, then didn't know what to do with it, so she pounded Marlena's hand with it. The girl pulled back with a yowl.

"Call the police!" Emma shouted in the direction of the girl cowering behind the desk. "Heather, now! Call them! We need an ambulance, too!"

"Emma, I already—" Billie was stopped by Marlena's nails, clawing her face, her arm, her hand holding the gun.

"No police!" Vincent shouted. "No police!"

"Are you out of your mind?"

"Self-defense." His words were muffled, because his head was being held flat on the floor, one cheek squashed.

"Who cares why?" Emma said gruffly.

The moaning grew weaker.

Billie smacked Marlena's hand off with the gun again, then held it, pointed at her, and Marlena grew quiet, her face pale against her scarlet lipstick.

Billie felt a rush. If she had to—if she wanted to—she could shoot this girl. She could shoot Vincent. Anyone. Everyone. Nobody could hurt her because she had a gun.

She heard herself and recoiled.

"Police! Call!" Emma shouted again from the tangle of arms and legs and bodies. Marlena grabbed—Emma caught—Billie pushed—Vincent twisted—Heather cried—Jeannie moaned. Emma punched—Marlena scratched—Billie pulled—Vincent bit—Heather sobbed.

"Give me the gun or hold him down and I'll call, dammit!" Emma shouted, and one second later, she shouted again: "Billie August, you're fired!" But even as she screamed that out, and through the grunts and curses and sobs and shouts—a siren, a screech of brakes.

"There's a gun," Emma shouted as they entered, her knee still on David Vincent's forearm and her other hand holding Marlena at bay.

"Down! Put the gun down. Slowly!"

They were shouting at Billie. "She means that—"

"Down! Now!"

She put the gun on the floor. "He shot his wife." Let the complicated rest of what he'd done wait a few minutes. Jeannie Vincent looked gray-skinned and barely conscious, her moans sporadic and ominously soft.

"You the one called this in?" the cop asked Emma.

"Me? No. Somebody on the street must have—"

"I did," Billie said. "I'm the one who called."

Emma glared, looked ready to wash Billie's mouth out with soap for lying.

"Before I came in."

"How could you have . . ." Emma let the sentence wander off.

Billie inhaled deeply, let her mind register that the police were here, David Vincent in handcuffs, paramedics working on his wife, and the danger over. "A hunch," she finally answered. "A bad feeling about how she was behaving outside. We PIs, we develop a sixth sense."

Emma didn't smile, didn't react.

"Okay," Billie said. "I *was* a pro. Or getting to be one, but I was just fired." She waited. Took a deep breath. Waited some more. "Okay, look—Jeannie Vincent's behavior made me nervous, but I also had a rock-solid fallback that would make a police visit worthwhile, even if nothing had happened here. Something you don't know about yet, Emma."

Emma's expression moved across incredulity, amusement— Emma's version of it, at least—to confusion, interest, and, upon being told there was something she didn't know, incredulity again, with annoyance added to it.

"You could have let me know," Emma said.

"What? I'm going to—it's complicated and long and I wanted—"

"You could have let me know you'd already called the police!"

"I tried, but you—"

Emma turned her back and took a step toward the desks.

"Emma?"

The older woman turned. Billie pointed at David Vincent, now handcuffed. She spoke softly. "He's a wild-animal smuggler. Tracy was part of it for a while, then wanted out. He killed her. She made a tape explaining it all. I have it."

Emma's expression was so unfamiliar, Billie couldn't translate it. Interest? Possibly . . . respect?

"Am I still fired?" Billie asked.

Emma waved the idea away, and then she turned again and walked back to where the brown-haired girl still cowered.

She hadn't exactly done back flips over Billie's cleverness.

But for five seconds she'd looked close to impressed. That was something.

Emma had nearly forgotten why she'd come here. She hadn't driven down to witness a face-off between the Vincents or to find out about Tracy Lester's death. She'd come here to tell Heather Wilson, once and for all, the truth.

"Stop sniveling," she told the young woman. "It doesn't help anything except your enemies. You want to be strong, girl. You are strong and nothing bad happened to you. It's a stupid job, anyway, so losing it isn't a bad thing, either."

Heather sniffled, looked around at the paramedics and police and nodded.

"Pay attention to me, now. We had a date. Do you still want coffee? I think you could use it." She herself wouldn't mind going back to the quiet café where people let you sit and think in peace.

The girl blew her nose and shook herself like a young animal. "No," Heather whispered. "No coffee. I'm okay. I was so scared. God, the screaming was enough, but then, the gun—the guns and the blood!"

"Do you feel calm enough to hear me now? Or should we wait for another time?"

"You found out about my mother?" Despite what she'd just been through, the thought of her birth mother brightened her expression. Emma could almost read the glorious images filling the girl's mind, the collected fantasies of Heather Wilson, and none remotely close to the truth. None of a negligent, drugged mother murdering her entire family. If she'd thought today's shooting was horrible . . .

And none of her fantasies had been about a teenager sacrificing her youth, her plans, and most of her life for the sake of a child she loved.

"Tell me, please," Heather said.

Emma cleared her throat and looked toward the ceiling. She walked the girl farther back into the storage area, away from the organized chaos of the outer office. She put her hand gently on the girl's arm. "Sometimes it hurts, or isn't what you wanted to hear, but the truth is always best. Do you agree?"

"I . . . I guess so." Heather's voice had shrunk and was unsure.

"Well, the truth is I did my very best, but I couldn't find your birth mother."

Heather's expectant smile faded. She took a deep breath and then another.

Emma put her hand on the girl's shoulder. "Listen to me. This is also the truth. You're going to be okay. You're like your mother—the one you know. The one you have. You're strong, the way she is, and you'll get your footing again and be fine. Trust me. Good strong women run in your family."

"You really couldn't find her?" Heather whispered.

"I really couldn't," Emma said.

The truth was: It wasn't a lie.

"Let's go hear the tape," Emma said. "And have a drink. How's that sound?"

Amazing. A friendly gesture? Tacit approval? "Good to both," she said.

"How's your arm? You're holding it funny."

"Not so good. I really slammed it. But I'm sure it's not broken."

Emma nodded approval. A broken bone would probably have offended her. "So you told her—Heather—about her mother?" Billie asked.

"Not exactly," Emma said. "Not really. I told her . . . what I'd learned."

Billie didn't understand, but it didn't bother her. She didn't have to understand everything, all at once.

They crossed the street together. Her arm felt a little better already.